MW00880727

Blood of Our Fathers

A novel by

J.A. Snow

Book Five in the An American Family Series.

Dedication

This entire series has been a labor of love.

And, while it is true it was I who spent the hours writing down the stories, based on over thirty years of genealogical research, there is another person who deserves recognition for the creation of *An American Family* as well.

Without my big brother, *Jim Snow*, who was the first to suggest that I try publishing on Kindle and who read every single book I put out, encouraging me to write another; who created the beautiful artwork for my children's book and two of my book covers, and, who, through every step of my journey into independent publishing, has been supportive of my work, I don't know that I would have had the courage to meet the challenge.

Jim has been my hero for as long as I can remember. I have cherished his artistic talents in drawing and music and from a very early age I put him on a well- deserved pedestal of admiration. I will always remember the portraits he drew for me of the Beatles, the tiny surfboard he carved and painted for my toy "troll." I will also never forget the wild adventures he took me on in his dune buggy and listening to his band rehearse in our living room.

Without him, this series might not have materialized. Thank you, Big Brother, for always being there for me!

Introduction

In this series, the Snow family has been on a long journey. From the fields of Porlock, England in *The Snows of Somerset County*, to the bloody streets of London in *Blood and Cobblestones*, and then across the Atlantic with the original *Pilgrim Girl*, they have suffered and endured what was to be their destiny. At the close of Book Four, *Escaping the Yoke,* we left Eddie Snow returning to Eastham after burying the body of his younger brother, Mickey, who had died in a skirmish with the Redcoats. Eddie has been given a temporary furlough to grieve and console his widowed mother, Lois, and then he must return to the war.

Although the residents of Eastham and the rest of Cape Cod have not seen much in the way of military battles on their home turf, the oppressive intrusion of the British army has long been a part of their lives. They have struggled to evade them by smuggling goods in and out to avoid the crown's taxation. They have suffered the constant surveillance and spying of the Redcoats. Many have sent their young men off to assist in the Revolution and some, like Mickey, will never return home alive.

As the war wears on, the tension is building toward a final climax. The French have finally given their support to the American Continental Army. To the east, over five thousand French troops are headed to Rhode Island, ready to assist them against the British army and, from the West Indies, the French Navy is sailing north to the Chesapeake Bay to confront British General Cornwallis who has garrisoned his army there. This could prove to be a turning point of the war.

Back in Eastham, Eddie Snow becomes aware of the plight of their cousins in the Wampanoag tribe who live south of town. For years, since King Phillip's War, the family of his great uncle Giles Hopkins and his great aunt Catone, the granddaughter of the great sachem *Massasoit*, have lived in peace with their white brothers. But, sentiments are turning; new residents of Eastham are not as open-minded as the Snows. At a time when the Cherokees and other tribes in the south are being driven from their homes and herded westward like cattle, the peaceful Wampanoag will begin to suffer as well.

It is a time of change, both good and bad, for the Snow family. For Eddie, it is a time of self-realization. Courage is not always developed in us until we are faced with overwhelming conflict or danger. Eddie goes off to war when he is not yet a man and when he comes home he is a very different person than he started out to be. War changes everyone it touches, just as love transforms every human heart and Eddie finds himself experiencing the effects of both on his life.

It is here we begin our story, in 1780, in what will be the final book in the An American Family historical series.

PART ONE *"PEOPLE OF THE DAWN"*

"Build a fire under them. When it gets hot enough, they'll move."

President Andrew Jackson

Chapter One *"Blood on His Hands"*

Private Eddie Snow leaned back against the wet, earthen wall behind him and cradled his little brother's bloody head in his lap. The militia had been stationed there, in the long gully that formed a natural trench alongside the road into Boston, where they would be unseen by unsuspecting British troops passing by; the perfect spot for ambushing the small garrisons. Lieutenant Knowles had instructed them to fire on the Redcoats at will and quickly change positions, moving up and down the gulley, fooling the enemy troops into thinking that they had more than the dozen men they actually had and diverting attention from the Continental troops who were traveling ahead of them. They had managed to kill at least a dozen soldiers that day, dragging their corpses off into the brush to hide them and retreating to their lair to await the next unfortunate group to pass by.

But, then, it had started to rain and the gulley became a river of rainwater, forcing the men to remain, cold and wet up to their shins, sloshing around in the slippery mud. At first, the ruse seemed to be working. Eddie noticed Mickey stand up beside him, holding his smoking musket in his hands, and turn to change his position. In an instant, another shot rang out, crackling through the air like a bolt of lightning. He watched Mickey fall and Eddie dropped his weapon to catch his brother as he sank down in the mud. He sat there for a moment. The sound of gunfire erupting around him became muffled in his ears as he saw blood pulsing from Mickey's temple. Pressing his hands against the flow, he could feel the blood oozing through his fingers and the rhythmic pumping of his brother's heart until, slowly, the pulsing stopped. He knew Mickey was dead. He couldn't move. The skirmish had ended in success but it was a hollow victory for Eddie. While the others were all gathering their gear and preparing to move up the road, Eddie reached down and forced his brother's frozen eyelids closed. His hands were sticky and red; his tears were flowing uncontrollably down his face......

He woke up sweating and trembling in his bed. *Damned nightmares!* Eddie wondered if he would *ever* sleep again; it was one of many dreams that haunted his nights. *Would his brother's death forever haunt him in his slumber?* He looked around the room in the early dawn; the blue linen curtains his mother had recently sewn for his room muted the morning sun's rays that were streaming through the eastern window panes and the aroma of charred oak firewood drifted in through the open doorway. *Ma is up,* he thought to himself.

He heaved himself up into a sitting position and swung his long legs over the side of the bed, pulling on his trousers and snapping his suspenders over his broad shoulders. He had only been home for a week after burying Mickey's lifeless body in the gulley outside Boston, returning his brother's musket and shot pouch to her, the only tangible things left of her son. Now was the time to get as much work done as he could around the place, while he had the chance. He knew the Eastham militia would be summoning him back to duty soon and he did not want to waste a moment's time.

Lois Snow had prepared her sons an ample breakfast of salt pork and eggs which she had laid out on the long family dining table. Only her younger son, Ephraim, remained living with her now; all Eddie's other siblings had married and moved into homes of their own. Ephraim had taken on the mail runs after the death of their father and Eddie worried about her being alone while Ephraim was away delivering the mail up and down the cape.

"Ma," he said as he kissed her sweetly and sat down to eat his breakfast. "I wish you would consider having someone come to live with you… to keep you company when Ephraim and I are gone. I worry about you."

"Fiddlesticks!" chirped Lois, dismissing her son's concern and reaching out to tussle his hair. "I don't need anyone watchin' over me! Why don't you let me cut your hair before you go back to the war? You look like a sheep that needs shearing!"

Eddie knew it was futile to pursue the subject; it seemed his mother grew more stubborn with each passing year. "My hair is fine, Ma. And, you don't have to press my coat and trousers," he said. "You don't have to do *everything* for me, you know!"

She smiled. "I've seen how you take care of your clothes," she said, shaking her head. "Your coat is hanging up, mended and pressed. It's a disgrace that they don't give you a proper uniform to wear! I darned the holes in your sleeves but I scrubbed like the devil and I could not get the stains out! *However* do you get so dirty?"

"We are just *militia*, Ma," said Eddie sourly. "Only the *real* soldiers rate a real uniform!"

"*Real* soldiers? *Fiddlesticks!*" said Lois. "My son is a *real* soldier no matter *what* he wears!"

Eddie didn't want to upset her. He knew exactly what caused the stains on his coat; the stains came from his brother's blood and probably from its previous owner as well. He was lucky to have a *second hand* uniform, bloodstained or not; most men in the militia wore their own civilian clothes.

Ephraim entered the room and sat down next to Eddie. "You always were her favorite, you know," he whispered. "That's why she pampers you, Eddie! No sense trying to deny it!"

Lois overheard him and laughed. "I have no favorites among my children!" she protested. "How can you say that?"

"I was just teasing him, Ma," Ephraim replied, amused that he could get a reaction from his mother who usually did the teasing. "I know you love *me* best!"

Lois had to smile at that. Her boys had inherited her sense of humor.

"I'm riding to Rock Harbor today," Ephraim said. "Do you want to ride along, Brother?"

Eddie thought for a moment. "Well, I had wanted to fix that broken shelf in the hen house, Ma," he replied. "And, the roof could use some pitch before winter."

"Those chickens can wait," said Lois, dismissing the idea. "Spend some time with your brother. You don't know how long you will be gone this time."

Eddie nodded. It was true; he expected word any day that he was to return to his post. Lieutenant Knowles had been more than accommodating, releasing him from duty long enough to bury Mickey and come home to his mother. His heart was not in it though; the thought of more killing bubbled up inside him and soured his stomach.

"I will saddle your horse, then," Ephraim said, rising from the table. "Better wear your coat; looks like we might get some rain today."

Eddie kindled the fire for his mother and kissed her cheek. "We won't be gone long," he assured her. "We'll be home for supper, I expect."

When the two brothers had mounted their horses and rode off down Skaket Road, Ephraim suddenly remembered he had one last minute delivery to make. "We'll have to make a stop at the Wampanoag camp," he said. "I have a letter to deliver to our cousins."

Chapter Two *"The Old Ones"*

It had been many years since Eddie had visited the Indian camp. He remembered, as a child, riding along with his father on other mail deliveries and the times his family attended the annual Wampanoag celebrations, when his young eyes and ears had seen and heard the sights and sounds of the brown-skinned men as they danced and chanted around a raging fire. He remembered hunting and fishing with his Wampanoag cousins and learning how to handle a bow and arrow long before he could shoot straight with a musket. Now, as he and Ephraim rode into the camp, at first glance, it didn't look as if much had changed. The crude *wetus* of generations past were exactly as he remembered them; a gathering of hickory-shingled igloo-like dwellings encircling a wide, dusty clearing where the tribe held their rituals, just as if time had not touched them. A few men in their leather were working on the inverted hull of a canoe while racks of drying deer hides were being tended by women in long fringed skirts and squaw boots. While the world around them was in constant turmoil, it *seemed* that life in the peaceful Wampanoag camp had been standing still.

But, then, he looked toward the east, toward the waves gently lapping on the eastern shore and noticed the old platform of the try pots, where the tribe had, for hundreds of years, butchered the whales they had trapped in the shallows, boiled their oil, and rendered the rest of the carcasses into something useful. Very little was wasted; most of the great bones, the teeth, even the skin had a purpose and was put to good use. The pots were quiet and cold now, rusting and abandoned, without the pungent smell of bubbling whale oil rising up in the air. The wooden platform was whitewashed with gull droppings and littered with the dead leaves of fall; idle, empty and non-productive.

"Why are there no men working on the try pots?" Eddie whispered. "Isn't it a little early in the season for whaling to be over?"

Ephraim shook his head. "The tribe has seen hard times, Brother," he whispered. "The crown has forbidden them to hunt whales from the shore any longer. They have declared all the blackfish caught close to shore *property of the king*. The punishment for poaching is hanging."

"What will they do? How will they sustain themselves without the blackfish?" Eddie asked but he was not shocked. The English never failed to surprise him with their greed.

Before Ephraim could reply, a young man, who appeared to be barely out of his teens, approached them.

"Welcome, friend!" he said and warmly locked arms with Ephraim as he got down off his horse. "Have you letters for us?"

The youth was tall and of a toned and well-muscled build; his hair was as black as jet and his head was shaved smooth on either side, with only an ebony tuft of hair that protruded from the very top of his head and fell down his back. He wore doeskin breeches that clung to his sinewy thighs and moccasins on his feet; around his neck were several strings of purple wampum shells that dangled just above the nipples on his bare chest.

"Yes, I do," replied Ephraim. "Do you remember my brother, Eddie? Eddie, this is Grey Eyes, nephew of Aquinnah."

"Yes," said Eddie, stepping forward. "I *do* remember you. But, it has been quite a while. How is your family?"

"*We are surviving*," said Grey Eyes with a serious tone to his voice and a somber cast in his eyes that were not really grey but more a silvery shade of blue, indicative of his mixed blood. There were many Wampanoag families now that had intermarried with the English settlers. "Come. Old Thomas will want to greet you."

Eddie looked quizzically toward his brother. "*Old Thomas?*" he whispered.

"Since his hair turned white, our cousin has gone by that name," Ephraim whispered back.

They followed Grey Eyes into a nearby wetu, bending slightly to keep their heads from bumping the low doorframe. Eddie looked around in the dim light. The room was small with benches cut from birch wood and covered with deer skins along each side. The fire in the center of the dirt-floored structure had dwindled down and was beginning to fill the room with smoke. Grey Eyes reached down and rekindled it by throwing a handful of pine chips on it, bringing the yellow flames snapping back to life and funneling the smoke toward the opening in the top of the wetu. Huddled near the fire pit, in only the light of a single whale oil lamp nearby, sat Old Thomas and two equally wrinkled old women. The man's snowy white hair was very long and braided down his back and the wings of a great bird were painted across his forehead. The women's eyes darted toward the three men approaching them just as Eddie recognized his cousins, Anne Hopkins and Rebecca Mayo, both granddaughters of his great Uncle Giles. *"Grey Eyes!"* said Rebecca. "I see you have brought our cousin to visit us!"

"Two cousins this time," replied the young Indian. "Ephraim and his big brother, Eddie. Do you remember?"

Old Thomas cleared his throat and spat a wet mouthful of tobacco juice on the dirt floor but did not utter a word.

"It is good to see you again," said Eddie, approaching Rebecca, reaching for her hand and squeezing it warmly.

Old Thomas still did not look directly at Eddie but seemed to stare over his shoulder when he finally spoke. "You have come back from the war?" he asked.

Eddie nodded sadly. "Aye," he replied. "But, the war is not over yet. Washington marches south with his troops and the French army is coming north to meet him. I expect to be back in the midst of it very soon."

Old Thomas looked discouraged by the news. "I look forward to the end of the fighting," he said. "There has been too much bloodshed. The Wampanoag want peace."

Eddie turned toward his cousin, Anne, and planted a kiss on her forehead. "It is good to see you again," he said. "How is your family?"

She reached out and squeezed her cousin's hand. "*We are surviving,*" she said.

That was *twice* he had heard that same phrase. *We are surviving* really meant the tribe was *suffering*, for it was not characteristic of Wampanoag to complain of the hardships of life.

"Oh, before I forget," said Ephraim. "This letter came for you."

He handed Old Thomas the official-looking envelope that had come all the way from the state capital. The old man's eyes narrowed, knowing it was not going to be good news. *Any news from the government was bound to be bad.*

"I heard what the king has done about the blackfish," said Eddie, turning back toward Old Thomas with concern. "What will you do now without the whales?"

Old Thomas raised his arm and thrust his hand holding the unopened letter toward the ceiling. "We are praying to the Three Sisters," he replied, "that our crops in the field and the *ottuck* in the forests will sustain us."

Apparently, Old Thomas was becoming disillusioned with the white *Christian* god they had accepted so long ago and was once again calling on the gods of his ancestors.

"Well, whatever we can do to help you," said Eddie. "You needn't worry. We will not let you starve."

Old Thomas' eyes twinkled and his yellowed teeth glowed in the lamplight. He held out a trembling, wrinkled hand and Eddie squeezed it in his. "Thank you, my son," he said. "And, we will pray for your safe return from the war."

Chapter Three *"Two Cemeteries"*

By the time they had ended their visit, the afternoon air had cooled and the ocean fog was already rolling silently across the salt marsh, cloaking it like an eiderdown quilt. Ephraim and Eddie put on their coats and again mounted their horses. Bidding goodbye to Grey Eyes and the old ones, they headed back down the western road under a rapidly darkening sky.

"When did Old Thomas go blind?" Eddie asked when they were far enough down the road to be out of earshot.

"His eyesight has been steadily failing over the years," replied Ephraim. "He is suffering from other ailments as well. I fear he won't be with us much longer."

"Without the whales they will have a difficult time," said Eddie. "How can the king take away their whaling rights when they were doing it long before the English ever *came* to America?"

"That's why we are fighting this war, I suppose," said Ephraim. "There isn't any one of us who hasn't been stripped of our rights."

Eddie was silent. He had left home the first time with his younger brother, Mickey, when their father was still alive and the pride in the old man's face was something he would never forget as they marched down Skaket Road with their muskets and shot pouches slung over their shoulders. *Go kill those bastard Red Coats!* he remembered his father whispering to him, *especially Captain Blood!* And, now, he would be called back any day to return to the war.

"Are you ready to return to the fighting?" his brother asked.

"No," Eddie replied dismally. "I have had enough of war. My heart is no longer in it."

Ephraim nodded. "Ma will be happy if you come home," he said. "She won't admit it to you but she sometimes paces the floor at night with worry."

"Well, word has it Washington intends to attack the British stronghold in New York and that he is calling for the French to support him. I expect that is where I will be headed next."

"Aye," Ephraim affirmed his brother's suggestion. "The *Newsletter* says the same. Washington is a stubborn old bird! He will pursue the Redcoats to the ends of the earth won't he?"

Eddie nodded. "Aye, I believe that he will do just that."

The sun broke through the mist for a few brief seconds, falling on Eddie's russet-red hair that had grown just as his physique had filled in from its adolescent gauntness. He was no longer the boy who had gone off to war with enthusiasm and youthful arrogance; he was now a man who had seen too much death and destruction for it to excite him anymore. The two brothers were different in many ways. Ephraim's hair was flaxen like their mother's and he was of a more slender stature than his older brother. His voice was softer and higher-pitched than Eddie's and Ephraim rarely showed anger; Eddie could not imagine his little brother would ever be capable of *killing*. There *were* similarities though; the sharp, chiseled nose and deep blue eyes that was inherent of the Snow family, and, in their hearts, their unwavering respect for the Wampanoag tribe. Eddie felt a twinge of jealousy, knowing that holding the position of messenger kept Ephraim from the obligation to enlist in the Eastham militia; his service was needed in the private sector and considered an exemption from military service.

"I am worried about Ma being alone so much," Eddie said after much thought. "Promise me you will encourage her to get a woman to move in with her; at least, while you are out delivering the mail."

Ephraim shook his head. "You know *Ma*," he said. "She likes her privacy and her solitude. It is in her nature, Eddie. At her age, there is no changing her I am afraid."

"She has always been stubborn," Eddie said, smiling.

"Our sisters check on her when I am gone," Ephraim assured him. "She refuses to leave her home so it is the best we can do. I tried to get Grandfather Freeman to move in with her; he isn't getting any younger either, you know. But, he insists on staying in that old shack past the dunes. Says he wants to die in his own bed or some such nonsense! I swear he is every bit as stubborn as his daughter!"

The road approached the old cemetery where their family were all buried and Eddie reined in his mount. "Give me a moment," he told Ephraim, who stayed in his saddle and held Eddie's horse. "I just want to pay my respects while I am here."

He jumped down and followed the path among the graves with their crude memorials, through the weeds that were now choking out the tender summer grass. The old cemetery was in a sorry state; Eddie had noticed it at his brother's funeral but it hadn't been the proper time to mention it. He passed by his resting grandparents, Micajah and Mercy, his great grandparents, Stephen and Susannah, and the newly carved headstone that marked Mickey's *mock* grave. The family had gathered there just days before to honor him even though his body was a hundred miles away in Boston. When he came to Jesse Snow's grave, he knelt down on one knee and, with his hands, gently touched the grass at the base of the headstone, feeling the spirit of his father in the cool wetness of the green blades between his fingers. "I'm off to kill the Redcoats, Pa" he whispered before he returned to his horse and his brother waiting on the road. "Why doesn't anyone clear away the weeds?" he asked. "The place is a disgrace even to the dead!"

Ephraim shook his head. "When we buried Pa, it was the first time anyone had used this cemetery since Grandfather took down the fence," he said. "Seems no one except the *Snows* want their dead to lie with the Indians. They have a new graveyard just north of town now, *just for the white folks*."

Eddie wasn't surprised at that either. The once proud Wampanoag tribe was no longer held in high esteem by the residents of Eastham.

"There's even talk of splitting the town," Ephraim went on. "Separating the whites from the Indians and the half-breeds and not allowing the others to shop at the mercantile with white folks."

"You mean *old man Clark's store?*" Eddie asked.

Ephraim nodded sadly.

"And, who are they calling *half-breeds?*" Eddie asked. "*Our cousins? The old ones?*" It made his blood boil. "The Wampanoag are our friends! Our *family*!" he said. "Perhaps we should open our *own* mercantile when the war is over and shut all the *bigots* out!"

"It's a thought," said Ephraim, smiling. "If only it could be resolved so easily! But, right now we have to high-tail it to Rock Harbor or we shall miss the boat with the mail and I'll lose a week's pay!"

They raced off, their horses at a gallop, just as they had done in their youth. But, instead of two boys engaged in a playful race, they were two grown men with serious thoughts in their minds, who were witnessing changes in their lives. War brought bloodshed. Prejudice brought division. Greed brought hardship. *Would it ever end?*

Chapter Four *"A Shameful Confession"*

The mail ship in Rock Harbor brought with it, as expected, the dreaded news: a letter summoning Eddie back to duty immediately. When they returned home, the three Snows spent their last quiet evening together, trying to avoid talk of the war. Eddie's heart was heavy; fleeting thoughts of running into the forest and deserting his post passed through his mind, although he would never admit it out loud. He hardly touched his supper; his stomach was twisted in knots over the prospect of returning to the battle trenches. After Ephraim had retired for the night, Eddie remained sitting by the fire with his mother.

"You look troubled, Son," Lois said. "Tell me. Are you afraid of going back into the battle?"

Eddie sighed deeply. "Of course, I am *afraid*, Ma" he said.

"Well, fear is nothing to be ashamed of!" Lois told him. "You will serve your country with honor I am sure. All soldiers must feel *some* fear before a battle! Any man who says otherwise is a liar! It seems like a natural thing to me."

How could he make her understand? Eddie thought frantically. *When she didn't understand at all?* "Ma," he replied. "It is not the fear of dying that torments me. It is my hatred of *killing*. I am *conflicted*. I am--- *ashamed!*"

He spit out the words as one would a mouthful of sour milk.

Lois reached out and took her son's hands in hers across the table. "*Ashamed?* How can that be? You are a hero in this town! You have fought bravely when your own brother lost his life!"

Eddie pulled his hands from his mother's grasp, shocked at his mother's romantic vision of war. *She knew nothing of war, of the awful reality of it!* "Ma, I have *never* fought bravely!" he said. "Mickey and I were not gallant soldiers in battle! We were nothing more than cowardly snipers in the shadows, ambushing unsuspecting Redcoats passing by! We were just *lackeys*; we dug trenches and watered the *real* army's horses and stole the boots off corpses. Where is the honor in that? It was nothing like I expected it to be!"

"Well, when you left you were very young," Lois replied. "Your expectations were probably set a bit high. We get smarter when we get older, after we have lived awhile, and then we begin to see things differently. I know your *father* would be proud of you."

Eddie suddenly broke down and a flood of pent-up emotion came forth. "Oh, Ma," he lamented. "I am just not cut out to be a soldier! It was *horrible*! The screams of men dying, the smell of stinking bodies everywhere! And, I expect it will get much worse before it is over."

Lois appeared to be deep in thought, searching for the right words of encouragement to offer her son. She had never seen him so distraught.

"I just don't like *killing*, Ma," he said. "How can I be a soldier and hate *killing* as much as I do?"

"You mustn't think of it as *killing*," said Lois. "You are defending our family, our friends, and our way of life. If we lose this war, we will be forever crushed under the boot of the British government. We will continue to pay rent to live on our own land and taxes on everything we produce with our own hands. We will be nothing more than slaves to the king!"

"Maybe," said Eddie dismally. "We should have never come to America."

"We *are Americans* now; there's no changin' that," his mother whispered. "And, we can never go back to being English ever again!"

Chapter Five *"Off to War"*

The great march had finally begun; Eddie had been ordered to report to Newport, Rhode Island, nearly a hundred miles away. He saddled his horse and rode out early the next morning, waving a stoic goodbye to his mother.

Before heading south along the King's Highway, however, he paid a visit to Clark's store in Eastham. It was early, barely dawn in the town and only a smattering of lamplights were beginning to flicker in the shop windows. He tied his horse to the railing and approached the entrance to the store where he could see a vague light emitting from within. Peering through the glass he saw a young woman stoking a fire in the corner of the room; an attractive woman he did not recognize. She had auburn hair, like his own, and it caught the light of the flames as it tumbled from beneath her bonnet, cascading down her back in dozens of curls. He paused for a moment, enjoying the very sight of her before he knocked lightly on the door to get her attention.

When she opened the door, she smiled at him. "I'm sorry, Sir," she said. "We are not quite ready for business yet."

"I apologize, Ma'am," said Eddie. "I am heading back to the war this morning and I just want to leave some money on my mother's account."

The woman looked bewildered.

"Lois Snow," said Eddie. "I am her son, *Eddie Snow."*

An expression of recognition came across her face. *"Eddie Snow!"* she said, opening the door wide for him to enter. "I know you! Don't you remember? We used to play together as children? I am Mary Clark!"

Eddie vaguely remembered a little freckle-faced girl who swam with the Snow children in the summertime and threw snowballs at them in the winter. But, now, here she was, all grown up and a beauty at that! "My word, it *is* you!" he said. "I thought you had moved away! Where have you been all these years?"

Her face took on a sad tone. "I have been away, caring for my grandmother," she said. "She has passed now and I am back to help Father with the store."

They lingered and reminisced for a short while until Eddie knew he had to be on his way or risk being late reporting for duty. He put his coin purse on the counter. "Please put this on my mother's account," he said. "For whatever she needs. If she needs more, be assured I will return from the war soon and make good any charges on her bill."

"Snow credit is always good with us," said Mary. "I am sure my father would agree. He speaks very highly of your service for our cause."

Eddie could not bear to entertain her unrealistic image of him as the brave soldier. "I wish you good day, Mary, and give my greetings to your father as well." He turned to leave when he remembered suddenly the discussion of the treatment of the Wampanoag he had had with his brother. "By the way," he said. "Is it true the Wampanoag are no longer allowed to do business in your father's store?"

Mary's face took on a concerned expression. She approached him and whispered in his ear, as if she were worried someone would hear her. "No," she said. "My father still sells to them; in the back, off the loading dock."

"But, why must they do that?" asked Eddie. "Why are they not treated like any other customer?"

"It isn't that my father *dislikes* them, Eddie," she replied. "The ladies in Eastham complain about the way they *smell*. So, to please everyone, he serves the Indians out back."

Eddie shook his head. "It seems kind of silly to me," he said. "Our town used to reek of boiling whale blubber eight months out of the year! And, now the ladies complain of a little *bear grease*?"

"Well, I thought you knew. They have cleaned up the *beach of bones* and the Indians are not allowed to slaughter whales on the shore any longer," said Mary. "I suspect they will move on one day to another place that is more hospitable."

"Aye, and where would *that* be, Mary?" asked Eddie. "The British have taken control of the shore up and down the cape and on the bay as well."

She shook her head sadly. "I don't know what will become of the Wampanoag," she said. "Perhaps this war will somehow resolve it."

Eddie voiced his sentiment silently: *This war won't resolve anything.* With that thought in his head, he went out and climbed on his horse, waving goodbye to Mary Clark, and cantered off down the King's Highway just as the morning sun was breaking over the blue Atlantic.

The journey took three full days. He first reached the little town of Barnstable, where he spent the first night in a loft over a livery stable and woke to the cackling of chickens and the braying of mules in his ears. Pushing his horse to its limits, he mounted up again and galloped on, reaching the shores of the Sakonnet River, where he spent another night huddling under the bridge as a shelter from the wind. But, Eddie did not travel alone; his vivid nightmares were with him every night as soon as he closed his eyes to sleep. If it had not been for his dear mother back home in Eastham, he might have spurred his horse westward, into the wilderness, to leave the bloody war behind him.

On the third day, he reined in his horse on a hill above Newport, the *city by the sea*, looking out over acres of tents and thousands of men in blue uniforms that spread out all the way from the main street to the Atlantic shore. In the bay, he could see a dozen or so American ships anchored, like bobbing sentinels, guarding the harbor. In the town square, where the British army had been garrisoned only a year before, now the red, white and blue flag of the thirteen colonies waved triumphantly. Never before had he seen so many soldiers all in one place! It took him almost an hour to find Lieutenant Knowles and his company in the endless mob of men.

"Good to see you, Snow!" shouted one of his comrades, Private Bradley Culpepper from Eastham.

"Aye," replied Eddie. "It looks as though I am late for the party."

He couldn't take his eyes off the crowd; soldiers mulling about and eating around fire pits, decorated officers engaged in serious conversation, the smell of thousands of horses.

"The party is just beginning," said Culpepper. "I hear we are breaking camp at daylight, marching south toward New York."

"Is that our destination then?" Eddie asked. "New York?"

"I expect so," said Culpepper. "Say, why don't we go into town and try some of that stout liquor and smoke a couple of fat cigars? One last night to relax before the war starts again! What do you say?"

Eddie felt the emptiness of his pocket, knowing he had left all the money he had with Mary Clark at the mercantile back in Eastham. "I-------" he mumbled sheepishly, embarrassed by his temporary state of poverty.

"Come on!" urged Culpepper. "The drinks are on me! I still have a *few* pennies left!" He leaned in and whispered. "I do hope they pay us soon, though. I don't fancy the idea of getting myself killed for free!"

It was true; the soldiers' pay had been delayed for many weeks now and there had been much grumbling on the subject. Eddie accepted his friend's offer humbly and they quickly left the camp before the shrill notes of a solitary bugle announced curfew.

The White Horse Tavern was their destination, a lively place that sat on the most prominent corner in the town of Newport. Three stories high it stood, with a gambrel roof hanging over shingles of barn red, with golden lanterns blazing from every window and the sounds of laughter and boots thumping on the oak floors, giving the old building its own heartbeat. Bradley and Eddie had left their horses behind at the camp and they walked down the street and into the smoky haze of the main room without turning any of the dozens of heads in the place. Continental soldiers and militia men alike mingled together without separation by dress code or social class; the war gave them all a shared uncertainty of tomorrow and the unspoken fear of impending death on the battlefield.

They drank their ale in silence, listening more to the conversations of others; suggestions of their next destination, complaints about their delayed compensation, remembrances of their fallen comrades. Eddie thought about Mickey who had died so very young and his heart ached. *Oh, how he hated war! Any war!* He couldn't help but wonder if Culpepper felt the same. "Are you anxious for all this to be over?" he asked, over the din of voices around them.

"Only if we win!" said Culpepper, smiling broadly. "Why? Are you suffering from battle fatigue, Snow?"

Eddie laughed. "I guess I am," he answered. "I worry about leaving my mother alone back in Eastham."

"How is she taking Mickey's death?" asked Culpepper.

"My mother is a strong woman," said Eddie. "Sometimes, *too* strong! But, my brother travels much of the time and she is all alone. I worry about her."

Culpepper put his tankard to his lips and emptied it, wiping his mouth with the back of his hand. "Well, perhaps it will all end soon," he said. "Rumor has it we are losing ground in the south. I hope all these months haven't been spent in vain."

"It's *all* in vain, if you ask me," said Eddie, not mincing his words.

"I expect Washington will make one last stand," Culpepper replied. "And, I intend to see it through to the end, regardless of the outcome."

Eddie swigged the last of his ale. He did not share Culpepper's enthusiasm. He wanted the war to be over. He wanted to go *home.* "I suppose we should go back to camp and get some sleep," he said to his comrade. "Dawn comes early!"

Chapter Six *"The March Begins"*

When dawn broke the next morning, half the camp was already saddled and ready, while the other half stumbled to their feet, rubbing the sleep from their eyes; Privates Eddie Snow and Bradley Culpepper were among the latter. Once on their horses, they followed Lieutenant Knowles and the rest of their company to the center of the encampment where the officers offered up a prayer for the troops. While their heads were still bowed, the sound of a lone horse's hooves clapping on the hard-pan clay plainly echoed across the clearing. When Eddie and the others looked around, a very tall, imposing officer entered their midst riding an impressive chestnut stallion with a white blaze and four white feet. The man appeared well over six feet in height, for his long legs dangled far below the horse's girth, with broad shoulders and a graying pony tail falling from beneath the back of his cap and he wore a royal blue coat adorned with gold medals that glistened in the morning sun. Someone in the crowd whispered that it was *General George Washington himself.* He was flanked by another officer in a powder-blue uniform, who, came another whisper, was the *Comte de Rochambeau*, commander of the French troops. The general made his way to the center of the clearing and adjusted himself in his saddle. Then, in a clear, deep voice very befitting of a military commander, he spoke to the soldiers.

"Men!" he said and immediately the camp was silent. *"The time is at hand which will probably determine whether Americans are to be free men or slaves; whether they are to have any property they can call their own. The fate of unborn millions will now depend, under God, on the courage and conduct of this army."*

He paused momentarily, clearing his throat, and went on.

"The eyes of all our countrymen are now upon us and we shall have their blessings and praises, if we are to be the instruments of saving them from the tyranny mediated against them. The enemy will endeavor to intimidate us by show and appearance; but, remember, they have been repulsed on various occasions by a few brave Americans! Every good soldier here will be silent and attentive and wait for orders, reserving his fire until he is sure of doing execution."

With that said, the general spoke down to his horse, patting the animal's muscular neck. "Come, Nelson," he said as he raised his sword from its scabbard and held it up, pointing toward the south. *"On to New York!"* he ordered and the entire army began to move as one massive juggernaut, following behind their leader down the streets of Newport. Company after company they marched; first the officers and Continental Calvary, with the din of a thousand horse hooves echoing across the cobblestones. Next, came the French troops behind *Rochambeau* followed by his infantry and the rest of the foot soldiers and then, finally, the militiamen in their rags. Eddie was one of the fortunate militiamen who had a horse to ride and someone shoved a flag in to his hands at the last minute. "Here, Snow," the soldier said. "Hoist the standard!"

As the people of Newport waved and cheered from the windows and doorways, Eddie steadied the butt of the pole against his thigh. The flag unfurled in the breeze and for the first time in his military experience Eddie Snow felt the slightest twinge of pride swell in his chest. *These people are depending on us!* He thought to himself. *If only he could find some honor in it!*

They rode from sunup to sundown, finally stopping to sleep on an elevated plateau from which they could watch the horizon for British troops. Exhausted and weary from the march, the men tended to their horses and gulped their suppers down quickly before they collapsed into their sleep sacks, only to be awakened before dawn to march again. And, on and on it went until they reached the Hudson River valley in New York, where some of the troops splintered off to remain behind to stand guard at strategic points along the river, while the others pushed on. Their new destination now appeared to be Philadelphia; to the *city of brotherly love*, where the troops, who still had not seen any monetary reward for their labors, finally received their long overdue pay vouchers. It boosted morale tremendously, as well as the coffers of the local innkeepers.

Somewhere along the way, Washington's strategy had obviously changed. Instead of launching attacks on New York or Philadelphia, they continued south, leaving all but those in high command confused as to where they were going. What Eddie and the other soldiers did *not* know was that Washington had received a secret dispatch that very morning, telling him that the French navy had finally arrived off the coast of Virginia. The dispatch went on to say that they had defeated the British navy in the Chesapeake Bay, and that the supreme commander of the British, General Charles Cornwallis, had garrisoned his troops nearby in Yorktown. It was obvious that Washington, like the cunning military jackal he was, was not about to bother himself with the *tail* of the snake in New York; he was going to lead his army directly to Yorktown to take off the snake's *head*!

For several more weeks, they marched on, through mosquito-infested swamps and lowlands, fording rivers and streams up to their waists. Virginia was experiencing an Indian summer. The weather had yet to turn cold which, under normal circumstances, would have made sleeping in the open air quite pleasant for the men, except for the biting insects that swarmed around them. Eddie himself was soon covered with itching bumps. Many of the men around him began to fall sick with fever and chills. At night, the camp smelled like a tannery from so many soggy boots drying on the campfires. By the time they reached Williamsburg, Eddie knew he, too, had contracted the disease; he could barely sit astride his horse, let alone have the strength to carry the flag. His body raged with the fever and his head ached acutely.

"You don't look so good, Snow," said Culpepper as he reached up to help Eddie down from his horse and they prepared to make camp on the outskirts of the town. Eddie dropped the flag in the dirt and literally *fell* into his friend's arms, lapsing into unconsciousness.

Chapter Seven *"Sleeping Through Yorktown"*

Eddie awoke briefly in a strange room and tried to focus his eyes on the objects around him. He noticed another man in a bed across the room but the man did not look familiar. Eddie closed his eyes to ease the dizziness in his head and leaned back against his pillow, drifting back into sleep. An hour later, he awakened again but his vision was still blurred. Clumsily, he pulled back the blanket and saw that someone had dressed him in a nightshirt. He could see yellow bruises on his right thigh and there were bandages on his arm that dangled off the edge of the bed over a blood-stained porcelain bowl but he remembered nothing. His mind was a blank slate.

Suddenly, he heard a woman's voice. "Well, Mister Snow," said a plump, middle-aged matron, who came to his bedside. "You have decided to join us again!"

She reached down and straightened his bedclothes, adjusting his pillow and wringing out a wet rag with which to wipe the sweat from his forehead.

"Hmmmm," she mumbled to herself, feeling his skin with the back of her hand. "Still a little feverish, but much better than yesterday."

"Where am I, Mistress?" he whispered; his throat was parched and he longed desperately for a drink of water.

"Williamsburg," she replied, and, as if she could read his mind, propped up his head and held a cup to his lips. "You were a very sick lad when they brought you to me."

"*Who* are *they*?" Eddie asked, still confused.

"Your friend, Mister Culpepper," said the woman. "You were so weak you fell from your horse. You must be quiet and rest now."

She crossed the room and sat beside the bed of the other patient. *Culpepper…. Culpepper…. Culpepper…* Eddie kept repeating the name in his mind. *Who in bloody hell was Culpepper?* Eddie could remember nothing. He watched as the woman tended to the other patient, sponging off his chest and arms with cool water.

He attempted to sit up but failed miserably and fell back when the pain shot through his head like a knife. Another woman, younger and much more attractive than the elder mistress entered the room and came to him, tucking his blanket back around him like a cocoon. "Shhhhh," she whispered. "You must rest. I will bring you some broth to sip and, if you behave yourself, I will tell you whatever you want to know."

The woman disappeared momentarily and returned with a large mug of steaming broth. She sat down in a chair beside his bed and began to gently spoon the broth into his mouth. The sensation of the warm liquid trickling down his throat was very pleasant. He wanted to sit upright, but his weakened condition forbade it. His sight was still blurry but he was aware that she was very pretty. "What is your name?" he asked between sips of broth.

"Susannah," she replied.

"And the other lady, is she your mother?" asked Eddie.

"No," said Susannah. "Her name is Gwendolyn. She is my aunt."

"Is she your only family?" Eddie asked.

He took a few more sips of the broth and felt a wave of nausea hit his gut.

"That's probably enough for now," she said sweetly. "Let's see if you can keep that down and I will bring you more later."

Susannah dropped the spoon into the half-empty cup and stood up, ready to leave. "My family lives in Chatham, Massachusetts," she told him. "I will be returning there soon, now that the war is over. There was a need for nurses to tend to the wounded and my aunt asked me to come and help her."

"Please," he begged. "Please, don't leave. I have so many questions. He put his hand on her forearm and she sat back down beside him. "What day is this?" he asked. "How long have I been here?"

"It is the eighteenth of October," said Susannah. "We have had the pleasure of your company for almost a month now."

"A month?" Eddie asked incredulously.

Susannah smiled and patted his hand. *"The war is over,"* she said. "Cornwallis surrendered to Washington at Yorktown."

"The *war*?" asked Eddie.

She laughed at that. *"Surely you remember the war!"*

Eddie tried to roll over under the restraint of the blankets, turning away from the young woman so she would not see the tears in his eyes. He was afraid to tell her that he remembered *nothing*.

"You have been sleeping for a long time now," she said soothingly. "Perhaps it will all come back to you after you have been awake awhile."

Eddie closed his eyes and tried to remember *something, anything.*

Susannah was his companion for many days; bathing him, spoon-feeding him liquid nourishment and keeping him warm and comfortable. At night, horrible nightmares haunted his sleep and he would wake up with his heart pounding and sweat rolling down his forehead.

"And, what are these dreams about?" Susannah asked him one morning when she brought him his breakfast. "Perhaps, they will help you to remember."

Eddie shuddered to re-live them. "One is of a British officer," he replied. "I can see him plainly coming toward me; smiling, as if we were old friends."

"And, *then* what?" asked Susannah.

Eddie swallowed hard. "I lunge at him and sink a dagger deep in his chest."

Susannah sighed. "Ah," she said. "Are you sure it wasn't a bayonet? Like the one on your rifle over there?"

Eddie turned and followed her glance across the room where a long rifle leaned against the wall. "That is mine?" he asked. "That means I must be a soldier. But, why can't I remember anything?"

"You hadn't any bumps on your head so my aunt seems to think it's the fever that's affected your memory," said Susannah. "Open your mouth and take this drop of mercury on your tongue and then you must rest. Malaria is a nasty disease. *You are lucky to be alive.*"

Chapter Eight *"The Journey Home"*

Several more days passed. Eddie's companion in the next bed was gone, leaving Eddie alone in the room. Eddie didn't miss him; the man slept all the time and rarely spoke. After he had left he found out why; the man was a French soldier and didn't speak a word of English.

When he was finally able to stand and walk about the room, on the faithful arm of his young nurse, they talked about many things and everything was new to Eddie. She told him his name was Eddie Snow, that he once had a friend named Culpepper and that he was from Massachusetts; that was all she knew. *That was all anyone knew.* "We wanted to notify your family of your whereabouts and we checked with the Continental army before they left Williamsburg," Susannah explained one morning, as she helped Eddie to his feet. "They said you must have belonged to one of the local militias so they didn't have any record of you." She helped him on with his tattered coat for their first walk outside. "It's not exactly a proper army uniform," she said. "But whoever darned and mended this for you did so with great care."

"My mother did that," Eddie said without a second thought.

When she realized he remembered something from his past, Susannah was encouraging. "That's good, Mister Snow," she said. "Your memory is returning!"

"Won't you please call me *Eddie*?" he asked. "You have nursed me for over a month now. I think we know each other well enough to be on a first name basis!"

Susannah smiled. She had become quite fond of the young militia man with no memory. They went outside and walked arm in arm along the cobblestoned street, looking up at rows of cone-shaped cypress trees on one side and, and on the other, silvery magnolias with their brilliant red seed pods hanging down like peeled pomegranates. Williamsburg was a pleasant town when it wasn't being ravaged by war. It was actually quite beautiful. They walked along in silence taking in the fresh autumn air. Susannah seemed to be subdued in quiet thought, Eddie observed, and he was about to find out why. "My work here is done," she said finally. "I will be returning to my home in Chatham next week."

Eddie felt the fear rise up in his chest. Susannah was the only person he felt he knew! *What will I do if she leaves me? Where will I go? How can I return to my home when I still cannot remember where home is?* He was at a loss for words and he stuttered a bit with the only reply he could think of. "Surely, you won't be travelling the roads alone!"

Susannah smiled and squeezed his arm. "No," she said. "My aunt would never allow that. She has enlisted a trusted gentleman friend to accompany me on my journey. Even in the best of times, it is unsafe for a woman to travel alone. You needn't worry about me, Eddie, for I will be well-protected."

"Your aunt will undoubtedly miss you," Eddie murmured, when what he *wanted* to say was that *he* would miss her.

"Aye," she replied. "And, I will miss you both as well."

There was a long pause. By the time they had reached the governor's palace at the end of the street, with its red brick walls and iron gates, the wind had come up, sending yellow leaves scattering across the cobblestones and causing her skirt to billow about her. "We should probably turn back," she said, looking up at the sky. "I'm afraid there won't be many more pleasant autumn days left for walks."

Eddie fell silent and his face drooped. The news that Susannah was leaving weighed heavy on his heart. He had to think of something to say! There would be no more opportunities to talk to her! He opened his mouth and the words that came out surprised even him. "Would you allow me to accompany you back to Massachusetts, Susannah?"

Susannah looked startled; even though she was aware of the bond of friendship that had developed between them, the idea seemed a little too personal. She looked at Eddie; so lost, so forlorn, so alone in the world. *Perhaps*, she thought, *returning to Massachusetts might jog his memory. Perhaps he would remember his home and be able to return to his family.* "It is a long journey," she said quietly, anticipating, in her mind, the objections her aunt would undoubtedly raise. "Several weeks of rough roads and contrary weather, I expect. Are you sure you feel up to travelling so soon?"

Eddie smiled. "Yes," he assured her. "I am feeling stronger every day, thanks to you."

It was an absurd notion! Her aunt would most certainly be opposed to the idea! Still, she could not help herself from sharing Eddie's enthusiasm. "My father owns a livery in Chatham," she told him. "Perhaps, he could put you to work there, just until your memory returns, of course. Then, you will want to return home."

Eddie's lips broke into a wide smile. "Perhaps," he said coyly. "Or, perhaps, I shall remain on in Chatham."

And, so, it was settled. The following week Susannah kissed her aunt goodbye despite the expected protests of the older woman. *I will have a military escort!* she had told Gwendolyn. *How much safer can I be?* And, she and Eddie rode out of town on two borrowed horses. It seemed the logical, practical thing to do; *returning a soldier to his home.* She was growing as much attached to him as he was to her and she could not bring herself to abandon him.

Susannah had been right about the weather. There was a distinct winter chill in the air on the morning they left. Susannah had cleaned Eddie's coat and trousers and her aunt gave them gloves to keep their hands from freezing and woolen scarves to wear around their necks to protect them from the wind. There was no snow yet; only the brittle cold air on their faces as, bundled in many layers of clothing and their other belongings rolled up behind their saddles, they rode out onto the King's Highway from Williamsburg to begin their long journey home.

Wherever *home* was.

Chapter Nine *"An Alternate Route"*

They had planned on their journey taking at least three weeks; their route stretched well over six hundred miles up and around the Chesapeake Bay, along the James River and northeast from there, through Philadelphia and New York, all the way to Cape Cod. They hoped to cover thirty miles a day if the weather was tolerable. With biscuits and jerky to sustain themselves and water stored in wineskins, they only planned to stop to rest their horses and sleep when there were decent accommodations. Susannah knew if it began to snow, their momentum could be delayed so, even though her concern for Eddie's health was foremost in her mind, she insisted they not stop to rest any more than necessary; getting caught in a blizzard was bound to be worse for her patient than *saddle sores*. Eddie followed along behind her doggedly as she forged ahead at a brisk trot. He knew she was anxious for home and family. His only desire was to stay close to Susannah; *the only person he knew in the world.*

A peculiar thought occurred to him as they rode along the very first day; *what if Susannah had a beau waiting for her at home?* They had never spoken of her personal life; he only knew she was unmarried from small scraps of information she had shared about her family. He watched her now, riding along on her horse with the wind flattening her bonnet against her hair and her calico skirt swelling out over her horse's tail. He had grown very fond of Susannah and yet the word *love* had not entered his mind. He knew he *needed* her desperately; she was the only reality he had in his life but he wondered what he would feel when he regained his memory. What if *he* had a woman waiting for him to return from the war at that very moment? What he did not know was that Susannah had also entertained the same thoughts. She knew she had no beau waiting for her in Chatham. *But what if Eddie had a wife and children?*

The King's Highway cut a wide swath through endless miles of harvested tobacco fields that were turned under for the winter, lying brown and sterile around them. They rode in silence for quite a while until Eddie found himself humming a tune to break the monotony. Soon, the words to the song came to him from somewhere deep in his fractured memory and, much to Susannah's amusement, he started singing:

"Farewell and adieu to you Spanish ladies;

Farewell and adieu to you ladies of Spain;

For we've received orders to sail from New England;

And we hope in a short time to see you again!"

"Pray, where did you learn that silly song, Eddie Snow?" she asked him. "Sounds like an old sea shanty to me!

Perhaps you were once a sailor before you joined the militia!"

Eddie could not for the life of him recall where he had heard the song but he was intrigued that he remembered the lyrics to *any* song at all! He lowered his voice to the lowest depth he could muster and he began again loudly in an exaggerated, mocking tone:

"We'll rant and we'll roar like true Yankee Whaler men;

We'll rant and we'll roar on deck and below;

Until we sight Gay Head off old Martha's Vineyard;

And straight up the channel to New Bedford we'll go!"

By now, Susannah was giggling uncontrollably at Eddie's ridiculous performance and the more he entertained her, the more of the old song he remembered:

"We have our old ship to the wind from sou'west, boys;

We have our old ship to deep soundings to take;

T'was forty-five fathoms with light sandy bottom;

We squared our main yard and up channel did make!"

"Stop!" she screeched, "Or I shall have to get off my horse and loosen my stays!"

Eddie stopped singing and began to laugh along with her. He hadn't laughed in ever so long; at least since he had taken sick. Susannah's cheeks were as pink as rose wine and her eyes were misted with tears of laughter. She had stopped her horse in the middle of the road, allowing Eddie to catch up to her. "There is a farmhouse up ahead," she said, when her laughter had subsided, pointing down the road ahead of them. "They will give us lodging for the night. I stayed here on my way to Williamsburg the last time. They are very nice people."

Eddie had stopped his singing and the smile on his face had evaporated into seriousness again. *Where had he learned a song of the sea? Gay Head? Martha's Vineyard? New Bedford? Could any of those towns be his home town?* he wondered as they approached the farmhouse and an old woman came out on the porch to see who her visitors were.

"Why, Miss Susannah!" the woman exclaimed happily. "Are you returning to Chatham?"

"Yes, indeed, Ma'am," replied Susannah. "Now that the war is over……"

The woman's face grew serious as Susannah dismounted from her horse and greeted her with an affectionate embrace. "Ah, Child," the woman said. "Don't be so sure it is *over*."

As she ushered Susannah and Eddie into the house, Susannah introduced them. "This is one of my patients," she said. "Eddie Snow from Massachusetts. I am returning him home to his family and he is protecting me on my journey."

"I am pleased to make your acquaintance," the woman said. "My husband is working in the fields but he will be happy to welcome a soldier at our table."

The three settled down at the kitchen table and the woman brought hot coffee from the hearth.

"What did you mean when you said that the war is not over?" asked Susannah. "I was told Cornwallis surrendered!"

Eddie was interested too. If it were true, should he be returning to the war instead of returning to Chatham with Susannah? He listened to the woman's words intently.

"Well," she continued, "It *is* true the British troops that were left after the battle at Yorktown were taken prisoner. But, *The Newsletter* says there are still thousands of Redcoats all over New England who haven't given up so easily. Why, just last week we had to run a couple out of our corn crib! Caught 'em sleepin' there ever so cozy! I had to hide the ammunition or my husband would've *blasted* them all the way back to England!"

Susannah's eyes were riveted to the woman's words. *The war was not over? How could that be? The Continental Army had left Williamsburg! She had presumed it was safe to travel the roads again! Had she led poor Eddie into the path of danger?*

Eddie glanced at Susannah, wondering much of the same. He was glad he had brought his musket that was now tied to his saddle. He might be forced to use it to protect them! *God, why couldn't he remember anything except a silly old sea shanty?* His memory was taking far too long to come back to him! He was lost in thought until he realized the woman had addressed him. Susannah answered for him. "Mister Snow has temporarily lost his memory," she explained to the woman. "He suffered from malaria for over a month."

"I suppose that is almost as bad as being *shot*," said the woman. "All the same, though, you two had better be careful riding all the way to Massachusetts alone. Stay off the King's Highway! They're out there, I assure you! The Redcoats will rise up again when we least expect it!"

Chapter Ten *"The Search"*

Back in Eastham, Lois Snow read and *re-read* the Boston Newsletter over and over to be sure she was reading it correctly. *The war was over! Cornwallis had surrendered! Surely that meant Eddie was on his way home!* But, when weeks and then months had gone by and Eddie still had not returned, she had begun to worry. *What if her son had died on the battlefield? What if he was lying wounded somewhere? Why, oh, why didn't she receive any news?*

She had wrapped her warmest shawl around her shoulders and marched down the icy Skaket Road, all the way to the armory where the militia men had congregated upon their return; *their return without one of their own!*

"We heard that Eddie took ill with malaria somewhere around Williamsburg," an apologetic young soldier told her. "Private Culpepper took him to a temporary hospital in town just before we marched on Yorktown."

"Well," said Lois insistently, "Where can I find this Private Culpepper? I want to know what has happened to my son!"

The soldier's face took on a somber expression. "Culpepper was killed at Yorktown," he told her. "I'm sorry, Missus Snow. That is all I can tell you."

Lois was livid. She gathered her skirts and marched home with bottled up anger that exploded into tears the minute she closed the door behind her. *Some efficient militia we have!* She voiced her thoughts to the empty room. *They can't even keep track of their own!* She paced the floor weeping and wringing her hands until Ephraim arrived home for supper and she met him at the door with desperation in her eyes. "We must go look for Eddie!" she said adamantly before poor Ephraim had a chance to remove his coat. "He is out there somewhere! I paid a visit to the armory this afternoon. They said he fell ill to malaria and was taken to a hospital in Williamsburg. Please, Ephraim! You must go find your brother!"

"I have already made plans to go, Ma," he said. "I finally got a replacement to deliver the mail in my absence. I can leave for Williamsburg tomorrow." He made her sit down while he kindled the fire and then made her some hot tea. "You must calm yourself, Ma," he told her. "You have your father to care for and you mustn't get sick yourself! Leave it to me. I will find Eddie, I promise."

She calmed a little. She hadn't slept well for weeks. Ephraim could hear her on many nights pacing and crying softly into her handkerchief; the swishing of her skirts and the padding of her slippers on the floor and the sniffling of her nose was a nightly occurrence.

"You need to rest, Ma," he said and insisted she go to bed.

"But your supper…." she tried to protest.

"Don't worry about me," he told her. "Go to bed now or I won't get any sleep myself! And, I have a long way to ride tomorrow!"

As long as he could convince her she was doing it for *him*, she agreed to lie down and rest and, soon, Ephraim was able to do the same. With the morning light, he was on his way, following the King's Highway around the upper cape, on the long road to Williamsburg. A light snow had fallen the night before but now the sun was up, glaring harshly on the stark whiteness before him that almost blinded him. Ephraim had brought with him his hunting rifle, but he was hoping he would not have to use it. His brother's comrades at the armory had warned him of the dangers when his mother wasn't listening, so as not to worry her needlessly. *Be careful,* they told him. *There was news of renegade Redcoats ambushing civilians all over Massachusetts, stealing their horses and weapons and shooting to kill if necessary.*

Ephraim knew he was not as brave as his older brothers. Mickey and Eddie were the *soldiers* in the family. He was just the meek little messenger, the one who stayed behind and took care of their mother. To say he was ashamed would be going too far, but he definitely felt a twinge of guilt now and then that he had sacrificed *nothing* for his country, when his brothers had sacrificed so much. Sure that he was branded a coward in the whispers of some, he pretended he had an important job to do. After all, *someone* had to deliver the mail! He suspected his brave brother Eddie would never understand his feelings; *his brother was cut out for war!* Now, perhaps, he could repair his sorry reputation by bringing Eddie home! *If only,* he prayed, *he was still alive!*

The King's Highway was once again a bustling thoroughfare. War had depleted most of the country's stores and they had to rebuild. Wagonloads of much-needed supplies were once again bouncing over the rutted road toward the cape. Farmers, who had been away fighting, were late in turning over their fields but they were determined to have a bounty crop come spring and he passed the frozen-whiskered men struggling behind their mules to turn under the hard ground before the heavy snows came. Ephraim was glad the road was so busy. It was a long journey at best; greeting passers-by helped to pass the tedious hours of riding.

He tried to keep his mind on finding his brother and tried to retrace his path; he remembered Eddie had been summoned to Newport so he started there, asking questions of everyone and, then, following the route he was told the army had taken. In every town, he was given the same answer: *follow the King's Highway all the way to Williamsburg.* No one could remember a single militia man out of the thousands that had marched through town with Washington. *Finding Eddie,* thought Ephraim dismally, *was going to be like finding a needle in a haystack.*

Chapter Eleven *"Scoundrels Along the Way"*

The road that turned off of the main highway meandered through a wooded grove, winding this way and that, under the cover of a canopy of tall cypress trees. Eddie took the lead in front of Susannah; in case they ran into wild animals or worse, he wanted to be in a position to defend her. The horses tensed up in the darkness, their black eyes darting from one peculiar sound to another and snorting nervously as they stepped carefully over the worn path, for they were animals accustomed to travelling the wide, well-lit highway and whatever lurked in the shadows kept them on constant alert. When light finally illuminated the path as they reached a clearing, their wary steeds broke into happy trots, eager to be out in the bright sunlight again.

"Have you had any more memories?" Susannah asked Eddie as she pulled her horse in beside him on the trail. "Do you remember where you heard that silly song?"

Eddie shook his head sadly. "No," he replied. "I have no idea where that came from."

"Perhaps your family lives on the outer cape," she said. "Eastham or Truro, perhaps?"

"Nothing comes to me," said Eddie. "It is like my life began on the morning when I awoke in that bed in your aunt's house. I fear I am no better than a newborn who has everything to learn!"

Susannah wanted to help him all she could but she had never dealt with an amnesia victim before and she had no idea of where to start. "Well," she said. "I think we should work on what you *do* remember. Like your mother mending your coat and the sea shanty and your dreams."

"Dreams are just dreams, Susannah," he said. "I doubt they have anything to do with the reality of my life."

"Well," she said. "Can you remember anything else about your mother? She must have loved you very much to mend your clothes so carefully. Can you see her in your mind? Can you hear her voice?"

Eddie focused his eyes on the road ahead of them, thinking about who his mother was. He had known that she had mended his coat but *how* had he known? Had he watched her thread her needle? Had she scolded him for tearing it and getting it soiled? He searched for the sound of her voice in his ears. Had she said goodbye to him when he went to war? Had she been proud of him?

Several minutes passed in silence. Susannah watched him as his eyes searched and his mind desperately sought out his past.

"Fiddlesticks!" she said suddenly. "I think my horse has thrown a shoe! He is walking *ever* so clumsily. We must stop and fix it or he will surely go lame."

"What did you say?" Eddie asked her.

"My horse...." she said, reining the beast in and jumping to the ground beside him. "Yes, he has surely thrown a shoe."

"No," said Eddie. "Not that. What was that *word* you used?"

Susannah thought for a moment. *"Fiddlesticks?"* she said. "Haven't you ever heard anyone say that before?"

"Yes," said Eddie. "My *mother* used to say that!"

He was beaming broadly as he got down from his horse and searched the path behind them for the lost shoe. Another piece of his memory had returned! *It is only a matter of time,* he thought to himself. When he returned to her, holding the piece of molded iron up for her to see. "I found it!" he said. "The nails are still intact! If I can only find an instrument to pound with I think I can straighten them and reattach it."

He searched and found a flat stone that would have to suffice as a makeshift hammer and he went to work getting the shoe back on the horse's hoof while Susannah stood beside him and held the reins. She looked at the sky and the clouded sun above them. It was getting late in the day and getting colder; the detour through the woods had cost them valuable time. Heaven only knew how long it would take them now to reach Chatham, going over winding roads and paths through the wilderness. She knew the King's Highway well, for she had travelled it many times, but she feared they might get lost out here in the woods. She couldn't rely on her traveling companion's memory since he had none. The concern on her face was not lost on Eddie. "Try not to worry," he told her as he helped her back on her horse. "I will get you home safely, Susannah! I may have lost my memory but I do have *some* useful skills."

At that moment, the bushes near them rustled and the horses started, pointing their ears toward the sound. Two soldiers clad in dirty red uniforms emerged from the thicket alongside the path, both holding rifles that were pointed directly at Eddie and Susannah.

"Now, that you have fixed that horseshoe," said one of the men with a cocky British accent, "My friend and I will relieve you of *both* your horses."

Eddie reached for his musket that was tied to his saddle.

"We'll take that musket too!" shouted the other soldier, rushing forward to snatch it from Eddie's reach.

"How dare you!" Susannah shot back at them. "You can't take our horses and leave us here in the middle of nowhere! What *cowards* you British are!"

Eddie glanced at her and shook his head in a silent warning but Susannah yanked on the reins of her horse's bridle and spun him around to run. The second soldier grabbed the reins from her and struggled to keep the horse from bolting. Before Eddie could do anything, a gunshot ripped through the silence of the open field and the first soldier was standing there with the barrel of his gun smoking before him. Eddie tried to turn his horse to reach Susannah when he saw the bullet hit her and knock her backwards off her horse. Just as he jumped down to assist her, the soldiers scrambled to retrieve the horses, swinging themselves into the saddles and galloping off across the field at lightning speed.

"Susannah!" Eddie screamed as he knelt beside her, lifted her head up and put his arms around her. Blood was rapidly turning the bodice of her pretty calico dress crimson and Eddie cradled her against him. She looked up at him with eyes that were drowsy and half-closed. "Eddie," she murmured.

"I'm here, Susannah," he said, trying to sound calm when his heart was pounding wildly in his chest.

"Our horses!" she whispered. "You must not let them take our horses!"

Her voice was raspy and uneven. Her eyes closed. Eddie stroked her hair gently and, at that moment, he knew how very much he loved her and how sorry he was that he had never told her so.

"Just get me home, Eddie," she said, so quietly he had to lean in close to hear her.

"I will, Susannah," he told her. "I will."

Chapter Twelve *"On His Brother's Trail"*

By the time Ephraim had reached Williamsburg, the snows had been steadily falling for weeks and the King's Highway was blanketed in white all the way south from Philadelphia. His hands were frozen to the reins as steadfastly as his eyes were focused on the road ahead; his horse's breath rose as white as smoke from a chimney fire above them. His heart lurched at the first sight of the town in which he hoped to find news of his brother, secretly hoping he would find him still alive in the hospital there. After being directed at the livery to the home of Mistress Gwendolyn Atkins, Ephraim quickly stabled his horse and went in search of his long lost brother.

When she greeted him at the door and he informed her who he was looking for, Gwendolyn's face took on a worried expression. "Aye," she said. "He was here. Had the fever real bad, he did. It was touch and go for long while."

"And, is he still here?" Ephraim asked anxiously.

"No," replied Gwendolyn. "He and my niece headed back to Chatham before the snows came."

"Chatham?" asked Ephraim. "My brother's home is in Eastham. Why ever would he be going to Chatham?"

The woman invited him in and poured him a cup of coffee so that she could explain. "I'd better warn you, Mister Snow. The fever took your brother's memory away," she told him, as Ephraim warmed himself by her fire. "He might not know you. He doesn't remember Eastham or anything of his past. That is why Susannah was a'takin him to Chatham. Just until his memory came back to him. But…." She paused and pursed her lips and her eyes darted away from Ephraim.

"But, *what*?" he asked her.

"I got a letter from my brother just yesterday," she said. "They ain't seen hide nor hair of either of them yet. They should've been there by now. I can't imagine what has happened to them!"

Ephraim remembered what the soldier at the armory had told him about the renegade Redcoats on the roads but he held his tongue, not wanting to frighten the lady. "What was your niece's *family* name, Ma'am?" he asked.

"Atkins. *Susannah Atkins*," replied Gwendolyn. "Will you go and look for them?"

Ephraim smiled and thanked her for the coffee. "You can rest assured that I will," he said. "I promise you I will get word back to you as soon as I find out anything."

Rushing back to the livery, he traded his tired horse for a fresh mount, gathered some food in his saddle pack and headed back down the King's Highway. By nightfall, he reached the farmhouse where Susannah and Eddie had rested and the woman remembered them well. "I told 'em to take the back roads, to avoid trouble," she told him. When she heard that they had not arrived in Chatham, she shook her head. "Seems as if I told them wrong."

"Do you know which road they took?" asked Ephraim, now so close on his brother's trail he was frantic for more information.

"Probably down the old plantation road," she surmised. "Down through the woods and out the other side."

Ephraim wanted to head out immediately but darkness had fallen around him, a deep moonless darkness, that told him it would be foolish to begin his journey before morning. The woman fed him and gave him leave to sleep in the hayloft over the barn and her husband offered his horse hay and water. Although the hay was soft and sweet-smelling and it would have made a pleasant place to rest, he could not bring himself to sleep. So rejuvenated with new hope, he tossed and turned until it was almost dawn and was cantering down the old plantation road before the sun made its first appearance on the horizon.

There was no path to follow, for the snow now covered everything. Still he forged on, until he was underneath the canopy of the trees where the bare ground finally revealed a well-worn path. He looked for signs, anything that they might have left behind like a cold fire pit or manure from their horses. But, the woods were as unyielding of information as the King's Highway had been. It was as if his brother and his companion had just *vanished.*

The snow had stopped falling and the air was warmed by a winter sun by the time he reached the edge of the woods. His horse's hooves made the only tracks in the pristine freshness of the snowy field where there were no signs of life anywhere; even the birds were silent in the trees and the creatures that made their homes there were nestled in their dens and burrows to keep warm. In the clearing, not much larger than their cornfield back home in Eastham, Ephraim spied some peculiar markings in the snow, two long straight lines, a foot apart and two footprints, as if someone was dragging a litter behind them. It led away from the clearing and up to the edge of a river, and then turned north along the riverbanks. *If they are afoot,* he thought hopefully, *I'll surely be able to catch up to them!" But, why were there not two sets of footprints in the snow?* The thought was disconcerting to him. *Was one of them injured or worse?*

Hours passed and the daylight faded away into night again. Ephraim unsaddled his horse and settled down in the shelter of a tree. This time he *did* sleep, soundly and relaxed, now that he was confident he would find Eddie soon. He awoke with renewed vigor and stamina and picked up the trail again that wound around several lakes and streams before it led into a salt-marsh and disappeared in a field of tall grass. *If only he had a hound!* he thought. *An animal that could smell them even without visible tracks.* His horse was of no use in that regard. It merely followed where Ephraim directed it, without a clue of where it was headed, and was more interested in grazing in the grass that was peeking through the patches of snow.

Another night and another day went by. He was now very near the ocean and Ephraim had run out of food, forcing him to dig for clams on the sandy shore to have anything to eat at all. He picked up the trail again on the beach and urged his horse into a gallop. By now, he could see he had help tracking his brother; he was now following several sets of wolf paw prints as well. He stopped briefly and readied his musket.

Finally, looking down from the top of a dune, he saw them; his brother was plodding along, pulling the body of his companion behind him on a litter made of two branches pushed through the sleeves of his coat that cradled her body between them. She appeared to be a petite thing; her feet barely protruded past the hem of Eddie's coat and he could see that she had lost one of her shoes. He could also see three wolves following close behind them. *Was she injured?* Ephraim wondered. As he got closer he *knew*; the woman must have been dead for days. His stomach lurched at the terrible smell in the air. The wolves were hovering, salivating, ready to strike when Ephraim came riding up behind them. Eddie turned around, half-expecting more thieving Redcoats; his eyes were dull and unafraid, however, for he had nothing left of value to steal. Ephraim could see his brother had lost weight, looking almost gaunt, and he was shivering in his bare shirtsleeves from the cold. He stared at Ephraim and Ephraim stared back; their eyes locked and widened. Ephraim aimed his gun and took a shot at the wolves. When the smoke cleared, the animals had vanished into the tall reeds and Eddie still hadn't moved.

"Eddie!" said Ephraim. "Eddie, it's *me, Ephraim!*"

Chapter Thirteen *"Edmund"*

Eighty-year-old Edmund Freeman opened his front door and breathed in the cold, salty mist off the ocean deeply into his lungs. He stepped out onto the tiny porch of his little house nestled in the sand dunes beyond Eastham and stretched himself. The tide was high and the waves were pounding the shoreline; there was still snow on the ground from the previous day and he expected it to be there for a long time to come. Temperatures weren't likely to rise again until spring.

He glanced down the rutted road between the dunes that led all the way to town, wondering if his daughter, Lois, would bring him breakfast or whether he should fix himself something to eat. *Poor Lois*, he thought. *She was getting forgetful. She was beside herself with worry about Eddie. Now she had sent Ephraim off to search for him.* He hoped she wouldn't have to bury three of her sons all in the same year!

 He bundled himself up in his woolen pea coat that had kept him warm for many years on the sea and sat down on the top step. He missed the sea. Missed it something *awful!* But, he knew his fishing days were over. His failing eyes scanned the beach up and down which was barren and gray for as far as he could see. No more *beach of bones*, he thought sourly. Ever since the king had taken away the Wampanoag's rights to herd the blackfish ashore the beach was a lonely, gray place, nothing more.

No more whales. Soon there will be no more Wampanoag.

He saw them up the beach a half mile or so, two brown-skinned figures, one old and one young, both with feathers in their black hair, coming toward him. He recognized one, Uriah Mayo, the son of Old Thomas. As they got nearer he could see the boy was his young son, Samuel. They were carrying bows and arrows over their shoulders, probably to hunt the deer that came to the shore to lick salt off the seaweed on the beach. Like horses drawn to salt, the deer craved it too. Edmund could never figure out why.

He waved to Uriah and the boy.

"You see any *ottuck* today?" the tall Wampanoag yelled up from the beach. Uriah spoke very good English, being married to a white woman, but often he used Wampanoag words mixed with English in his speech. *Ottuck* was the Wampanoag word for *deer.*

Edmund shook his head and yelled back. "Not today."

He knew the once sea-going tribe now hunted deer and fished for cod along the coast ever since their whaling rights had been taken away. Winter was a harsh time on the cape, even for those families who had their larders stuffed with food.

Uriah waved back at the old man and, without stopping, they continued down the beach.

"Stop by for a visit on your way back," called Edmund. "My daughter will have something cooking on the fire by then!"

He watched as the two Wampanoag slowly disappeared in the distance and went back inside to stoke the fire. *Where was Lois anyway*? He wondered. *He was hungry.* He pulled a loaf of three-day-old bread from the cupboard and sawed off two slices, smearing them with the blackberry jam his daughter had made for him in the spring. He remembered the resentment he had felt when Lois had gone off and married Jesse Snow, how he missed having her around so much he slept in her bed for weeks after the wedding. Outsiders would have thought it strange, very improper, but he knew his feelings for his daughter were pure; she *had* been like a wife to him in many ways since her mother had died, when Lois was so very young. She had cooked and cleaned, she had laundered and mended his clothes; she always had a hot meal waiting for him when he returned from the sea. But, Lois needed a husband; it was her right. There were just things a father could not provide, like children of her own. He just missed her smile, her voice, her very presence in the little house they had called home. Now, he often wished she would come home, now that all her children were grown and he was all alone out here midst the sand dunes and the surf.

At that moment, Lois threw open the door and entered, carrying an armload of bread and other sweet-smelling things wrapped up in a kitchen cloth. "Hello, Pa," she said, planting a quick kiss on his cheek. She noticed the bread and jam in his hands. "I brought you some fresh bread. That old loaf must be tough as shoe leather by now! Remember your teeth aren't as strong as they used to be!"

She laughed and went to the kitchen, where she put down her bundle and sliced him some fresh, still warm, bread and put some coffee on to boil. "It's *freezing* out there," she continued to chatter while the old man consumed his fresh bread with vigor. "I do hope Ephraim and Eddie have not been caught in the snow."

Edmund shook his head. "They are grown men, Lois," he said. "They can take care of themselves. My word, you still treat them like little boys!" He realized he had touched a nerve with his careless words as soon as he had said them and he was immediately sorry. "Forgive me, child," he said. "I know you are going through a difficult time right now. That wasn't very sensitive of me."

"Oh, you needn't apologize, Pa," she said. "I know my Eddie will be coming home. Ephraim will find him! I will have my boys home with me very soon!"

Edmund had his doubts. Eddie had been gone too long and the war was over with no word of him. It didn't look promising. But he held his tongue and let his daughter have her hope. "I invited Uriah and the boy for supper," he said. "Will we have enough to feed two starving Indians?"

Lois smiled at her father. He spent so much time with the Wampanoag men it wouldn't have surprised her if he moved to the Indian camp south of town. For as long as she could remember, they had fished together, back when they herded the blackfish into the shallows and when they had shared their catch of cod and shellfish in the off-season. They were kindred spirits, blood brothers joined by the sea. "Of course," she said. "I brought enough meat to make a fine stew for you to warm over but if you wish to share it, that is fine too."

She busied herself putting the stew together and finally put the pot on the fire, joining her father at the kitchen table. *He looked tired,* she thought to herself, *haggard and grey.* How long could she keep this up, trekking all the way from Skaket Road out here to the dunes to care for him? She wasn't getting any younger herself! "Why don't you come live with me in town, Pa?" she asked him for the hundredth time, knowing the answer he had given her ninety-nine times before.

"Not till you bury me," he said. "I want to die in my own bed."

Chapter Fourteen *"The Wampanoag Way"*

Eddie seemed to be in a trance as his brother approached him. "Eddie?" Ephraim said again. "Don't you know me? It's Ephraim, *your brother*!"

He put a hand on Eddie's shoulder and removed the branches of wood that held up the makeshift litter from his hands, letting the corpse of the woman gently down on the sand. Eddie blinked and the haze seemed to clear from his eyes for a moment. His expression was empty but slowly a distant smile came across his lips and he reached out and touched Ephraim's face. "Brother!" he said with quiet wonder. "I remember you! *You're my brother! Ephraim!*" He threw his arms around Ephraim and cried tears of joy.

"My God," said Ephraim. "What has happened to you? Why are you clear out here on the shore? Why didn't you come back on the King's Highway? Do you know how hard it was to find you?"

They laughed and cried together, Eddie mumbling out what had happened to him and Susannah on the road. With the mention of her name, he looked down and began to weep again, sinking to the sand on his knees. Ephraim took him by his shoulders and pulled him away. "We have to bury her," he said firmly. "Eddie, for God's sake, you can't drag a *rotting corpse* all the way back to Chatham!"

Eddie shook his head. "I promised her I would get her home," he said adamantly. "I *promised* her, Ephraim!"

"She needs to be buried," said Ephraim. "It would be disgraceful to bring her home to her family like this!"

Eddie looked up, focusing on the field of reeds and swamp grass beyond the sandy shore, knowing eyes were watching them. "And, as soon as we leave, they will dig her up!" he said. "I can't let her be supper for a pack of wolves!"

Ephraim could see his brother was not rational about the subject. His mind raced, reaching for any solution to the problem at hand. "Do you remember when we used to attend the Wampanoag funerals with Pa?" he asked, not knowing if Eddie's memory of their childhood was completely gone. "Do you remember the pyres they built?"

Eddie struggled to remember. *Funeral? Pyres? Wampanoag?* Slowly, trickles of memory seeped into his brain. "Yes!" he replied, astonished that he could recall something that had happened so long ago. "They burned the bodies and buried their bones wrapped in deerskin!"

"Yes!" said Ephraim. "I knew you would remember! We can bury Susannah the *Wampanoag* way! That way the wolves won't get to her!"

Ephraim turned and scanned the clearing around them for driftwood and began collecting all he could find. "Come help me, Eddie," he said. "The sooner we take care of Susannah the sooner I can get you home! Ma is *ever* so worried about you!"

When they had gathered a goodly amount of driftwood and dried reeds, Ephraim pulled a flint from his saddlebag while Eddie knelt and took Susannah's body in his arms and laid her gently on the bed of wood. Ephraim pushed his brother away to a safe distance and lit the fire under her and the flames soon consumed her, crackling and snapping in the cold ocean air. Ephraim could see that his brother was weeping softly; the reflections of the fire danced in the tears that ran down his face and the wolves watched from a distance, as their prey went up in smoke.

When the fire had dwindled, they gathered up her bones and wrapped them in a blanket from Ephraim's saddle bag. Ephraim tied the small bundle to the back of his saddle. He handed the reins to Eddie. "Here, Brother," he said. "You have walked holes in your shoes. You take my horse and let me walk awhile. We can take her to Chatham for a proper burial and *then we're going home!*"

Chapter Fifteen *"Lois"*

Lois finished preparing her father's supper and gathered up his laundry to take home for a good scrubbing. She noticed Edmund had gone back outside and she found him sitting on the stoop in front of the house, staring at the horizon. *He has never been the same,* she thought, *since he came home from the sea.* The sea had been his life's blood; it seemed as if it had given him a reason to live after her mother died. She understood completely. *The sea is to my father as my children are to me.* The words did not upset her. She knew he loved her too. But the sea ran through his veins just as surely as the blood that ran through her own. "Pa," she said quietly. "I've got to get back to town now. It's nigh on to dark and the wolves will be out."

He nodded as she bent over to kiss his cheek.

"Enjoy your supper with Uriah," she said. "I will check in on you again tomorrow."

He nodded again. "Thank you, Child, for the stew. I am sure Uriah and his boy will be grateful."

She smiled, half-heartedly at best, for she knew the plight of the Wampanoag tribe and she knew how concerned her father was about his friends. She waved before she walked away down the path to town. Halfway to the highway she paused to rest. Her hips ached from walking several miles every day to care for her father.

She hoped against hope that her father would agree to come inland and live with her but she knew better. *This was his home.*

She stopped in at the mercantile when she reached the main street, finding Mary Clark behind the counter, and greeted her warmly. "And, how are you today?" she asked.

"I'm just fine, Missus Snow," replied Mary. "Is there any word of Eddie and Ephraim yet?"

Lois shook her head. "No," she answered. "But, I expect them home any day now!"

Mary is such a sweet girl, thought Lois. *She would make a perfect wife for her Eddie.*

"Oh, I do hope so, Missus Snow," said Mary. "I pray for their safe return every night."

Prayers! thought Lois. *What good do prayers do?* She had prayed for years but it still didn't save her Jesse, or her boy, Mickey. Why would it save Eddie and Ephraim now? Her faith had suffered in the years since the war started. Instead of the hope she had once felt, she was feeling bitterness, as if her family was dying around her, being snatched from her bosom, leaving her alone. Still, it was comforting that someone else cared. *Mary cared.*

"What can I get for you today?" Mary was talking but Lois' mind was far away.

"Oh, just some soap," she said, patting the bundle she held in one hand. "I must do my father's laundry tomorrow. He is just like my boys, always gets his clothes so dirty…."

Her mind wandered off again. Mary retrieved a box of soap flakes from the shelf while Lois dug in her purse for change.

"You don't owe anything, Missus Snow," said Mary. "Eddie left plenty on your account for your purchases."

Lois smiled. "He's a good boy, my Eddie," she said.

"And he will be home very soon, I'm sure," Mary told her as the old woman left the store and set out for Skaket Road.

It was dark by now. The moon had risen high above the little town; big and round, it lit up her path as she hurried toward home. She hugged the bundle of laundry close to her chest for warmth against the chill in the night air. In the distance she heard owls hooting in the tall trees and wolves howling from beyond the kettle ponds and she hurried even faster, despite her aching hip. Ahead, she could see the house; its white paint picked up the moonbeams and set it apart from the forest beyond it. In the window, she thought she saw the flicker of light; *had she left a candle burning*? Surely not! Even though her memory was not as good as it used to be, she was more careful than that, never leaving anything burning that could catch the house on fire while she was gone. *It must be the reflection of the moon in the window pane*, she reasoned, unless…. oh, she dared not hope for what was running through her head at that moment!

But, as she neared the house, the light became clearer; it *was* a lamp burning in the kitchen window! It wasn't the moon's reflection! Someone was there! *Could it be? Could it be?* She quickened her pace and by the time she reached the path across the yard she was almost running. "Eddie! Ephraim!" she called out in the darkness. The door opened and her sons stepped out to meet her as she flew up the steps.

Maybe prayers did work after all! Her boys were finally home!

Chapter Sixteen *"The Old Man Returns to the Sea"*

They sat up almost all night at the kitchen table, listening to Eddie's story. Lois was beside herself with joy and couldn't seem to stop bursting into tears. As Eddie recounted what had happened to him, he seemed preoccupied with his surroundings, wandering around the rooms he grew up in, touching and studying objects, as if his mind was reaching out for every memory he could find. It was coming back slowly; he had recognized his mother and his brother immediately. When the other family members came to welcome him home the following day, he stumbled over their names, even though he knew their faces. "I still don't remember much about the war," he told Lois, after Ephraim had gone off to deliver the mail and they were finally alone.

"Do you remember your brother, Mickey?" she asked.

Eddie's face looked puzzled. "Mickey?" he asked.

"He died in the war," she told him gently. "I know you had nightmares about it after you came home."

"I still have the nightmares," Eddie replied. "But, nothing seems real in them."

Lois disliked speaking of her dead son and quickly changed the subject. "Perhaps its better you *don't* remember that," she told him. "Now, you must come

84

with me to visit your grandfather. He will be ever so glad to see you!"

She bundled up the clean laundry and Eddie carried it under his arm.

"We need to get you a buggy, Ma," he said. "And, another horse to replace the one the Redcoats stole from me. This is a long walk for you to make every day! Especially in the wintertime!"

"I feel fine," said Lois. "It's good to get outside in the fresh air. Besides, we can't afford a buggy. Buggies are for fancy folks, not people like us."

"Still," said Eddie. "I am going to look into it. We'll have more money soon. Now that my enlistment in the militia is fulfilled, I need to get back to work to make a living."

They stopped briefly at the mercantile, to pick up groceries for Grandfather and Mary Clark waited on them. "I am so glad you have come home, Eddie," she said happily. "Your mother has been so worried about you."

Eddie stared at the pretty young woman behind the counter. She looked somehow familiar but he could not remember her name. "I'm sorry – I don't remember your name," he apologized to her.

Mary dismissed the idea. "That's perfectly all right, Eddie. It's been a long time since we played together in the kettle ponds."

"This is Mary Clark," Lois interjected. "She used to come with us at berry-picking time. Don't you remember, Son?"

Eddie shook his head. Lois explained about the malaria.

"Well," said Mary, as she bundled up their groceries, "Perhaps we can go gather berries again when the weather gets warmer. We always had such fun!"

Lois was pleased, *very* pleased, in fact. She had been keeping her eye on Miss Mary Clark for quite a while now as a suitable wife for her son. "I want you to come to supper soon, Mary," she said. "You can help Eddie remember his childhood!"

They said good-bye and began the long walk out beyond the dunes. The sun was shining brightly above them, giving the impression of warmth, but the ground around them was still frozen and hard and the air was bitterly cold coming off the ocean. Eddie scanned the old shack that belonged to his grandfather with dismay. "I should spend some time out here fixing things," he said. "Now that I am home, there is a lot to be done around here!"

Lois agreed. The house and yard *did* look a bit shabby and cluttered. "Pa!" she called when they reached the front porch. "Look who I have brought to visit you!"

The door creaked open and the inside of the house was dark behind the shuttered windows.

"Pa?" Lois made her way to the kitchen and lit a lamp. She turned toward her father's bed and could see him lying there in the shadows; still and quiet. "Pa?" she said again. "You asleep?"

Eddie took one look at his grandfather and froze. *He knew that look. He had seen it on Susannah's face.*

"Ma, I don't think he can hear you," he said. Eddie remembered well the smell of death; the scent of it still lingered in his nostrils.

Eddie watched his mother cross the room and approach the bed where Edmund lay. Without a tear, she leaned in and kissed his face tenderly before she pulled the blanket up over his head. Turning to Eddie, her voice took a calm, collected tone as she instructed him what to do. "Go to town and let your brothers and sisters know," she said. "You must collect several heavy stones for me from the kettle ponds and get his boat ready for sailing. We will take him back to the sea in the morning and put him to rest." She turned back to the corpse of her father and, as if she were speaking to him directly, said quietly, "You can spend your last night in your own bed, Pa."

By nightfall, the word had reached all in Eastham; the old man of the sea, Edmund Freeman, was dead at the ripe old age of eighty. Lois and Eddie stayed with him all that night. She prepared what she called "his last meal" for any guests who might come calling, especially the band of Wampanoag who appeared on the beach and built an enormous bonfire on the sand that stretched between the ocean and the old shack. Until well after midnight, they sat around the fire, chanting in slow, rhythmic, mournful voices that could be heard all the way back to town. They had lost a dear friend. They had hunted whales together, they had shared their bounties, they had broken bread together. When the fire began to die down, Lois invited them all to sleep inside out of the cold and they sprawled across the floor of the little shack, rolled up in their blankets, at the foot of Edmund's bed.

In the morning, Lois again prepared food for her father's mourners and Eddie helped her into the boat along with Edmund's wrapped body. Uriah got into the boat with them and, with the others watching from the beach, they rowed out past the breaking waves. She had dressed him in his pea coat and filled the lining and the pockets with the heavy stones. Gently, Eddie and Uriah lowered him over the side of the boat and they all watched as his body slowly disappeared beneath the water.

Softly, Lois began to sing one of her father's favorite songs,

Farewell and adieu to you Spanish ladies….

Uriah joined in and then Eddie, with a glimmer of realization,

Farewell and adieu to you ladies of Spain…

Chapter Seventeen *"The Unopened Letter"*

The official government letter that Ephraim had delivered to Old Thomas months before still sat on a dusty shelf, high up on the wall of his wetu, unopened and ignored. It wasn't until his daughter-in-law, Bethia, wife of his son Uriah, had been doing her weekly cleaning that she noticed it and took it directly to her husband. Uriah had ripped open the envelope immediately and read its contents. His face showed his concern and Bethia was worried too. "What is it?" she asked him. "What is the English king taking from us now?"

Uriah sat down on the deer-skin covered cot beside the fire. Shaking his head, he sighed deeply and re-read the letter. "It's not the *king* this time," he said. "This time it is the *governor's council* in Boston."

"Why can't they just leave us in peace?" she said; her voice was sharp and annoyed. "What can they possibly do to us now?"

"They are revoking our right to govern ourselves," said Uriah. "That means……"

"I *know* that that means!" his wife snapped. "They will send their troops to rule over us! In our very own camp! They will stand in judgment over our own council. They will…." Her voice trailed off into angry thoughts, as she watched for her husband's reaction to the news. For hundreds of years the Wampanoag had governed themselves, punished their own criminals, laid down their own laws. It was their *right* as a free and independent nation that had lived in America long before the arrival of the English.

"Surely, this will not set well with my father," said Uriah. "This will go against the very treaty they signed with Massasoit."

"These men don't remember your great grandfather," said Bethia. "How conveniently they forget how he helped them! How he kept them from starving that first winter! How he was their friend for many decades!"

He knew his wife was right. The royal governor of Massachusetts was not much different than the king across the sea; he was just another demagogue in fancy silks who drank tea in the afternoon and was only interested in pursuing his lavish lifestyle. And, yet, Uriah himself came from mixed blood, the son of Old Thomas, a direct descendant of Massasoit through the *sachem's* daughter who married an Englishman. "They say he was pleased," Uriah told her. "He thought *joining* our houses would make us stronger. After all these years, it has only weakened us. It has made us dependent on their charity. We take what meager amounts they dole out to us. We can no longer hunt our blackfish. They treat us like second-class citizens in Eastham, when it was my grandfather who allowed them to settle here in the first place!"

His angry words followed him and drifted off as he left the wetu and went to speak to Old Thomas, leaving Bethia standing there shaking her head. They couldn't just *ignore* the Governor's letter. Even *Indians* had some God-given rights; they had to speak up for themselves, regardless of the consequences. His father had been silent for too long. He had ignored their blatant disregard for the treaty signed with Massasoit; closing his eyes and refusing to open the letter, as if that would make the problem go away! It was time to speak. It was time to call the *old ones* together and discuss a plan of action before it was too late!

At the urging of his son, Old Thomas dispatched a messenger to go to the other Wampanoag settlements in Chappaquiddick, Christian town, and Gay Head, inviting the other tribes to a meeting and by the next day the small camp just south of Eastham was crowded with a hundred newcomers. At sunset, another bonfire was lit from a pile of dried cornstalks and driftwood in the center of the camp. Old Thomas took his place with the other sachems, with Uriah at his side, and opened the discussion. As the fire blazed, angry words were exchanged over the governor's decision. Hadn't they obeyed all the English laws since King Phillip's War? Hadn't they lived in peace with the people for now over a hundred years? What right did the new American governor have now to revoke their treaty with Massasoit? What could they do now, now that they were so few of them left and hardly a force to be feared?

"It is true," said Old Thomas. "There are not enough of us left to wage war on the Americans. But, my son is right; *something must be done*. But we must wage a war with *words*, not *weapons*; that is our only hope to remain independent."

"We must send a message to Boston," said the sachem from Gay Head. "We must insist that we be heard! Perhaps this new American governor will not close his ears to us as the English king did."

The others agreed. But who would go? And how many?

"It must be done in a peaceful way," said Old Thomas, "Or else they will answer us with their muskets! Only cool heads will prevail!"

Uriah agreed to accompany the old ones to Boston. "I will take my wife and my son with me," he told the others. "I will go unarmed. That way they will not see us as a threat."

"Do you think that is wise, Son?" asked Old Thomas. "To take Bethia and the boy?"

"We go in peace, Father, just as you suggested," said Uriah. "We will honor the words of the treaty my grandfather signed and bring no weapons. Surely they will not attack an unarmed man and his family!"

"Still," said Old Thomas. "I think it's best to leave the boy at home."

Uriah's voice was firm however. "He will not be a boy forever," he said. "Someday, he will be the *sachem* of his tribe!"

Old Thomas and the others were of the same sentiment. The decision to go to Boston was made, formalized by handshakes and clasped forearms. They rose to their feet and began to dance around the fire. The *stomp dance* they called it; for many generations it was their way of releasing their anger peacefully. Many of the men took hollow turtle shells filled with gravel from the kettle ponds and tied them to their legs. To the rhythm of a drum they began to stomp the ground. The children joined them shaking small gourds filled with water, making a gurgling sound. The women clapped their hands and moaned in mournful high-pitched voices. More wood was thrown on the fire until the flames rose high in the air and the dancing continued far into the night.

From the porch on Skaket Road, Eddie was just returning from locking up the chickens in their coop for the night. As he stepped on the porch step he suddenly noticed the glow of the great fire in the distance, looming orange and brilliant against the night sky. He knew something was amiss. *What had happened now?* he wondered. "I have to ride to the Indian camp," he went in and told his mother. "Something is up."

Chapter Eighteen *"The Governor"*

They owned no horses; from the beginning of their existence, the Eastham Wampanoag were hunters and gatherers and *men of the sea*. Wherever they needed to go, they had their three-man canoes, which were easily carried on their shoulders from shore to shore on the cape, for they were never very far from water. When they hunted in the woods they used their own feet to propel them. And, although the tribe had purchased a few mules, back when they had heavy barrels of oil to transport to the mercantile in Eastham, they now used them only to plow their cornfields. By the time Eddie had saddled his horse and reached the tribal meeting, and had learned of the newest threat to his cousins, he was willing to accompany them to Boston as well, to support their cause.

They launched their canoes from Rock Harbor the next morning, with Grey Eyes rowing for Old Thomas, Uriah taking the oars for Bethia and little Samuel. Eddie captained the boat in which the old ones, Ann Hopkins and Rebecca Mayo, sat. The current from the northeast was brisk and rowing against it was difficult at first, but soon they reached the main channel from the sea, and they rested a bit, using their oars only for steering north and letting the water propel them toward Boston on the other side of the bay.

Old Thomas held in his lap an oval-shaped box carved from birch-wood that had been passed down in his family since Massasoit; the box that contained the original treaty signed by his great-grandfather and the then-governor of Massachusetts, William Bradford. The box had the appearance of a huge walnut, held together with leather straps. Nothing in the Wampanoag culture had straight edges or corners; it was not a *natural* shape, they believed, for nothing in *nature* had straight, square lines. Their homes had curved roofs and even the wood from which they built their funeral pyres was curved. Just like the ancient Chinese, who called the concept *Feng shui* centuries before, everything in the Wampanoag world also had to be in harmony with nature. The old man sat there with his aging hands holding and gently stroking the box as if it was a treasure which, in a way, it was; it was the written word of their great leader, Massasoit. His eyes were staring into space at nothing while he rehearsed in his mind what he wanted to say to the governor of Massachusetts.

Meanwhile, in Boston, the governor, John Hancock, sat at his oversized desk in the capital, pouring over reports, signing his name to a pile of documents before him that had been overlooked with all the recent turmoil in government. He paid only the slightest of attention to the details of the documents, skimming over them hastily and scrawling his name with a quill until his fingers were stained blue.

He was tall and thin, not a robust-looking man by any stretch of the imagination. But, there was a reason for that; his health had been steadily failing for a long time. Suffering from the gout and other maladies, Hancock looked much older than his fifty-one years. The pressures of government only added to his poor health. Only a few weeks after the British surrender at Yorktown, he had begun to catch up on the stale matters that crowded his desk. The Indian situation was the subject of many letters he had received from the local officials across Massachusetts. Since the restrictions put upon them by the British government, they had been displaced in society. From many towns, there were complaints of public drunkenness and vagrancy, of thievery and other unsavory behavior. While it had not occurred to the governor to reinstate the Indian's whaling rights as a possible solution to problem, he instead agreed that the Indians' practice of self-government was not working and that something had to be done; taking control of them seemed the only practical answer.

When the group from Eastham marched into his office that cold December afternoon and seated themselves in his outer office, demanding to be seen, he had silently wished for a trap door under his desk into which he could escape. Indian matters were distasteful to him and he was more than happy to delegate their business to his assistants. "No," he overheard a man's voice say beyond his closed door. "We want to speak to the governor himself. This is a matter of importance."

His Lieutenant Governor had announced the group and escorted them inside the little office, collecting up extra chairs on which the women could sit. It was a diverse group staring at him from across the room: one old blind Indian man and two elderly Indian women, two younger Indian men with paler skin, obviously half-breeds, a white woman and a white man, though apparently not married to each other for they sat at opposite ends of the room and one small boy, sitting cross-legged in the corner of the room. The old man introduced everyone. "I am *Thomas*," he said, "the great grandson of the sachem, Massasoit. We represent the Wampanoag tribes of the lower cape, from Eastham and the islands to the south of Chappaquiddick and Gay Head."

The governor shook the men's hands and settled back in his high-backed, leather chair to listen to their complaints. Old Thomas spoke clearly even though his English was broken in parts and he waved his hands a lot in expression; the governor waited politely, letting the old man have his say.

"I understand that you have governed yourselves for many years," he began, when Old Thomas had finished, and the men in the room heaved a collective sigh. Their sachem might as well have been reading the governor Indian folklore for all the interest he was showing.

"But, you must understand that we have received many complaints from our citizens. From the town of Eastham, there have been reports of drunken Indians roaming the streets at night, frightening the ladies."

It was a ludicrous allegation at best and everyone in the room, with the exception of the governor, knew it was untrue. While it *was* true that more liquor was being consumed by the Wampanoag men than in days past, there was a reason for it. There were more idle hours, between corn harvests and hunting seasons. Whaling had once kept them busy to the point of exhaustion. But, the men of the tribe would *never* venture through the streets of Eastham at night for fear of being shot. Where was the governor getting his information? Old Thomas wanted to know.

"I cannot reveal the names of the complainants," said Hancock. "But I can assure you that I have appointed a council of my very best men to handle the problem. They will be visiting Eastham very soon. It has taken much time to catch up with domestic matters since the war has kept us busy for so long."

Old Thomas cleared his throat. "I promise I will find out if there is any kernel of truth in these allegations and, if it has merit, I will punish the perpetrators severely. We are a peaceful people. We wish to live in harmony with the Americans."

Governor Hancock nodded in agreement. "Then, there is no reason for concern. I am sure we can work together to address the concerns of the citizens of Eastham."

There was a moment of silence before Old Thomas spoke again. "Now that we have won the war against the British, when can we expect to have our whaling rights restored?" he asked.

The governor squirmed in his chair. Old Thomas untied the leather straps that secured the wooden box in his lap and produced the treaty signed by Massasoit with trembling hands.

"I have brought the original treaty," he said. "Will your council honor its promises to do no harm and take nothing from our people?"

The governor took the rolled up parchment in his hands and took a moment to read the words scrawled on it. He handed it back to Old Thomas. "The beaches up and down the cape were becoming most foul," he explained. "Many complained of the stench. The beaches are much cleaner now, and the air as well, wouldn't you agree?"

Uriah laughed out loud before he could stop himself. "Yes," he said. "Our town used to smell of whale oil in the summertime. Still, there is a need for lamp oil and candles, is there not?"

"It is a matter of *where* the whales are butchered," said the Governor. "Is it not more practical to perform such distasteful chores out to sea?"

"Yes," agreed Uriah. "But, we do not wish to leave our families alone for months at a time. Our women and children would be most vulnerable. And, besides that, we have neither ships nor the means with which to build them. We can hardly go to sea with our small canoes!"

"Again," said the Governor, standing up as if to adjourn the meeting. "I assure you I will address the matter with my council. You will be hearing from us very soon!"

"And, will the Wampanoag have a seat on this council of yours?" asked Uriah, with obvious contempt seething in him.

"We will work on that," the governor assured them. "Now, please, you must give me time to come up with a solution that we can all live with."

Chapter Nineteen *"The Price of a Stick of Cinnamon"*

Eddie's memory was coming back in bits and pieces, jagged flashbacks and dreams that both frustrated and delighted him. On some days, a particular sight or sound or smell would conjure up remembrances of his past life with vivid clarity. On other days, his mind seemed clouded and his demeanor down-trodden, especially when he could not remember someone's name whom he had known in his past life. Most difficult of all to retrieve were his memories of the war and, beyond that, to his childhood, and he struggled with it, afraid he would never be the same man he used to be.

The one memory that remained alive with intensity was that of *Susannah*. Lois had asked him often about the woman who died at the hands of the Redcoats and she listened intently as Eddie described her; it was obvious her son had been quite smitten with the woman who had nursed him back to health. His entire face would burst forth in a smile as he spoke of her and it warmed Lois' heart to see her son so happy. But, she worried too. She had continued to nurture the relationship between Eddie and the storekeeper's daughter, Mary Clark, hoping the two would become fond of each other. *What if Eddie will never get over his lost love Susannah?* she wondered. *Would he waste away his entire life dreaming of a dead woman?*

Determined to see her plan through to fruition, she began inviting Mary over for supper often, after which they did needlework and, together with Eddie and Ephraim, engaged in lively discussions on almost every subject. Both of the brothers obviously enjoyed Mary's company and while Lois thought she would make an excellent wife for *either* of her sons, she worried more about Eddie; he would need someone to be by his side when his mother could no longer be there. While outward appearances showed him to be a strong, energetic young man, she knew, inside, he was still in a fragile condition. It seemed as if his mind would never be whole again.

After his return from Boston, Mary seemed most interested to know what had happened with the Governor.

"He said he has appointed a council to oversee the matter," Eddie told them. "They are supposed to be here any day now."

"How are the *old ones* taking it?" she asked.

"Not well," replied Eddie. "We shall just have to wait and see what happens next. At least, we have made our voices heard."

"For all the good *that* will do," said Lois sourly.

Winter had finally withdrawn itself to lie in wait for another year; spring was bursting forth with abundance, painting the cape in luscious green. The men, including Eddie, returned to the fields to plant more crops and Eastham was soon abuzz with activity again. The war was behind them now; the fledgling country called America was now standing on her own, proudly waving her own flag. While the new government officials scurried to get the newly adopted laws in place, the matter of the Indians' right to self-govern was again shoved to the bottom of the pile of other *more pressing matters*.

Spring also brought new settlers to Eastham. Clark's store was hardly able to keep up with its new customers and Mary had her hands full fulfilling orders for goods, while her father worked frantically on the loading dock to keep up with the demands of the growing town. But, as welcome as the additional business was to their little enterprise, the Clarks were not entirely happy about their new clientele. The streets of Eastham soon went from *bustling* to *raucous*; the men, who had always congregated at the Inn across the street after work in the afternoons, had become boisterous and offensive. While her father had refrained from selling hard liquor as a matter of conscience, the innkeeper had no qualms about selling ale and whiskey by the bottle to anyone who had money. *Drunken Indians?* Mary thought to herself one afternoon, observing a bunch of white men who sat across the street on the steps of the inn, swilling from their bottles and being most disrespectful to the women who passed by. She was standing there at the window watching their disgraceful activity when Bethia Mayo and little Samuel walked into the store.

Bethia and Mary were old friends, from back when she was *Bethia Knowles.* The Knowles family had been among of the first in Eastham, along with the Snows and the Clarks and the other founding families whose ancestors had migrated from old Plymouth. For generations, they had endured the presence of the Redcoats together, teaming up to smuggle goods in and out of town to avoid the royal taxes. Their families had broken bread with each other and shared holidays together. When Bethia had married Uriah Mayo it was no surprise to them. Indeed, the Mayos had a long history of intermarrying with the Wampanoag tribe, dating all the way back to the days of Massasoit. The Clarks, like the Snows and the Knowles, remembered a time when the Wampanoag had walked freely on the streets of Eastham, when they had supplied the precious whale oil to the mercantile that kept the town out of the darkness and meat to their tables when crops failed and hunting was sparse. Mary, like Eddie, remembered and respected the Wampanoag people for their contribution to the very existence of the town. They were glad to see each other that afternoon and hugged each other affectionately.

"My goodness, how Samuel is growing!" remarked Mary. She remembered well the day little Samuel was born, how proud Bethia was of him when she brought him the first time to introduce him to her. He had been a tiny little creature with wiggling hands and feet, a shock of dark hair and Bethia's big, round eyes.

"Yes, he is," said Bethia. "The *old ones* say he will be taller than even his father one day."

"No more trouble with the governor?" Mary asked hopefully.

"It's been quiet," said Bethia. "It is like they have forgotten about us altogether. But perhaps that is a *good* thing!"

"Aye," Mary said, nodding her head. "The less often they visit us out here, the better off we are!"

She took Bethia's list of items and went about filling her order. "You must be making something special," she remarked, wrapping a half stick of cinnamon carefully in tissue paper and placing it in Bethia's bag so as not to crumble it. She remembered visiting her friend at the camp and the salivating aroma of Indian fry bread sizzling on the fire and then sprinkled with sugar and cinnamon while it was still warm. There was just no *American* desert that smelled so luscious, not even American apple pie!

Bethia nodded. She had learned to prepare many traditional Wampanoag dishes for her husband and she had introduced him to American food as well. Now, they enjoyed both. "Yes," she said. "We are having a little celebration tonight."

Mary watched as Bethia opened her shawl and placed her hand on her slightly protruding stomach.

"That is wonderful news," Mary gushed. "I am so happy for you!"

They laughed and hugged each other again and Mary watched as Bethia and Samuel walked out into the afternoon sunshine before she went to assist another customer.

They walked hand in hand, mother and son, along the southern road that led to the camp, taking in the sights and smells of springtime on the cape. The thimble weed and bearded beggar-ticks were blooming along the roadside and the mockingbirds argued with each other from the pine branches above. Samuel was happy that school was out for spring. Although the children of the tribe were still not allowed to attend class in the big schoolhouse in town, Bethia insisted he study with the other Indian children nevertheless. They gathered together in the Mayo wetu over the winter just as the American boys did in Eastham, studying mathematics and spelling. Bethia was determined that her son would be as well-educated as any *white* boy in town.

"Will I one day be able to go to the university in Boston?" young Samuel asked.

"We will see about that," said Bethia, knowing the American universities were not integrated as yet, but she did not want to discourage her boy. "You have many years of study before you are ready for the university!"

They walked on, chattering about school, about the American war, about many things, so engrossed in their conversation that they did not hear horses behind them. By the time Bethia turned around, the men from town were almost upon them.

"What's a purty white woman doin' out here all alone?" he asked, the liquor on his breath evident from far away.

A second man riding beside him cackled. "She ain't alone!" he said. "She's got her half-breed kid with her! She must like her men painted and stinking of bear grease!"

The two passed a bottle between themselves, drinking sloppily and wiping their mouths on their sleeves. Bethia kept walking straight ahead, her hand clasped tightly on Samuel's, trying not to make eye contact, but the first man hurried his horse around in front of them.

"What's your hurry, little white squaw?" he taunted her. "Have you been livin' with the savages for so long you forgot how to speak English?"

Fear was rising up in her chest until she thought she would have to gasp for air. *Why oh why had she gone to town alone? Why hadn't she waited for Uriah to accompany her?* She stared back at the man on the horse and tried to muster courage from somewhere deep inside her. "Please let us be on our way," she said.

"That's not very friendly," said the man, with an evil leer on his face. "Don't you like *white* men?"

Bethia searched frantically for words. Again, she repeated. "Please, Sir, leave us be. We have done you no harm."

"Did you hear that?" the second man came forward on his horse; so close Bethia had to pull Samuel back lest he be trampled by the horse's hooves. "She called you *Sir!*"

"Well, that's better," said the first man, as he swung his leg over the saddle and dismounted. Handing the reins to his companion, the man stepped forward and boxed Bethia in between the two horses. She dropped her bag of groceries and pulled Samuel to her breast, trembling in fear. The man was in her face; his reeking breath was hot in her nostrils. He grabbed her arms and shoved little Samuel aside, into the grasp of the second man.

"Now," he said, grabbing her by her chin and covering her mouth with his, nauseating her with the vile taste of whiskey. "You be nice to me and I'll be nice to you."

She struggled against him and felt the sting of his hand across her face just as Samuel broke free and ran down the road toward home.

Ripping at her clothes, he hardly noticed that Bethia was carrying a child.

But, by then, it didn't matter.

Chapter Twenty *"The White Savages"*

"Uriah! What is it?"

When Eddie opened the door, he could instantly see that something was terribly wrong.

Uriah and Grey Eyes entered the room in a frenzy. Eddie could see that they had painted their faces with red clay and their eyes were ablaze with anger. Uriah was on the verge of tears. When he was told what had happened to Bethia on the road, Eddie felt their rage, but he knew he had to calm them down. Dashing off to town to confront the two drunken men who had assaulted his wife was something that had to be done with care. Their best bet was to go directly to the armory and get the militia's help in handling the matter.

"I know that it is not a good time to push our rights," Uriah said, shaking his head. "That is why we have come to you first, Eddie. You *know* the men in the militia. You must speak to them on our behalf! We will abide by the law. But, the laws must apply to *both* the Americans and the Wampanoag fairly! Why is it they come down on us so harshly when it is their *own* they need to discipline?"

Eddie agreed. Lois, who had been listening to the conversation from the kitchen, came forward and put a comforting hand on Uriah's arm.

"Is Bethia all right?" she asked. "Do you want me to go care for her?"

"She is with the *old ones* now," replied Uriah, and then, almost in a whisper, he added, "She was carrying my child. They fear she will lose the baby!"

Lois turned to her son. "Eddie, you must convince your friends down at the armory to arrest these men! The streets are becoming too dangerous for our women to venture outside."

Grey Eyes had been silent up until that point. "If you visit our camp, Missus Snow, you must not travel alone," he warned. "Wait until we can accompany you."

"He is right, Ma," said Eddie. "You must stay here and be safe. Bethia is with the *old ones*; she is in good hands. Come, Uriah, and we will pay a visit on the militia. I will do everything I can to help you get justice." He looked at the two men before him and motioned toward the kitchen. "But, first, wash that war paint off your faces before we go to town!"

The three men left the house and walked briskly toward town but not before Eddie had tucked his father's pistol in his belt just in case there was trouble. When they reached the armory, Eddie was greeted by his former comrades, who took his words very seriously.

"That place has become quite a nuisance," said his old corporal. "We have to break up fights almost every night."

"But, this goes far beyond public drunkenness!" said Eddie vehemently. "These men have raped a pregnant woman! They should *hang* for this!"

"Eddie, you come with us. *You two*," he spoke directly to Uriah and Grey Eyes, "*You stay here and let us handle it.*"

The two soldiers armed themselves and, with Eddie close behind them, left the armory. By the time they reached the inn, it seemed as if the whole town knew there was going to be trouble. Shutters were quickly fastened shut; people disappeared behind closed doors and peeked through the cracks to see what was about to transpire. Mary Clark looked out the store window and saw Eddie marching beside the two soldiers. Her father came up behind her and watched over her shoulder. "Trouble again?" he asked his daughter.

"It looks that way," she said.

"Isn't that *your* Eddie Snow with them?" asked Clark.

Mary blushed. "Father!" she protested. "He is hardly *my* Eddie Snow!" Silently pleased, she turned back toward the window and watched as Eddie and the soldiers disappeared inside the inn. *If only….* she thought to herself.

The crowd was mulling about when the three men stepped into the establishment, but, upon seeing the officers, there was a hush that came over the room. From the description Uriah had given them, they foraged through the crowd, looking for the guilty faces.

"There," said Eddie. *"Those two over by the window."*

With hands gripping their pistols tightly, the two militia men stepped ahead of Eddie and cornered the two men between them. *"You two,"* said the corporal. "You are under arrest."

One of the men stood up and looked around the room for an escape route. The other, in a lazy drawl, took a swig of his drink and stared mockingly at the officers. *"Why* are we under arrest?" he asked. "What is it we are being accused of?"

"Assaulting a woman this afternoon on the southern road," said the corporal.

The man shook his head. "Didn't assault no *woman*," he replied. "Didn't see no woman on the southern road, neither, only one *white Injun squaw* and her half-breed kid."

Eddie was fuming inside. These two reminded him of the pair of Redcoats on the road to Chatham, the two who had murdered Susannah. *"Bethia Mayo is no Injun squaw, you dirty, rotten…."*

"You're wasting your breath, Eddie," said the corporal. "These men have no consciences."

From the inn, they escorted the two prisoners back to the armory, where they were locked in a cell. As they entered the room where Grey Eyes and Uriah were waiting, the man who had done all the talking remarked, "I don't understand what a white woman sees in savages like you!"

Uriah stood up from his chair and approached the bars of the cell. His eyes looked down at the man with such hatred he was shaking. *"The only savages here are the ones who would commit such a disgusting crime!"*

Eddie and the others had to restrain him from grabbing the man's neck through the bars and strangling him. "They will get justice, I assure you, Uriah," said Eddie. "Come. You need to go home. Your wife needs you."

Chapter Twenty-One *"Ma's Will"*

Uriah and Grey Eyes returned to the Wampanoag camp, where Uriah remained at his wife's side until the dawn. When the *old ones* had done all they knew to do, they left them alone and Uriah sat down on the dirt floor beside her bed, laying his head against her heart and holding her hand tightly as she slept. There was quiet chanting outside, as the others in the tribe mourned the loss of Bethia's baby. It was an eerie and yet comforting sound to their ears. *Their child was now in the hands of the gods.*

Back in the house on Skaket Road, the Snow family mourned as well. When Ephraim returned home from his mail deliveries and they all sat down to a late supper, the mood was subdued and sad.

"Something has to be done," said Lois to her sons. "These men must be punished! *Hanging* is too good for them in my opinion!"

"They *will* be punished, Ma," said Eddie. "There will be a trial and they will be convicted, I am sure of it."

"Somehow, the Wampanoag will get the blame for this," she said. "The governor will use this as another reason to persecute them. You can mark my words!"

"And, this incident will bolster the bigotry that is already rampant in Eastham," Ephraim remarked.

"What else can they do to them that they haven't done already?" Lois asked.

Ephraim's voice took a somber tone. "They can drive them from their land," he said. "The *old ones* told me they are relocating many of the other tribes inland to Mashpee against their will and selling off their land to the Americans."

"That land belonged to them since the beginning of time," said Lois bitterly. "What can we do, Eddie? How can we help them?"

"We will think of a way, Ma," said Eddie. "Try not to worry about it."

"Do you know why they call themselves the *people of the dawn*?" she asked. "Your grandfather told me about it a long time ago."

"No," said Eddie. "I don't believe I have ever heard that story."

"They believe the ocean gives birth to the sun in the east every morning," she explained. "They remain near the ocean, for it has provided blackfish for them for their sustenance and the sun has kept them from freezing in the winter. They fear moving west, away from the sun and the ocean. They believe the earth swallows the sun every night in the west, bringing darkness and death."

"I thought the Wampanoag became Christians a long time ago," said Eddie. "Surely, they don't believe that superstitious nonsense any longer!"

Lois shook her head. "Old customs and traditions are hard to break," she said. "Especially, since praying to the *white Christian God* hasn't helped them much."

Lois stood up and walked across the room quietly. She returned with a quill and paper and sat down at the table.

"If you are planning to write a letter to the governor," said Eddie, "It won't do any good. He is not concerned with the Wampanoag tribe. He will ignore the issue until someone *dies*. We will just have to wait on this *council* he has appointed to act."

"Someone *did* die. *Bethia's child*," Lois said quietly. "But, we may not have to wait that long for justice."

"What do you mean, Ma?" Ephraim asked, intrigued at his mother's mysterious tone.

She began to scratch furiously on the paper in front of her. "You boys will have to correct my grammar on this," she mumbled. "Ain't never written a legal document before."

"What are you writing, Ma?" Eddie finally asked. "Just *what* are you up to?"

"My will," Lois replied. "I am writing my *will*."

Eddie laughed out loud. "And, how, pray tell, is that going to help the Wampanoag?" he asked.

"I'm leavin' your grandfather's house and land to Uriah," she said stubbornly. "It's *mine* now and I can do what I want with it. But, no one must know about it until the time comes, when they try to take them off their land. That way, no one can interfere!"

Her sons smiled at her and then at each other. *Leave it to Ma to come up with a plan.*

Chapter Twenty-Two *"A Walk in the Moonlight"*

By August, things had settled back into a predictable routine in Eastham. The two men who had assaulted Bethia were tried and found guilty by the magistrate; they were whisked away to a prison on the mainland and forbidden to ever set foot in Eastham again. Soon, the incident was forgotten by everyone except those personally touched by it. Clark's store continued to profit from the increased population in and around Eastham. Eddie, who had yet to find gainful employment, agreed to go to work for them to help Mary's father with the shipments of goods going in and out of town, delivering orders by wagon to the outlying towns. In turn, Mary had agreed to watch over Lois when deliveries called Eddie out of town. She spent most evenings in the house on Skaket Road, keeping the now fifty-eight-year-old widow company and becoming increasingly close to the other members of the family as well. Eddie began to walk her to and from her little apartment she shared with her father above the mercantile, for her safety, of course, but also because she was beginning to hold a special place in his life. While he still mourned for Susannah, long after her death, the ache in his heart had subsided somewhat, and Eddie was intent on making new memories. His memory of the war had never completely returned; it was as if his mind went back to the house in Williamsburg and remembered very little beyond that.

Mary was doing her best to help Eddie regain his earlier memories, of their lives together as children playing on the sea shore and splashing in the kettle ponds, of playing stick ball on Skaket Road and digging for clams in the saltwater marshes. Summer had been the best time for every youngster in Eastham; it was a time of innocence and carefree hearts before the concerns of adulthood took hold and laughter became tempered with responsibilities.

This night was reminiscent of those days. It was particularly warm and humid, so humid and still, in fact, it seemed that even the crickets were sleeping in the grass along the road to town. The moon was but a sliver of what is had been just days before but still bright enough to shimmer in jagged echoes across the salt water inlets at the bottom of the sloping hill, beyond which were the lights of Eastham.

The road had been recently graveled by the highway men and was slippery under their feet making a crunching sound as they made their way in the dark. Suddenly, Mary took a step that sent her legs sliding out from under her. She would have fallen had Eddie not reached for her and caught her fall.

"Thank you, Eddie," she said, when she up-righted herself. "I will have to be more careful where I step."

As assurance, Eddie reached out and cupped her arm in his to guide her. It was a comfortable feeling, to have their arms linked in the moonlight. Beneath his shirt she could feel the hardness of his muscled arm, the dampness of sweat on his shirt. She had never felt so close to him before and her hand held tight to the crook of his arm.

"It is *ever* so hot tonight," she said. "I am sure the house will be *stifling* when I get home."

Eddie nodded in the dark. "Aye," he agreed. "And, it is so quiet and still. I'll bet our voices can be heard all the way to town."

"Let's go walk on the beach," Mary suggested. "And, get our feet wet! It is the perfect weather for it."

By the time they had reached the bottom of the hill and stopped to remove their shoes, Eddie took Mary's hand in his. They started running along the moonlit trail that led to the eastern shore, digging their toes deep into the sand, just as they had done as children. They could hear the surf pounding just ahead of them, down the banks of orange clay and beyond, filling the void in the stillness of the hot night. They reached the place where the sea met the sand, their feet welcoming the coolness beneath them, letting the water swirl around their ankles and feeling the sandy grit between their toes.

"Doesn't that feel wonderful, Eddie?" Mary asked.

"Aye," he replied. A rogue wave rushed in around them. Mary hoisted her skirts high and they retreated, but not before his trousers were wet to the knees and her hems were soaked. He laughed out loud at first, still clasping Mary's hand tightly in his own. They ran down the beach until they were out of breath and collapsed on a dry bank of sand to rest.

"It reminds me of...." Eddie began to say and then stopped.

"What?" asked Mary. "*What* does it remind you of, Eddie?"

"Oh, nothing," he replied. His voice was suddenly sullen and she could tell his mood had changed.

He started to rise, brushing the sand from his trousers. Mary's heart plummeted in her chest. For so long now, she had hoped he would break free of the past that haunted him, to shed himself once and for all of the elusive pieces of his life that he struggled to remember.

"Tell me, Eddie," she said, clutching his hand in hers to keep him from leaving. "*Tell me what you remember!*"

He was silent for a moment. There was a lull in the waves and above the gentle lapping of the water she could hear him crying softly in the darkness.

"What is it, Eddie?" she asked, pulling at his hand until he sat back down beside her. "You can tell me. Talking about it might help."

"*I remember the day my brother died*," he said slowly, in a hoarse whisper.

Another wave crashed on the shore.

"Tell me what happened," Mary said. "*Talk* to me, Eddie!"

Eddie sat staring out over the surf. "We were caught in a rainstorm," he said. "Up to our knees in mud."

"The waves reminded you," she remarked. "That's good, Eddie. You must remember. The only way you can forget it is to remember it and then let it go."

In his mind, he could see that muddy trench alongside the road to Boston, the flour sacks filled with bloodied boots stolen from soldiers' corpses, the acrid smell of gunpowder and sweat and death all around him. He remembered the corporal who had tried to take Mickey's boots before they buried him and how he refused to let them put his brother in the cold ground with bare feet. "He died in my arms, Mary," he said, with tears streaming down his face that she wiped away. "I couldn't save him. *I was his big brother, and I couldn't save him!*"

She put her arm around his shoulders.

"And, I couldn't save Susannah either," he said. "What kind of a man am I?"

Mary turned and sat back on her knees in the sand. *Maybe this is the moment that he will finally be able to let Susannah go and see that I have been right here all this time!* she thought hopefully. She had loved him as child, worshipped the red-haired boy they called *Captain Ginger*, when the boys played their mock-war games in the streets. She would watch with the other girls, sitting on the steps of her father's store, cheering them on and laughing as the boys toppled and fell on the cobblestones, feigning mortal wounds, and cavorted about like carefree, gangly colts. When he had reappeared in her life, the love of her youth was rekindled. She had been waiting for him to say something, for some encouragement that she was special to him too. But, no matter what his mother or she wanted, it didn't matter until *he* felt it himself. "You are a good man, Eddie Snow!" she said. "Saving your brother and Susannah was something only *God* could do. You must not blame yourself!"

Eddie heaved a long sigh, as if a weight had finally been lifted off his shoulders. The faint scent of lavender water on Mary's skin filled the air between them. His memory of her was returning too, sweet Mary Clark, the doe-eyed girl who shared iced cookies and lemonade with the other children on the loading docks of the mercantile. The quiet one who sat side by side on the steps of the store with little Bethia Knowles, braiding each other's hair "Indian style" in the shade of the summer sun. It was because of her he had showed off so much, acting bravely when he tumbled around in the street with the other boys and then going home to nurse his bruised kneecaps and elbows in secrecy. The memory came back to him of that morning, before he had returned to the war, of seeing her in the firelight with her hair cascading down her back, realizing the little girl had grown into a beautiful young woman.

The moonlight tonight brought out the white of the lace bodice of her dress and, although her face remained in the darkness, he could see the faint sparkle in her eyes. With one impulsive move, he took her in his arms and kissed her with all the emotion he had kept in check for so long. *All* the emotions, the sorrow, the pain, the shame, all escaped from him and became passion. Mary's body collapsed against his chest and she clung to him.

Finally, she thought before her mind lost itself in his embrace. *Finally, he has noticed me!*

Chapter Twenty-Three *"The Forgotten Ones"*

The news was of no surprise to Lois and Ephraim, nor to anyone who knew them. It seemed the most natural occurrence, something that had been fated since childhood.

"It's about time," his mother chided him when they told him of their plans to marry. Inside, Lois couldn't have been more pleased.

The nuptials were brief, vows spoken in the office of the Town Clerk in Eastham that fall. Eddie placed a plain silver band on Mary's finger and she moved into the house on Skaket Road. Although he still suffered lapses in his memory, Eddie was finally able to move forward in his life. He occasionally had nightmares, but much less frequently than before, and he was hopeful they would go away with time. He worked harder at the mercantile than ever before, shoulder to shoulder with his new father-in-law. He expanded their corn crop; he and Ephraim were able to clear away several more acres of raw land behind the house. Bethia and Uriah were welcome guests in the Snow house. Bethia, too, was emerging from her own haunting memories and it was a time of rebirth for both of them.

Little Samuel often joined the families too, although the label of *little* hardly described him any longer. He had grown tall, almost as tall as his father, and the pride of the Wampanoag tribe was apparent in his demeanor. *He was more Indian than white.* And, although he clearly had affection for the Snows and the others who were related to him by blood, he showed a marked intolerance for the snobbish whites in Eastham.

"He worries me," Bethia confided in Mary and Lois one evening, while the men were outside enjoying their tobacco on the front porch and the three women were sewing by the fire. "After what happened on the road that day, he has developed a hatred for the white people."

"He seems all right around *us*," said Mary. "Surely, he does not hate *all* the whites!"

"Of course," replied Bethia. "He loves his family. You all are his family. But, there is a darkness in his soul that I fear will come out if ever he is confronted."

Lois looked up from her sewing. "Have you had more trouble with the governor?" she asked.

"Not directly," said Bethia, keeping her voice low so that Samuel would not hear her. "But, they have finally forced the tribe on Noepe off their land and some in Gay Head, as well. I fear *we* will be next. A few Wampanoag came through our camp just the other night, running away from the white men who were rounding them all up to move inland to the settlement at Mashpee."

"What will you do?" asked Mary, horrified at the thought of the tribe being driven from their homes.

"What *can* we do?" asked Bethia sadly. "We sent the *old ones* to Boston to speak to the governor. What good did that do? We never even heard from him again! Now, the militia is coming in with their guns aimed at us. What other choice do we have but to move on or die?"

"They have no right," said Mary. "You have lived on this land since before the days of old Plymouth. The bones of your dead are buried here. We would not *be* here if it hadn't been for the Wampanoag tribe!"

"No one remembers that, I am afraid," replied Bethia. "We are the *forgotten ones.*"

Lois put down her needle and thread and looked directly into Bethia's eyes. "You don't need to worry," she said adamantly. "We won't let them send you away to Mashpee."

"I don't want anyone to get hurt, Lois," said Bethia. "I don't want our men to have to take up arms to defend us. I would rather take Uriah and Samuel and go peacefully than to see them shot and killed."

"What about the *old ones*?" asked Lois. "They are too frail to move such a long way and rebuild! What will happen to them?"

"I don't know," said Bethia sadly. "It will certainly break their spirit."

The following day the distant smoke from a funeral pyre could be seen all the way to Eastham. The *old one* Anne Hopkins had died.

It wasn't long before there was another pyre for *old one* Rebecca Mayo. The granddaughters of Massasoit were the last of the matriarchal line and now they were gone, leaving Old Thomas as the last elder of the tribe. Those of pure blood were dying off, leaving only those with mixed blood, and that blood was becoming more diluted with every generation.

Was extinction on the horizon for the Wampanoag?

Chapter Twenty-Four *"Music to her Ears"*

Lois Snow had not been this happy since the days of her marriage to Jesse Snow.

Young Mary unburdened her of the heavier housekeeping tasks, giving her a welcome respite, but it was much more than that. There was a definite bond growing between the two women, an intimacy she had never known with another of her own gender. Growing up the only child of the widower, Edmund Freeman, and living so far out on the eastern shore, she rarely met girls her age. Less educated than the other girls, for she had no mother to teach her reading and writing by the fireside, she sometimes felt inadequate around others.

Even after she had married Jesse and moved to the house on Skaket Road, becoming part of the large Snow family, there was always so much to do, so little time to socialize. She had lost two of her daughters prematurely, one-year-old Sarah, who had succumbed to the spotted fever and her namesake, Lois, who had been sickly since birth and died at twenty. Even now, her two grown daughters, Louise and Thankful, were so busy raising their own families that free time was a luxury neither of them had. They checked in on their mother, of course, when Ephraim was away on his mail runs, before Eddie came back from the war. But, having Mary in the house was so comforting to her, she couldn't remember a time when she felt more content.

Mary continued to help out at the store and frequently brought home new and unusual foods imported from the West Indies, now that the British no longer blockaded their ships in the harbor. Items like wild forest mushrooms and strong, dark chocolate were especially appealing to Lois, who had grown up poor, living on shellfish and chowder made from flour and water, for most of her childhood. She and Mary enjoyed experimenting with new recipes and provided Eddie and Ephraim with dishes they had created from their own imaginations. When Uriah and Bethia would come for supper, they would enjoy seeing the faces of their guests when they tasted their latest concoctions.

It was on one such evening, when Uriah and Bethia had come to visit, that more surprises than just the food on the table were announced. Eddie, who had been bursting to tell his news, was the first.

"Mother," he said, standing up at the head of the table and raising his glass in a toast. "And family and friends. Mary and I have an announcement to make."

Eyes turned to Mary and the blush on her cheeks revealed all, even before Eddie could continue.

"We are going to have a baby in the spring!"

Lois clapped her hands together, wondering how Mary had managed to keep the secret from her. But, it was only proper that the father be informed of the news first. Smiling, she looked around the table, her eyes pausing briefly on Bethia, remembering that awful day in summer and those awful men....

Bethia was quiet at first, then she looked up. Even Uriah was caught by surprise when she said, "That is wonderful news, Mary. Uriah and I are expecting again too!"

It was definitely a night for celebration. For Uriah, it was especially bittersweet. For many months after his wife had been attacked so brutally, he had found it difficult to touch her, for fear it would conjure up bad memories. He had held her close to him every night, of course, cradling her in a comforting yet loving way. But, it had only been recently that he had allowed his passion to rise, that she had been able to respond to him again. The announcement of this baby was *welcome* news. It did not bother him in the least that she had shared it among the others first. The Snows were their family. Now that all the *old ones* were gone except his father, it was only right that she share their happiness with them.

When Lois went to her bed that night, Mary had come to her room and sat down beside her.

"You will be a grandmother again," she said. "I hope he won't be one that cries at night and keeps the whole house awake!"

Lois reached out and took her daughter-in-law's hand. "I will *welcome* that sound," she said. "It will be music to my old ears!"

But, it was not to be. In the morning, there was no fire lit in the hearth; Eddie had awakened to find the house cold and still. They had stayed up late the night before; *Ma must have overtired herself*, he thought as he stoked and kindled the embers until there were flames snapping and rising up the chimney. When Mary had dressed and joined him, she was surprised that the old woman had not risen before her. Never had she known Lois Snow to sleep in late in the morning! She waited awhile and then tiptoed into Lois' room to check on her, when she discovered her dear mother-in-law had passed away in her sleep.

The cries of her grandchild would never awaken her again.

Chapter Twenty-Five *"It's All Stealing"*

Mary Snow heard the sound of wagon wheels outside and she glanced through the windows of the store, expecting to see a merchant coming to deliver goods. But, the sound she heard was not that of a loaded wagon; from the squeaking of the wheels and the creaking of the floorboards across the cobblestoned street, she recognized the sound of an empty wagon. First one, and then another, until a half dozen wagons pulled by large, black mules lumbered through town, going south. She didn't recognize any of the drivers, *out-of-towners from Truro or Fresh Brook*, she reasoned to herself as she went about her work.

She was especially *tired* today. In the last stages of her pregnancy, Eddie had wanted her to stay home, to rest and not work so hard. But, Mary was a worker; she grew bored staying at home. She loved to work at her father's store, dusting shelves and stacking cans, sweeping the floor and polishing the window panes. She felt content when the store was tidy and neat and proud when customers came to shop. But, today, she forced herself to sit down in a chair by the fire; she felt an odd ache in her lower back, a feeling she had not felt before. When Eddie came in from the loading docks, he was immediately concerned and insisted on taking her home. He helped her into his delivery wagon that was loaded with goods headed for Rock Harbor and they rode off together.

"Where were all the wagons going this morning?" she asked, as they bounced along the southern road.

"I'm not sure," Eddie replied. "They're probably from the new store up north."

"But, they were empty," she said. "As if they were going to pick up a load. They didn't head toward the docks and it's too early for any crops to be ready for harvest. Where do you think they went?"

Eddie rubbed his chin thoughtfully. He wasn't sure. It *was* odd, though. Clark's store now had competition from the north; a new establishment had sprung up just after the winter thaw in the wealthier part of town. Mary's father wasn't really worried; he had all the business he could handle and loyal customers he wasn't afraid of losing. Still, it was peculiar to see so many empty wagons heading out the road that led to the Wampanoag camp.

Grey Eyes wondered the same thing when he saw the wagons pull up between the camp and the beach. The man on the first wagon jumped down and took the path toward the *try works* the Indians had built many years before and the little dock where they moored their canoes. He watched them from the rise above the camp as they maneuvered the wagons around, backing them in closer to the wooden platform. Two of the men jumped down from their wagons, with sledges and axes in their hands and they immediately started tearing the try works apart.

Grey Eyes ran back to the camp to inform Old Thomas, who joined him on the hill. By that time, the men had the heavy iron cauldrons loaded on the wagons and they continued to chop away at the platform until they had busted up all the lumber.

Old Thomas leaned against his crooked walking stick and hobbled his way down the path. *"You, there!"* he shouted when he had reached the beach. "Where are you taking our pots? And, who has given you the right to tear up what we have built here?"

The anger was apparent in his words; but, he was a harmless, old man and no threat to the men. The one who seemed to be in charge laughed at him, waving him away as if it were none of Old Thomas' business *what* they were doing.

"Been told to tear down these try works," he said. "No need to bother yourself, old man. We can handle it."

"Who gave you permission…." Old Thomas began again, waving his stick in the air defiantly.

"The governor's council," said the man, cutting him off rudely. "Your whaling rights have been suspended. Now, they want us to clean up the beaches. This mess is nothing but an eyesore. It has to go."

It was true they had been clearing the beaches all along the eastern shore. What had once been called the *beach of bones* for all the whale carcasses that had laid there rotting, was now a pristine stretch of silver sand for as far as the eye could see. Men in boats had come ashore and tied ropes to all the corpses and hauled them out to sink them in the deep waters. But, tearing down their try works was another matter. What if the new American government decided to reinstate the Wampanoag right to hunt the blackfish? The try works were their property, the pots, the blubber hooks, the lumber they had cut and hewn themselves and nailed together. Old Thomas was not pleased.

"Those pots belong to *us*," he shouted. "And, all the hooks and nets and other equipment you have loaded onto your wagons. We should be compensated for it, at least. You cannot just come in and steal our property!"

"It's not being *stolen*," replied the man. "The government is *confiscating* it."

"It all looks like stealing to me," said Old Thomas.

Grey Eyes watched the men nervously for their reaction. Old Thomas spoke as if he had a hundred warriors to back him up in case there was trouble, when, in fact, the tribe now consisted of mostly widows and orphans. Grey Eyes, Uriah and Samuel were among the few dozen men left and all the others, at that moment, were out fishing and hunting. He wasn't sure he alone would offer much defense against the six men with their muskets.

"You can keep the wood for your fires," the man finally said. "If I have your word you will haul it all away from the beach. But, you have no use for the try pots and whaling gear any longer if you cannot hunt whales. We must remove them. *Orders of the council.*"

"But, this is *our* land," argued Old Thomas. "We have lived here for many generations."

The man turned toward the old *sachem*. With a scowl on his face, he spit out his words, "It's not your land any longer! The other tribes have moved on to the Indian settlement at Mashpee. Haven't you heard? It's only a matter of time before it's your turn to go."

Old Thomas's face went rigid; he gritted the few teeth he had left. "I'll *never* move to Mashpee!" he said defiantly and moved closer to the white men, as Grey Eyes followed close behind him, ready to defend Old Thomas if necessary.

"You, boy!" the man shouted at Grey Eyes. "You'd best get busy hauling this wood away or we will load it up and take it too!"

Old Thomas had moved dangerously close to the white men and stood stubbornly blocking the path between what was left of the try platform and the wagons.

Swiftly, the man who had been doing all the talking stepped forward and pushed the old man out of the way.

"Get on with you, Injun!" he yelled. "We have work to do here!"

Suddenly, from the top of a nearby sand dune, a shrill war cry pierced the silence. All the men looked up to see young Samuel standing there, with his father's tomahawk held high in the air. His face and arms were vividly painted with black charcoal from the fire pits and red clay from the coastal cliffs; he had attached more eagle feathers to his blue-black hair. *He was all decked out for war.* Before anyone could move, the boy rushed down off the rise, swinging the tomahawk wildly at the men. Two of the men ran for the wagons and their loaded muskets, while the others fended off the blows of the young, inexperienced warrior. The first shot was fired into the air to frighten the boy, while the second gun was aimed directly at Samuel.

"Drop the tomahawk, boy," said the man with the gun. "I don't want to have to shoot you."

"What is going on here?" came a booming voice from behind them; a canoe had silently slipped up to the dock and Uriah disembarked, running toward the crowd of men on the beach. "Put those muskets down before someone gets killed!"

Uriah turned toward Samuel; instantly the boy dropped his father's tomahawk and ran off up the beach, disappearing behind the mounds of sand.

Old Thomas came forward to greet Uriah. "They are stealing our try works!" he said frantically. "Uriah, what can we do?"

Uriah's eyes were focused on the men holding the muskets near the wagons. Anger bubbled inside of him but he knew he had to keep a cool head to avoid bloodshed. "You can put down your guns, men," he said. "My people will offer you no resistance. *Take* the pots. We don't have use for them any longer."

Old Thomas gasped and his eyes widened in surprise. "But, Uriah...." he began.

"Leave it alone, Father," said Uriah. "*These rusty old pots are not worth dying for.*"

Chapter Twenty-Six *"Hard Choices"*

Thatcher Snow came into the world squalling, with a shock of red hair like his parents' and fists that were clenched like those of a prize fighter.

"That boy certainly has a set of lungs," joked Eddie when Uriah came to visit and get a look at the new baby.

"He reminds me of *you*, Eddie," said Uriah. "Another *Captain Ginger!*"

Mary was finally content to leave the store to her husband and her father; staying home with her new son filled her days with pleasure but she missed Bethia, who had not visited in recent weeks due to her own confinement.

"How is Bethia feeling?" she asked Uriah. "She is due any day now is she not?"

Uriah had been staying close to the Wampanoag camp for several weeks, fearing his wife would go into labor and he would not be close when the time came. With the *old ones,* Rebecca and Anne, gone, he did not trust the birth of his child to the younger women of the tribe. "Yes," he replied. "She has grown very large, and is very uncomfortable."

"I can understand that," said Mary. "But, oh, it is worth every discomfort! Just look at our son! Isn't he the most handsome boy you've ever seen?"

Uriah's face twitched and Mary instantly regretted her words. Uriah, too, had a handsome son. She knew that young Samuel had not returned to the Wampanoag camp since the day of the altercation over the try pots. Word was he was out in the forest somewhere, refusing to be driven away to Mashpee. The *wild one,* people in town were calling him. Folks could occasionally see the glow of a lone campfire in the distance and women were warned not to venture too far into the woods to gather berries and mushrooms. *There was no telling what the crazy Indian boy would do.* Mary had to laugh at that; she had known Samuel since his birth. She could never *fear* him.

"Have you heard from him?" asked Eddie. "Any word at all?"

Uriah nodded sadly. "Aye," he said quietly. "He has been staying out of sight, but he comes in the night and leaves gifts at our door."

"Gifts?" asked Mary. "What kind of gifts?"

"Game birds he has killed. Strings of fish he has caught," said Uriah. "At least, we know he is not starving."

"Bethia must be beside herself with worry," Mary said. "He is so young to be out on his own."

143

"He has made his choice," said Uriah. "I have taught him to fish and hunt. If he chooses to live free as his forefathers did, I cannot stop him."

Eddie poured himself ale from a cask and moved from the baby's cradle to the fire. "And, you," he asked. "Have there been any more incidents?"

"No," said Uriah. "But, we keep expecting to hear from the governor, if nothing else, a decision as to where our tribe will be living. My father is determined not to go to Mashpee, but I fear he will not have much say in the matter."

Eddie reached down and pulled the latest copy of the *Boston Newsletter* from beside his chair. He handed it to Uriah. "I guess you have not heard, then," he said, tapping his finger on the headline. "The governor is dead. I doubt you will be hearing from him."

Uriah stared at the newspaper blankly. He stood up and shook his head. "I suppose it is hopeless then," he answered. "I should be getting back to Bethia. I don't want to leave her alone too long. Thank you for the ale. I will tell my wife you have a fine son!"

"You must bring her to supper soon, Uriah," said Mary. "And, the baby too!"

Now is the time, thought Eddie, *to tell him.* "Uriah, I have some news for you that might make the future look a little brighter," he said. "Come sit back down. There is something I want to show you."

Uriah again took his seat beside the fire and Eddie retrieved a document from a bureau drawer. When he sat down, he unrolled the paper and handed it to his friend. Uriah read the words of the last will and testament of Lois Snow and he pursed his lips tightly together to hold back tears. "This was good of your mother, Eddie," he said. "To know we have a place to go when the time comes will be welcome news to my wife. But...." A down-trodden expression crept across his face.

"But?" asked Eddie. "I thought you would be pleased! Ma wanted to be sure our family would stay together, here in Eastham. What's the problem?"

"You and Mary are our family, that is true," said Uriah. "But the Wampanoag are our family too. How would it look if *we* were allowed to stay and had to watch them all leave for Mashpee? Our hearts would be torn in two."

Mary had been listening from across the room where she sat rocking the cradle. She stood up and approached Uriah, placing her hand on his shoulder. "Discuss it with Bethia first," she said. "See what she has to say. We will certainly understand if you decide to go with the tribe to Mashpee when the time comes. Lois just wanted you to be *able* to stay if you *wanted* to stay. She wanted you to have that choice."

"And, I appreciate that," Uriah replied as he rose from his chair to leave. "If only the other white folks in Eastham felt the same."

He started out, down the southern road toward the Wampanoag camp, walking along silently in the dark, his deer skin moccasins crunching on the gravel road. He passed the spot on the road where Bethia had been attacked and his heart ached. Life had certainly taken strange turns in his life, in the life of his family. And, yet, he had to force himself to have hope with the thought of the new baby they were bringing into the world, another baby of mixed blood who would have ties to both whites and Indians. Perhaps it was a *good* thing. Perhaps one day the roots of prejudice would be drowned out by mixed blood. But, it wasn't going to happen overnight.

The woods loomed on either side of the dark road and he thought of Samuel, out there somewhere, living with the animals of the forest, with hatred festering in his soul. He could not cut out the piece of his son's heart that hated the whites and he was not sure he wanted to. The whites had done bad things to his family. His son had witnessed it firsthand. Who was he to tell his son he had no right to *hate*? Was he a coward to give in to them? He wanted peace with the whites but at what price?

When he finally reached the crest where the road fell off into the camp clearing, he could see a fire burning in the outdoor fire pit. He could hear chanting, quiet, somber chanting which he recognized as the mournful songs of the dead! His pace quickened, his heart raced. *Not again*! *They could not lose another baby! Who was the tribe mourning for?* He rushed across the camp toward the wetu he shared with Bethia and burst through the doorway, expecting the worst.

Bethia was lying on their cot, cradling a small bundle in the crook of her arm. On her face was a sad smile.

"Is he dead?" Uriah blurted out. *"Is my son dead?"*

"No," she replied. "Your *daughter* is quite healthy. Come see."

Uriah looked down at the tiny creature sleeping in his wife's arms, a beautiful olive-skinned infant with shiny black hair. *"Then, why….?"* he asked, turning back toward the doorway. *"Who are they mourning?"*

"Old Thomas is dead," said Bethia, reaching out for her husband's hand. "I am so sorry, my love. Your father did not get to meet his granddaughter."

Chapter Twenty-Seven *"Orleans"*

It was only a matter of time before the town of Eastham
formally divided into social classes. Like water in the
crevices of a rock when it freezes, it would split into
separate, shattered pieces a community that had once
been bound together by hard work and common goals.
To the north, the affluent gathered, building elaborate
two and three story homes that overlooked the ocean
and modern stores that catered to the sophisticated
tastes of the rich. The aristocratic families of the wealthy
sea captains who now owned fleets of ships that were
moored to the docks in the newly built harbor, who
dined lavishly and dressed in big city finery, now called
their part of town *Wellfleet*. To the south, the area
between Rock Harbor on the west and the Wampanoag
camp on the east was hereafter to be called *Orleans*. No
one knew exactly where the idea came from; someone
suggested it was named after a city in the north of France
that once marked the spot of Joan of Arc's first victory.
Ironically, it was also the name of a *woven* fabric that
came from that same area of France; now it represented
the *woven*, blended population of whites and
Wampanoag, of half-breeds and mixed-bloods who were
shunned by the folks to the north. Meanwhile, in
between, the original nucleus of old Eastham withered
away in obscurity, like a town bypassed by a new and
better road, a forgotten and abandoned *no-man's land*.

With still no word from the government in Boston, the Wampanoag soon put the prospect of forced relocation out of their minds, hoping they would be allowed to stay. They worked, side by side, with the folks of Orleans, planting crops they expected to harvest in the fall, building up their new little town, in which they could trade openly, without issue. A new mercantile and even a tiny one-room post office sprouted up, hardly bigger than a postage stamp itself; they improved their little harbor and tilled more acreage. A new school was built that welcomed not only the children from the Wampanoag camp but began to accept *girls* as well, an idea that before had been unheard of.

They fished for cod, built a new salt-works and harvested quahogs in the marshlands and kettle ponds. Ephraim resumed his position as mail carrier and, with his experience working for his father-in-law, Eddie was soon running the mercantile to provide for his growing family. Thatcher soon had two brothers, Joel and Jesse, and a fourth child was on the way. When the baby was born, and turned out to be a girl, Eddie told Mary he wanted her to pick a name for their daughter. "I know nothing of girl's names," he said. "A little girl should have a beautiful name. You would be the best to make that decision."

Mary did not need time to ponder. She already had a name in mind. "I think we should name her Susannah," she told him, "After your friend who lost her life bringing you home to me."

Eddie had no words. He had, for years, tried to keep the one memory he *wanted* to forget from his mind. His love for Mary had grown slowly but, in the years they had spent together, it had developed into a strong, lasting union; he couldn't imagine his life without her. She seemed to understand him better than anyone else, even his own mother. He was touched by her sentiment. "I am sure Susannah would be honored," he told her, embracing her tenderly.

In the Wampanoag camp, Uriah and Bethia had decided on the name Mercy for *their* little girl. Their happiness was short-lived, however. Bethia's health began to deteriorate soon after the birth and she would never conceive again. Before long, she succumbed to the unknown illness that ravaged her body, leaving young Mercy to take over her mother's duties at a very young age. And, yet, life went on.

The families continued to spend a great deal of time together. Little Mercy played with the Snow children from the time she could walk. The families, especially after Bethia's untimely death, shared frequent suppers together and Mary watched over Mercy when the men went on hunting trips. It was a peaceful time for the two families joined by blood and spirit.

But, just when life appeared to have settled back into a comfortable routine, when the strong arm of government seemed far away in Boston and the harbor was finally free of English interference, events were transpiring over three thousand miles away in London that would have a disastrous effect on America. The Treaty of Paris, which had officially put an end to the Revolution in the colonies, was soon violated. England and France were once again at war and trade restrictions were once again forced on the Americans by the English government that did not want them trading with the French. America had to take sides in the new war, they were told, and their allegiance to their mother country was not only *expected*, it was *demanded*. Before long, the English were once again blockading all the harbors and bays up and down New England; Massachusetts, depending greatly on its sea-going businesses, was hit especially hard. Soon, American ships were gathering moss and barnacles, tied to the docks, and thousands of men found themselves out of work. Opposition grew at the prospect of Americans being forced into the middle of a war they hadn't started. Tempers from Boston to Chatham flared. Ships delivering goods *locally* were also halted by the British fleet; only those captains who were willing to pay a ransom, in goods or money, were allowed to pass. Those who would not were turned around to return to their home ports, with their ships' bellies still full of rotting goods. It wasn't long before Orleans was pulled into the midst of it.

Captain Matthew Mayo and Captain Winslow Knowles came from old Eastham stock, whose families had become joined by their mutual relationships with the Wampanoag. Formerly long-distance whalers, the uncles of both Bethia Knowles and Uriah Mayo were soon caught up in the business of smuggling goods across Cape Cod Bay under the noses of the British fleet. Several times each week, Eddie, often with the help of Uriah and Grey Eyes, loaded up goods from the loading dock behind the mercantile, transporting them personally to the docks at Rock Harbor. There, Mayo and Knowles' ship would be waiting to pick up the contraband and sneak it through the blockade under the cloak of darkness, all the way to Boston, on their ship loaded down with rye. In Boston, where more local smugglers were waiting, they exchanged their cargo for supplies needed back in Orleans. Knowles and Mayo also traded their large whaler for a smaller, less noticeable craft but, on one return voyage, they were captured by the British.

Once on board the British ship, they were shuttled into the captain's quarters, where a ransom was demanded of them. Captain Knowles argued that he hadn't any money on board, that he would have to return to port to obtain the money. Accompanied by two British midshipmen, they did not steer for the port at Rock Harbor, however, but took them instead to Billingsgate Point, north of Wellfleet. While Mayo went ashore to supposedly obtain the ransom money, he managed to get a message back to Orleans. In their pre-conceived plan, Mayo's crew secretly slipped the boat from its moorings. When Mayo and his captors returned, the vessel was gone; it had drifted down the coast, going aground just north of Rock Harbor where Eddie, Uriah and Grey Eyes were waiting for them. The British crew were taken prisoner and held in a barn until a ransom was paid by the British for *their* release. The residents of Orleans shared a good laugh after the incident. The smuggling went on, however, for several years, until the end of the British blockades.

Chapter Twenty-Eight *"The Woman Who Reads the Stars"*

Old Eastham had been divided for years now. But, there would always be some things that they shared. The white residents of Wellfleet could not deny they still had kin that resided in Orleans, while those of mixed blood still carried the family names of the aristocratic families in the north. Even families that had been torn apart by bigotry and prejudice shared a blood tie that could never be completely severed. Although they kept their interactions to a minimum, it was impossible, in the course of conducting everyday business, for the people of Wellfleet not to have *some* contact with the people of Orleans. Disease was something that spread, regardless of the economic or social class of people. And, in the year that followed, an epidemic struck harder than any war they had ever seen. At its height, the undertakers in *both* towns were burying two to three people every day. They had experienced epidemics before but this one was devastatingly powerful. It had a new name; they called it *typhoid.*

It started innocently enough in the Snow house on Skaket Road. Mary Snow was not surprised when their three boys came home one afternoon feeling ill; she knew that children often came down with colds and fevers from their contacts at school and she wasn't overly alarmed. A good dose of honeysuckle and rose water and a few days of hot chicken broth and warm blankets and the patients were usually clamoring to be outside playing with their friends again. So, when their boys all came home that day with headaches and chills, she dosed them promptly and put them all to bed in the upstairs loft.

When Eddie and Uriah came in that night and found only girls at the supper table, they were surprised that the female members of the family had not come down with the illness.

"We women are far stronger than you know," said young Mercy.

Susannah couldn't resist adding her opinion. "Aye," she said, smiling at the girl who was like a sister to her. "Women give birth to babies! You can't get much stronger than that!"

Eddie and Uriah had to agree. But Eddie was skeptical. "And, you say all *three* of the boys caught it at the same time?" he asked. "Are you sure the schoolmaster isn't giving a test tomorrow and this is their clever way of getting out of it?"

"No," said Mary. "They are definitely sick this time. We put them all to bed."

By the next day, it was no joke. Half the students, boys and girls alike, were kept home from school. By the end of the week, ten of their neighbors had died from the fever. Thatcher, Joel and Jesse were still weak but at least their fevers had lessened and they were able to keep their food down. Ephraim reported that the epidemic had spread up and down the cape. Uriah came from the Wampanoag camp and informed them that the fever had hit there as well. He brought with him a basket of cranberries; *an old Indian cure for fever.* "My mother used to swear by it," he told Mary and Eddie.

"It couldn't hurt," Mary told him and served cranberries to her patients with their supper that night. The news that people were dying from this disease gave the boys no qualms about puckering up and eating the sour fruit.

Uriah and Mercy returned to the Wampanoag camp to assist with the sick there; by then several had died and the funeral pyres were burning almost every day. They stayed away from town for weeks after burying the bones of their dead, waiting for the disease to hopefully run its course. By the time Uriah paid a visit to the Snow family again, and was greeted by Eddie at the door with a frozen smile on his face, Uriah could tell all was not well.

"Mary has come down with it now," Eddie said sadly. "I am not sure it is safe to invite you in to supper."

"I am not worried. I have been exposed to it back at the camp," Uriah told him.

"Nevertheless," replied Eddie. "I would feel terrible if you got sick. Perhaps it is better to wait until Mary is well."

Uriah agreed and he returned to the Wampanoag camp to tell his daughter the dreadful news. "She is a strong woman, remember?" he said to her to cheer her up.

Mercy shook her head. "Yes, she is," she said. "She has been like a second mother to me. I don't know what I would do if we lost her."

Uriah knew his daughter had become close to Mary Snow; from the tone of her voice he could tell just *how* close they truly were. "We will pray to the gods," he said. *"To all the gods."*

Mercy disappeared immediately after supper and Uriah went out into the night and down to the dock, where he knew she liked to spend her evenings, gazing up at the stars. *It was her special place.*

"Look, Father!" said Mercy, pointing upward as he approached her. "There is *Ursa Major!*"

"Who?" asked Uriah, sitting down beside her and letting his legs dangle out over the water next to hers.

Mercy laughed. "We learned about it at school," she said. "We are studying the constellations. *Ursa Major.* They sometimes call it the Big Dipper. See, there…. how the stars form the shape of a ladle? And, over there, is Orion the Hunter. And, there, is the North Star. It never moves. The Vikings used it to navigate their ships hundreds of years ago."

Uriah looked up and tried to see the pictures his daughter was painting for him. It just looked like a bunch of stars to him.

"You are growing to be a very wise woman," he said. "Perhaps you will be sachem of our tribe one day; a woman who can read the stars!"

Mercy laughed. "I have no desire to be *sachem*," she said. "I want to marry and have children. Besides, we are becoming a very *small* tribe, with the help of the typhoid, smaller every day. Soon, we won't have to worry about going to Mashpee; this disease has taken care of that."

"Yes," replied Uriah. "I suppose that is true."

There was a quiet lull in their conversation. The waves lapping gently against the pilings beneath them and an occasional call from one of the gulls that flew overhead were the only sounds in the darkness.

"The gods are silent tonight," said Uriah.

"Perhaps they are busy making Missus Snow well," Mercy replied. "I am going to visit her tomorrow, Father."

"Eddie said to wait," he said. "And, I agree. I don't want my daughter to get sick!"

"I helped nurse Thatcher and Jesse and Joel when they were sick," she insisted. "It will be all right. I won't get sick, Father! You mustn't worry about me."

Uriah could see strength in his daughter. How she had grown since her mother died! Had it really been nineteen years since her birth? *I will lose her one day,* he thought. *She already has dreams of marriage and children.* "Do you have a particular candidate in mind to marry?" he asked, wondering if there was a secret she wasn't telling him.

He could not see her smile in the darkness but somehow he sensed she was amused at his curiosity.

"Yes," she said matter-of-factly. "I do."

Uriah waited for her to continue. "Well?" he said. "Do you intend to keep your old father wondering who his future son-in-law might be? I might not approve of him you know!"

Mercy sat up and brushed the sand from her skirt. "Oh, I think you will approve of him," she said confidently. *"I am going to marry Thatcher Snow!"*

Chapter Twenty-Nine *"The Dream Catcher"*

Eddie awoke in the middle of the night with his heart pounding and his face dripping with sweat. He pushed the blanket away from himself and laid there in the dark. The nightmares had not plagued him in many years; since he had regained most of his memory and had dealt with the "demons" of his past, he was able to sleep soundly again. Still, *something* had awakened him suddenly. For an instant, he worried that he had contracted the typhoid fever but when he rose and went to the open window, his body had cooled. It was no fever. *It had to be a dream!*

Mary was sleeping peacefully beside him. In recent days, her condition seemed to have improved and Eddie was hopeful the worst was over. Knowing he could not go back to sleep, he didn't want to toss and turn and wake his wife, so he threw on a robe and tip-toed out of the bedroom. He re-kindled the fire and sat in Mary's rocking chair, stretching his feet out toward the flames. In quiet times like these, he often thought of Susannah; the flames reminded him of the pyre they had put her body on to keep her from the wolves. Poor Susannah, who had nursed him back to health only to lose her life so tragically. *And, yet, if Susannah had lived, what would his life have been like?* he wondered. *Would they have married? Would she have been as devoted to him as*

Mary had been all these years? These were questions that would never be answered. He leaned back in Mary's chair and closed his eyes, when the fire suddenly popped and crackled, igniting a bit of sap in the crevices of the fresh log, and he was wide awake again. When the fire had settled down again, Eddie did too, returning to his bed when his eyes began to feel heavy.

When morning came, he overslept. He opened his eyes and could hear the boys' footsteps upstairs and marveled at how three boys could sound like a herd of moose, lumbering across the ceiling. *Boys.* He could hardly call them *boys* any longer. They were almost of marrying age and could soon make him a grandfather! The thought was enough to make him get out of bed. "Mary?" he reached down and lovingly squeezed his wife's buttocks through the blanket. "Time to get up! The herd is awake above us. Can't you hear them? They'll be tearing your kitchen apart to make their own breakfast if you don't rise."

Mary did not stir. She had been so very tired; the fever had taken its toll on her body. *Maybe, I should let her sleep*, he thought. Then, he heard the boys galloping down the stairs.

"Mary," he said again. Still there was no movement.

He crossed around to the other side of the bed and placed his hand on her shoulder; he reached up and felt her face. It was cold, *cold, just like Susannah's.*

The realization rocked him like a bullet to the chest; he sank down on the bed and pulled Mary to him. Her limp, lifeless body leaned against him like a rag doll. *This can't be happening to me again*, he thought. *How many wives will I have to bury?* For even though he and Susannah had never married, he suddenly realized he thought of her in that way. He laid Mary back down on her pillow and pulled the blankets up around her before he leaned over and kissed her; his lips lingered on hers and he tasted the saltiness of his own tears. He could hear the boys' voices in the other room and Susannah taking out pots and pans to start breakfast. *How was he going to tell his children? What was he going to say?*

It was Ephraim who delivered the sad news to the Wampanoag camp the next day. "My brother is beside himself with grief," he told Uriah and Mercy. "His nightmares have returned. He was positively *hysterical* last night and refused to go to bed. I don't think he will ever sleep again."

Uriah and Mercy stood at her graveside the following day with the Snow family and laid her to rest. After the preacher had said his final words, they all returned to the house on Skaket Road to share a somber supper together. Mercy left Susannah in the kitchen and found a distraught Eddie sitting alone on the porch, staring into the nothingness that he felt his life had become. She took his hand and smiled at the man she hoped would one day be her father-in-law, although her heart was aching with such intensity she feared she would burst into tears at any moment.

"She was a wonderful woman," said Mercy. "She was a mother to me, when my own mother died. I will never forget her."

Eddie nodded sadly. "She loved you too, Mercy," he told her.

"Ephraim says you are not sleeping at night," she said. "He says your nightmares have returned to you."

Again, Eddie nodded. It was true; he was terrified of closing his eyes, terrified of the images that haunted him in the darkness.

"I have brought you a gift," said Mercy, holding a small object in her hands and offering it to Eddie.

Eddie took the object and stared down at it, a circular piece of pliable bark, woven together and intertwined with threads colored from berries and flowers, with feathers and beads dangling down from it. "It is beautiful," he said. "What is it?"

"It is a *dream catcher,*" Mercy replied. With her fingers she pointed to the intricate design in the center the object Eddie held in his hands. "I made it myself. You must hang it over your bed at night. It will catch and trap the bad dreams before they can get to you. It is an old Wampanoag legend but I believe it works."

Eddie was touched at Mercy's gift, although he doubted it would be of much use. "Thank you, Mercy," he said.

"Indian customs and beliefs probably sound silly to many people," she said. "But, there are things no one can explain, even the learned men in the universities. I have learned much in my schooling, but sometimes the old remedies of my people seem to be the ones that bring me the most comfort."

"I will try it," said Eddie.

Mercy smiled and kissed his cheek lightly. "I promise you will sleep soundly tonight."

Chapter Thirty *"The Wild One"*

Mercy had seen it several times from her favorite evening perch on the little Wampanoag dock her ancestors had built, where the tribe now tied up their canoes. Night after night, she would escape the summer heat inside the wetu to come study the stars in the heavens; on some nights she took an oil lamp and an old school tablet with her so that she could sketch the stars as they twinkled above her. The first night she had seen it, she had lowered the wick in the lamp to get a better view, afraid her eyes were somehow tricking her. But, no! On this night she had seen it again! Looking north, past the beach of bones, beyond the dunes and the fields of reeds, she saw the unmistakable glimmer of a campfire burning. So enthralled by the mystery of it all, she put her own safety out of her mind and ventured off the dock and began to walk toward the firelight in the distance. She removed her squaw boots and hurried along, immersing her feet in the swirling water. The moon was big and full tonight and its reflection turned the white waves to silver. She could hear the far-off howling of wolves but her curiosity outweighed her fears; *who was on the beach at this hour?* she wondered. *Was there another solitary soul who shared her passion for the sound of the surf and the umbrella of the stars above her head at midnight? Had she a kindred spirit?*

She stopped momentarily when she lost sight of the flame but, when she took a few steps more, she realized it was only hidden behind a mound of sand. It was still there, flickering orange and bright against the ink-blue of the night sky. Finally, she reached a high dune, a great mound of sand that had blown in from the sea and piled high against a tall bank. She was glad she had left her lamp and tablet behind, for it took both her hands and feet to pull herself up the steep rise. And, there, she saw it; down below her was a large bonfire on the beach with three Wampanoag men seated around it. There was laughter and conversation in her native tongue. Mercy sat down and watched the strange men for a while, listening to what they were saying. *They were running away from something, from the re-location most likely,* she surmised. The one who had his back to her had a well-built body, with powerful shoulders and a long black braid down his bare back. She felt drawn to him. When he spoke, his words were sometimes in Wampanoag, sometimes in English and his voice had a familiar ring to it. She could not see his face; *was he someone she knew?* She moved her body slightly, making herself more comfortable so she could sit and listen longer. She leaned forward, folding her legs up underneath her and rustling a pile of dead reeds, when they crackled under the pressure of her body. The silence was broken and the man whose back was turned reeled around in her direction. She panicked, knowing she had been discovered. She stared back at the man, recognizing something in his face. *But, who were these men?* she wondered. The man who had seen her stood up and smiled at her and suddenly she realized who he was. *He had their father's smile!* She stood up and dashed down the steep embankment, stumbling and falling forward in the deep sand, but she could not stop. Samuel recognized her too and ran toward her, catching her in his arms.

"I do believe it is my baby sister!" he told the others.

"Samuel!" Mercy mumbled excitedly. "Where have you been? Why have you not come home?"

Samuel led her to the fire and introduced her to the others. "This is *Cloud Dancer* and *Soft Wing*," he said. "And, what name did they give you, Little Sister?"

"They named me Mercy," she told him. She stared at the two other men. She did not recognize them as any in their tribe. "You men are not from Orleans?" she asked.

The men stared back at her nervously.

"You can trust my sister," Samuel assured them. "She would not betray my trust."

She stared at him, seeing her father in both his physical appearance and his demeanor. Here was the man her parents had whispered about all of her life, her own brother who had run away before she was born. He looked healthy enough; she remembered how her mother worried that he would not have enough to eat in the woods. He appeared in good form, lean and brown from the sun. *The wild one*, the people of Orleans had nicknamed him, whose campfires could be seen in the night skies. *Her own brother!*

"These men are escaping the relocation in the south," explained Samuel. "I am acting as their guide on their journey to Canada where they will be beyond the American government that wants to ship them off to the desert in the west."

Mercy's face took on a serious expression. "That is very dangerous, isn't it?" she asked. "What if you are caught? They will ship you off to a prison instead!"

"The desert beyond the great river *is* a prison," said the one called Cloud Dancer. "It has high fences and guarded gates. They say once you go in you will never come out again."

The other man agreed. "I would rather they just *shoot* me than to cage me like an animal for the rest of my life," he said.

Samuel shook his head. "You need not worry about me, Little Sister," he said. "I have evaded the white people all these years. We only travel by night. The white people are fat and lazy and once they have eaten their suppers they don't leave their houses."

Mercy was silent for a moment. "Do you know that our mother died?" she asked. "And, Old Thomas too. And, that we lost many from the typhoid?"

Samuel's eyes clouded. "I saw the funeral pyres from the distance," he replied. "I knew not who they were for."

"Our father grows old," she said. "It would warm his heart to see you again, Samuel."

Samuel took a long piece of wood and poked at the fire, sending sparks scattering into the sand. "Tell him for me," he said, "That I am well, that I am helping our people. That will make him happy."

"Not as happy as seeing you again," said Mercy. She looked around in the firelight and spotted an old house only yards away from the fire pit, a place she did not recognize. "What is this place?" she asked. "Who lives here?"

"No one," said Samuel. "It used to belong to Eddie Snow's grandfather. It's been abandoned since he died." He turned the attention toward his little sister. "But, what about you, Mercy? You are all grown up now! Have you a husband yet? And children?"

Mercy felt her face flush with embarrassment in front of the strange men. "No," she replied. "But, I hope to marry soon."

"Is this so?" asked Samuel. "And, who is your intended?"

"Thatcher Snow," she announced proudly.

"Thatcher......?" Samuel's eyes darkened and the smile on his face disappeared.

"A white man?" he asked, his words laced with angry venom. "You are going to marry a *white* man?"

"Have you forgotten that the Snows are our family? That our own *mother* was white?" said Mercy. "The Snows are our cousins on our father's side."

"Yes," said Samuel. "But, I do not see them as *family* any longer. They have weakened our bloodline! They are the reason the Wampanoag are dying out!"

Mercy felt anger rising up within her. Where had her brother learned such bigotry? "I can't believe you would say such a thing about the Snows!" she said. "They have supported us for many years! They have treated us as equals!" Mercy was at a loss for words except for one burning question. "Did you hate our mother as well, Samuel? Is that why you never came home?"

Samuel shook his head and the other two men stared menacingly at her. "You should go home now," he said. "It is late and not safe for you to be out alone."

Mercy could sense the change in her brother's mood. She could see that he had developed such hatred for the white people that he had forgotten that the Snow family were their kin! "I do not understand you, Brother," she said, rising to leave. "But, I am glad I got to meet you nevertheless. Take care that you don't get yourself *hanged.*"

She ran back up the sandy hill and did not stop until she reached the dock at the Wampanoag camp.

Chapter Thirty-One *"Strange Inheritances"*

*"*You actually *saw* your brother?*"* Uriah asked a second time, in awe of what his daughter had just told him and needing reassurance that his ears were not playing tricks on him. "And, Samuel is well?"

"Yes, Father," Mercy replied. "He looks a lot like you. That was why I recognized him so quickly!"

Uriah could tell she was leaving something out, something she was holding back. "There is something else?" he asked.

Mercy tried to pick the right words for her father to hear; for him to *understand.* "He is helping our people from the south escape the forced re-location. He is guiding them north to Canada."

Uriah sighed deeply. "That is a very dangerous occupation," he said. "But, it does not surprise me. Your brother was very angry with the American government."

"His hatred has not lessened, I am afraid," replied Mercy. "When I told him I planned to marry Thatcher Snow, he shut down completely and did not want to talk any more. I am afraid I upset him greatly."

"Twas not your fault," her father said. "Your brother has not taken the treatment of our people lightly. We cannot fault him for that. He must see me as weak for giving in to it."

Mercy approached her father and put her arm affectionately around his shoulder. *"You? Weak?"* she asked incredulously. "You have protected us, our family, from harm. You have tried to live in peace with the white people. What would Samuel have you do? Fight the American government on your own?"

"Samuel has seen things that you have not," Uriah said sadly. "When he was very young and impressionable. He cannot forgive those things."

"I know about what happened to Mother," Mercy whispered. "Susannah told me about it a long time ago. Samuel must have felt helpless."

It was a memory that did not conjure up happy feelings and Uriah was anxious to change the topic of conversation to something else. "And, *you*, young lady," his voice suddenly sounded cross. "You should not be wandering on the beach alone at night! What if you had run upon someone else? Thieves or poachers or worse? Do you not see how dangerous that could be?"

Mercy made a grimacing face. "Oh, Father...." she began.

"No arguments!" he said. "I forbid you to take such risks in the future. How far did you walk? Just *where* did you find your brother?"

"On the beach, near Mister Snow's grandfather's house," she replied.

"You walked all the way out there in the dark?" asked Uriah incredulously. "Have you lost your mind, girl?"

"Samuel says house is abandoned," said Mercy. "He says no one ever goes there."

Uriah knew the place well. So did Samuel. They had shared many meals there with Edmund Freeman, the old man of the sea. He had never told anyone beside his dead wife that he had inherited that house and land from Lois Snow. Inwardly, he laughed; how ironic that Samuel had found sanctuary on the very land of the white family he disdained so! On the very land that *he* would inherit someday! "There is something I have never told you," he said, "About that old house."

Mercy's ears perked. *Her father was going to tell her something exciting* and she loved a good mystery! "What is it, Father? What about that old house?"

"It belongs to *us* now," said Uriah. "It was left to us by Eddie's mother. She considered us family and she wanted to be sure we had a place to go if the government takes away our land here."

Mercy was surprised and a bit disappointed. She expected him to tell her something much more interesting, like the house had once been a pirate's lair or it had ghosts or something equally provocative. "Is that all?" she asked. "What will we do with an old abandoned house?"

Uriah smiled at his daughter's innocence. *How wonderful it must be,* he thought, *to feel so secure when at any moment they could lose everything they held dear? How wonderful, and how dangerous!* "That old house may save us from the re-location someday," he told her sternly. "You must not make light of it!"

Mercy did not fully understand the politics of it all, but she could see the seriousness in her father's face as he spoke. The matter of the re-location had been discussed her entire life and nothing ever became of it, so she had put it out of her mind. Perhaps, she had not seen the gravity of the situation.

"Promise me," Uriah said firmly. "Promise me you will not wander up the beach at night ever again!"

"I promise," she said.

Inwardly, however, she knew she was not being truthful. She was suddenly *fascinated* with the old house beyond the dunes, especially now that she knew it belonged to her family! She secretly wanted to get a look inside the place!

Chapter Thirty-Two *"A Spittin' Image"*

"I can't believe you are serious!" Susannah said. *"You want to marry Thatcher?"*

Mercy put her finger to her lips to silence her.

"Shhhh! They could walk through the door at any minute!" she whispered.

The two were alone in the kitchen in the house on Skaket Road, preparing supper for the Snow men who were due to come home from a hunting trip in the woods and Uriah who had work to do back at the Wampanoag camp.

"I don't know what on earth you find attractive about him," said Susannah, not worried at all about anyone overhearing their conversation. She leaned over to taste the stew and replaced the lid back on the kettle. "He's lazy and vulgar! And, he has to be reminded to wash his hands before supper! How can you possibly be in love with someone like that?"

Mercy was smiling as she slid a batch of biscuits off a hot tray. It was not the reaction she had expected from her cousin, but since Bethia's death, they had become so close they confided everything in each other. "I don't know why," she replied. "Love is like a mild form of insanity, I suppose. Besides, *you* are his sister. Sisters *always* think their brothers are disgusting."

"You wouldn't say that if you had brothers!" Susannah said. "Believe me, it is like living with a cage of unclean birds. I don't know how my mother survived it so long!"

Mercy bit her lip and Susannah realized she had said too much.

"You forget that I *do* have a brother," she said sadly. "And, I would have given anything to have known him growing up. It was very lonely after my mother died."

Susannah moved closer to her best friend and put a comforting arm around her. "I'm sorry, Mercy," she said. "I sometimes forget about Samuel."

"I will never forget him," Mercy replied. "Did I tell you I met him once on the beach?"

She told Susannah about her chance encounter with Samuel on the beach but left out the part about her brother's hatred for the Snow family.

"What did he say when you spoke to him?" Susannah asked. "What on earth did you have to say to each other after all these years?"

"Just that he was helping the Indians who are escaping re-location in the south," Mercy answered.

"Did he ask about your parents? Did he tell you when he plans to return to the camp?"

Mercy shook her head. "I am afraid he will never come back," she said. "He is quite content living free."

The girls covered the supper to keep it warm and retreated to Susannah's room until the men returned. Susannah pulled out a dress she was making and showed it to Mercy.

"Why, it's beautiful, Susannah!" Mercy told her. "I love the color and the…."

"Would you like to try it on?" Susannah asked. "I have no one to help me with the fittings so I have to take it on and off myself to mark the seams. It takes me *ever* so long to get it right! That is one of the problems of living with a house full of men! They know nothing of dressmaking!"

Mercy slipped out of her soft doe-skin dress and stepped into Susannah's stiff new one made of starched gingham, pulling it up around her. The strange fabric felt odd against her skin. She had worn clothing made from animal hides all of her life.

"Here," said Susannah, fetching a small mirror and positioning it on the window sill so that Mercy could see herself.

Mercy gasped at her reflection. She and Susannah were almost the same size and the dress fit her perfectly. The green material brought out the hazel color of her eyes.

Quickly, she untied her braid and let her hair fall down in curly ringlets around her shoulders.

"You look just like your mother," said Susannah. "Why, you could almost pass for…." She stopped herself.

"I could almost pass for a *white woman*?" asked Mercy. "Is that what you were going to say?"

Susannah was ashamed of herself and immediately apologized. "I didn't mean anything by it, Mercy," she said. "You know how much I love you and your family! It's just that you don't look *Indian* at all, dressed like that with your hair down. No one except those who knew you would ever guess!"

Mercy knew it to be true. Every summer the sun lightened her dark brown hair, giving it a warm glow; it was now almost the color of her mother's hair and, without the tight braid, she looked like a completely different person. "Susannah," she said. "Would you make a dress for me?"

Susannah crossed the room and found her sewing basket. "I'll do better than that," she said happily. "I'll let you have this one! Come and we will put the finishing touches on it. Won't your father be surprised?"

When Eddie and the boys finally arrived home and Mercy made her entrance into the room, their eyes followed her.

"Doesn't she look just like her mother?" Susannah asked. "Don't you think Uriah will be pleased?"

Eddie was not so sure about that. Conjuring up memories was not always a pleasant task. Still he nodded and sat down to eat his supper. "She surely does, Susannah!" he said. "She's the spittin' image of Bethia herself!"

The boys were more interested in the food on the table, except for Thatcher, who glanced her way several times, which pleased Mercy immensely. It was not the first time he had noticed how pretty Mercy Mayo was, but she was even prettier in white girls' clothes, with her hair down around her shoulders, *very pretty indeed!*

When they had cleared the dishes from the table, and Uriah still had not arrived to fetch his daughter, Mercy shared her concern with Eddie. "It's not like him to be late in coming for me," she said. "I hope everything is all right at the camp."

"Has there been trouble lately?" Eddie asked.

"Not that I know of," replied Mercy. "But, my father does not always tell me when there is trouble. He tries to protect me from such things, as if keeping me ignorant will protect me!"

Another hour passed and the boys went off to bed. Eddie considered taking Mercy home himself but decided against it. There was no telling what was going on at the camp. He didn't want to take her home if there was trouble.

"You are welcome to stay here," he told her. "I am sure your father must have a good reason for being delayed."

He sat by the fire until well past eleven, hoping that he would hear a knock at the door, but no knock came. Just as he was about to give up and go to bed, the door swung wide open and Ephraim came bursting in. His eyes were wide and his expression was not one of weariness and eagerness for sleep.

"What is it?" Eddie asked his brother.

Ephraim crossed the room and handed Eddie the latest copy of the *Boston Newsletter*. "*This* was delivered today," he said. "There will be trouble, Eddie. They must be doin' their war dances out at the camp. The fires are burning hot!"

Eddie read the first few lines of the article in the paper. The President had finally signed a law, *ordering the re-location of all Indian tribes*! It had finally happened! He dropped the paper and stood up, reaching for his coat and weapon. He had to reason with Uriah before he did anything stupid! "We can't leave the girls alone," he said. "The boys should stay here. I'll wake Thatcher and tell him to stay by the door after we leave."

Thatcher was sleeping soundly when Eddie shook his shoulder gently and whispered to him. "Wake up, Son!"

he said, trying not to wake the other boys sleeping in the room.

Thatcher rubbed his eyes and followed his father into the other room. "What is it, Pa?" he asked, yawning.

"Your uncle says there is trouble brewing at the Wampanoag camp. We have to go check it out," said Eddie. "I need you to bar the door as soon as we leave and not open it for *anyone* until we return!"

"All right, Pa," answered Thatcher. "But, what has happened?"

"Trouble with the government again," replied Eddie as he and Ephraim stepped out onto the porch. "We won't know how *much* trouble until we get there. *Whatever you do*, do not let your sister or Mercy leave this house!"

When Eddie turned, he saw what Ephraim had seen earlier. In the distance, he could see flames against the night sky, *many flames*. It looked as if the entire Wampanoag camp was on fire!

Chapter Thirty-Three *"President's Orders"*

With loaded muskets, they saddled their horses and spurred them to a gallop down Skaket Road. The closer they came to the camp, the higher the flames were shooting up into the sky.

"That's more than a *war* dance," yelled Eddie.

It was apparent the entire camp was burning to the ground. Strangely, when they finally reined in their horses on the rise above the camp, there were no dancing Indians either; there were no Indians at all, only a few men in state militia uniforms who were just mounting their horses and preparing to leave the scene. Every wetu in the camp was ablaze; everything that was not in flames was already a smoldering ruin! Eddie and Ephraim rode up to the soldiers.

"What has happened here?" Eddie demanded. "Where are the people of the Wampanoag tribe?"

"They are on their way to Mashpee," said the soldier. "Cleared 'em out just this morning, by order of the President himself."

"But, why are you burning their homes?" asked Ephraim who came riding up behind Eddie. "Weren't they allowed to take their belongings with them?"

The man stuck a wad of tobacco in his cheek and began to chew. "They were allowed to take only what they could carry," he said. "We're not in the business of moving huts and canoes halfway across the state! Besides, they won't be a'needin' them anymore. The government is gonna feed them and set them up in nice little houses in Mashpee. They'll be taken care of real good. They won't want to come back here."

"Do you actually *believe* that hogwash?" asked Eddie, deeply incensed. "And, what of their dead lying in the cemetery? What about them?"

The second man swung his horse around to face Eddie squarely. "We're not movin' corpses! That's for *damned* sure!" he said, laughing. "What's *your* interest in these Injuns anyway?"

Eddie held his tongue, when he wanted to lash out at the soldiers, but he knew it would not do to anger them. "They are my family," he said.

The man squinted his eyes and stared back at Eddie. "You don't look Injun' to me," he said.

"We were related by marriage," said Eddie, although he did not feel the man deserved an explanation. "How long ago did they leave?"

"Early this mornin'," he said. "I hope you don't have any stupid ideas about rescuing them! They have a full company of soldiers guardin' them. So I advise you not to do anything crazy."

The soldiers turned and rode off down the road toward town, leaving Eddie and Ephraim sitting astride their horses, side by side, watching the remnants of the *wetus* crumble and fall into heaps of spent ash and embers.

"We have to go to Mashpee," Eddie said. "The children will be all right. I told Thatcher to be sure the girls did not leave the house."

"I'm with you, Brother," Ephraim assured him. "I'm not sure how much we can do about it, though. We can't fight the government all by ourselves and no one else seems to care."

Eddie spurred his horse and took off, stirring up clouds of dust and ash behind him and Ephraim followed. No matter how they looked at it, *it was going to be a long night.*

Chapter Thirty-Four *"Sad News for Mercy"*

"But, Pa said you girls were to stay in the house!"

Thatcher was standing with arms crossed and feet spread wide, guarding the door and Susannah was openly defying her older brother.

"Pa would certainly let us go outside to empty our chamber pots and collect the eggs before the weasels get them!" Susannah shot back. "Use your head, Brother! Something has undoubtedly happened to delay Pa and Uncle Ephraim. Now, get out of my way, or I will *push* you out of my way!"

Thatcher knew his sister's logic was most likely accurate. It had been two days since their father and uncle had left for the Wampanoag camp. Susannah was right; something must have gone terribly wrong! With a sigh, he stepped aside and unbarred the door.

"Thank you!" said Susannah, brushing past him. "Now, go and open up all the windows! With the three of you cooped up in this house all this time, it is beginning to *stink* in here!"

Mercy followed quietly behind Susannah, helping her take the reeking chamber pots outside for a thorough cleansing. When she passed Thatcher, she smiled ever so slightly and he smiled back at her. "I can't imagine what has happened to them," he said. "It's not like Pa to stay away unless there was trouble. I think I will go to town and ask at the armory. Surely, if there has been trouble, they will know about it!"

When he returned, a half hour later, he delivered the bad news; news that he knew would be particularly devastating to Mercy.

"The militia has destroyed the Wampanoag camp," he told the rest of the family. "Burned everything to the ground! And, they have taken the tribe away to Mashpee."

He glanced at Mercy, who had her eyes closed and appeared to be weeping. "I'm sorry, Mercy," he said. "But, try not to worry. Pa and Uncle Ephraim must have followed them. They'll be sure nothing happens to your father."

"I suppose they will be coming for me, too," Mercy replied. "I should leave before I cause your family any more trouble."

Thatcher was unyielding. "You will do no such thing! You will stay here and out of sight until my father returns or he will take a lash to my backside!"

Susannah rolled her eyes at her brother. "Pa has *never* whipped you, Thatcher Snow, and you *know* it! Quit telling such lies just to impress Mercy!"

Embarrassed and caught in his own embellishment, Thatcher barred the door again and picked up the Boston Newsletter, sitting down on the floor near the fire. "Yep!" he said. "Here it is in black and white! President Jackson signed the re-location act into law!"

Susannah crossed the room and snatched the paper from her brother's hands. "We have heard enough of the *bad* news," she said sourly. "Why don't you boys go down to the pond and bring us fresh fish for supper?"

Thatcher stared at her warily.

"Don't worry," she replied sarcastically. "Mercy and I will be good little girls until you return."

When Thatcher had left with Jesse and Joel, with their fishing poles slung over their shoulders, Susannah took Mercy into her arms and hugged her tightly. *What else can the wretched government do to make them suffer?* she wondered to herself. "There is rarely any truth in what my brother has to say," she said, trying to make her dear cousin smile. "But, he *is* correct about Pa. He will stand by your father no matter what! Try not to worry, Mercy. He will bring us news soon."

Mercy sighed deeply as she began to change back into her own clothing.

"Don't you want to keep the dress?" Susannah asked.

"It is a beautiful dress," replied Mercy. "But, it would look best on you. I must remember who I am."

"Don't talk like that," Susannah pleaded.

"Your father and your entire family have always watched out for us," Mercy said. "I have no doubts in the matter. But, it seems that the government, English or American, will not stop until it has destroyed the Wampanoag and all the other tribes. Still, we have not suffered as much as the Cherokees in Georgia or the Seminoles in Florida. At least, we are still alive! I suppose I should be grateful we are only being moved as far as Mashpee and not to the deserts west of the great river!"

Susannah's heart ached for Mercy. *How could she say or do anything that would help at all?* "Try not to worry," she said again, realizing the emptiness of her words no sooner had they left her mouth.

Chapter Thirty-Five *"Mashpee"*

They had ridden all night, taking the King's Highway to Barnstable and then south on a rutted trail that wound its way through the salt marshes all the way to Mashpee.

"There ain't no way they could've got wagons over this road," said Ephraim. "Do you suppose they made 'em *walk* all the way to Mashpee?"

"Wouldn't surprise me," replied Eddie. "Soldiers in the militia now aren't in it for honor anymore; they're in it for money! *Nothing but hired thugs*, if you ask me." He paused and thought of Mercy, safe back home with his children. "I'm glad the girl is with us, at least."

Dawn was breaking by the time they reached their destination; the fingers of sunlight were creeping slowly across the sleeping plantation. It hardly looked like a town at all, but a scattering of structures called *wigwams*, built from sedge, that dotted the shores of a large freshwater pond and beyond them, fields of corn and beans and squash all the way to the seashore and Waquoiit Bay. Half-naked Wampanoag men were beginning to stir; making their way down the road to tend their crops and women were lighting campfires. It hadn't the *look* of a prison; in contrast, it appeared quite peaceful and serene. Was it possible the people were happy with their lives here? Was it not such an awful place after all?

With their flared nostrils breathing heavily and their necks lathered in white sweat, the horses were eager for rest; Eddie and Ephraim were exhausted from the long ride as well, but they were determined to keep going until they found Uriah and the rest of the tribe. The road followed along the shore of the pond, past an old meetinghouse and several sheds and lean-to's, until several canvas tents came into view. It was there they finally saw Uriah and Grey Eyes, standing outside the entrance to the first tent, like guardian angels watching over their flock. Uriah's eyes flashed and his mouth broke into a sad smile when he saw them approaching. At that moment, a pair of soldiers with muskets drawn appeared and watched as Eddie and Ephraim rode toward them.

The soldiers walked out into the road and stood between them and the tent.

"State your business here," said one of them.

Eddie, once a soldier himself, almost laughed out loud. "You can put away your weapons, Corporal," he said. "We are no threat to you. We have come to be sure our family arrived at their destination safely."

"*Your* family?" the second soldier asked. "I don't think you'll find any of *your* family here. These are all Injuns, come to live at Mashpee; President Jackson's orders!"

"Are guns *really* necessary?" Eddie asked the soldier, whose musket was still aimed at them. "I assure you we are not looking for trouble and, surely, these peaceful people are not giving you cause to shoot any of them!"

The soldier looked at Eddie with a scowl. "You never know what Injuns' will do," he said. "What business is it of *yours* anyhow?"

"I am Eddie Snow," said Eddie, getting down from his horse. "This is my brother, Ephraim. We have ridden all the way from Orleans to catch up to you. And, you are mistaken, sir. These are *indeed* my family. You have several of my cousins. We share blood."

"Half-breeds!" mumbled one of the soldiers under his breath, walking away in disgust.

Uriah and Grey Eyes walked past the soldiers and greeted the Snows.

"How are you faring?" asked Eddie. "Has the army been treating you well?"

"It will be good now that the women and children can rest," said Grey Eyes. "They are all quite weary."

When Uriah came toward him, they locked arms and Eddie could see fear in his eyes. Uriah moved closer and whispered in his ear, "Don't say anything about my daughter."

"There's to be no whispering!" the soldier snapped.

"I knew this was coming," said Uriah, loudly enough for the soldiers to hear him. "I just didn't know *when*. We will just have to make the best of it, I suppose." He could sense that the soldiers were listening to every word, so he went on talking, hoping to convince the men with guns that his people would give them no trouble. "They say we will have our own land here. Plenty of land to grow our own crops and forests to hunt. The more I hear about it, the better it sounds!"

Eddie nodded even though he knew Uriah was lying through his teeth. He played the game just long enough that the soldiers returned to their posts outside the tent.

"We have to re-build our homes, of course," Uriah continued. "These tents will have to do until then. Come inside and sit a spell. We have coffee and we will find something for you to eat."

"Leave your guns with your horses," the corporal told them.

"No problem with that," Eddie assured him.

Eddie and Ephraim followed Uriah through the maze of Indians sleeping on the ground. At the rear of the tent, Grey Eyes fetched them some cups of strong brew and a couple of cold biscuits and they all sat down together. Eddie looked at the sleeping faces of the gentle Wampanoag around them. *At least, they are safe,* he thought. *At least there were no casualties; only their pride has suffered so far.*

"How is she?" Uriah asked quietly.

"She is fine," Eddie replied. "My boys are watching over her. I told Thatcher not to let her leave the house."

Uriah nodded. "I don't want her to come here just yet," he said. "I want to see how my people are treated. I will send for her as soon as I know it is safe."

"You still have Grandfather's house," Eddie said sadly. "It will always belong to you and your family."

"I am the sachem of my tribe. As much as I appreciate your mother's generosity, my place is with them. Tell my daughter I have not forgotten her," Uriah replied. "When it is safe, I will send for her. We will have to wait and see what happens here."

Chapter Thirty-Six *"Under Guard"*

Eddie and Ephraim stayed long enough to help the men of the tribe begin the job of gathering the makings of what were to be their homes. With no hickory bark available, they used the dried reeds and rushes that the other dwellings were made of, although the pickings were sparse. They were not allowed to venture out of the sight of the soldiers; they had to make do with whatever they could find in the immediate vicinity.

"When I think of all the usable wood that went up in flames," said Eddie. "If only they had let you bring the wood with you."

"The journey was long enough," replied Uriah. "We would have never made it carrying wood on our backs. No, we will just have to use what we have here."

The young corporal was watching them, sitting astride his horse with his musket lying across his lap. He found it curious that these two white men had such an interest in the Indians when his own inclinations were to shoot them all and be done with it. He had enlisted in the army to *protect* the whites from the savages, not to be a *nursemaid* to them! Eddie watched the man, wondering what his thoughts were, the thoughts of a soldier assigned distasteful duties. Eddie could surely commiserate with that. He approached him, hoping they could find a common bond, something that would assure Eddie that the Wampanoag would be treated decently.

"How long have you been in the militia, Corporal?" he asked. "I don't think I caught your name."

"Six months," the soldier replied. "Name's Sparrow. *Isaac Sparrow.*"

"I was in for a year," said Eddie. "I was with Washington when we marched south to Yorktown."

The soldier seemed interested. He nodded and offered Eddie some tobacco from a greasy-looking pouch he pulled from his pocket. He was young, just about the age Eddie had been when he had enlisted years before.

"Are you happy with your military life?" Eddie asked. "I remember how disappointed I was in the beginning."

Sparrow cocked his head. "I suppose I am, a little," he said. "Not much excitement in this job, but I reckon *someone* has to round up these Injuns."

"How long is your assignment?" Eddie inquired. "Will you be staying on through winter here?"

"I hope not!" said the corporal. "Once we get this last bunch settled in, I expect I'll be sent back to Boston. Back to civilization!"

"My brother and I will be returning to Orleans soon," said Eddie. "I feel much better knowing they have you to watch over them."

The corporal laughed. "Oh, we will watch over them," he said. "Once it starts snowing, they won't be wandering too far. If they make it through winter, they'll have a good chance."

And, you destroyed their homes in Orleans to be sure they couldn't go back there, Eddie thought dismally. His disgust with Corporal Sparrow was difficult to hide. Still, he wanted to strike a note of camaraderie with him, some assurance that Uriah and the others would not be harmed. "The Wampanoag are strong," he said. "They have survived many hardships. If they receive fair treatment, I doubt you will have any trouble with them."

Corporal Sparrow patted the butt of his gun. "They will answer to my musket if they do."

It was a disconcerting thought for Eddie.

Chapter Thirty-Seven "His Grandfather's House"

Mercy could not sleep. Susannah's bed was much too soft and yet the rug on the floor did not offer any comfort either. The house was not a place that conjured up slumber; its walls were uniform and straight, structured and without a natural flow. The shutters were shut tight against the night air. She needed nature around her, the softness of sand under her feet and the canopy of open air over her head. After lying there for hours, listening to her cousin's soft breathing, she dressed silently and slipped out of room on tiptoe and headed for the front door. As soon as she had stepped out onto the porch, she wished she had brought her warm mantle made of raccoon fur, for the night air was raw against her bare arms. But, her mantle had been most likely burned to the ground along with the rest of her belongings. She would need new clothes, now that winter was coming.

The sky was clear and pocked with silver stars, just the kind of night she loved. Making her way quietly down the path through the dunes, she could hear the surf in the distance calling to her. She knew her father would scold her for doing it, for venturing out in the darkness to seek the sanctity of the seashore again. He would never understand her need for it. But, her father was far away in Mashpee, performing his duties as sachem. She was not afraid. Like her brother had once felt, Mercy, too, felt restrained and imprisoned. Her home had been destroyed and the prospect of Mashpee was dismal. She yearned for the freedom of the shore, knowing it might be her last chance to feel it! The thought of searching for her brother passed through her mind but she was wise enough to know she'd probably never be able to track him. Samuel left no traces; for years he had been a master of concealment. She could follow the coast all the way to Canada and most likely never find him. The house beyond the dunes was where she found him before. She found herself walking toward the old place and held her breath when the shadow of it came into view.

The fire pit on the shore was cold. No one had been there in a long time. She sat down on one of the rocks that circled the belly of ash and charred wood to star-gaze for a while. It gave her a special comfort; the characters in the great constellations spoke to her. With eyes that were weary from lack of sleep, she searched for her celestial friends who always seemed to bring her peace; *Andromeda*, the chained maiden, twinkled down at her in empathy. *Aquila,* the eagle, offered its wings to flee, and Indus, the *Indian*, reminded her of her heritage. She said a prayer, silently, to the gods, to *any* god who would listen. *Please bring my father home safely. Please let me see my brother again.*

After a while, Mercy stood up and made her way from the fire pit toward the old house. The old steps creaked and stretched beneath her feet as she climbed them. Reaching out, she touched the door knob and turned it and it opened to her, groaning on its hinges like an old sick woman. The darkness inside was like pitch, with only small pockets of light streaming in from the windows and the doorway from the moon that had finally risen. She felt her way toward the first window, wiping away the cob webs from her face and tasting dust on her tongue. Something with claws scurried across the floor. The dim rays from outside reflected on a table on which the rusty old utensils and primitive wooden bowls that belonged to the previous owner lay. *Thatcher's grandfather had once lived here,* she thought, feeling a special closeness to him. *And, now it belonged to her.* A deep intense longing came over her to live here, to make the old house her own! She did not want to go to Mashpee, to be herded and corralled like mindless cattle. She wanted to marry Thatcher and settle here on the eastern shore! It was a fantasy, an impossible dream. They were driving all the Wampanoag away. They would never let her stay in Orleans! She desperately wanted to break the invisible chains of bondage and live free like her brother Samuel! Mercy straddled the divide; she wasn't white, she was only *half-white.* Part of her belonged in the old world of the Wampanoag, while the other part lived the life of her white family. *But, why should that matter anyway?* she wondered. *She was Wampanoag but she was American too!*

Tears welled up in her eyes, there in the darkness, and she moved away from the window, touching the crudely-made furniture, feeling her way along in a blind man's world and it made her think about her *own* grandfather, Old Thomas. Although she had never met him, because he had died on the very day of her birth, she had heard her father speak of him often and she felt as if she *had* known him, and from what she had heard, her father was like him in his loyalty to the tribe, never wavering. She knew Uriah would never abandon his Wampanoag family in Mashpee to return to Orleans, even if he was given the choice. She turned around and started back toward the doorway, stepping carefully around strange obstacles that bumped against her in the dark. Suddenly, the illumination from the doorway that lighted her path was filled with a shadow, *a shadow in the shape of a person.* The floorboards creaked again with strange footsteps that were not her own. Mercy held her breath as the shadow moved toward her and she opened her mouth to scream as an arm in the darkness reached out for her.

Chapter Thirty-Eight *"Preparing for Winter"*

The soldiers, after much prodding by Eddie and Ephraim, finally allowed Uriah and the others to fell some of the trees in the nearby woods, under their watchful eyes, of course. Eddie and Ephraim worked alongside the Wampanoag men in a desperate attempt to get shelters erected before it began to snow. The women and children gathered dried reeds and rocks and any other building materials they could find along the shore of the pond. Other families, who had been in Mashpee awhile and had already raised their *wigwams,* joined them to help. Some came from the north, some from the south and they spoke in slightly different dialects, but there was enough similarity in their words for understanding. It was a slight comfort to know they were not alone.

They had brought as many blankets and rugs as they could carry on their backs but there would not be enough; there had been no time to pack properly. The men had been forced to leave most of their larger tools behind at the camp. Erecting dwellings that were fit to live in, in such a short time, was going to be quite a challenge but the Wampanoag had never run away from challenges.

"Ephraim and I will go back to the camp," Eddie assured Uriah. "We will salvage what we can and bring you whatever else you need from our tool shed. We will pack up as much food as we can load on the wagon"

Uriah nodded. "Perhaps you should leave now, before the bad weather comes," he said. "You need to check on the *children*." He was careful not to mention his daughter's name. "We will be fine for now."

"They are hardly *children* any longer," replied Eddie. "I expect we will both be *grandfathers* one day soon."

The idea resonated with Uriah. *Grandchildren*, he thought, *to be raised in captivity, to be deprived of their God-given freedom*. It was not a happy expectation. He pushed it to the back of his mind. "Go," he said to Eddie. "Bring us whatever you can spare. We will be most grateful."

Eddie and Ephraim headed out shortly after, trying to offer *hope* to their cousins in the *hopeless* circumstance in which they found themselves. First, they needed to retrieve the wagon from the mercantile and hitch up the mules. Then, they would salvage what they could from the burned Wampanoag camp and bring as many supplies as they could load on board back to Mashpee.

"We will have to find a better road," Ephraim told his brother, as they maneuvered their horses around the deep ruts in the road. "Or repair it as we go. The wagon wheels will never make it this way without breaking."

Eddie had to agree. "We will bring shovels and planks," he said hopefully. "We will just have to fill in the holes as we go."

By the time they arrived at the mercantile, it was midnight and the town of Orleans was asleep. Nevertheless, they woke the sleeping mules in their pens and hitched them to the wagon. Loading the wagon bed half full of goods from the mercantile, they paused to rest before going on.

"It's probably best to let the children sleep," Eddie said. "No need to wake them in the middle of the night. Why don't we just head out to the camp? It will be dawn by then and we will see what we can glean from the ashes."

"I don't know about you, Brother," said Ephraim. "But, I am about to fall down from lack of sleep. Perhaps, we should go home and start our journey in the morning."

Eddie pointed to several sacks of flour in the wagon. "There is a comfortable bed right there," he said. "One of us can sleep while the other drives. That way we can cover twice as much territory."

"You would make a great *slave* master," Ephraim said, laughing half-heartedly as he climbed up into the wagon and they headed south in the few hours before the dawn. By the time the sun emerged on the Atlantic horizon, Eddie and Ephraim were already sifting through the rubble of the Wampanoag camp, foraging for anything that had not been destroyed by the fire.

"Damned government," Eddie snarled. "Why destroy everything? We could have used the materials to rebuild in Mashpee!"

Ephraim, who had just awakened from his brief nap in the back of the wagon and was energized again, agreed. "My fear is that they won't get decent shelters built before the snows," he said.

"That's probably part of the plan," replied Eddie. "If the government can't kill them outright, they'll just take their homes instead and freeze them to death!"

They worked for over an hour, collecting a few farming instruments, some cooking pots and pieces of charred pottery. At one point, Eddie reached down and picked up a small dream catcher buried in the grey mire. Its edges were singed and he blew away the ash and put it in the wagon. "Mercy made one of these for me, when Mary died," he said sadly. "It worked for me. Maybe this one will work for Uriah."

They turned the wagon westward and whipped the mules into action. It wasn't *much* they were bringing; it wouldn't be nearly enough to last the winter. *But it was a start.*

Chapter Thirty-Nine *"Watching the Sun Rise"*

"Mercy?" a familiar voice called out, and again, "Mercy? Are you here?"

She moved toward the shadow in the doorway. *"Thatcher Snow!"* she said. "You almost scared me to death! What are you doing here?"

"Pa said I was to watch over you," he said. "You shouldn't be out here all by yourself."

The darkness gave her the courage to reach out and touch his arm, pretending to lean on it for support. *Sweet, thoughtful Thatcher!* The closeness to the man she was secretly in love with was intoxicating. "I'm all right, Thatcher," she said. "Thank you for your concern. But, you needn't have worried about me."

"But, why did you come out here in the dark?"

"I could not sleep," she replied. "I always used to sit on the dock at our camp at night and watch the stars."

"You can't see any stars from inside a dark house," said Thatcher. "Come and I will take you home."

"I wanted to see the house," she said. "It's my family's house now, did you know? Your grandmother left it to us. Did you know that?"

Thatcher did not know. There was a lot he did not know about Mercy, *a lot he wished he knew.* He had been smitten with her for a while now. "So, is this where you plan to live, now that your Father has moved on to Mashpee?" he asked.

She followed him back outside into the moonlight. "The government will probably force me to go to Mashpee with the others," she said. "I think I would *like* to live here though. It's such a quiet, peaceful place, don't you think?"

Thatcher touched her hand that was clinging to his arm. "Yes," he said. "I suppose so."

There was silence for several moments as they emerged from the old house. She slid her hand down his arm and he gripped it in his palm, gently, firmly, confidently. She felt her fingers entwined with his as she stopped and looked upward. The moon was directly above them now and the stars were less visible. The surf was ebbing and flowing at their feet. Mercy was caught up in the beauty of the moment. She had everything she wanted right here, right now: the old house, the ocean and the stars, and, most of all, *Thatcher.*

"Let's stay awhile," she whispered. "Let's sit on the beach and watch the sun rise."

Thatcher, too, was affected by the romantic scene, but his common sense struggled against his emotions. "We should get back to the house," he said quietly, but he knew, at that moment, he would do whatever she wanted him to do; he was at her *mercy.*

"Please?" she asked in a tone so sweet and innocent he thought his legs would buckle underneath him.

"Well, Susannah will be furious with me," he said as she led him to a nearby dune and seated herself, leaning back against the cold gray wall of sand.

"I will deal with Susannah," she said. "She won't stay angry for long. Come, Thatcher, and watch the sunrise with me."

In a tender act of chivalry, Thatcher removed his coat and placed it around Mercy's shoulders. He sat down beside her and she leaned against him for warmth. Gradually, the sky lightened and the stars faded. The moon slipped quietly behind them and, before long, the golden glow of the sun began to rise above the blue horizon, burning off the mist that lingered over the water. Swarms of squawking gulls now flew in circles above their heads in their quest for breakfast, as the sunshine slowly began to warm the beach around them. The warmth was comforting to her chilled face and Mercy closed her eyes for a moment to savor it. She looked over at Thatcher to say something.

But, Thatcher had already drifted off to sleep.

Chapter Forty *"The Killing Tree"*

By the time Eddie and Ephraim arrived back at Mashpee, the weather had grown colder. Amazed by the amount of work the men had accomplished in their absence, Eddie was encouraged. After unloading the wagon, they returned to the woods to help with the heavy lumbering.

"Is everything all right at home?" Uriah asked anxiously.

"Everything is fine," Eddie replied, failing to mention that they had not actually *gone* to the house on Skaket Road. "Let us worry about getting your shelters up for now!"

The daylight hours were short, so they worked without stopping. With only a few decent saws and axes, they attacked the fallen trees with a vengeance, removing the outer bark for roofing material and branches for other uses and hewing the green wood into beams and supports of somewhat uniform lengths. The methods of working with tall timber were more familiar to Eddie and Ephraim than to the Wampanoag, who had little knowledge of American construction, but they learned quickly. After all, it wasn't the *style* of the dwelling that mattered; wetu, wigwam or stick built house, whatever would serve to keep the snow off their heads, was all that really mattered for now.

In the evening, the women were finally able to prepare a proper meal for the weary men; they gathered together in the big tent to eat and make plans for the following day's work. Sleeping on the dirt floor beneath the tent seemed a natural thing to Uriah and the other Wampanoag men. For Eddie and Ephraim, however, it translated into rising in the morning with stiff backs and aching heads. With brave smiles on their faces, they were willing to do their share of the work, and, clearly, seeing the strength and toughness of their Indian cousins only added to the respect they already felt.

"I don't think even Mercy's dream catchers can cure what ails me," Eddie whispered to Ephraim, as they finished their breakfast and headed out once again to the woods.

Ephraim agreed and Uriah made light of the whole thing. "It's *good* for you to sleep on the ground," he told them. "I could never sleep on those feather-stuffed things you call mattresses!"

"You only say that because you have never *tried* sleeping in a *real* bed, Uriah," said Eddie, rubbing his backside. "Believe me, you would change your opinion!"

Laughing, they went about their work. By now, Corporal Sparrow had developed enough trust in Eddie and Ephraim, that he did not follow them, but, rather, preferred to remain in his warm bed for a while longer. The sun had not shown itself, hiding behind thick, gray clouds. The air was crisp and still; it looked like snow was looming. There was no movement on the surface of the pond, not even a ripple from the ducks that made their homes in the tall reeds. With the framework for only two small houses completed, and many more that remained to be built, half the men stayed behind in the camp to finish the roofing while Eddie and Ephraim accompanied Uriah and a half dozen others into the woods.

When they spied a sixty-foot pitch pine, the men quickly chose it, for the one tree alone would supply more wood than several of the smaller ones. It stood on the edge of the wooded area, its three-foot girth leaning slightly toward the west from the patterns of the wind that blew up the valley. Pine was soft wood, easier to work with, and preferred by the Indians for the pitch to start their fires and the sticky resin they used for sweetening their food. Its only flaw was that pine was frequently pocked with knots and swirls within the trunk that did not conform to the natural grain of the wood, making it difficult to cut uniform pieces for construction.

Ephraim and Eddie took a two-man saw and began to saw away at the trunk.

Uriah and Grey Eyes watched from a safe distance as Eddie cut a notch in the thick trunk on the east side of the tree that faced the open space and the shore of the pond. With that accomplished he made a second cut, below the first, making a wedge, which he pulled from the body of the tree.

"Stand clear, everyone!" yelled Eddie as he began to undercut the massive trunk from the opposite side with a smaller saw. Ephraim joined Uriah in the shade of the woods behind the tree and watched as Eddie worked. The other Indians hid behind them, afraid that the huge tree would come down upon them.

The tree made a strange, crackling sound, tilting slightly forward toward the pond, precisely where Eddie wanted it to go. It hovered there, motionless, as if pondering which way it wanted to fall. Eddie gave the tree an encouraging push with his foot. The tree tilted again toward the east and Eddie backed away, waiting for it to fall. But, then, something went terribly wrong. The tree shifted and began to fall away from the clearing, directly toward where Eddie and the other men were standing. The crackling of the wood was so loud they couldn't hear him as he called out a warning. "Move!" he shouted, as he dove out of the path of the falling tree. "It's going to fall the wrong way!"

Uriah looked upward just in time to see tons of wood and a forest of pine branches coming down on him. Eddie yelled again. With a horrific thud, the tree hit the ground, taking several smaller trees with it.

"My God," whispered Eddie, running toward the spot where Uriah had been standing. All he could see were Uriah's moccasins protruding from under the massive trunk. He climbed over the top of the tree and saw his head on the other side of the tree, with blood trickling from the corner of his mouth. Grey Eyes came running up behind him but he could see there was nothing anyone could do. Uriah was dead.

"Where is my brother?" asked Eddie.

He climbed over several thick branches until he saw the face of his brother, looking up at him from beneath a canopy of green needles and pine cones. "Ephraim," he said, taking his brother's hand that was near his head. "Don't move! We will get you out!"

Eddie ran to grab his saw to cut away the part of the tree that covered Ephraim's body. Grey Eyes took another saw and started to cut from the other side.

"Hold on, Ephraim!" he said as he started sawing frantically. *"You just hold on!"*

With tears blinding him, he sawed away, pitching pieces of the wood over his shoulder. Ephraim did not move. He had closed his eyes.

"Ephraim!" yelled Eddie. "Stay with me! Hang on!"

Grey Eyes was the first to let his saw rest on the bark of the tree. He had done all that he could do. He reached out and took Eddie by the arm. "Your brother is gone, Eddie," he said. "We cannot save him."

Eddie looked down at Ephraim's face that had turned a peculiar shade of blue. He dropped his saw and ran off into the woods screaming.

Grey Eyes did not follow him.

"Let him have his grief," he told the Wampanoag men who were watching in horror.

Chapter Forty-One *"The Sacrifice Rock"*

Winter had finally come to the cape; one again, the houses were cloaked in white, their eaves scalloped in sparkling icicles, their fireplaces billowing clouds of smoke against the frigid blue sky. The people of Orleans hid themselves beneath heavy layers of clothing while the farm animals huddled together in the pastures for warmth. In bountiful years, when the harvests had been good, it was a time for families to gather together in thanks, to congregate in their parishes to worship, to replenish themselves for the spring planting ahead. Babies were conceived, by both man and beast, during the long, cold nights and life renewed itself year after year.

This winter in the Snow house was not a joyous one, however. Grief permeated the rooms like an evil spirit; silence loomed within its walls. The family went through their normal daily routines mindlessly; by rote they did what needed to be done. Susannah and Mercy prepared and put food on the table. Thatcher and his brothers kept the fires burning and the livestock fed. But, *death* had once again come to the house on Skaket Road and the place would never again be the same.

Eddie's mind had once again drifted back into the oblivion; he wandered around aimlessly, like a lost soul.

He rarely ate anything or slept in his bed and his nights were haunted with dreams no *dream catcher* could cure. After witnessing the funeral pyre for Uriah in Mashpee, he had brought Ephraim's body home to be buried with his family. After that, he would often disappear for hours, only to be found sitting in the cemetery, weeping over the graves of his loved ones. He had finally lost the will to remain among the living.

Mercy had taken on a transformation of her own. With news of her father's death, and the ever-present threat of being forced to move to Mashpee, it now seemed the safest thing to do was to accept Susannah's offer to make her some suitable dresses, so as not to call attention to herself when she had to venture outside. And, she had a new project that required her to be outside; with the help of Thatcher, she was spending most of her time refurbishing the old house beyond the dunes. She continued to sketch; now her collection included seascapes and birds in addition to the stars and constellations. Her art was becoming her solace in the solitary world in which she found herself. The house beyond the dunes became her studio. Soon, she had removed herself from the Snow house altogether, reclusing herself from everyone except Susannah and Thatcher.

Susannah, Joel and Jesse found themselves in the middle of all the raw emotions that were surrounding them. Although they grieved as well, their grief was tempered with the reality that death was a part of life, and *life went on*.

That new life was soon infused into the old house beyond the dunes and it came alive again. Mercy refused to live in grief; her father would not have wanted that. In the spring, she planned to whitewash the dingy clapboards that were cracking and peeling from the ocean winds but, for now, she busied herself with making the inside warm and cozy against the cold outside. With hand-me-downs that Susannah pulled from the Snows' dusty old attic trunks and throwaways from anywhere she could find them, she stitched and pieced together new curtains and rugs. She polished the windows to a sheen and oiled the wood floors. She would send Thatcher on excursions into town to glean anything of use from the garbage behind the town businesses to further add to the strange collection of furnishings she had acquired.

"I think it is wonderful," Susannah told her one afternoon, surveying the improvements Mercy had made in the old house. "It's *different*, but it is unique. It is *you*, Mercy."

Stepping down from a ladder, with a paintbrush in her stained hands, Mercy had stopped to rest awhile. "I haven't much to offer you, Susannah, but I have some tea," she said, putting on a kettle to boil in the hearth. "How is your father doing? Thatcher tells me he still does not sleep at night."

Susannah shook her head. "I don't think he even remembers *why* he is so unhappy," she said sadly. "He was like this after Mother died, but not nearly so pronounced." Her face grew serious. *"Mercy, I do believe he has lost his mind."*

Mercy was shocked and immediately concerned. "He has seen too much death," she replied, pouring hot tea into two cups, while the two women sat down together. "There are some old Wampanoag spells that I can cast upon him."

Susannah's eyes narrowed and her brows pinched together in disbelief. "Surely, you don't think that *spells* can cure a broken heart," she said. "You are much too intelligent to believe such nonsense."

Mercy sipped on her tea thoughtfully. "Call it nonsense, if you will," she said. "But, there are many things we can't *logically* explain, *spiritual* things that are beyond human understanding."

"It is more than just grief with my father," said Susannah. "It is as if his mind is in another place. Sometimes, he stares at me as if he doesn't know who I am."

At that moment, Thatcher came through the door, his arms full of firewood. He greeted his sister with a kiss on the cheek and proceeded to stack the wood near the hearth.

"There is work to be done at home too, Thatcher," said Susannah. "Jesse and Joel have been complaining that you have not been shouldering your share of it."

"Tell them I am only helping Mercy to get this old place livable again," he said.

"They understand that, Brother," said Susannah. "But, our father is no longer of any use in that regard. Everything has been left to them."

"I will be home soon," he promised as Susannah stood up and prepared to leave.

"I will tell them," she said with a slight smile to her lips. "It seems as if this house has become *your* home too."

Susannah did not wait for an answer; going out into the snow and folding her mittened hands tightly under her arms, she left Mercy and Thatcher alone, with a knowing smile on her face. She knew there was strong affection between her cousin and her brother and it pleased her immensely. *Perhaps grandchildren could lift her father out of his abyss of sadness,* she thought. *Something* had to make him want to live again!

As soon as the door closed against the cold wind coming off the ocean, Thatcher immediately took Mercy into his arms. She let him kiss her and she kissed him back, but her mind was on his father. "Why didn't you tell me your father was so ill?" she asked, pulling herself away and clearing away the empty cups from the table.

"Pa has gone senile," said Thatcher. "You can't talk sense to him."

He followed her into the kitchen and stood behind her; she could feel his breath hot on the back of her neck.

"Thatcher, you need to go help your brothers," she said, pushing him away. "I don't want your family thinking you care more for me."

"But, I *do* care more for you," he replied, with a grin. "I love you!"

Mercy laughed. "And, I love you as well. But, I have work to do and so do you! Now, off with you so I can get these walls painted."

She followed him to the door and he kissed her again in the doorway. She watched him as he disappeared among the snowy dunes and went back inside the house, only to emerge moments later in a cloak Susannah had given her and a small bundle in her hands. Walking briskly, she went in the opposite direction, up the beach toward the little dock near what was left of the burned Wampanoag camp. There was something she knew she had to do; something she had been putting off. *Now was the time.*

The shoreline was frozen; the sand was covered in a thick blanket of snow all the way to the water's edge, where it turned to shimmering sheets of ice. The coast of Orleans was stark and barren; its steep banks and flat beaches stretched out for as far as her eyes could see. The imprint of her footsteps formed a solitary trail through the snow, the only sign of life anywhere. When she had finally reached the place where the dock had been, she realized the soldiers had torn it down too; nothing was left but an empty beach. She walked a little further and then took a path that led inland toward the camp and, there, in the shade of some trees, she found what might have escaped the notice of another; it was a wide flat piece of granite, now covered in snow and split down the middle from a lightning bolt ages before.

All her life she had been taught about the *sacrifice rock*; she knew its legend better than she knew the lessons she had been taught at school. The gods honored anything offered on a sacrifice rock, *anything except human beings*, which was a hard lesson her Wampanoag ancestors had learned long before she was born. The gods did not approve of murder, but anything else offered from nature was considered a gift to the gods; in their eyes, even sticks of driftwood and pebbles from the shore were as valuable as gold or silver. It was the *spirit* in which the gift was given that was important.

She took the small bundle she was carrying and opened it, placing the torn pieces of her old doeskin dress along with the leather ties with which she had once braided her hair on the rock among the many other "offerings" laid there.

"Mister Snow needs comfort," she whispered. "He needs to rest. He needs peace in his life. He has always helped our people. He needs help now for *himself.*"

For several moments, she knelt there, feeling her knees grow numb from the snow, before she rose and started back toward the house. She had given up something precious to the gods, something she would never have again. *She had given up her heritage.*

Chapter Forty-Two *"The Gift of Morning"*

As soon as Thatcher lost sight of the house, and started up the slippery path toward town, the sun suddenly came out from behind the clouds and he shielded his eyes from the glare of it. He could see the smoke spiraling from the chimney in the house on Skaket Road. It was a time of change in his life, a time when he needed a father he could talk to, *man to man*. But, his father was only a shell of a man now, unable to comprehend problems or offer advice, which Thatcher desperately needed.

When he entered the house, the family was already seated at the table and he realized he was late for supper. "I'm sorry, Susannah," he said apologetically. "I know I am late."

He could see that his sister had set a place for him and he quickly took his seat between his brothers.

"There were some soldiers here today," Susannah said in a serious tone. "They were looking for Samuel."

Eddie sat at the end of the table, staring at his plate, and said nothing.

"Why do they think *we* would know his whereabouts?" Thatcher asked. "Even Mercy has only seen him *once* in all these years."

"They seem to think, since we are related to his family, we might know something," Susannah replied. "They suspect him of stealing chickens up north. They think of him as a renegade and a danger to the town."

"What else did they say?" asked Thatcher carefully.

"They didn't mention Mercy, if that's what you mean," replied Susannah. "But, I think it is not a good time for her to be alone in that house on the beach. I think she needs to come back and live with us where it is safe."

"Yes, Brother," said Joel sarcastically. "Then you can spend more time helping with the work around here."

Thatcher knew it was time to tell them. "I'm sorry if I have not carried my share of the load lately," he said to his brothers. "There has been a lot of work to get that old house livable again."

"But, that's my point," said Susannah. "She is not safe out there all by herself! You must convince her to think about her own safety, Thatcher!"

Thatcher cleared his throat. He looked across the table at his father for reassurance that he was listening. There was none. He cleared his throat again nervously.

"Have you something to say, Thatcher?" Susannah asked.

"Yes, I do," Thatcher replied. He turned toward Eddie with a sheepish smile. "I am going to marry Mercy!" he blurted out.

Eddie had no reaction, but kept staring at his food. Joel and Jesse laughed, slapping their brother on the back in congratulation. Susannah smiled a knowing smile.

"And, you will be moving into Grandfather's house?" she asked. "Is that what you are telling us?"

"Yes," said Thatcher. "So, you see, Sister, you needn't worry about Mercy. I will be there to protect her! She will be my wife! With our marriage made legal and her claim to the property, they can't force her to go to Mashpee!"

Susannah wasn't so sure. "The government can't be trusted. They have a way of deciding what they *can* and *can't* do," she warned. "Just be careful. Don't provoke them unnecessarily."

Thatcher shook his head and finished his supper. "We won't bother anyone, I promise you," he said with confidence. "No one will even know we are there!"

Mercy and Thatcher were married the very next day in a quiet ceremony in front of a city clerk who just happened to be half Wampanoag himself, after which they returned to the house on Skaket Road for supper and quiet celebration. But, this time, it was the *bride* who brought a gift; she had something special for her new father-in-law.

Mercy's emotions had been see-sawing since she had visited the sacrifice rock. Although she had given away her Wampanoag clothing in sincerity, she was questioning whether the gods would see it as a purely *selfless* gesture. *Just what was she giving up?* she wondered. The doubts had come to her the night before, as she spent the night alone in the old house beyond the dunes. *Would the true sacrifice for her be going to Mashpee with the others? Was she only doing what she wanted to do to secure her own freedom?* Somehow, she felt she had to do more, just to let the gods know her prayers were real and heartfelt.

Eddie did not join in the wedding party, nor did he sit down to supper with the others that night.

"He has been bedridden for days now," explained Susannah. "I can barely get him to eat anymore."

Mercy had a small parchment, rolled up in twine, a special gift for Eddie. "May I go in and see him?" she asked Susannah. "I have something for him."

She opened the door to Eddie's bedroom, carrying a candle to burn away the darkness. Eddie was lying on the bed, rigid and fully clothed, his eyes wide open.

"Mister Snow?" Mercy said quietly. "It's me, *Mercy.*"

She walked softly to the edge of the bed, placed the candle on the small table there and sat down beside him. Above the bed she could see the dream catcher she had made for him so many years before, when his wife had died. "Are you still having the nightmares?" she asked, not expecting him to answer. She knew he had barely uttered two words in weeks.

She unrolled the parchment and pulled several sewing pins from her pocket and, with the tips of her fingers, repaired the parts that had been smudged. She looked around the room for the perfect spot to hang it, and decided on the wall at the foot of his bed where he could see it every day as he opened his eyes. Crossing the room, she positioned it on the wall and returned to Eddie's bedside. Eddie stared at the picture blankly, without emotion.

The picture was of the sunrise on the cape. She had drawn it when she had first started visiting her new home. With chalk made from the coastal mud and crushed flowers and seeds, the same ingredients her father had used in his face paint, she had captured the essence of the brilliance in the morning sun as it rose above the ocean. It was a beautiful piece, one she was very proud of and had originally planned to hang on the wall of her own bedroom, but, when she heard of Eddie's lapse into inconsolable grief, she knew he needed it more than she. She could see the sunrise every morning from her front porch. In this room, from his bed, Eddie could see nothing but four square walls. "What do you think, Mister Snow?" she asked him. "Do you like it?"

Eddie stirred slightly. His eyes blinked and he slowly turned toward Mercy sitting beside him. Silently, he reached out and took her hand in his.

"Now, you shall have the sunrise every morning," she said happily.

"Thank you," he murmured and drifted off to sleep.

Little did she know that it would be the last words Eddie Snow would ever utter.

Chapter Forty-Three *"A Wild Wedding Night"*

The new bride and groom returned to their home on the beach later that night, merry from wine and celebration. Thatcher had thrown together a satchel of clothes, his hunting rifle, and fishing pole. They were as natural together as brother and sister, for, indeed, they had grown up together, and their new home was a part of *both* of them. They entered the darkened house and Mercy lit a lamp on the kitchen table while Thatcher re-kindled the fire in the hearth. His heart was overwhelmed with love for his new wife; her gesture toward his father was one of the reasons he loved her so much. *What a sweet, wonderful woman he had married!*

She had put his clothes away in a drawer of the old dresser that had been his grandfather's, and her hands lingered on the fabric of his shirts as she folded them. *This was to be her life*, she thought happily. She turned to see Thatcher standing in the doorway and she crossed the room and enveloped herself in his arms.

"I love you Mercy *Snow*," he said proudly.

"And, I you," she replied as he kissed her.

They stood there for a few moments, lost in their embrace, when suddenly the door to the house burst open and a man was in the room with them. He was dressed in Wampanoag clothing, with feathers in his hair and paint on his face. Thatcher stepped in front of Mercy to protect her from the intruder and prepared himself to fight. "What do you want here?" he demanded. The man was nearly his height, but he was much older; Thatcher wasn't concerned about confronting him. "How *dare* you break into our home!"

The Indian moved closer, menacingly, but Thatcher stood his ground. Mercy tried to come between them but he held her back with his arm and prevented her from doing so.

"Take your hands off my sister!" the Indian yelled and lurched forward, taking Thatcher by the shoulders and throwing him to the floor. Mercy let out a scream and tried to separate them as they wrestled with each other. Wildly, they punched and kicked at each other; they were well-matched, but when Mercy saw the glow of a knife blade in the lamplight she gasped and screamed. *"Samuel! He is my husband! Stop this nonsense!"*

She grabbed onto his arm and fell on the floor between them. The Indian let go of Thatcher and sheathed his knife. He stood up and stared down at his little sister, while Thatcher helped her stand up.

"You are Samuel?" Thatcher asked, tasting blood in his mouth from a punch.

Samuel was reeling as well, nursing a bruised eye that was beginning to swell. "You must be Thatcher Snow," he said, his voice cold and still threatening.

Mercy stood firmly between them. "Samuel, you have no right to come into my home and attack my husband," she said.

"*Your* home?" asked Samuel. "How did *that* come about?" He stared with disgust at Mercy's American attire. "And, look at you! Are you a *white* woman now? Have you completely abandoned your Wampanoag ways?"

"If you would sit down and *listen*, perhaps we could discuss it like adults," said Mercy.

She stood her ground until Samuel had retreated to one side of the table and Thatcher to the other, before she sat down herself. "Our father is dead, Samuel. I inherited this house from Thatcher's grandmother," she explained. "And, Thatcher and I were just married today. Is this your way of congratulating us?"

Thatcher rubbed his chin. "A handshake would have been fine with me," he said, trying to make light of the painful situation.

"Samuel," Mercy said. "I think you owe my husband an apology."

Samuel's face was still dark with rage. He was not accustomed to making apologies. He did not think he had done anything wrong. A white man was touching his sister. He was only defending her. Mercy's words, *our father is dead,* were just beginning to sink into his brain.

"Samuel!" said Mercy again. *"Apologize or leave this house!"*

She crossed the room and opened the door, letting a gust of icy wind blow in. Samuel's ego was bruised. His pride was wounded. He started for the door to escape the eyes on him. Pausing only briefly in the doorway, he looked at Mercy as if he wanted to say something, but the words were left unsaid.

And, Samuel disappeared again into the night.

Chapter Forty-Four *"Mercy's Epiphany"*

The announcement came the next day that Eddie Snow had died; Joel had come knocking in the early morn on the door of the house beyond the dunes with the sad news. He took one look at Thatcher's face when his brother opened the door and his eyes widened. "What happened to you, Brother?" he asked, noticing Thatcher's split lip and swollen jaw.

"Nothing," Thatcher murmured. He would have made a joke, but he was not in a jovial mood.

Mercy appeared behind Thatcher, curious why her brother-in-law was paying such an early visit.

"Pa is dead," said Joel. "He died in his sleep last night."

"No!" Mercy screamed. "I don't believe it!"

Thatcher sat down in a chair by the door in a state of shock.

"Jesse and I will take care of his grave," said Joel. "Mercy, it would be good of you to come comfort our sister. She is quite distraught."

"Of course," Mercy replied. "We will come straightaway."

When the door closed, and Joel had left, Mercy fell into Thatcher's arms. "I am so sorry, my love," she said.

She thought about the day before and marveled at how so many vastly different events could transpire in one short twenty-four-hour piece of time. It had taken its toll on Mercy and she knew it had also affected Thatcher. First, their wedding, followed by her last poignant visit with her father-in-law; then, Samuel's sudden attack on her new husband and the hours of tender lovemaking in their darkened room. And, now, *this.* Her mind could not comprehend so much all at once. Mister Snow was gone. Had she *cursed* him instead of *blessing* him as she had wanted to do? Were the gods punishing her for her selfish sacrifice by punishing *him?* Tears welled up inside of her, but they were angry tears, tears full of rage. *No,* she told herself. *Mister Snow was with the gods now*; his suffering had been taken away. It was a *good* thing, although her husband was mourning and she needed to comfort him. Her head was spinning; nothing made any sense. She forced herself to remain calm as they dressed and left the house for town.

Susannah was happy to see them when they reached the house, although her tear-stained cheeks revealed the telltale sign of many hours of anguish. While the men went out to prepare a new grave in the cemetery, she and Mercy prepared Eddie's body for burial. They bathed him and dressed him in his best suit of clothes. Mercy combed his hair and looked affectionately into the face of the man who had become so important to her.

"I don't think I grieved so much at the death of my own father," she whispered.

Susannah touched her hand. "That was only because your father was far away," she said. "You had just spoken to Pa last night." She paused and noticed for the first time the drawing on the wall. "Did you make this for him?"

Mercy nodded.

"That was very sweet of you, Mercy," said Susannah.

"I thought it would bring him some happiness," she said. "The sunrise is a blessing in Wampanoag culture. The closer we are to the sun, the happier we are."

"And, now you will see the sunrise every morning from your front porch," replied Susannah. "You truly are *the people of the dawn*."

She smiled and reached out to hug her new sister-in-law. Together, the family walked through the events of the day in a shared state of shock and sadness. After Eddie's burial, they shared supper together and Thatcher and Mercy retreated to their house, exhausted and spent. Lying close together in their shadowy room, listening to the surf outside their window, Mercy's eyes would not close. When she heard Thatcher begin to snore softly, she rose from their bed and wrapped herself in Susannah's cloak. She made her way to the fire pit outside the house and sat down. There were no stars; the sky was overcast and it hovered oppressively over her. Her spirit was heavy; her heart ached with sadness as she stared blindly out over the waves. She wanted to feel happy and free but her emotions were tied together like a wet knot of twine. *Did life need to be so hard? So confusing?*

She heard movement, footsteps in the snow, behind her, in a lull between the waves, and turned, expecting to see that her new husband had come to search for her. To her surprise, it was Samuel who stepped out of the shadows. She frowned at him. "Have you come to apologize to my husband?" she asked, not mincing her words. With all the events of the past twenty-four hours she hadn't the strength to argue with her brother.

"I came to apologize to *you*, Sister," said Samuel. "Your husband is a strong man. I didn't hurt him that much."

"That's hardly an apology," Mercy replied as Samuel sat down on a rock beside her. "I *love* Thatcher. When you attack *him* you attack *me*."

Samuel sat in stubborn silence for a few moments. He had no desire to hurt his sister, but he had lived too long nurturing a hatred for the white man that it was impossible for him to concede that a white man was now his kin. He remembered the Snow family. He remembered old man Freeman, whose house his sister had inherited. He admitted to himself that they had been good to him, good to his father. "I have always had hatred for the white men who hurt our mother," he said finally. "You don't know how strong hatred can be."

Mercy's heart softened. "I know what happened to our mother," she replied. "Those men were evil and they were punished, Samuel. But, you can't go on hating *all* white people because of the bad deeds of just a few! You can't make that your *purpose* in life! You certainly can't blame *Thatcher* for what happened to our mother!"

Samuel knew she was right. He just couldn't find the words to express himself.

Mercy fell silent herself. In her heart, she felt the gods speaking to her. *His purpose in life. Every man has a purpose,* they whispered in her ear. *"And, every woman!"* she said aloud.

"What?" asked Samuel, confused at her sudden utterance. "What are you talking about, Mercy?"

Mercy! she thought. *The gods gave me that name for a reason!* Suddenly, she knew what they were trying to tell her! It became ever so clear in her mind. She *had* sacrificed in good faith to the gods; she knew it in her *heart*. But, she had more to do. And, she didn't need to sacrifice her heritage at all! "Samuel," she said quietly. "I will help you."

By now, Samuel was thoroughly confused. *Had his sister gone mad?* "Help me with what?" he asked.

"Our house will be open to you and the others escaping the re-location. It is the perfect spot; no one ever comes out here. They can rest here on their journey."

Samuel was wary. "And, what will your husband think of this plan?" he asked. "Don't you think you should ask him first, before you make such a commitment?"

Mercy shook her head. "Come, Brother," she said. "You can sleep by our fire tonight. We will discuss our plans in the morning."

Chapter Forty-Five *"A Foot in Both Worlds"*

Spring came early that year. The snow melted, the air grew warmer and Mercy was soon aware that she was with child. It was the beauty of spring, when everything in nature renewed itself. Thatcher had awakened that cold morning after his father's funeral to find his brother-in-law sleeping on his hearth, and he had merely laughed out loud at the sight. When Samuel had clumsily tried to apologize to him for bloodying his lip, he shook his head.

"My own brothers have punched me twice as hard," he said. "Is that not so, Mercy?"

Mercy smiled and agreed with him. She had seen Thatcher and his brothers in many a scuffle in the house on Skaket Road, and, then, an hour later, be the closest of friends again. It was peculiar to her, as a woman, to understand men's strange behaviors. But, she was pleased that there would no longer be animosity between the two men she loved the most.

Her plan was a risky one, which they plotted out over the next several weeks. Thatcher was concerned about her safety, and rightly so; the militia had the power to arrest anyone caught assisting escaped Indians who ventured off their restricted homelands. He did not want to go to prison! He wanted more details before he would agree to anything.

"It occurred to me that night," she told him. "I am of no use to my people as long as I am *one* of them. That would be sort of like helping someone out of a six-foot hole when you're standing in the hole yourself! But, if people see me as a *white* woman, married to a *white* man, they will have more respect for me. They can't tell me what to do or where to go. I can use that as leverage. They can't just barge in and take me away!"

Thatcher still wasn't convinced. He wanted to know *precisely* what she was planning to do.

"First," she said. "I want to visit Mashpee. I want to see for myself how my people are being treated. Then, we can decide how best we can help."

"Do you think that is wise?" Thatcher counseled. "In your *condition*, I mean." She had only the night before informed him that he was soon to be a father.

"It will be much easier to make the trip now than *after* the baby comes," she said matter-of-factly. "Besides, I want to visit my father's grave. I want to see Grey Eyes again."

Thatcher knew there was no arguing with his wife when she set her mind on something.

It became her passion. As a new life blossomed in her womb and her dainty body had yet to grow clumsy and awkward, she first accompanied Thatcher in a journey to the Mashpee colony a few days later. No longer were there soldiers standing vigil outside the camp as Samuel had warned them there would be. Now, the Wampanoag seemed to have given up the desire to escape and the need for guards was no longer an issue. It wasn't *contentment* that had changed her people; it was *surrender.* The once exotic, brave men and women who roamed Cape Cod and beyond as free spirits, were now fated to living in captivity, prisoners behind *invisible* but very *real* prison walls.

Grey Eyes, whose hair had also turned grey in the years since she had seen him last, came forward and hardly recognized her. Dressed in her calico, with high-buttoned boots and a bright bonnet covering her loose brown hair, Mercy surprised all those who knew her with her new *American* appearance.

"Before you think of me as a *traitor*," she told Grey Eyes, "Hear what I have to say first. Believe that I love my people as much as I ever did. But, I have decided I can do them more good as a white woman than I ever could as a Wampanoag."

"I would never think of you as a traitor," he said. "I knew you too well. You are your father's daughter. Wampanoag blood runs through your veins as much as mine."

With Thatcher and Grey Eyes, she visited all the wigwam-homes of the tribe. While there were a few of the older women who looked at her clothes with disapproving frowns, Mercy's warmth and sincerity soon won over their hearts. She made scribbled lists of what the tribe needed: seed corn, wool for weaving, lamp oil to light their homes, anything they lacked, she promised, they would have.

"Now, I want to visit my father's grave," she said finally.

They walked up the road toward an old meetinghouse at what seemed to be the nucleus of the town of Mashpee. It sat on a slightly elevated plateau, looking down on a little cemetery and surrounded by a grove of pines and oaks. At the first sight of the cemetery, Mercy paused. "Where is he buried?" she asked Grey Eyes.

"Over there," replied Grey Eyes. "We wanted for you to come to his funeral pyre, but Eddie thought it might be dangerous. The soldiers were still around back then."

He led Mercy and Thatcher across the grass to a simple stone that was covered with sticks and pebbles. Apparently, others had already been there to pay their respects. She reached down and picked a tiny yellow dandelion that had sprung up in the grass and placed it on her father's headstone.

"I understand why Mister Snow kept me away," said Mercy. "He was only trying to protect me."

Thatcher and Grey Eyes watched as Mercy knelt down and ran her hand over the stone, as if caressing it.

"Kwe noeshow," she said softly and began a conversation with her father's spirit which only Grey Eyes could understand. When she started to weep and appeared on the verge of collapse, Thatcher rushed forward and helped her to her feet.

At that moment, an old white-haired man came walking toward them on the path. He was tall and thin and slightly hunched over; his spectacles were crooked with one glass covered by a ragged patch. Obviously blind, he walked with a crooked walking stick to guide his steps and it reminded Mercy of Old Thomas' walking stick that had stood in the corner of her family's wetu for years after his death. The man was smiling. "Welcome my dear," he said, reaching for her hand in the void between them.

Mercy took his hand in hers and answered. "You must be Reverend Amos whom I have heard so much about. I understand you spoke at my father's funeral."

"Yes," said the old man. "A better man I can't remember. We were sorry that you could not be here, but we understand."

"That is going to change, Reverend," said Mercy. "You will be seeing more of me. I am determined to help you all I can to minister to my people."

Thatcher looked over his shoulder to be sure no one was nearby. "Mercy," he whispered. "Please be careful what you say here."

Amos nodded his head. "Your companion is correct," he said in Mercy's direction. "I think what you are doing is very admirable but you must not endanger yourself. You must be cautious in your conversations. Keep your freedom if you can. I understand Uriah's grandchild is due at any time."

"Let me introduce you to my *companion*," she said. "This is my *husband,* Thatcher Snow." She paused for a moment. "But, how did you know that I was going to have a child?" She was surprised that such news had reached Mashpee.

"Your brother visits us quite frequently," he said. "He comes and goes in the night so as not to arouse suspicion. He keeps us informed of your well-being."

They sat on the grass and talked at great lengths about the plight of the Wampanoag people, of the misery of the first winter her tribe spent in the bitter cold before adequate houses could be erected.

"They were piled in, three to a cot," said Amos. "The women put the little ones between them for warmth. But, we lost a few to the cold nevertheless."

Mercy quickly wrote *blankets* on her list.

"Mercy," Thatcher interrupted. "We must start on the road for Orleans. That road can be treacherous in the dark."

"Yes," answered Mercy. She took the old man's hand in hers once again. "We will help you," she said. "I am grateful you are here to look over my people."

The wagon set out on the rutted road back to Orleans just as the sun was beginning to set.

"I hope we don't break a wheel," said Thatcher. "This is no place to be stranded in your condition."

"I liked the reverend," Mercy replied, happily oblivious to the danger. "Didn't you?"

"Yes," Thatcher answered. "I suppose so. But, Mercy, you must be careful not to promise more than we can deliver! Just how are we going to *pay* for everything you promised? Where will we find the money?"

"With Susannah's help," Mercy answered. "I've already spoken to your brothers, too."

She knew that the mercantile now belonged to Thatcher and his siblings and that, somehow, they would get the needed supplies. The next day, Susannah came to visit and was happy to take part in Mercy's *mission.*

"Your name truly fits you," she told Mercy. "It is as if your parents knew your destiny. But, you must be careful using your house to hide those who are escaping. Especially now, that you will have children to protect. Promise me, you won't act recklessly."

Mercy assured her. "I promise I will be as wily as a *fox*," she said.

Chapter Forty-Six *"His Tell-Tale Red Hair"*

Their plan was beginning to work well. The Snow siblings had agreed to raise their prices at the store by a few pennies, prices that were still much less than the mercantile in Wellfleet. With the little profit they made, they were able to send supplies every week to Mashpee to help the Wampanoag get back on their feet, and the residents of Orleans were happy to help once they knew it was for a good cause. Joel and Jesse made the deliveries so that Thatcher could remain close to Mercy who was expecting the birth of their child any day. And Samuel arrived every week or so, with a new gaggle of escapees; some were Seminoles from as far away as Florida, Cherokees from Georgia running from the dreaded Trail of Tears and Choctaws from Alabama, all making their way northward along the eastern shore. On those nights the little house was lively with conversation and Mercy would flutter about like a plump little hen, feeding them and nursing blistered feet and tucking them into bed around the fire. And, by morning, they would be gone, north to Provincetown, where they would slip undetected into canoes and paddle under the cloak of darkness across to Cape Anne and, finally, Canada and *freedom*.

On one such evening, only a day after Samuel and the others had departed, there was a loud knock on the door.

When Thatcher opened it he was met with the cold stares of several uniformed soldiers.

"Is this the home of Thatcher Snow?" asked the one in charge.

"Yes," Thatcher answered. "How can I help you?"

The soldier brushed past Thatcher and pushed his way into the house, glancing over at Mercy who was sketching near the fire, balancing a tablet across her swollen belly.

"Anyone here except you and the Missus?" he asked, while the others were poking their noses through the bedroom door and rummaging through the kitchen.

"No, Sir," said Thatcher. "Who *exactly* are you looking for?"

"The Injun' they call the *wild one*," said the soldier. "Hear he's been seen comin' this way with some other renegades. You haven't run across them, have you?"

Thatcher shook his head, trying to act casual. "No, we haven't seen anyone," he replied.

The soldier looked around the room and made a second sweep of the bedroom. He tipped his hat to Mercy. "Well," he said. "Better lock your doors and keep an eye out if you want to keep your scalps. These Injuns will steal anything that ain't nailed down, that's fer sure!"

"Thank you for the warning," Thatcher said, escorting them to the door. "We'll sure be on the lookout."

As soon as the door closed, Mercy put down her tablet and began to pace across the floor in a worried state. "Do you think Samuel and the others have made it as far as Provincetown yet?" she asked.

Thatcher shrugged. "Depends on a lot of things, I guess," he said. "I wouldn't worry about it, Mercy. Your brother has been doing this kind of thing for years. He's not stupid."

"But, they've never come looking for him *here* before!" said Mercy. "Do you think they suspect something?"

"I don't see how they could," said Thatcher. "It's hard to track footprints in the sand, even for a Wampanoag!"

"I'm too tired tonight to worry," said Mercy. "I'll worry about it tomorrow."

Thatcher put out the lamp on the kitchen table and the couple made their way into the bedroom, where Mercy began to pull back the quilt on the bed. For a moment, her eyes darted to the wall above the headboard.

"Oh, Thatcher," she said. "You don't think they noticed *that*, do you?"

Thatcher followed her glance; there, hanging above the bed, was the little dream catcher that Mercy had made for his father, the one they kept in remembrance after Eddie's death.

"Perhaps," he said. "Perhaps, not. But, just to be safe, let's put it away in a drawer." He reached up and removed it from the wall. "There's no sense taking chances."

Back in Orleans, the soldiers had stopped at the livery to bed their horses for the night. As the men dismounted, a young corporal looked at his sergeant quizzically. "What do you think, Sergeant Sparrow?" he asked. "Do you think they were telling the truth?"

Isaac Sparrow, who had been promoted since his days standing watch over the Indians at Mashpee, scratched his head. "I'm not sure," he said. "But, that fellow sure looked familiar! That red hair! I just know I've seen him somewhere before."

"And, didn't you think it strange," asked one of the other soldiers, "That they had that Injun thing hangin' over their bed? They didn't look Injun to me! Him nor the missus!"

A light went off in Sparrow's head. He remembered where he had seen that red hair before! "They're *half-breeds*," he quipped sarcastically. "And, I'm sure they *weren't* telling the truth! We'll have to watch that house from now on. There is something going on there. We'll get to the bottom of it."

Chapter Forty-Seven *"All in an Afternoon"*

Mercy was sitting on the porch of the old house. In front of her was a wooden easel Thatcher had built for her so that she could sketch without having to balance her tablet on her growing belly. She was eager to try her new *pastels*, the dry crayons that Thatcher had ordered all the way from France, and her fingers had already set to work capturing the summer seascape before her. The day was balmy and still; a pod of playful dolphins frolicked just beyond the surf and she was watching them in between strokes on her paper. Thatcher was away tending to business at the mercantile and Samuel had been gone for weeks up north but Mercy was not lonely; this was the perfect opportunity to do her best work. As she watched the sun and the dolphins dance on the surface of the water, she could not have been more content.

Susannah had visited just the day before, checking on the welfare of the expectant mother. They had put the finishing touches on a cradle for the baby that was due any day. The two women had become closer than ever now that the birth was imminent. For the first time in a long while, the Snow family was experiencing a period of peace and tranquility. The tribe in Mashpee seemed to be settling in to their new domain quite well and Thatcher assured her that all their physical needs had been met. They were now allowed to move about more freely within the boundaries of the Mashpee compound and, although they would never again be *truly* free, they seemed to have accepted it. Mercy had taken it upon herself to pay visits to the cemetery in Orleans, to lay offerings on the graves of Old Thomas and the others who slept there and she knew Reverend Amos was doing the same for her father. They had not had any more visits from the soldiers searching for Samuel. *Life was good.*

She put her crayon down on the lip of the easel and leaned back in her chair to rest for a moment. Her back ached acutely today; she knew the time was near for her to meet her new baby. Scanning the beach with her eyes, for a brief moment she thought she saw someone walking toward her but the sun's glare sometimes played tricks on her. When she looked again, she saw no one, only mounds of hot sand, the sun's silvery reflection on the ocean beyond and a few gulls and terns, waddling about among the bubbles of the retreating tide. *Nothing but a mirage*, she thought to herself. Then, she saw it again; there *was* someone walking on the beach! She rose from her chair and squinted to see who it was. *"Samuel!"* she whispered in horror. She could not imagine why her brother would be coming home in broad daylight, leaving himself open to discovery by the spying soldiers. As he drew closer, she could see he was walking very slowly. It was not the way of her brave Wampanoag brother; his stride did not have its usual confident air. Then, she saw why. With one arm tied up in a bloody sling across his chest and his head drooped low, he staggered across the yard and collapsed at the foot of the porch.

"Samuel, what has happened to you?" she said, rushing down to him as quickly as her delicate condition would allow. His face was white and his eyes dull as he looked up into her horrified stare. "Come," she said. "We need to get you into the house quickly."

Leaning on her for support, Samuel limped up the steps and into the house, where he immediately slumped down in front of the hearth. Mercy brought him a cushion for his head. With fingers still stained blue, she pulled apart the makeshift sling and saw his wounded arm was swollen and purple and crusted with dried blood. She could tell he had been shot. His fingers were a hideous shade of black. *Gangrene!* She had seen it before, in the days when she still lived in the Wampanoag camp and she knew the consequences of it. *Her brother would have to lose his arm to save his life!*

She stoked the coals in the fireplace and put a pot of water over them to boil. She pulled clean cloth from a drawer in the kitchen and began to wipe away the blood to wash out the wound. She found the spot where the bullet had entered but nowhere could she see where it *had exited. The bullet was obviously still lodged in his arm and needed to be cut out. Where, oh where was Thatcher?* she wondered frantically. She knew what to do; she had watched the *shaman* of their tribe many times remove bullets and perform amputations. She knew *what* to do; she just wasn't sure she would be *able* to do it. She was already feeling nauseous and light-headed.

"I need to get you up off the floor," she mumbled, for kneeling over him was giving her great pain. "You must get up, Samuel. We need to get you onto the bed so we can get the bullet out of your arm."

It was a struggle. Samuel was lapsing in and out of consciousness and she was afraid she would not be strong enough to support him if he fell, but slowly they managed to hobble to the bedside, where he collapsed onto the mattress and into a deep sleep. Mercy brought the kettle of boiling water and placed it on the bedside table. *At least, I don't need to sedate him*, she thought, remembering how the shaman had to have two grown men from the tribe hold down patients for the excruciating procedure. *At least Samuel would feel no pain.*

She opened the window to let in the fresh air for the room was quite stifling. She went to the kitchen and found her sharpest knife, the small one with the narrow blade that she used to filet and clean fish, and cleaned it with the boiling water. *First the bullet*, she thought, *then the arm.* She looked down at his arm and began to probe her brother's flesh just above his elbow to find the bullet, cringing as she dug deeper. Fresh blood began to dribble onto the bed sheets and she stopped to hold her fingers against the flow. Each time his blood would clot and hold, she would start again, searching for the tiny piece of metal, until she finally felt something hard with the tip of the blade; the bullet emerged and she held it in her shaking hand.

When the bleeding had stopped, she examined Samuel's arm carefully, but it was impossible to determine how far up the infection had spread. *His hand would have to go;* of that she was sure. But, how much of his arm would have to be removed was a mystery to her. *Does it matter?* she wondered to herself, *when his arm would be useless without his hand anyway? Does it matter how much I cut away?* She knew if she did not cut enough she would be needlessly butchering him only to have him die anyway.

She left the room momentarily and went out to the porch for a breath of fresh, summer air for the heat and her nervousness was making her feel quite queasy. She looked hopefully up the path between the dunes, hoping to see Thatcher returning from town, but there was no one for miles; she was all alone with the hard decision she had to make. She sank down on the porch steps and began to weep. A day that had begun so beautifully had turned into a nightmare. Suddenly, and without warning, a pain caught her unaware and she gripped her abdomen just as she felt a rush of fluid creeping down her legs and trickling onto the step. *Not the baby!* she thought. *Where, oh, where was Thatcher?*

As if the gods were answering her, she looked up at that moment and saw her husband walking along the pathway to the house; she raised her hand to wave to him. She tried to stand but another pain struck her and she hunched over until it passed. When she looked up again, she saw two soldiers riding close behind Thatcher. *No!* she thought wildly. *This can't be happening!* She was not going to let them take her wounded brother away!

Thatcher rushed forward, seeing that something was terribly wrong. "Mercy?" he asked. "Are you ill?"

She looked up into her husband's eyes. "The baby is coming," she said flatly.

"We need to get you into the house," he said, reaching down and scooping her up into his arms gently. He noticed her stockings were stained a dark pink and a worried frown pinched his face. He turned toward the soldiers.

"May I beg a favor of one of you gentlemen?" he pleaded. "Could one of you ride to the old house at the end of Skaket Road and fetch my sister-in-law? My wife needs help with the birth of our child."

"I'll go," said one of the soldiers, turning his horse around, while the one who had introduced himself as Sergeant Sparrow dismounted and followed them.

"No," Mercy whispered to Thatcher, her eyes growing wide. *"You don't understand.* Leave me here for a moment. I will be fine."

Thatcher shook his head. "Don't be silly," he told her. "You need to be in bed."

A breeze blew up from the ocean then; the paper on Mercy's easel began to flap and her crayons began to roll off onto the floor.

"Sergeant," said Thatcher. "Would you mind bringing my wife's easel inside the house? She won't be doing any more sketching for a while."

He carried her down the hallway.

"No, Thatcher," she kept whispering. "Put me down here. It's terribly hot in the bedroom. I'll simply *stifle* in there."

"Why are you acting so strangely?" asked Thatcher as he pushed open the door to the bedroom. He could see the bed covers had already been turned back. He noticed the pile of bloody rags on the floor beside the bed. Panic rose in his chest. *"My god, Mercy,"* he said. "What..........?"

Mercy looked over her shoulder, following her husband's glance. The bed was empty. The curtains were fluttering in the open window. *Samuel was gone!* At that moment, they heard the rhythmic thudding of Sergeant Sparrow's boots in the next room. Just as Thatcher laid Mercy down on the bed, the soldier peered in through the doorway.

"I'm sorry to intrude, Ma'am," he said. His eyes surveyed the room, lingering for a moment on the pile of bloody rags on the floor. "We think that Injun is headed this way. We've been trailing him for a while now. We wanted to warn you to be on the lookout."

Thatcher turned toward him. "As you can see, Sergeant, we have more pressing issues to worry about at the moment." His eyes grew dark with impatience. "Now," he said. "Could you please leave and give my wife some privacy?"

Chapter Forty-Eight *"Little Susie"*

By the time Susannah arrived and the soldiers had finally departed, Mercy was already in the throes of strong labor. Thatcher paced about the room nervously, wringing his hands, not knowing what to do.

"Why is there so much blood?" he asked. "Is the baby going to be all right?"

Susannah finally ushered him out of the room. "You must leave me to tend to her," she said. "Sit down and try to calm yourself. Read a book. Sit on the porch. You must not worry, Thatcher. Your wife and baby will be fine."

She retreated into the bedroom and closed the door. Mercy was lying there with sweat beading across her forehead. Susannah blotted it away with a damp cloth. She, too, had wondered about the bloody rags on the floor, wondering if she had come too late to save the baby.

"It's not *my* blood," Mercy whispered. "Samuel was here. He had been shot. I had to remove a bullet from his arm."

Susannah's face took on an expression of relief. "So, *that's* why the soldiers were here," she said. "But, where did he go? How did he escape?"

Mercy raised her arm and pointed toward the open window. "I suppose he went out *that* way," she whispered, as another contraction came upon her.

Susannah sat down beside the bed and held Mercy's hand in hers as the pains continued and grew in intensity. "It's almost over," she said finally. "The baby is almost here."

In a few more moments, and a few more pushes on Mercy's part, a perfect little girl came into the world. Thatcher heard the baby cry from the next room and his heart leaped with joy. "Can I come in now?" he asked through the closed door.

"Let me bathe and swaddle her first," said Susannah. "And, then we will introduce you to your new daughter!"

A *daughter*! Thatcher hadn't really thought about what gender the baby would be. It wasn't important. What *was* important was that Mercy and the baby were all right. So many emotions were running amuck in him. He had managed to hide his annoyance with the soldiers, who had followed him all the way from town. Lately, they were popping up in the oddest of places, stalking him, watching his daily movements. He had not shared that information with Mercy; he didn't want to worry her unnecessarily. But, he needed to warn Samuel at their next meeting that it was no longer a safe place for him to be.

When Susannah finally opened the bedroom door and allowed Thatcher to enter, she tiptoed out to leave the couple alone in that special moment.

Thatcher was speechless as he peeled back the tiny blanket and looked for the first time into the face of his daughter.

"There is something I have to tell you," Mercy said. "Have the soldiers gone?"

Thatcher nodded. "Yes, they left some time ago."

"Samuel was here," she said. "The blood you saw on the rags was *his* blood. He came home with a bullet in his arm."

"But, where….?"

"He must have heard the soldiers coming and climbed out the window," she replied. "But, I am very worried about him, Thatcher. I managed to remove the bullet but his hand has developed gangrene. He needs to have his arm amputated soon or he will die!"

"What would you have me do?" he asked.

"*Find* him," she said with a pleading stare.

"But, I can't leave you and the baby now," Thatcher replied.

"Susannah will stay with me until you return," she said.

He was worried but he finally agreed. He sat on the edge of the bed and kissed Mercy tenderly. "What shall we name her?" he asked, touching the baby's nose with the tip of his finger.

Mercy smiled. "I think we should name her Susannah after your sister," she said. "We could call her *Susie* for short."

"I like that," he replied. "And, my sister would be most pleased."

There was a knock at the bedroom door. "May I come in?" Susannah asked.

"Of course," said Mercy happily. "We were just picking out a name for our daughter. We want to name her after you."

Susannah beamed. "Will you be leaving to search for Samuel?" she asked. "If so, I will run home and collect a few of my things. And, let your brothers know where I have gone."

Thatcher rose from the bed. "I will leave first thing in the morning," he said.

"No," Mercy said adamantly. "I think you should leave *now*, Thatcher. There is no time to waste. Samuel needs surgery *immediately* or he will die."

"Very well, then," he said. "I will walk with you as far as town, Susannah. I will need to saddle a horse. I do not know how far I will have to go or what condition Samuel will be in when I find him." He looked at Mercy. "Are you sure you will be all right until Susannah returns?"

"Yes," was her reply. "Off with you now! *Find Samuel before it is too late!*"

Chapter Forty-Nine *"Blind Joe Amos"*

The back of the wagon was hard and unyielding; every pot hole the wheels found in the surface of the road kicked like a mule's hoof to Samuel's festering arm. Thatcher had only agreed to transport his brother-in-law under certain conditions; first, Samuel was to remain in Mashpee, under the protection of Reverend Amos, until his wounds had fully healed and, second, he would submit to the surgery that was necessary to save his life.

Thatcher had found Samuel by chance, hiding there in the stable behind the mercantile where he had gone to get his horse, sick and in terrible pain. Taking him back to the house where Mercy and the baby were was out of the question; Sergeant Sparrow already suspected the Snows of harboring him. He refused to put his wife and child in danger any more than necessary. No, the only other place they could find safety was in Mashpee, the only place Samuel had sworn he would never go. *Now, his life depended upon it.*

As a diversion, Thatcher had loaded up supplies in the back of the wagon after he had helped Samuel into a small concealed space between the boxes and bags. They had left Orleans as soon as darkness had fallen while, hopefully, the soldiers had retired for the day. It was a long, painful journey for Samuel, so painful, in fact, that he passed out shortly after they had started down the King's Highway and, thankfully, remained unconscious the rest of the way.

In his weekly visits to deliver supplies, Thatcher had been learning a great deal about the Mashpee settlement and the people who lived there. In years past, it had been home to a long string of missionaries and traveling preachers who were seeking to "save" the Indians from their *heathen* ways. From the early English Puritan, John Eliot, who was also in the business of dispossessing the Indians of their lands, to Richard Bourne and Gideon Hawley who had helped to build the Mashpee Meeting House that now served as the tribal church, the Wampanoag had seen their share of do-gooders and charlatans. It wasn't until Reverend William Apess, a Methodist minister, who was also a native *Pequot* Indian, arrived in 1833 that things began to change.

First of all, the Massachusetts legislature had appointed a minister named Phineas Fish from nearby Santuit to preside over the church at Mashpee. But, contrary to his vows of love for all humanity, Fish was deeply prejudiced against the Wampanoag and was soon forbidding them entrance to the meeting house. The result was the old man named Joe Amos, the blind, Baptist Wampanoag preacher they had met in the cemetery on their first visit, who started giving sermons every Sunday under a nearby oak tree in defiance of Phineas Fish. After all, Amos told his people, *God does not require a roof over our heads to worship!*

Amos was truly a man of God. He baptized many new Christians in nearby Wakeby Pond. Not only could he recite the entire King James Bible from memory, he could do so in both English and Wampanoag. Soon, there were more parishioners attending his outdoor services than were seated in the pews of the Mashpee meeting house. By the time Apess came to town, the whole congregation had literally shifted from Fish to Amos, and, together, the two Indian ministers, held the community together against any more attempts to prey upon its members. Fish was run out of town, and, after that, Amos and Apess helped to organize a council of twelve Wampanoag men to represent them in Boston and drafted a list of demands to free them from their *white masters.*

But, there were other problems. Not long after Massachusetts had taken part in the Indian Removal Act, the sovereignty of Mashpee as an Indian refuge began to crumble. Whites freely trespassed on the Mashpee lands, harvesting lumber and grazing their livestock with no concern over the rights of the Wampanoag people who made their livelihood there. When a group of white farmers from nearby Barnstable arrived early one morning to cut wood, the Wampanoag, including Reverend Apess, firmly stood their ground. As quickly as the white farmers filled their wagons with the stolen lumber, the men of Mashpee *unloaded* it, stacking it among their own stores. Tempers flared and angry words were exchanged but the farmers, wanting to keep their scalps, finally left, complaining all the way to the office of the Governor, Levi Lincoln, in Boston.

Governor Lincoln, fearing more serious hostilities from the Indians, had recently sent a delegation to investigate the source of the trouble. The state militia came and arrested Apess, charging him with rioting, assault and trespassing for which he spent thirty days in jail. Soon after, abolitionist William Lloyd Garrison got involved in the matter, pressuring the Massachusetts legislature to reinstate the Mashpee Indians the right to govern themselves. So, such was the early history of Mashpee.

By the time Thatcher arrived in Mashpee that night, Samuel was still sleeping in the back of the wagon and he had lost an enormous amount of blood. He reined in the mules near the rear of the old meeting house and knocked on the door. Reverend Amos appeared in his nightshirt and, together, they carried Samuel's unconscious body inside. The shaman was quickly summoned and there, in the dim lamplight of the preacher's quarters, Samuel's arm was removed and the stump where his arm had once been was sutured. Indian healing herbs were applied. Prayers were offered up to the gods.

Thatcher sat in the corner of the room, while the reverend prayed and the shaman chanted old mournful songs in his native tongue. For an hour or so, Thatcher napped, slumped over in his chair but he awakened at the sound of Samuel's moaning. "He's coming out of it!" he said excitedly and rushed over to the edge of the bed where Samuel lay.

The expression on the face of the medicine man was serious and intense. He leaned over his patient, feeling for the strength of Samuel's pulse. Samuel opened his eyes for a few moments; he looked down at his mutilated arm and then up at Thatcher. "Looks like you will win all of our fights from now on," he whispered with a weak smile.

Thatcher smiled back. "We'll just have to teach you to fight *left-handed*," he told his brother-in-law playfully but feeling raw emotion rising in his chest. He had become fond of Samuel since their first unfortunate meeting.

"He has lost a lot of blood," the shaman said. "He must sleep if he is to regain his strength."

There were more hours of waiting and Thatcher finally curled up near the fire and slept.

As daylight approached, when the people of Mashpee awakened, they were unaware that one of their own was lying perilously close to death on a cot in the back of the meeting house. And, by the time the sun had risen high above the trees, Samuel, *the wild one*, was dead.

Chapter Fifty *"The Artist and the Horseman"*

Thomas Snow came into the world exactly three hundred and sixty-two days after the birth of his sister, Susie. The house that had once been the quiet and isolated home of the old man of the sea now resonated with the sounds of children's laughter; its walls pulsed with the bustling, busy world of the growing family. Mercy had mourned deeply for her brother when Thatcher had returned home with the sad news but she knew her husband had done all he could do. She knew Reverend Amos and the shaman had tried valiantly to save Samuel's life and she had come to terms with his death. As quickly as old lives were being lost, she was bringing new life into the world and there just wasn't enough time to dwell on the past.

Susie was a precocious child, much like her mother had been. Mercy could see herself in the toddler's antics and proclivities. When Mercy would sit and sketch on the porch, Susie would sit at her feet, doodling on the floor with the worn-down stubs of used crayons. When Thatcher came home each night from his work at the mercantile, there would be new murals drawn on the floors and walls. *I see our little artist has been at it again*, he would say, laughing when his daughter would climb into his lap and show him her stained fingers. *We must have the most colorful house in all of Orleans*, Mercy would reply, proud of the work of her young protégé.

As she grew older, her artistic talents bloomed even more. When they enrolled her in the Orleans school, her teacher encouraged her to pursue her passion. Soon, Susie's works of art graced not only the walls of the schoolhouse, but, as soon as Thatcher hung some of them up at the mercantile, customers were asking to buy the pictures; her colorful seascapes captured the hearts of many, as did her depictions of the local wildlife. She would sometimes sit for hours on the shore, watching the movements of the seabirds so she could capture them on paper. Mercy was pleased that her daughter showed far more talent than she ever could; the girl truly had a special gift. She silently wished they had the means to send her away to study in one of the fine French schools where they valued art, but she kept it to herself, knowing they would never be able to never afford such a thing.

As for Thomas, as he grew, the boy was far more interested in his father's horses and mules than in academic pursuits. When he was old enough to accompany Thatcher to the mercantile, the boy would disappear into the stable behind the store and his father would find him brushing the horses and feeding them carrots he had pilfered from the produce bins inside. It wasn't very long until he was itching to be in the saddle on his father's lap, riding around Orleans and, soon after, he was riding alone up and down the King's Highway, accompanying Thatcher on his deliveries to Mashpee. It was because of his talent at horsemanship that he soon became involved in the underground practice of *moon cussing*.

The town of Orleans was growing at a slower pace these days than its neighboring towns. With the removal of the last of the Wampanoag tribe to Mashpee, many of the families of mixed-blood drifted that way also, settling there on the upper cape. As the population grew older, the younger generation began to diminish also. The classes at the Orleans school had only half the number of pupils than they had in years past. Businesses began to grow stagnant in the shadow of the bustling economy of Wellfleet to the north and people grew steadily poorer. The Snow family hung on to the mercantile but took outside work when the opportunity arose and there was one business that never failed to reap profits.

The eastern coast of Cape Cod, from Brewster to Truro, had long been a graveyard for ships that wrecked in its blinding fogs and treacherous currents. Indeed, Mercy and Thatcher had, on more than one occasion, taken in sailors stranded along the beach of bones when their ships ran aground. Sometimes the ships could be salvaged but, more often than not, once they were beached with damaged hulls, their holds filled with sea water, getting them back out to sea was an almost impossible task. Waiting in the dunes like *sand vultures* were the *moon-cussers,* the under-employed men and women of struggling Orleans who would brave the cold ocean waves to scavenge the abandoned ships, gleaning anything of value and hauling it ashore to be sold on the black market. Unwittingly, Thatcher and his brothers became a part of it and, although they did not *personally* rob the ships, they nevertheless became *middlemen* in the exchange of the pirated goods.

Mercy did not wholeheartedly approve of what her husband was doing. She worried that he would be caught and arrested. But, she was a practical woman too, and she knew the criminal activity was widespread; Thatcher was only one of many who supplemented their earnings by obtaining cheap goods to sell. They would have had to arrest the entire town of Orleans in order to catch them all, which seemed highly unlikely.

The Snows had acquired, over the years, a small stable of horses and mules which they used to make deliveries and rented out to others on occasion. It was because of *one* horse in particular, which was Thomas' special favorite, that the boy got involved at all. He had named the young gelding *Glimmer*, because of his shiny grey coat, that appeared silver in the dark. It also made the animal the perfect vehicle for *deception*.

At that time, there were only three lighthouses on the coast of Cape Cod, two lights were built in Chatham to the south and one in Truro to the north, at the mouth of Cape Cod Bay. But, in between, was a fifteen-mile stretch of dark coastline and the potential for ships running aground on the invisible sand shoals, which made the wary captains stay far out to sea until they saw a signaling beacon. If the ships traveling between the two lighthouses, using them as markers, could be fooled into losing their way, more ships would end up on the shore and be ripe for the pickings.

A man, whom Thatcher knew only casually around town, came into the mercantile one evening to inquire about renting a horse. Thatcher was just sweeping up the floors and young Thomas was helping with the smaller chores. It was almost time for supper.

"I'd like to rent that *white* one you've got out back," said the man, and young Thomas' ears pricked. *His horse? His father was going to rent out his horse?* He came around the counter and Thatcher could tell by the expression on his face the boy was not fond of the idea.

"When would you need him?" Thatcher asked. "Tomorrow?"

"Oh, no," replied the man. "I will need him *tonight.* I will bring him back in the morning. If it works out well, I may be using him again in a month or so."

To Thomas the idea was immediately suspect. *Who rented a horse for the night?*

"And, how far do you intend to take him?" asked Thatcher.

"Not far," said the man. "Only south to Chatham."

Thatcher was worried that the man intended to steal Glimmer and ride out of town, never to be seen again and he knew how heartbroken his son would be if that happened. "No, I'm afraid not," he told the man. "He is my son's horse, you see, and if he were to stumble and break a leg in the dark, it would be most grievous to my family."

Thomas puffed up his chest. *No one was going to take his horse out for a moonlight ride!*

"Well, would your son be agreeable if we paid for *his* time as well then?"

Thatcher was confused. "You want to rent my *son* too?" he asked. *"Whatever for?"*

"I just need him to ride up the coast to make a delivery," the man said, growing agitated.

Thomas was suddenly interested. He could ride Glimmer in the dark! He had ridden up and down the beach many times. He knew the coast as well as anyone!

"I don't know," said Thatcher, thinking of what Mercy would have to say. He knew it had something to do with delivering stolen goods.

The man was losing his patience. He was ready to walk out. He finally laid down a fair sum of money on the counter. "I'm willing to pay you a good price," he said.

"With business being what it is around here lately, I would think you could use a few extra dollars."

Thatcher stared at the money on the counter. Thomas was already halfway out the door.

"I can do it, Pa," he said. "I'll go and saddle Glimmer right now!"

Chapter Fifty-One *"The Moon-cussers"*

Mercy was beside herself with worry the minute Thatcher returned home and told her about the man's strange request. "How could you have been so careless, Thatcher Snow?" she asked.

Thatcher reached into his pocket and produced the money the man had paid him.

"Are we in the *slavery* business now?" she said, staring at the bills in Thatcher's hand. "Have you sold our son to a stranger? What's next? Will you sell our little Susie too?"

Thatcher was annoyed. Mercy had never spoken to him in such a caustic tone before. "I didn't *sell* anyone," he said. "The man simply hired Thomas to make a delivery. That's all."

"Thomas is much too young to be out working for strangers in the night," Mercy replied.

"I was no older than he when I started helping Pa," he said. "And, since when did *you* become afraid of the dark? You, *the girl who wandered the beach at midnight?*"

Mercy bit her lip. *Perhaps he was right*. Perhaps, she was being too protective of her son. She knew her son could ride like the wind, she knew he could handle Glimmer, but she had other concerns.

"Surely, you realize this has something to do with the *moon-cussers*," she said, with a somber tone in her voice. Everyone in town was aware of the thieves who carried on their illegal trade in the darkness of moonless nights.

"I deal with them every day," said Thatcher. "They keep our shelves stocked with goods we could not afford by any other means. They are no different than any of us; they are just men trying to make a living. Besides, this money will help pay to have the mules shoed and the wagon fitted for a new wheel."

It was certainly true. In recent years, they had been barely eking out a living and the Snows had worried they might have to close the mercantile. Ironically, it was the Wampanoag at Mashpee who were now helping *them*, supplying baskets and brooms and produce for the Snows to sell, in repayment of all the years of support the Snow family had given them. Thatcher and Mercy finally went off to bed but it was a sleepless night for both of them, listening for the sound of Thomas returning. When daylight came and Thomas came walking in, he sat down at the breakfast table and began to eat hungrily, without saying a word.

"Well?" asked Mercy. "Aren't you going to tell us about your midnight adventure?"

"Not much to tell," said Thomas. "All I did was deliver a lantern to a man in Chatham."

"A *lantern?*" asked Thatcher. "That's all? Did you pick up goods in Chatham?"

Thomas shook his head. "Nope," he said. "The man there gave me another lantern and told me to bring it back to the man who hired me."

Thatcher and Mercy exchanged perplexing stares.

"So, what you are telling us is that he paid for yo u to ride all the way to Chatham and back, carrying nothing but a *lantern?*"

"Yep," said Thomas, finishing his breakfast. "And, it's a good thing they gave it to me too! There was no moon at all last night and it was awfully dark! Luckily, ol' Glimmer is sure-footed!" He paused and took his last bite. "Can I go to bed now? I'm awful sleepy."

When he had gone off to his room, Mercy voiced her sentiments about the whole situation. "I don't want him to do this again, Thatcher," she said. "Something is very strange about it. Why couldn't this man ride himself to Chatham? Why involve our boy?"

Thatcher was confused as well. "He seemed to be only interested in Glimmer," he said. "And, he could see that Thomas was not happy about renting out his horse."

"Why *Glimmer?*" she asked. "Why not another horse?"

278

Thatcher shrugged his shoulders and kissed his wife on the cheek before he headed out the door for the mercantile. "It is all very strange," he said in parting. "I hope we have seen the last of him!"

The next day, Thatcher was extremely busy at the mercantile with a new shipment of goods he purchased from the man who had hired Thomas. The man made him a very good deal and the goods exchanged hands and Thatcher tried not to think any more about it. But, a month later, the same man paid them another visit, wanting to know if Glimmer and Thomas were available. And, Thomas had, once again, saddled for another midnight ride. It was the same as before; there was no moon and the beaches were as dark as pitch. And, the following day, more bargain-priced goods arrived.

Only hours earlier, a few miles out to sea, Captain Roger Nelson was standing on the fo'c'sle on the merchant ship *Prince,* scanning the shoreline off Orleans with his spy glass. Without the moon that night, the scattered stars were pitiful purveyors of illumination; the captain's eyes were fixed toward land as they sailed northward, hoping the Truro light would soon come into view.

All at once, he saw a faraway flickering. He checked his maps; the currents were swift that night but it didn't seem as if the ship had travelled that far. But, surely, *it had to be the light at Truro he was seeing through his glass!* He lowered the wick in the oil lamp hanging from the foremast behind him to get a better look and focused his eyes intently on the light. There, on the beach, he could see something silvery-white and a yellow light that seemed to be moving. He immediately gave orders to bring the ship about, confident they were about to make the turn toward Cape Cod Bay. By the time he realized his mistake, the *Prince* had run aground with a heavy thud, lodging itself deep in a bar of sand. There was much scurrying on deck and the crew finally abandoned ship and went ashore to seek help, planning to come back the next morning in the daylight, when the damages could be ascertained.

Soon after the crew had departed, however, in the darkness of the moonless night, several small boats silently rowed out toward the ship and the boats' occupants, climbing over the side, quickly began to unload the ship's cargo.

The moon-cussers had moved in to collect their bounty.

Chapter Fifty-Two *"The Three Sisters"*

Since the writing of the Constitution and the Bill of Rights, the Congress, in the newly formed nation, had done little in the way of improving on the lives of its citizens. But, after the ravages of war, the epidemics of disease and the poverty of the struggling economy, the legislators in Boston finally made a decision that would help the ship owners on Cape Cod; they agreed to set aside $10,000 in tax money to build three lighthouses on the beach outside Orleans.

Why *three* lighthouses? As the ship captains, especially *Mad Jack Percival* of Barnstable who frequently sailed the route between his home port and Cape Cod Bay, explained, there was nothing midpoint on the cape to guide ships and keep them from running aground on the sandbars outside Orleans. If the captains saw *two* lights, they could assume they were in the vicinity of Chatham; if they saw a *single* light, they knew they would be rounding the cape at Truro. So, Mad Jack argued, if they built *three* smaller lighthouses midway, between the other two, they would know precisely when they had reached the midway point and could no longer be fooled by the *moon-cussers* and their phantom lights on the beach.

And, so the work began, high on the cliffs above Nauset Beach, to erect three tiny round structures, standing only fifteen feet tall, built of white-washed brick with shiny black lantern decks, each boasting ten oil lanterns and narrow spiral staircases made of iron. They would stand only one hundred and fifty feet apart and give much-needed employment to four local masons, two carpenters, a cook, and three young laborers, one of whom was *Thomas Snow*.

Mercy was not at all pleased with the project; she savored the peacefulness and remoteness of the dunes, fearing months of intrusion by the lighthouse builders. Besides, she told Thatcher, with three blinding lights practically in their backyard, this was worse than the moon; she would never again be able to see the stars! But, she had no say in the matter. The land at the top of the cliffs adjacent to their property belonged to another and that person quickly accepted the government's money. It was inevitable that the dreaded lighthouses would soon be their new neighbors!

Despite his mother's misgivings, Thomas was eager on the first morning he was to report to work. With a shovel from his grandfather's tool shed, he made his way through the dunes toward the cliffs. All that day, he piled sand into a wide flat wooden tray and then, with the other boys, hauled buckets of sea water to make a kind of sandy mortar for the masons to secure the bricks in place.

"They used nothing but *sand* to make the mortar?" asked Thatcher that night at supper. "Once the sand dries out that won't hold together!"

"That's what they told me to do, Pa," Thomas told him. "I just do as I am told."

Mercy smiled. "Perhaps they will all fall down," she said happily. "And, they will choose another spot to build."

"We're to build a little house for the light-keeper too," said Thomas. "I expect we will be quite busy for a while."

"Well, don't stand *too close to* them," warned Thatcher, "Lest the darned things come down on your head! Leave it to the government to make such a mess of things!"

And, day after day, until thirty-eight days had passed, Thomas worked on the light houses and came home each night with stories to tell. Shortly after the construction began, the supervisor walked off the job, objecting to the poor quality materials and the makeshift methods allowed them by the government that did not want to pay an extra penny for safety. He refused to guarantee that the poorly-built foundations and the weak mortar used to secure the bricks would hold.

"They are calling them the *three sisters*," Thomas told them.

"How dare they name those monstrosities after the *Wampanoag* gods!" complained Mercy. "They know nothing of tradition!"

"They are calling them that because, when we finished the first one, it looked like a little girl in a white dress and a black bonnet," Thomas tried to explain, wondering why his mother took such offense to the name. "Besides, it's just a *name*, Mother."

"Thomas," she told him, "It's *more* than just a name. Your ancestors worshipped the *three sisters*. They represented the crops that sustained us, corn, beans and squash. The *three sisters* were sacred to us."

Thomas had never heard his mother speak of her people before and he was intrigued.

It seemed as if enough time had gone by for Mercy to be completely honest with her children. That night after supper, she sat down and told Thomas and Susie the stories of her past, of the once-proud Wampanoag tribe of Cape Cod, of their removal to Mashpee, of her own father.

"I never knew my grandfather was the *sachem* of his tribe," Susie said in wonderment. "Why have you not told us these things before, Mother?"

"We thought it best not to talk too much about it," replied Mercy.

"We were afraid the government would come and take your mother away from me," said Thatcher. "After all these years, I don't think they much care anymore."

Susie and Thomas learned that night of the struggle of their ancestors. After they had gone to bed, Thatcher found Mercy standing at their open bedroom window in her nightgown. He walked up behind her and encircled her in his arms. "I am glad you finally told our children the truth about your heritage," he whispered.

"It is probably the only *good* that will come of those lighthouses," she replied, "Having to explain about the *three sisters*."

"Why are you so *opposed* to them?" Thatcher asked. "You should be pleased that our son has *honest* work now, that he no longer has to accept ill-gotten wages."

Mercy smiled at that, although he could not see her face in the darkness of their room. "It's like I explained to you before," she said "I love being able to see the stars and the constellations. I am afraid I agree with the pirates on one issue; I love the splendor of a moonless night, when all the stars come out."

Thatcher kissed the back of her neck tenderly.

"They will be shining right into our bedroom window, you know," she said.

"I sort of like the sound of that," said Thatcher. "I will be able to see you when we make love."

She turned toward him. "Only a *man* would say that," she replied. "Women like the mystique of a darkened room. It's so much more romantic!"

"You are a nothing but a *charlatan*, Mercy Snow!" he said. "After all the years of our marriage, I find that I have married a true *moon-cusser!*"

Their laughter erupted and he scooped her up and carried her to their bed, where he kissed her again, many times, in the darkness that she loved so. Had there been any moonlight streaming through the open window, he would have seen, on his wife's face, a look of passion and yearning, as she clung to him. He was *her Thatcher*, the man she had waited for patiently for most of her childhood, the man whose children she had bore, the man she would love *forever*. White or Indian, she cared not; he was more than her *blood*, he was her *soul*.

By morning, with the sun, their life resumed its normal routine and romance was temporarily put aside. Thomas went off to work on the three sisters and Thatcher to the mercantile. Soon, however, it seemed as if the lighthouse project was somehow *cursed*. Shortly after, the crew building the three sisters was stricken with an outbreak of small pox and two of them died. Mercy refused to let Thomas go to work until the sickness seemed to have moved on. The disease had spread to the town of Orleans quickly and Mercy was devastated to hear that her dear sister-in-law, Susannah, had succumbed to it also. She ran all the way to Skaket Road when she received the news and found Susannah in her bed, covered with sores and burning with fever. "I will stay here until you get well," she promised.

For a week, she remained in the house her husband had grown up in, nursing Susannah. On the seventh day, Susannah succumbed to the disease.

The Snows had lost another of their own.

Chapter Fifty-Three *"Emeline"*

When the familiar face first appeared in the mercantile the following day, Thatcher remembered the conversation of the previous night, when Mercy had finally revealed the secrets they had been keeping from their children. Now that Samuel was gone, now that the tribe in Mashpee was doing very well on its own and he no longer had to deliver needed supplies to them, the subject had been put aside in place of more pressing matters. *There was no need to worry about it any longer,* thought Thatcher, until now, when the man standing at the counter next to an attractive young woman brought it all back. "May I help you?" Thatcher asked.

The man had visibly aged since their last meeting and he no longer wore a militia uniform, but Thatcher would never forget his face. With eyes narrowed more from perplexity than from bad vision, he stared at Thatcher. "Don't I know you?" the man asked. Then, as if a light had been lit inside his head, he added, "Yes! I remember! You used to live out in that old house in the dunes!"

"Yes," Thatcher replied. "I still do. And, you, *Sparrow* was it? Are you still in the militia?"

Sparrow laughed. *"Gods, no!"* he said. "Too old for that now. Have a family of my own to raise. By the way, how is your missus? I remember she was having a difficult time the last time I saw you. Havin' a baby as I recall."

"She is quite well, thank you," Thatcher replied.

"And, the baby?" asked Sparrow, with an unexpected hint of compassion in his voice.

"The baby is all grown up and quite healthy," said Thatcher.

Suddenly, it seemed as if the man standing before him had changed. He was no longer the arrogant sergeant who had invaded their home looking for poor Samuel. He actually seemed to be a quite likeable fellow.

"That's fine," said Sparrow. "This is *my* daughter, *Emeline*. She is helping me with the shopping. Settled down in a house by the kettle ponds, we did, just this spring."

The young woman smiled and went about perusing the shelves of goods while the men talked. She was but a wisp of a thing, tiny and frail, with skin so white it was almost translucent. Her blond hair against her skin made her look all the paler; Thatcher couldn't help but wonder where her mother was. "I didn't think I'd seen you around in a very long time," he said.

"I must be losing my memory," said Sparrow. "I can't seem to remember your name."

"Snow," said Thatcher. "*Thatcher Snow.*"

"Snow, you say? Now, that's peculiar! My wife's name was Snow before I married her! Has your family been in Orleans for a long time?"

"We were one of the original families who settled here," said Thatcher proudly.

"Well, isn't this a day for surprises?" he looked for his daughter among the aisles of groceries. "Emmy! This man is our cousin! He's a *Snow* just like your mother!"

The girl smiled at her father with tired, sad eyes.

For an hour, the two men sat and discussed their common heritage until Thatcher was convinced the man had not come spying on them. As far as they could figure, both Thatcher and the sergeant's wife had descended from common ancestors, *Stephen and Susannah Snow.*

"You *must* come to supper tomorrow!" Thatcher said. "Bring your wife and family! I would love to connect with kin again; so many of us have moved away from the cape. I'll invite my brothers; we can make a night of it!"

Mercy was not so excited about the reunion, when Thatcher returned home.

"I've brought you extra food," he said. "I'm telling you, Mercy, the man has changed! He is not in the militia any longer. I don't think he even remembers why he was *here* that day!"

Mercy had not concerned herself in ever so long about being "discovered". The tribe had settled in Mashpee without further incident. Now, the proud Wampanoag tribe refused any more charity from Thatcher; they insisted, instead, on repaying the Snow's generosity by supplying marketable goods to the mercantile. She had not assisted in the hiding of escapees since Samuel had died, with the exception of offering food to an occasional wanderer on the beach. But, somehow, she felt uneasy about meeting this man's family, even if he *was* Thatcher's long lost cousin. This man had once sought to arrest her brother. Had enough time gone by that the government was no longer interested in an Indian woman living *clandestine* among the whites?

But, trying to be agreeable to her husband, she prepared enough food for guests and, just as a safety precaution, removed the dream catcher from their bedroom wall once again, where they had re-hung it months before.

When their company had arrived the next night, the little house was suddenly full of people and, with so many introductions, no one knew *exactly* who was who. Emeline sat quietly visiting with Susie. Missus Sparrow was not feeling well, she explained, and had not accompanied them. The men, of course, were seeped deeply into conversations about business and politics. The only one who seemed slightly aloof was Thomas, who sat with the men but who was watching the women out of the corner of his eye, particularly Emeline

Sparrow. From the very moment he first saw her, he was smitten with the pale, angelic-looking creature.

It proved to be a pleasant evening all around. As the Sparrows were leaving, Isaac pulled Thatcher aside for a brief moment. "By the way," he whispered. "I hope there are no hard feelings between us. I mean, about that *Injun* thing."

Thatcher cringed. *Now that he had welcomed the man into their home, was he going to reveal his sinister motives?*

"I knew all along," said Isaac. "That your missus belonged to that bunch we moved to Mashpee. I knew the *wild one* was her brother."

Thatcher's mouth gaped in astonishment. "And, you didn't report us?"

"Naw," said Isaac. "What do I care if you have Injun blood in your veins? You people weren't doin' any harm to nobody. And, I was just doin' my job. I hope you understand." He paused. "I met your father, you know, out at Mashpee. You have his red hair. That's how I knew who you were."

Thatcher smiled. The militia no longer stood between families.

At least, *between the Snow and Sparrow families!*

Chapter Fifty-Four *"The Fledglings Leave the Nest"*

Susie's art continued to be her passion, as it was to her mother in her own youth, and, after the *three sisters* were built, Thomas went back to helping Thatcher at the mercantile. But, times continued to be hard; the family business was barely covering the expense to remain open, and, soon, Joel and Jesse had decided to leave Orleans to seek employment in one of the bigger cities on the mainland. They had come to supper one evening to explain their plans to Thatcher and discuss the subject of what was to be done with their parents' house on Skaket Road.

"I hate to sell the old place," Thatcher admitted. "Even though, heaven knows, we could all use the money."

"That house has been in your family too long," Mercy told them. "Let us hold on to it if we can. You must never forget where you came from!"

But, Joel and Jesse were adamant on the subject. "Sell it if you can," they told Thatcher. "We don't intend to move back home anytime soon."

After his brothers had departed, Mercy asked Thatcher, "How do you feel about selling the home you were raised in?"

Thatcher had to admit the prospect bothered him. "I just keep thinking about Pa," he said. "And, my grandparents before them. The Snows have lived in that house for hundreds of years. It will seem very strange to see someone else take up residence there."

Mercy nodded in agreement. "I don't think you should sell it," she said. "I think we should sell *this* place and move to Skaket Road ourselves."

Thatcher knew that ever since the completion of the *three sisters* next door, his wife had been unhappy. Every night, the shafts of yellow lantern light pierced the darkness of their bedroom, a steady, unrelenting light that did not fade until the dawn. She *detested* it. She could not seem to sleep. Their love-life had become strained because of its intrusion, as well. "Are you serious?" he asked her. "I thought you loved being near to the shore."

"Everything changed when those monstrous lights were built," she replied. "It doesn't feel like it used to. Besides, Skaket Road is still within walking distance of the shore."

"Well," Thatcher said. "If that is what you want, Mercy."

"There is something else I want," she replied. "Something I want more than anything in the world."

What was it? Thatcher wondered. *Anything! Anything to make his wife smile again!* He waited anxiously to hear what she had to say.

"It's for *Susie*," were her words. "I want to sell this house and send Susie to college in the fall."

"College?" asked Thatcher. *"What on earth for? Women don't go to college!"*

Mercy's face fell. She had expected a more positive reaction from Thatcher. *"To learn!"* she said, with more sharpness to her voice than usual. "There is a women's college she has mentioned. With the money we make on selling this house, we could send her, Thatcher! It would pay for her tuition and her board."

"You mean she would have to *live* at this school?" Thatcher asked, not at all enthusiastic about losing his only daughter. "And be away from us?"

"Only while school is in session," Mercy said. "She could come home in the summertime."

Thatcher could not wrap his mind around it. *A girl going to college! The idea was preposterous!* "It would make more sense to send *Thomas*," he said.

"Thomas is only interested in horses and the livery business," said Mercy. "He *hates* the classroom, you know that."

"But, what would she learn? Wouldn't it all be a waste of time and money, when she gets married and settles down to raise a family?"

Mercy took a deep breath. She had to make Thatcher understand on some level. He was still living in the past, when girls didn't even attend *primary* school, when Indians were considered *unworthy* of an education. She remembered the thrill she felt on *her* first day at the white school in Orleans, how her heart felt like it would burst wide open with pride! "Our daughter is *gifted*," she said finally. "It would be a shame to waste that gift."

Thatcher knew Susie was special in many ways. With her artistic talent, she was much like her mother. He saw an infectious sparkle in Mercy's eyes when she spoke of it. He knew he couldn't fight both his wife and his daughter, and, it appeared that Mercy's mind was made up. The next day, they began to pack their belongings for the move to the house on Skaket Road, but not before Mercy had written a letter to the women's college, regarding their daughter's enrollment there.

Thomas had no reaction to the news that his sister would be going away to college. He seemed agreeable to the idea of moving the family to Skaket Road. Thatcher had noticed a positive change in his son, who seemed eager, all of a sudden, to take on adult responsibilities. He didn't know that *Thomas had something else entirely on his mind.*

Chapter Fifty-Five *"The New Old House"*

If only walls could talk, thought Mercy, as she wandered throughout the old house that was to be her new home, *what stories would they tell me?* The house that had been originally built by Constance and Nick Snow over two hundred years before, with rooms and lofts added on in subsequent years for their growing family, knew all the family secrets and scandals. If it had a voice, the house would be able to describe the bitter arguments between spouses, the parents' anguish over babies that died prematurely, the nights of passionate love-making that created those babies. This old house had seen many wars, had weathered many brutal winters and had baked in the relentless sun during endless droughts; it had a tale all its own.

There was much cleaning to be done. After Susannah's death, it had been the home of two young bachelors and her brothers-in-law were not overly concerned with dust on the floor or cobwebs clinging to the window sills. She decided to start on the downstairs, opening up all the windows to rid the rooms of the stagnant air of winter, stripping all the beds of their linens for a thorough washing in lye soap, wiping all the window glass, and taking a stiff broom to the floors. *Mercy had her work cut out for her.*

Susie had, just days before, been accepted at the women's college, and now she waited anxiously for the end of summer, while she helped her mother settle into the new "old" house on Skaket Road. The house beyond the dunes sold quickly; never before had Mercy seen that amount of money, but she placed it in an envelope and sent it off immediately for her daughter's tuition. Thatcher's doubts lingered; he still was not sure it was a good idea. Business continued to be slow at the mercantile; indeed, their livery business seemed to be their mainstay.

Thomas had taken a temporary job helping their cousin, Isaac Sparrow, plowing under more of his land and doing improvements on the Sparrow property. His dedication to responsibility that his father attributed to him, had another motive, however. From the field where he worked every day, he had a clear view of the Sparrow house and could easily watch the comings and goings. Every morning, Isaac Sparrow would emerge in his work clothes and make his way down the road to another field he was working on. Missus Sparrow never seemed to go anywhere, except, occasionally, onto the front porch, where she would sit with her needlework in a rocking chair. It was the fragile, young Emeline he looked for, however, the diminutive girl with the white-blond hair, who would come out to launder clothes in the back yard or beat the dust from rugs with a broom. With her hair tied up in a ribbon, and white apron covering her skirt, she would hang the clothes on the line and, when she had finished, she would shade her eyes and wave to Thomas in the field. *She seemed to know that he was always watching her.*

It was blazingly hot that day. The late summer sun burned though his cotton shirt as he followed along in the furrow behind his father's mule, steering the plough through the dry earth. *"Heyahh!"* he shouted to keep the animal moving, slapping the ends of the reins against the mule's rump. *"Get on there!"* The old mule was sweating as much as Thomas was and they were both eyeing the cool kettle pond just across the field. Finally, Thomas pulled in the reins, wiped the sweat from his brow and unhitched the mule. "You and I need a drink," he told the animal and led him down the road toward the water's edge, where they both waded in, knee-deep. While the mule sucked in a long drink of water, Thomas cupped his hands and splashed water over his head and then drank also.

"It is *devilishly* hot today, isn't it, Tom?"

Thomas spun around and saw Emeline Sparrow standing on the shore with a bucket in her hands. "Here," he said, "Let me help you with that."

He left the mule and quickly retrieved the bucket from her hands. After he had filled it, he offered to carry it back to the house for her.

"Thank you, Tom," she replied. "But, I can manage. You have more important work to do than carry my water for me."

Thomas stared at her, now with the rare opportunity to be so close to her. Her blond hair had turned almost white from days of doing laundry in the sun; her cheeks were the only part of her that had color. She was like a porcelain doll, pale and lovely and delicate.

"You have no business toting heavy buckets," he told her gallantly. "What would your father think of me if I stood by and watched you labor?"

She smiled at him. "My father has no qualms about my working. Especially since my mother has been ill."

"How is she?" asked Thomas. "I see her come out on the porch once in a while. Is she feeling a bit better?"

Emeline shook her head. "No," she replied. "She is very weak. Just walking out to the porch wears the poor dear out."

Thomas set the bucket down next to her laundry tub in the shade of the house.

"Thank you," she said. She reached for the bucket and Thomas noticed her hands, so tiny and white.

"You just wave to me in the field whenever you need me to tote another bucket of water for you," he said and went back to retrieve the mule.

When he returned home that night, after he had bedded the mule down in the livery behind the mercantile, he thought about her again over supper. While the conversation at the table droned on about Susie's departure for college, Thomas was staring at his food absent-mindedly.

"Isn't that right, Thomas?" his father was saying.

Thomas blinked. "I'm sorry, Pa," he said. "I wasn't really listening."

"I was saying that your work at Sparrow's is almost finished," said Thatcher, "so you will be able to accompany your sister to her new school."

"Yes, Pa," said Thomas. "I should be finishing up by tomorrow. Only two more rows and I'll be done."

"That's good," said Thatcher. "I hate to close the mercantile. We can't afford to lose any business."

Thomas had mixed feelings about his sister going off to school. It seemed *frivolous* to him, like she was taking a holiday while the rest of the family labored to put a few more pennies into the family money jar. And, he wasn't excited about taking the journey with her. He would miss being away from Emeline. "I don't see what all the fuss is about," he said. "What's so important about *school* anyway? What do you intend to learn, Susie?"

Susie's eyes widened and she gazed at him condescendingly. "There is more to life than *mules and horses*, Brother, dear," she said. "I intend to learn everything I can about the world."

"And, come home and do *what*, exactly?" said Thomas. "Teach your *dolls* to read and write?"

Thomas laughed and Mercy admonished him. "Thomas Snow! Don't speak like that to your sister!" she said sharply. "Perhaps, she will teach school herself when she has graduated."

"*A woman school teacher?*" Thomas mocked her. "*That* I shall have to see!"

"All right, all right," said Thatcher. "*That's enough* between you two. Who will you have to argue with when you are separated for nine whole months, I wonder!"

Thatcher had his own doubts about spending so much money for this faraway school and he wondered, too, just how much *value* there was to Susie's education. The Snow women had managed to raise families for centuries without the benefit of book learning. *Why was anything different now?*

Chapter Fifty-Six *"Isaac"*

They were gone for several days but it seemed like an *eternity* to Thomas, who thought of Emeline and nothing else for the entire journey. There was little conversation between them; both Susie and Thomas were lost in completely separate worlds of thought. Before he left his sister on the front steps of the school, kissing her awkwardly on the cheek, he had helped her get her bags down the long hall to the dormitory, not realizing how much he would miss her. Lingering just long enough to not appear rude, he made a weak excuse about his work that was waiting for him at home and high-tailed it back to Orleans.

When he arrived, Thatcher was unloading crates on the loading dock. He smiled; he was glad to have his son back. "How was the trip?" he asked Thomas.

"Long," said Thomas flatly, weary from his one hundred and eighty-six mile ride.

"What was the school like?" asked Thatcher. "Did Susie seem pleased? Was it like the school in Orleans?"

Thomas laughed. "No, Pa," he said. "It is nothing like the Orleans schoolhouse. It was enormous! Four stories high of red brick! And, iron gates. It looked like a big castle!"

Thatcher thought about the three sisters' lighthouses. "Well," he replied, "Let's hope they didn't use *sand* for the mortar!"

After Thomas had unhitched the mules and put them away, he joined his father on the dock. "Has Mister Sparrow been asking for me?" he asked eagerly. "Does he have any more work for me?"

"I haven't seen him since you left," said Thatcher. "But, his daughter came in yesterday. Buying medicine, she was, for that mother of hers."

"Missus Sparrow doesn't look at all well, Pa," said Thomas. "She doesn't even leave the house most days."

Thomas went to the stable and began mucking the stalls that had not been touched since he had been gone, but his mind was wandering. He just couldn't take his mind off Emeline and when he would see her again.

"Did you do a good job for him?" asked Mercy at supper that night, sensing her son's disappointment at not hearing from Isaac Sparrow. "You didn't take shortcuts, did you?"

"No, Mother," he replied. "I ploughed him a fine field. I know that he has more land to clear. I hope he will hire me to do that too."

"Well," said Mercy, "Maybe you should pay him a visit. Maybe he doesn't know you have returned. It couldn't hurt."

Thomas followed her suggestion the very next day. After his morning chores, he walked down Skaket Road toward the kettle ponds again and found Isaac Sparrow in the fields. "Hello, Mister Sparrow," he called. "I just thought I would let you know I am back from taking my sister off to school. I will be available if you need me again."

Sparrow's face was hard. He barely glanced at Thomas and continued his work clearing away a stubborn stump from the field. His demeanor was so peculiar, Thomas wondered what he had done to displease him. Surely, he couldn't be dissatisfied with his work! He looked beyond the Sparrow house at the brown, even rows he had turned under.

"I can handle the rest of it myself," said Sparrow. "Can't afford to pay anyone else now."

Thomas lingered for a moment. "Is everything all right, Mister Sparrow?" he asked. "Has your wife's illness gotten worse?"

Sparrow glared at Thomas. "My wife is of no concern of yours, Boy!" he spat. "Nor my daughter neither! Now, off with you! I have work to do."

Thomas was shocked and surprised at the contempt in the man's voice. He *had* somehow offended the man but he couldn't imagine why. He turned and retreated down the road, the disappointment showing in his slumped shoulders. Thatcher noticed the look on his son's face when he walked into the mercantile.

"I don't know what I could have possibly done to *displease* him, Pa," said Thomas. "I did my very best work, *honestly* I did! I even helped tote water for Emeline to do her laundry."

Thatcher scratched his chin in thought. "H'mmm," he said. "Perhaps, I will pay him a visit this afternoon. He is our cousin, after all. If he is going through a tough time, maybe I can help."

Thatcher headed out to the Sparrow farm after he had closed the mercantile for the day. The place was looking fine, he thought to himself, noticing the fields Thomas had ploughed. Surely, the man couldn't be displeased with his son's work! Young Emeline answered his knock on the door, and showed him into the house, where Isaac was just finishing his supper.

"Hello, Isaac," said Thatcher. "I thought I would check in with you and make sure my son did a satisfactory job for you."

Thatcher watched Emeline as she carried a tray of food into an adjoining bedroom. "Is your wife terribly ill?" he asked.

"She's *dying*," said Sparrow bluntly. "Can't do nothin' else for her. Emeline just tries to ease her pain."

"How long has she been like this?" asked Thatcher.

"A year or so," was Isaac's reply. "Doctor says it's something in her blood. He says it's just a matter of time."

"I'm sorry, Isaac," Thatcher said. "Is there anything we can do? Perhaps Mercy can come and give Emeline a break for a spell. Young'uns need to get out of the house every now and then."

"Emeline is perfectly content taking care of her mother," said Isaac. "No need to trouble your missus."

"It's no trouble, Isaac," said Thatcher. "We are *family* after all! That's what families are for!"

"No," said Isaac. "Thank you, Thatcher, but *no.*"

Chapter Fifty-Seven *"An Offer of Help"*

Thomas was beside himself; he was still confused by Mister Sparrow's sudden coldness.

"Some people are just that way, Thomas," Thatcher told him. "He didn't want any help tending to his wife either. I told him your mother would be happy to come and spell Emeline for a while."

"There is something else," said Thomas. "His wife has been sick for a long time and he has acted fine. I just know there is something more to it, Pa."

"Well, we just have to give the man his privacy," said Thatcher. "Another job will come along."

But, Thomas was determined to get to the bottom of it. He was desperate to see Emeline again. The next day, after he had finished his chores around the stable, he walked down the road toward the Sparrow farm, with a shovel over his shoulder. When he arrived at the lower field, where Mister Sparrow had been working clearing stumps, he began to finish the job, taking on every stump he could find, piling up stones off to one side and making a way for the mule and plough to pass through. After an hour had passed, he heard someone walking toward him and looked up to see Mister Sparrow approaching with a frown on his face.

"I told your Pa I didn't need your help anymore, Thomas," he said angrily. "If you must know, I can't afford to *pay* you. The medicines for my wife are costing me a pretty penny right now. I just don't have any extra to pay for help."

Thomas stopped his work momentarily and smiled. "You don't owe me anything, Mister Sparrow," he said. "I just want to help out. Look, we can have this field ready for the plough in no time!"

Sparrow shook his head. "I can't expect you to work for *nothin'*" he said. "No, this just isn't right."

Thomas put his shovel into the dirt again and continued working. "You need help, Sir," he said. "I don't expect any pay."

From the front porch, Thomas could see Emeline had come outside and was watching them. He raised his hand to wave at her, but she quickly went back inside. Isaac's eyes followed Thomas' gaze. "You must go on home now, Boy," he said. "I appreciate the thought, but you must go on home."

He turned and made his way back to the house, with his head hung low. Thomas was confused and disappointed. He had tried to do something *nice* for the man. Was Isaac Sparrow such a proud man he would not accept help? He couldn't help wondering if he had done something wrong, something to upset him. He gave up and returned home.

"That was thoughtful of you, Son" Mercy told him. "Some people are very peculiar when it comes to accepting help. Try not to worry about it. I am sure it is nothing that you did wrong."

"I'm not so sure, Mother," he said. "He just seems so angry all of a sudden! And, Emeline didn't even wave to me today like she usually does! I *know* I haven't done anything to offend *her*! I don't know what's come over the entire family!"

"Her mother is dying," said Mercy. "That must be very hard for her. Give them time. They are going through a difficult time right now."

"Do you have a special interest in the girl?" Thatcher asked. "Is *that* what this is all about?"

Thomas blushed and he averted his eyes from his father's stare. "I like her a lot, Pa," he said.

Thatcher and Mercy exchanged glances.

"Maybe, that is why Isaac is acting so strangely," Thatcher said. "Maybe, he thinks you are getting too familiar with Emeline!"

"All I did was carry a bucket of water for her," said Thomas. "That's all."

Thatcher recognized the look in his son's eyes. He once had that look when he spoke about Mercy. "Well, like your mother says, give them time," he said. *"Time will tell."*

Chapter Fifty-Eight *"The Subject of Pride"*

But, Thomas could not help himself. He couldn't stay away from the Sparrow farm. Every day when he had finished his work at the mercantile, he would take his fishing pole out to the kettle ponds and sit on the shore at the spot where Emeline usually fetched water. But, day after day, he was disappointed. Emeline had either come and gone before he arrived or she was avoiding him. He was desperate to know *why*. After a frustrating week, he decided to take his catch of fish and offer it to the Sparrow family.

Emeline answered the door and Thomas was suddenly tongue-tied, standing there, smiling sheepishly, with a smelly, dripping string of fish in his hands. "I caught these today," he said. "I thought your mother might like some fresh fish for supper."

Emeline peered out over Thomas' shoulder toward the field where her father was usually working. "Thank you, Tom," she whispered. "But, you must go now."

She started to close the door but Thomas stuck his foot out and stopped her. "Emeline!" he said. "What is wrong? What have I done to make you and your father so angry with me?"

Emeline's eyes softened. "Oh, Tom," she said. "It is nothing that you have done. It is my father. He is so worried about my mother. I don't know what he will do when the time comes to bury her."

"But, all I want to do is *help* him," replied Thomas. "He won't even let me help him with the stumps in the field and everyone knows that is a two-man job! Can't you talk to him?" He swallowed hard. *"I miss seeing you every day."*

Emeline reached out her hand and touched his. "I have missed you too," she whispered. "But, my father is not in the best frame of mind right now. Something is bothering him. Maybe it would be best if you stayed away. Just for a while."

Thomas nodded. "I will do what you think best, Emeline," he said. "I don't want to anger your father."

"He will enjoy the fish tonight," she said, pushing him gently away from the door. "Let's start with that. Give him some time, Tom. *You must give him some time."*

That night supper in the Snow house was subdued. Thomas played with his food for so long it was cold, before Mercy finally put an end to the uncomfortable silence. "I wonder what Susie is doing right now," she said. "It is so quiet around here without her."

Thatcher stared across the table at his son. "Is Isaac still acting strangely?" he asked. "I see you go out to the kettle ponds every afternoon. You aren't annoying him, are you, Son?"

Thomas shook his head. "No, Pa. I offered them my catch today. Emeline says he just needs time."

"It must be horrible to sit and wait for someone to die," Mercy said. "I can't imagine how the poor man faces every day."

"It's not right to keep that girl a prisoner, though," said Thatcher. "He doesn't even bring her to the mercantile lately. Comes by himself, he does, and only buys a few pennies worth. Either they have a lot packed away in their larder or they are not eating much."

Thomas thought about it. Emeline *did* look a little paler and thinner that day than he remembered her. "You mean they're *starving*?" he asked in horror.

"Pride is a funny thing, Son," said Thatcher. "I can't imagine he would make his family go without food. Still, I'm glad you gave them your fish. Did he say anything?"

"He wasn't there, Pa," replied Thomas. "I gave them to Emeline. She seemed pleased with them."

When it came time to retire, Mercy closed the door to their bedroom, while Thatcher sat on the bed pulling off his boots. She went to the window as she did every night, looking up at the stars. "I can smell the salt spray roses on the breeze tonight," she said, breathing in the aroma of the flowers that bloomed wild in the marshes. "I think I miss that even more than I miss the sound of the surf."

"Are you *truly* happy here, Mercy?" Thatcher asked. "Do you miss the old house beyond the dunes?"

She smiled. "I am happy wherever *you* are, Thatcher," she said. "You know that."

"You looked a little sad at supper," he said, climbing into bed and propping himself up on one elbow. "What is troubling you?"

Mercy came away from the window and sat down beside him. "Our son is in love," she said simply.

"Aye," Thatcher replied. "I do believe he is, at that."

"You don't think…" she began and stopped abruptly.

"What?"

"You don't think Isaac disapproves of our son because of my *heritage*, do you?"

Thatcher reached out and pulled Mercy to him, holding her in his arms. "You must remember that he did not report us when he could have easily taken you away from me," he said. "He knew all along who you were."

Mercy nodded. "Well," she said. "That may be true. Turning a blind eye to our little secret is a bit different than the prospect of his own daughter marrying our son. Perhaps, his *good will* only goes so deep."

Thatcher hadn't thought of that. Sparrow had seemed to take the subject of intermarriage with the Wampanoag lightly in the beginning. *Was Thomas bringing the subject a little too close for comfort?*

"I am going to pay Missus Sparrow a visit," said Mercy. "Maybe she will confide in me."

She blew out the lamp beside the bed and sank down into Thatcher's arms.

Chapter Fifty-Nine *"A Mission of Mercy"*

She packed a basket full of food the next day, wrapping up the still-warm Indian frybread and some jars of berry jam and string beans she had put up the previous spring. She had made a dream catcher for Missus Sparrow too, hoping it would ease her pain. As Mercy set out down Skaket Road with the basket swinging from her arm, the summer sun was warm on her back. She could see the Atlantic in the distance, blue and shimmering, and her heart was full of peace.

Isaac was already working in the field. He spotted her walking up the road and she waved at him, only to see him turn quickly back to his labors. Undaunted, she hastened up the road toward the house and knocked on the door.

"Hello, Missus Snow," Emeline said.

"Good morning, Emeline," Mercy replied, walking confidently past her. "I brought your mother some fresh frybread and a few other things. I know how difficult it must be to leave her to go to town for supplies."

Emeline's eyes watched the door warily, expecting her father to come in at any moment. "That was very kind of you, Missus Snow," she said politely. "Mother is asleep, but I am sure she will enjoy it."

There was a moaning sound from the bedroom. "Emmy?" said a tiny voice. "Do we have guests?"

"Yes, Mother," Emeline replied. "Missus Snow brought you a basket of delightful food."

There was a pause. Then, the tiny voice spoke again. "Please, bring her in, Emmy."

Emeline led the way into the bedroom and Mercy followed.

"Hello, Missus Sparrow," she said. "I am so sorry to hear that you are ill. I have brought you something I hope will peak your appetite."

The woman was the most delicate thing Mercy had ever seen; like a ghost of a ghost, she was lying there in the little room, with a wisp of white hair spread out over her pillow that made her look far older than her forty years. Her hands were not yet wrinkled, but the transparency of her skin showed every vein; her arms were so thin it hung from her bones like moss from the limbs of trees. She looked up at Mercy and tried to smile through her pale lips.

"I hope you will enjoy the food," said Mercy. "I was sorry you could not join our family for supper awhile back. It is nice to find long lost family!"

"Aye," said the woman. "Your husband and I share a pair of grandparents, I understand."

Mercy pulled the dream catcher out of the basket. "If my son has his way, we may share *grandchildren* one day," said Mercy, giving a wink to Emeline.

There was an uncomfortable pause.

"I was brought up in the *Wampanoag* tribe," Mercy said. "I have brought you this to hang on your wall. It will bring you peace and help you sleep."

The woman closed her eyes, obviously tired from the slightest conversation, as Emeline found a place on the wall above the bed on which to hang Mercy's gift. For a fleeting moment, Mercy remembered the dream catcher that hung over her own bed, the one she had given to Thatcher's father just before he died. *Had it been a curse?* It gave her pause to think. *No,* she told herself. *Peace. It brings peace.*

"It was good of you to come visit me," the woman said. "I hope you will come again."

It was her cue to exit; Mercy could sense that the woman tired very quickly and wanted to rest so she made her way to the front door with Emeline following close behind. "Whatever your mother needs, Emeline," she whispered. "You let us know."

"My father doesn't take kindly to charity," Emeline said, shaking her head. "But, I appreciate what you have done for my mother. And, tell Thomas that we really enjoyed the fish last night. It was delicious."

"My son is very fond of you, Emeline," Mercy replied. "He has been so worried that he has done something to anger your father."

"No," said Emeline, with a sad sigh. "With my mother so ill for so long, I think Father worries about losing us *both*."

"Try to convince him that he is not all alone,Child," said Mercy. "He has *kin* who care about him and you and your mother. We are here if you need us."

She put her arms around the girl then, holding her as tightly as she had held Susie on the day she had gone off to school. Perhaps, she thought, she needed *them* as much as they needed *her*.

Chapter Sixty *"Love in a Kettle"*

"I think it is time for us to leave that poor family alone." Thatcher noticed the disappointed expression on his son's face across the supper table. "Thomas," he said, "You have tried. Your mother and I have tried. The man wants to be left alone and we have to honor that."

"But, *Pa*," Thomas protested. "I don't think they have enough food to get through the winter. Missus Sparrow is *dying*. He doesn't have the right to make them suffer when we want to help."

Thatcher raised his tankard and emptied the last of his ale; his gullet bobbed up and down as he drank. "Isaac Sparrow is the head of his family," he said. "Just as I am the head of mine. I want you to stay away from that girl. We don't need any more trouble."

The chair scraped loudly across the floor as he left the table. Mercy cleared the dishes away and reached down to put a gentle hand on Thomas's shoulder. "Give it time, son," she whispered. "If you love this girl, it will last. I loved your father for many years before we could be together. *Patience is a virtue*; try to remember that."

But, after darkness had fallen, and Thomas tossed and turned in his bed, unable to sleep, he dressed silently and slipped outside. Thatcher and Mercy heard his footsteps.

"Maybe, he is like his mother," she said. "He likes his *midnight walks*."

"He won't stay away from her, I am afraid," said Thatcher.

Mercy smiled in the darkness of their room. "Love doesn't just *stop*, Thatcher," she said. "Even if you *want* it to."

"I'm afraid our boy will have to answer to Isaac's musket if he doesn't take care."

"Emeline is of marriageable age," Mercy replied. "She could leave if she wanted to. But, I don't think she will leave her mother."

Outside, Thomas followed the road down to the kettle ponds. The air was warm and thick; the dragonflies whirred and the bullfrogs croaked along the shoreline. When he came to his fishing spot, he sat down on the grass a few feet from the water's edge. He removed his shoes and stretched out his legs, letting the water lap against his bare feet. Set against the backdrop of the night sky, he could see the Sparrow house in the distance and the light that flickered in the windows; she was so close and yet so far away. *Was his father right? Did he need to walk away and leave Emeline alone?*

Stupid old man, he thought about Isaac Sparrow. Maybe, it wasn't sickness at all that was killing his wife; maybe she was just *starving* to death. Thomas was angry. He was jealous that another man *controlled* the girl he loved. Suddenly needing to clear his head, he pulled off his shirt and trousers, leaving them lying on the beach, and dove into the water, swimming with long strokes until he finally reached the middle of the pond. In what, centuries before, had once been a glacier of ice, he rolled over in the melted water that remained and floated on his back, looking up at the clear sky. The water was cold and invigorating on his skin; he could feel his scalp tingle like the pricks of a thousand needles. He closed his eyes and let his body relax, his arms outspread on the surface of the water that was as calm as a pane of window glass. A few feet away from him, a fish broke the calm, jumping at a bug, and the water began to ripple around him. He dove down into the black depths and surfaced again when he could no longer hold his breath; he rolled over and began to swim back toward the shore. Then, out of the corner of his eye, he noticed a shape moving toward him in the moonlight.

Emeline! Was he dreaming? He could not make out her face, only the faint outline of her head above the water. "How did you know I was here?" he asked when she swam nearer and he could see that she was no dream.

"I watch for you every day," she said. "And, I often come here at night and think about you."

He reached for her and she moved toward him silently; her tiny naked body came between him and the cool water, clinging like a vine around him. Without words, his lips sought hers and found them, eager and willing. The feel of her skin against his, the taste of her mouth was so new and intoxicating, he thought his heart would burst from his chest. Around and around they spun, reaching, searching, responding to each other beyond their wildest imaginations. *Thomas knew he could never give her up now.*

"I want to marry you," he whispered hoarsely, pulling his mouth away from her face and burying it in the fold of her neck, nibbling on the lobe of her ear. He wanted to *consume* her, to absorb her very being into him, to touch every inch of her and linger there. Her only answer was a murmur of contentment. For an hour, they languished in each other's arms, floating, kissing, caressing in the cool water.

When they finally swam back and dressed together on the beach, it was without modesty or shame; they felt *right* together, as if they were pieces of a puzzle that was now complete. As she ran her fingers through her damp hair and pulled her nightgown back over her head, she finally spoke. "Father will be angry," she said. "But, if I can convince him that he isn't losing a *daughter*, but gaining a *son*, perhaps he will listen."

"I will speak to him tomorrow," said Thomas, pulling her close to him one more time. "I will never let you go!"

He watched her disappear into the darkness and he began his walk back up Skaket Road, deep in thought.

With his head finally clearing from the haze of their lovemaking, his future was suddenly clear to him; he would not take *no* as an answer from Isaac Sparrow! When he reached the front porch of the house, he found his mother sitting on the step in her robe and he sat down beside her. Mercy reached out and touched his damp hair. "A midnight swim?" she asked, not seeing his blush in the darkness.

"Mother, I am going to marry Emeline," he said. "I am going to speak to her father tomorrow."

Mercy was remembering the night that she had spent with Thatcher, watching the sun rise. She knew how her son was feeling and she didn't want to take it away from him. "You must tell him how much you love her," she said. "He has grown cold but once there must have been passion in him. You must revive his memory."

"I don't know that I can change his way of thinking," said Thomas. "But, I am going to marry her no matter what he says!"

"I am happy for you, Son," said Mercy. "And, for Emeline."

Chapter Sixty-One *"A Changed Man"*

Thomas awoke on the morning following his night of love in the kettle pond filled with a new purpose. He quickly finished his morning chores, feeding the horses and mules behind the mercantile and filling their troughs with water, before he set out once again on the road to the Sparrow house. When he spied Isaac in the field, he puffed out his chest and strode across the furrows bravely. "Mister Sparrow, Sir," he said. "I would like to have a word with you."

Isaac withdrew his shovel from beneath the root of a stubborn oak stump and turned toward Thomas.

"I have asked Emeline to marry me," said Thomas.

Isaac's eyes darkened but he did not speak.

"The way we see it," continued Thomas, borrowing Emeline's words. "Is that you won't be losing a daughter, you will be gaining a son who can help you with the work around this place. And, you won't have to pay me; *I will be part of the family.*"

Still, Isaac did not speak, but his eyes glazed over as if tears were hovering there, ready to fall.

"I love your daughter, Sir," said Thomas. "I want to take care of her. We are going to be married. I have no desire to take her away from you. If I have done something to displease you, won't you tell me so that I can apologize?"

Isaac put down his shovel. "I will come to speak to your parents, tonight," he said, turning away from Thomas, walking toward the Sparrow house.

Thomas hurried home and told Mercy what had transpired.

"Well," she said, "I guess we will know what his feelings are tonight, then. You have done all you can do, Son."

Thomas spent the afternoon nervously helping Thatcher around the store, unable to think of anything but the coming visit.

"Don't worry, Son," Thatcher tried to calm him. "You will soon know, one way or the other, and we will all breathe easier."

The anticipated knock on the door came just after supper. Isaac Sparrow entered the room, with Emeline following behind him in silence. She gave Thomas a half-smile and it was obvious she was nervous too, but, in her eyes, Thomas could see the light of love shining through. When they had all taken their seats around the table, Isaac was the first to speak. "I have something to say to all of you," he began in a raggedy voice. "Now that your son has taken a fancy to my Emeline, there are things that must be said."

Mercy held her breath. *Please don't call my boy a half-breed*, she thought to herself, worried that he was going to offend Thomas in a condescending way she knew only too well. Thatcher waited to hear what the man had to say, sure that it was manly pride that had changed Isaac's attitude toward Thomas. Thomas just wanted to bring an end to the suspense.

"I knew your father," he said directly at Thatcher. "And, I knew yours too, Missus Snow, from my days at Mashpee. They were both good, decent men."

"Mercy," she replied, *"Please, call me Mercy."*

Isaac took a deep breath. *He's going to say it*, thought Mercy; *he's going to call us Injuns or half-breeds and tell us to remember our place.* She looked across the table at her son, at his face that was so full of innocence and hope. She had never raised him as a *Wampanoag*. Since his birth, she had tried to protect him from the cruel truth.

"I was a different man, *then*, than I am today," Isaac went on. "What we did to your people, Missus.... *Mercy*, was a terrible thing. And, I was a part of it, just as sure as I am sitting here now. I have no excuses; couldn't use 'em if I had 'em, because there *was* no excuse for what we done."

"Isaac, all of that is behind us now," said Thatcher. "My wife and I know that none of it was your fault."

"You don't understand," replied Isaac. "I am truly ashamed of the way we treated your people. Of the way I...."

He looked as if he were going to burst into tears at any moment. It was Mercy's turn to say something, to ease the poor man's mind. "Isaac, you did my husband and I an invaluable service; you could have reported me for not following the others to Mashpee. Because of you, we were able to stay here in Orleans and raise our children here. Because of you, we were able to help my people survive the re-location."

Isaac stood up suddenly. His eyes darted around the room, as if seeking to find the courage to say what he had come to say somewhere in the walls around him. "If we are to join our families, there is something you need to know, somethin' I need to get off my chest," he said. "I don't want no *misunderstandings* if it comes up later."

Thatcher was growing exasperated by Isaac's procrastination. "If *what* comes up later, Isaac?" he asked. *"Get on with it, Man!"*

"I was the one who shot your brother, Mercy," he finally spit out the words. "I was responsible for his death. *And, for that, I am truly sorry."*

Chapter Sixty-Two *"Warriors and Peace-Makers"*

Mercy had gone out into the night, as was her way. Isaac and Emeline had left quietly, without words; *no more words needed to be said.* When Thatcher went to look for her, he found her on the path toward the dunes; he knew she would go toward the ocean to be alone.

"I need to see Grey Eyes," she mumbled when he tried to get her to come home. "I need to speak to him about this. I don't know how to *feel*, Thatcher."

All at once, she collapsed into her husband's arms, sobbing and clawing at his shirt.

"Shhhhhhhhh," Thatcher whispered against her wet cheek. "We will go to Mashpee, if that is what you want to do. Come home and get some sleep. I will harness the horses to the wagon at first light. Don't cry, Mercy. *Please, don't cry.*"

"No, Thatcher," she said adamantly. "I need to go *now. Tonight.*"

But, her tears still had not dried, even when they had pulled the wagon up behind the meetinghouse in Mashpee. They had travelled all night and the bright morning sun cast a harsh light on the bedraggled, weary pair when Reverend Amos came to the door to greet them. "He is here," said Amos, when they asked the whereabouts of Grey Eyes. "His health has been failing, but seeing you will cheer him I am sure."

Amos could see there was anguish in Mercy's eyes. "What troubles you, my child? Is there anything I can do?"

He escorted them into a little room at the back of the building; Thatcher recognized it as the same room where Samuel had died but, out of love, he spared Mercy that gruesome detail. They found Grey Eyes, sitting in a chair eating his breakfast and, after they had greeted each other, Thatcher withdrew from the room, to leave them alone. "She needs his counsel," he told the reverend. "Something happened last night that has her very distraught."

"No more death in your family, I hope," said Amos. "Your children, they are well?"

Thatcher nodded. "Yes," he said, "Our children are quite well. Our son, Thomas, has asked a girl to marry him. And, she and her father came to visit us."

"That sounds like *good* news," replied Amos. "Does your wife not approve of this girl? Is that why she is so upset? It must be something serious for you to travel all night to get here."

Thatcher's face was drawn. He rubbed his eyes from lack of sleep and sat down at a table near the door, as he explained about Isaac's heartbreaking confession.

Inside the room, Mercy had just finished telling Grey Eyes the very same story. She looked at his face, now wrinkled and aged by the years, and she saw the sparkle of wisdom in his mixed-blood eyes. *The same wisdom she had once seen in her father.*

"Tell me, Grey Eyes," she said pitifully. "What shall I do?"

Grey Eyes thought for a few moments, letting Mercy cry on his shoulder, before he spoke. "Your brother chose to live as a *warrior*," he said finally. "And, he chose to die a *warrior's* death. It was what he would have wanted, to die, feeling he was defending his people."

Mercy blinked as she tried to comprehend what Grey Eyes was saying. It was true that Samuel had lived his entire life fighting the white man's laws.

"*You* have chosen to be a *peacemaker*," he continued. "And, so it is *you* who must make *peace* with this man who has asked for your forgiveness."

"I don't know if I can do that," she replied. "I don't know if I *can* forgive him."

"You *must*, Mercy," Grey Eyes replied. "Hatred is not good for your spirit. And, your son *loves* this girl. You must do it for your *son and for yourself.*"

Yes, Mercy thought. *Thomas would be heartbroken if she forbade him to marry Emeline. He would never forgive her and she didn't think she could bear that.*

"You cannot put the sins of the father on this poor girl," said Grey Eyes. "She has no blame in it. *Peace* in your family is what is most important."

Mercy's mind ventured back to the day she had uttered almost the same sentiment to Samuel, when he wanted to blame all the whites for their mother's savage assault. The *logic* she understood. But, *forgiving Isaac*, now that he had confessed he had been the one who pulled the trigger, when he was the very *reason* Samuel was dead, would not be an easy task.

Grey Eyes began to moan softly in a voice barely above a whisper, calling on the gods. Mercy closed her eyes and her voice joined his. Outside the room, Thatcher could hear their chanting in Wampanoag, *soulful* words, the meaning of which he did not understand, but he knew, somehow, would comfort his wife. He looked across the table at the reverend and saw that old man's eyes were closed as well. It was an *Indian* thing; it was part of the mystery of the great *Wampanoag.*

When Mercy finally emerged from the room, an hour later, they walked with Reverend Amos down the hill to the little cemetery, to the graves of Uriah and Samuel, who now lay side by side, cradled in the arms of their Mother earth. As she knelt down at the foot of her brother's grave, she knew, instinctively, that Samuel was finally at peace. His heart was no longer in turmoil. There was no more war in his spirit. He had finally reconciled with their father.

It was good.

Chapter Sixty-Three *"Solomon's Prophesy"*

To everything there is a season and a time to every purpose under the heaven, King Solomon once said, *a time to be born and a time to die*. The next few years, in the Snow family of Orleans, would prove to be *their* season.

It had started out pleasant enough. The wedding, joining Thomas and Emeline, turned out to be a joyous event, despite the events of the previous week. Putting confessions and forgiveness behind them, the two families were able to move on from the past, for the sake of the two young people who were so much in love. Mercy had visited Isaac, upon her return from Mashpee, and told him they would not speak of it again. She prayed for many nights, giving her grief and anger up to the gods, cleansing her mind of the hate she *wanted* to feel toward Isaac, keeping the wisdom of Grey Eyes' foremost in her heart. She knew it would not be easy to forget what Isaac had done, but her love for her son triumphed over it. Susie came home for the occasion, and Mercy truly felt as if she had birthed another daughter in Emeline, as she watched her son place a ring on the girl's finger and made her his wife.

By the time fall had come to the cape, the three men, Thatcher, Isaac and Thomas, soon left their womenfolk to pick up their rifles, to hunt in the woods together. When Susie returned to school, Emeline filled the hollow void she left behind and kept Mercy company through the long weeks, when the temperatures around Orleans dropped lower and lower, when the days became shorter and the skies grayer and gloomier.

The wedding had come just in the nick of time, for exactly nine months later, a son was born whom they named Albert, after what had been a difficult pregnancy. Emeline, who had always been thin and frail like her mother, struggled to eat enough to nourish the child she was carrying, as she suffered through months of agonizing morning sickness. The town doctor told them she was anemic. *Give her red meat*, he said, *and fish, three times a day if you can.* But, poor Emeline, was unable to keep much of it down. After the baby was born, the nausea continued and, month after month she grew thinner and weaker.

"Her mother was just like this," Isaac told Thomas. "When she carried Emmy. She just never seemed to have the strength most women have."

Missus Sparrow, while still bed-ridden, was delighted in her new grandchild, however. Just having the baby in the house seemed to improve her mental condition, if not her physical health. Thomas had promptly moved out of the house on Skaket Road and in with the Sparrow family, helping with the household chores and the farming, so that Isaac could spend more time with his wife. The two families had finally blended into one and both households seemed to revolve around little Albert, the dark-haired infant who, without ever knowing it, kept both the Snows and the Sparrows from falling apart. While her mother lingered on, it wasn't long before Emeline became ill as well.

Thomas soon learned how to feed and diaper the baby, although his first attempts were quite clumsy and made Emeline laugh out loud. That was the *good* part, making her smile and laugh again. There were other times when she and Missus Sparrow slept throughout the day. Isaac tried his hand at cooking, but it was Mercy who stepped in and saved them.

"The name *Sparrow* certainly suits them," Mercy complained to Thatcher, after spending the previous day nursing the two sick women and helping with the baby. "They pick at their food just like *birds.* Emeline has no strength to fight whatever this illness is. I fear she will linger just like her mother does and never get any better."

 Thatcher was worried that his own wife might catch the illness too.

"You needn't worry about me, Thatcher," she told him. "I don't think what they have is contagious. Besides, you must remember that I have *Wampanoag* blood in my veins. My people don't die without putting up a fight!"

Her words had a bitter-sweetness to them and she tasted it as soon as she had uttered them, *remembering Samuel.*

"I am *more* worried about our boy," said Thatcher. "I don't think he is ready to raise a baby on his own."

Mercy smiled at that. "He has *me*," she said. "And, *you*. Try not to worry about it. It is time for our son to grow strong. Remember, *that which does not kill us makes us stronger.*"

Thatcher looked around the room that was so full of happy memories; so many generations of the Snows had come and gone through this very space. *Had been born, had lived, had married, had died.*

At that moment, the door flew open and Thomas was standing there, with tears streaming down his face. He was holding little Albert in his arms.

Mercy jumped up. "Thomas!" she said. "Here, bring that baby in out of the cold!"

She pulled Albert from her son's arms and cradled him in her own. "What has happened?" she asked him. "Have they gotten worse?"

"They're all down with the *fever* now," Thomas said wearily. "I'm not feeling so good myself."

"I'll put the baby to bed and then I will go tend to them," said Mercy.

"I heard the typhoid had returned to Wellfleet," Thatcher said. "I didn't know it had come this far. Mercy, I don't want you to go. You must think about your *own* health."

"You forget I nursed you and your brothers through it once," she replied. "I will be fine. *Someone* has to care for them!" She turned to Thomas. "You get into bed and let your father care for little Albert until I get back."

She put the baby down in the worn cradle that her own children had slept in and put on her shawl. "Don't you worry, Son," she said, with more conviction than she was feeling. "Everything will be all right."

Chapter Sixty-Four *"His Final Forgiveness"*

Isaac was screaming. When Mercy had arrived at the Sparrow house, all three family members had taken to their beds. She had expected the women, in their already-weakened state, to be the worst, but the typhoid had taken hold of Isaac quick and hard. The disease seemed much deadlier than she remembered; his fever raged hotter and more virulently. Isaac already had the tell-tale rose-colored spots all over his body and delirium had already set in. He was raving and thrashing about in his bed so violently, Mercy had a difficult time keeping him lying down. Mumbling incoherently over and over about *his work in the fields*, it took every ounce of strength she had to calm him.

When, finally, sleep overtook him, she left him to tend to Missus Sparrow and Emeline, only to find them sleeping peacefully.

"Where is my baby?" Emeline said, when she awoke and saw Mercy standing over her. "What has happened to Albert?"

"Albert is fine," Mercy assured her. "Thatcher is caring for him. We must get *you* well first."

"Tom is ill too, isn't he? And, Father?" Emeline asked.

Mercy nodded. "You just rest, Emeline," she said. "You need to *rest* to get well. I will care for your parents."

For a brief hour, somewhere in the middle of the night, all her *patients* were finally sleeping and Mercy sank down in a chair near the fire that had long since gone out. The air was so cold in the house her body was trembling. *There was no time for rest*, she told herself; she needed to get the fire going again and quickly. She brought in wood from the kindling pile behind the house and, when she had coaxed the little flames to finally ignite into a real fire, she sat down again, soon drifting off into sleep herself.

Just before dawn, Mercy awakened to the sound of Isaac coughing in the next room. She jumped up and went to him, trying to raise him up into a sitting position so he wouldn't choke. His body was so hot and dry it seemed as if it would burn clean through his nightshirt. When the coughing spell subsided, and he fell back against his pillow, he looked up at her in surprise. "Mercy?" he asked, staring through drooping eyelids. "Why are *you* here? Where is Thomas?"

"Shhhhhh," she said. "Thomas took the baby to my house. Thatcher is looking after them."

His eyes were clouded and he closed them as Mercy ran a wet rag over his forehead. *"You must rest,"* she said, for what seemed like the hundredth time.

He opened his eyes again slowly. "My wife? Emmy?"

"They are sleeping just in the next room," Mercy replied.

"It is too much to ask you to do this," he murmured; his voice was raspy and withered.

"We are *family*," said Mercy. "This is what *families* do."

Their eyes met and locked for an instant; both of them were thinking about Samuel. With a shaking hand, he reached out for her. *"Thank you,"* he whispered, *"for forgiving me."* Then, his mouth formed a weak smile and his eyes misted with tears, *just before his heart stopped beating.*

She stood up and lingered there beside the bed for a moment, searching for the words she would use to tell Missus Sparrow and Emeline that he was gone. Walking softly into the next room, where the sunlight was finally shining through the easterly windows, she put some water on the fire to boil. *Tea would be soothing,* she thought, both for herself and the women sleeping in the next room. She thought about Thatcher and Thomas and baby Albert, wondering if they needed her. But, *worrying* was a luxury she couldn't afford. The men in the Snow family were strong; *they would have to muddle through a few days without her.*

She sipped her tea in the silence of the house that was now a *tomb*. She knew she would have to send for someone to retrieve Isaac's body and she ventured out onto the porch, hoping to flag someone down on the road, but there was not a soul about. Little did she know, the typhoid was spreading and nearly every house in Orleans had been affected by it.

When an hour passed, she finally opened the door to the bedroom where Missus Sparrow and Emeline were sleeping. She pulled back the shutters on the window to let in what little warmth was offered by the winter sunshine, still wondering how she was going to tell them the sad news.

She needn't have worried. From the frozen expressions on their faces, one look was all it took for her to know that the typhoid had taken Missus Sparrow and Emeline too.

Mercy ran from the house and all the way down Skaket Road, not stopping until she reached the front door and Thatcher's waiting arms.

Chapter Sixty-Five *"Grey Eyes"*

Thirty-three miles away, in Mashpee, the typhoid had also paid a deadly visit, most likely hitch-hiking to town with travelling merchants and sailors from the ships docking in one of the nearby harbors. Over the years the ethnic balance of the once-Wampanoag village had changed drastically. Many of the Wampanoag men had taken sea-faring jobs to support their families; some never returned from the sea, and some succumbed to the typhoid, leaving their women and children behind to fend for themselves. The *good* news was that, despite many setbacks, the legislature in Boston was finally giving the people of Mashpee limited rights to represent themselves; ever since the wood-lot revolt, the governor had exercised more leniency in dealing with the Wampanoag people. In an effort to keep peace, he allowed them to go back to making their own local laws, as long as they did not conflict with state and federal laws, and gave them temporary ownership of the lands they occupied. The widows of the men who had died at sea held on to their land deeds tightly, seeing them as footholds in their quest to regain their autonomy.

Unfortunately, there were white men, with no scruples, who began to move in to Mashpee, wooing the land-owning widows into marriage and, thereby, gaining rights to the land, and, like locusts in a field of corn, they came to devour and consume. Once married, many of them treated the women no better than slaves in their own houses. Mercy was appalled at the metamorphosis that had taken place on their next visit to Grey Eyes and Reverend Amos. Mashpee had, once again, become an unhappy place for many.

They had weathered the winter and she had comforted Thomas over the loss of his young bride. Little Albert continued to be their bright spot, a welcome blessing in Mercy's world. With the spring, she had bundled the baby up and Thatcher had driven them over the rugged road to Mashpee. This time, she insisted Thomas come along with them. She wanted him to know something of his heritage. She wanted him to meet his people before they were all gone. "Mashpee hardly looks like the same place," she said to Grey Eyes, as they entered his little room behind the meeting house. "Who are all these *new* people?"

The once robust Wampanoag was growing even more frail and thin than before, and his hair had turned the color of snow. His hands were now marbled with blue veins and crisscrossed with lines; his handshake was weak. "We have many more widows now," he said. "The numbers of Wampanoag men are becoming fewer every year. Our blood is growing weak."

"Blood is just blood," Mercy said, smiling. She looked at Thatcher, who was sitting beside her. "As long as we *remember* our heritage and honor it, it doesn't matter if our children have blue eyes or brown. *Surviving* is the most important thing."

Grey Eyes nodded his head. "Yes," he replied weakly. "I suppose that is true for those like *you*, Mercy, who have married for love. I fear many of these outsiders do not do the same. *They marry our women for their land.* Many of them are suffering in these marriages. It is a sorry sight to see."

"Well, why don't they *do* something about it?" Mercy asked. "Why don't they stand up for themselves?"

Grey Eyes smiled, remembering Mercy as a little girl again, the free-spirited, fearless daughter of his good friend, Uriah and the great granddaughter of the great sachem.

"They are doing what they feel they need to do to survive," he said. "All Wampanoag women are not as strong as you are, Mercy."

Mercy unwrapped the bundle in her arms and little Albert was introduced to Grey Eyes for the first time. When he heard the news of the typhoid in Orleans, he was saddened. "It certainly took its toll here," he said. "I am glad you came through it, Thomas. I am sorry that you lost your wife."

"Thank you," Thomas mumbled.

"Thomas will be fine," said Mercy, casting a sad smile at her son. "Once his heart has healed. It was quite a shock to lose Emeline so soon. They were very much in love."

"And, how is the mercantile business?" asked Grey Eyes, turning toward Thatcher. "Doing well, I hope."

Thatcher shook his head. "Not so much," he admitted. "Sales dropped so drastically I had to finally close the doors. Thomas and I kept the livery. Renting out horses and mules is much more profitable than selling dry goods and groceries. We have purchased more mules and have a steady line of customers when ploughing time comes. It may not make us rich but it will sustain us."

"And, your daughter?" asked Grey Eyes. "Is she married now too?"

He could see the longing in Mercy's eyes when he spoke of her daughter. "No. She has finished her college and has taken a teaching job," she replied.

"In Orleans?" the old Indian asked. "No," said Mercy with a deep sigh. "In Boston. We don't see very much of her these days."

It was not Mercy's favorite subject; she missed her daughter greatly.

They visited for over an hour and then said their goodbyes so that Grey Eyes could rest. Mercy lingered at his bedside. After the others had left the room, he reached for her hand. The invisible bond between them pulsated in their clasped palms. "I fear I may not see you again, Child," he whispered. "The time is near for me to meet the gods. They are calling me. I can feel it in my bones."

Mercy leaned over and kissed the old man's forehead. She understood. *It was his time.* "You have been a good friend," she said. "I will never forget you."

A week later Grey Eyes was dead.

Chapter Sixty-Six *"The Boy"*

He quickly outshined all the stars in Mercy's heavens.
From the moment he came into her world, little Albert
became the center of her life, her reason for living.
Everywhere she went, she carried him on her hip; she
didn't sleep, she didn't eat, she didn't do anything at all
until she had first tended to *the boy.*

"It is a good thing I am not a jealous man," Thatcher said
to her, one night as they prepared to go to bed. "I do
think your heart belongs to another."

He said it in jest. He enjoyed seeing the loving way his
wife had taken on her grandchild and, with the exception
of nursing him at her own breast, she became the only
mother the child would ever know. The child seemed to
be thriving on goat milk and his grandmother's love; his
tiny cheeks were soon robust and rosy, his little belly was
plump and supple, with no trace of the Sparrow paleness.
She sang to him in Wampanoag and, when he grew older,
told him bedtime stories she remembered from her
childhood in the Indian camp.

The boy began to talk very early, before he was even a
year old, probably because Mercy constantly carried on
conversations with him. While Thomas and Thatcher
were busy running the livery, she would often visit them,
giving the boy his first exposure to horses and mules,
setting the stage for his future life. He seemed drawn to

the animals. Mercy became obsessed with caring for him, even more than she had with her own children.

But, it is not in a man's nature to be second in the heart of his wife for very long. Even when the boy had begun to sleep through the night, Thatcher would hear his wife rise from their bed and take her post, in the rocking chair by the fire, just in case Albert cried out for her. Sometimes, he would find her there, asleep in her chair, covered with a quilt, the ever-vigil *mother-bird* listening for the call of her *adopted chick.*

As he grew older, Albert's sweet baby nature began to change, *toward everyone except Mercy.* She noticed the difference too; he reminded her very much of her older brother, Samuel. Strong, stubborn and fierce. He had become almost defiant toward his own father and grandfather, fearing no repercussions, knowing his doting grandmother would always cloak him in the folds of her skirt and shield him from punishment. It wasn't long before Thatcher had words with his wife about the situation. "You are *spoiling* the boy," he warned her, waiting until little Albert had finally fallen asleep in the next room, where she could hear him easily if he woke in the night. "He has no respect for Thomas. The only one he will listen to is *you*, Mercy."

Mercy immediately dismissed her husband's concern. "He is growing up, that's all," she whispered. "He is testing his wings."

Thatcher was growing impatient at his wife's refusal to admit the boy was out of control. "Well, he had better test them somewhere else," he snapped. "Or else he will feel the sting of a buggy whip on his backside!"

"Don't you dare touch my boy, Thatcher Snow!" said Mercy, surprising even herself with the curt tone of her voice. She looked toward the door, worried she might have awakened Albert.

Thatcher stared at her in a state of disbelief. Who was this woman who now ranted and raved in front of him? Where was his loving wife, who had once clung to him in the night but who, now, only waited in the darkness with her ears listening for little Albert to cry out? She had not been nearly as protective of Susie and Thomas when they had been growing up. He was becoming disgusted with himself; what kind of man would let a woman, let alone a small child, trample on his status as head of his own household? He would *not* stand for it! "Mercy," he said firmly, "Albert is *not* your boy. *Thomas* is his father. You are *only* his grandmother."

"Only his grandmother?" she spat the words out at him like a cheek-full of bitter tobacco. "I have raised that boy almost since birth! I am the only mother he will ever know!"

Thatcher turned away from her; he had escape his wife's wrath. Too much had been said already. "And, what if

Thomas decides to marry again?" he asked. "Have you considered that?"

She *hadn't*. And, she *wouldn't*. Thomas was still a child himself who knew *nothing* of child-rearing. She was sure she knew what was best for the boy. She put out the light and climbed into their bed, as far away from Thatcher as she could without falling out on the floor.

There followed a week-long silence between Mercy and Thatcher. While his father stayed late at the livery every night to avoid going home, Thomas grew concerned. He knew that his son was the cause of the friction between his parents. "Maybe, I should move away," he told his father, as they fed the horses one evening. "And, take Albert with me. Perhaps that would be best. Then, you and Mother will start speaking to each other again."

Thatcher refused to believe they had to break up the family to have peace. "That is not the answer, Thomas," he replied. "Your mother and I will get over this. We have been through worse."

"I haven't been much of a father to him," said Thomas. "I will admit I didn't know exactly what to do after Emeline died. It was just easier to let Mother take over."

"I think it is time the boy got to know his *father*," said Thatcher. "You need to get him out of the house more often. Teach him to ride. We'll take him hunting in the woods. We'll turn him into a man."

Chapter Sixty-Seven *"And, Then There Were Three"*

By the time Mercy had forgiven Thatcher, for her heart would not allow her to stay angry at him for long, she had agreed to start correcting young Albert's bad behavior and Thatcher hoped their life would get back to normal again. Once again, the Snow household was peaceful. While Mercy still spent her evenings by the fire, reading to her grandson, she allowed him to accompany Thomas and Thatcher to the livery in the daytime. At first, it was difficult to draw him away from the grandmother who had become his rock, but Thatcher knew the boy had to one day become a man in a man's world. And, he had the perfect solution waiting for Albert in a stall in the livery on a clear, bright morning in May, just after school had let out for the summer.

"We have a surprise for you, Albert," Thomas told his son at breakfast. "Hurry and eat. It's waiting for you at the livery."

The boy ran all the way down Skaket Road to town, with Thomas and Thatcher following behind with happy smiles on their faces. When Albert entered the stable, not knowing what to expect, he eagerly searched among the bales of straw and bags of grain. "Where is my surprise?" he asked Thomas.

At that point, Thatcher opened one of the stall doors. "It's in here, Albert," he said. "Come see."

In the stall, sleeping in the straw beside his mother, was a newborn foal, a tiny thing with a fuzzy red coat and long legs that were folded up underneath him. Thatcher took hold of the mare's halter as Albert knelt down beside the new baby, delivered only hours before.

"He's mine?" asked Albert. His eyes were popping with wonder. "Really, Father? He's *really* mine?"

"He is all yours, son," said Thomas. "Every boy needs his own horse."

"Why is he all wet?" asked Albert. "Has he been swimming?"

"He's still wet behind the ears," replied Thatcher, *"Just like you!"*

Albert reached and out and stroked the sleeping foal's head gently. Suddenly awakened, the little animal struggled to get to its feet, fearful of the boy's scent. The mare nickered softly and the foal ran clumsily behind its mother.

"It will take time for him to get to know you, Albert," said Thomas. "You must be patient with him."

"But, I want to *pet* him," said Albert. "Why is he so afraid of me?"

Thomas walked to the corner of the stall and sat down, motioning for the boy to join him. "Sit here with me," he said, "And, let the foal come to you, when he is ready."

They had sat there in the straw most of the morning, waiting for the timid newborn to overcome its fear of the strange two-legged creatures who had invaded his world. Gradually, they became friends, two youngsters in a strange new world. In the coming months, the boy would bolt down his breakfast and run for the stable every morning and rush home to supper every night, with stories to tell his grandmother.

Albert named him *Goblin*.

"Why *Goblin*?" his father asked him.

"Because he just appeared in the night!" was Albert's answer. "That's what goblins do!"

They let Albert halter the foal and lead him around the pen. They taught him the firm commands to use when training him. They showed him how to give rewards when the colt obeyed. Now, the boy who had once been unruly and undisciplined himself, was now teaching the same lessons to his horse. Over the next several months, the two bonded. And, still, every night young Albert would rush home to his grandmother, who was always waiting to hear of his daily adventures.

"He sure loves that colt," Mercy told Thatcher one night after she had cleared the supper dishes away. "I have never seen him quite so happy."

"He has turned out to be good boy," said Thatcher. "Even though his grandmother spoils him."

Mercy looked tired. The dark circles under her eyes told Thatcher she hadn't been sleeping.

"Are you all right?" he asked her. "Don't you feel well?"

He followed her into the bedroom and watched her as she readied herself for bed.

"I'm sorry I spoil him," she said somberly. "I want him to be a good boy and grow up to be a good man, like Thomas is becoming."

Thatcher put his arms around her. "I know you do," he said. "You've done a good job with Albert."

"It's sometimes hard for a mother to let go," Mercy replied. "I miss Susie so much."

"You should be very proud of our children," he said. "It was because of *you* that they are so strong and independent. I had very little to do with it."

"That's not true, Thatcher!" said Mercy. "You have been a good father and a good husband."

"I never had *your* special gifts," he answered her. "It was from *you*, they learned about the stars in the sky, about the *Wampanoag* traditions; because of you our children see beauty in everything around them."

She fell asleep in Thatcher's arms that night and she had a dream. In the dream, she was a little girl again. She was running through the Indian camp in her bare feet. When she looked down, she saw her feet were covered with black soot. She kept running all the way to the Sacrifice Rock and stopped. Her doe-skin dress was right there where she had left it so many years before, but, strangely, it had mended itself back together. She pulled off her white-woman clothes and slipped into the softness of the deer-hide; she put her feet into her comfortable, worn squaw boots. Then, she climbed up onto the rock and stood there, looking out at the ocean. She could hear Reverend Amos preaching under his oak tree all the way from Mashpee. She could hear her father chanting around the great fire pit. She could see Samuel hunting in the woods with *two* good arms. Suddenly, everything made sense. *To everything there was a season.*

And, it was good.

Chapter Sixty-Eight *"Alfred Rose"*

It was the most difficult decision Thatcher Snow had ever had to make, *what to do with Mercy's body.* Common sense told him she should be buried in the Orleans cemetery in a proper coffin where she would be near to her husband, her son and her grandson. But, knowing his wife's mind, he knew instinctively what she would have wanted and he followed his instincts. He had Thomas hitch the mules to the wagon and asked Albert to run to the tanner at the edge of town to purchase several deer hides. Then, the three Snow men began their sad journey to Mashpee on the King's Highway to seek out Reverend Amos, with Mercy's body in the back of the wagon.

It was almost dusk by the time they arrived. It was a clear night, the kind he knew she would have approved of. The stars were just coming out overhead. Reverend Amos guided them to the field below the little cemetery, where there was a wooden pyre built for her. As they placed her on the platform of birch branches, Thatcher could not control his emotions any longer; tears flooded down his face and, sobbing, he sunk to his knees in the dirt. Thomas and Albert helped him to his feet and escorted him away to a nearby log on which to sit.

Reverend Amos spoke of Mercy Snow in English for the Snows and in Wampanoag for the benefit of the others who had gathered.

"She was a blessing to her people," he told the group. "Our beloved Mercy truly had a foot in two worlds for, although she lived in the world of her adopted American family, she never forgot her Wampanoag blood. If not for her courage and compassion, her people might not have survived the re-location. She risked her own life to see that her people were cared for. For that she has our respect and gratitude."

He went on to speak of the gods and, when the fire was finally lit under her, the three Snow men clasped hands there in the glow of the flames, saying farewell to her for the last time. They wrapped her bones in the deer-skins and buried them in between the graves of Samuel and Uriah.

"It is where she belongs," Thatcher explained to young Albert, who was confused about the whole ritual and wondered why they were burying her so far away from home. "Your grandmother will rest peacefully here." He looked up and pointed to a clearing in the tree branches above them. "Right here where she can see the stars."

It was a long, silent journey home in the wagon. Thomas could not find words to describe how he was feeling. Albert soon fell asleep in the bed of the wagon, having silently cried himself to sleep. When they had returned to the livery in Orleans, they found an unexpected visitor waiting for them; sitting on the corral fence was a skinny, dark-skinned boy. "Are you Mister Snow?" the boy asked, when he saw them approach.

Thomas nodded and turned to his father, but Thatcher was not yet ready for conversation; he had jumped down from the wagon and was walking away toward Skaket Road.

"Aye," said Thomas. "We are *all* Mister Snow. And, who are *you*? You aren't from around here are you?"

"I'm from *Noepe*," said the boy. "My name's *Alfred Rose*. I need a job. They told me you might put me to work."

Noepe had once been a Wampanoag village, off the coast of Nantucket. From what Thomas had heard, the Noepe tribe had moved on to Mashpee years before. Thomas studied the boy's features; he sure enough *looked* pure blood.

"You *Wampanoag*?" asked Thomas.

"Yes," replied the boy defensively. "But, I can work as hard as any *white* boy."

Thomas laughed half-heartedly. "I didn't mean nothin' by it, Son," he said. "We're half-breeds too. My mother's kin all live in Mashpee now."

Alfred Rose was slightly younger than Albert, but not by much, and he was taller by a few inches. *There isn't much meat on his bones*, Thomas thought to himself as he introduced the boy to Albert. He was pleased when the two seemed to get along right off and Thomas agreed to take the boy on, thinking it would be good to give his son a companion his own age, someone to fill the empty space left behind now that his grandmother was gone. *It would have made Mercy happy*, he thought, his hiring a *Wampanoag* boy.

"I'll have to be sure it is all right with my father," he said. "You'll have to forgive him right now. We have just come from burying my mother."

"I'm sorry," the boy mumbled, not knowing quite what to say. "Do you want me to come back another day?"

"No," replied Thomas. "Today is as good as any. Albert can show you around. If you don't have a place to sleep, you are welcome to bed down in the hayloft tonight."

"Are you all right with that, Albert?" he asked, just as the boy was awakening from his nap in the back of the wagon.

"Yeah, Pa," Albert replied, yawning and wiping the remnants of dried tears from his eyes. "I'll show him around."

When Thomas had departed to check on his father, Albert took Alfred Rose on a tour of the livery. "You ever been to a funeral pyre?" he asked. "That's where we just came from, burying my grandmother in Mashpee."

"I have kin in Mashpee too," said Alfred Rose. "But, my father refused to be told where he would live. We hid out on the island until the soldiers had gone. We had pyres back home. But, you and your father sure don't look Wampanoag."

"I am a half-breed," Albert explained. "Just like a lot of folks here in Orleans. My grandmother had Wampanoag blood. My grandfather is American." He shook his head. "I don't really understand the whole Wampanoag funeral thing, though."

"It is the only way our souls can be set free," explained Alfred Rose. "They are pulled up in the smoke toward the sun's warmth so our spirits can fly away."

"*You* gonna be buried like that?" asked Albert.

Alfred Rose sighed. "I sure hope so," he said quietly. "I can't imagine rotting in a dark grave. I want to ride a chariot across the night sky. That's what shooting stars are, you know. *Spirits riding their chariots.*"

Albert was doubtful about that. They had made their way outside and he looked up at the sky; just at that moment a light streaked across the heavens. "Wow! Did you see that?" he asked.

Alfred Rose nodded in the dark. "That might have been *your grandmother.*"

Albert was silent. He wanted to believe it; he felt tears well up in his eyes and he turned away to hide them from Alfred Rose. "Come home with me and have supper with us," he said finally, after he had shown him everything.

And, as the weeks went by, the boy learned the livery business quickly, even though his experience with horses and mules was limited. He was a hard worker and he didn't mind taking on the most menial of tasks. Every night he was an eager guest at the Snow supper table; from the way he gulped his food it didn't look like he had eaten a full meal in a long time.

"We'll have to teach you to ride," Albert told Alfred Rose, one morning after they had finished their chores. "I've been riding almost since I could walk. Goblin, over there, is *my* horse. We can saddle one of the other horses for you."

Alfred Rose planted his rake into the dirt and stopped in his tracks. *Cleaning up after horses and feeding them was one thing. Riding them was quite another*! He wasn't sure he *wanted* to learn to ride. "I dunno," he told Albert warily. "My family didn't have horses back in Noepe. I'm a little afraid of them, Albert."

"Don't be afraid," said Albert. "I'll show you how. *It's easy*."

Every afternoon for the next few weeks, they practiced with bridles and saddles and Albert showed Alfred Rose how to insert the bit into the horse's mouth and how to tighten the cinch just right. "You've got to get it good and tight," Albert said. "Make 'em move around a little to be sure they aren't holding their breath and puffing up their lungs. If you don't get the cinch as tight as you can, the saddle with slip right off with you in it!"

Alfred Rose was terrified at the thought.

"Now," said Albert, demonstrating with Goblin. "You use your left foot on the horse's left side. Pull yourself up." He mounted his horse and sat back in the saddle. "You see? That's all there is to it!"

They practiced mounting Goblin two or three times and then they rode up and down Skaket Road and back, with Alfred Rose riding a reliable old mare and Albert taking the lead on Goblin.

"Alfred Rose did just fine!" Albert told Thomas when they had returned to the livery after their first ride. "He'll be as good as me before you know it!"

Albert had run into the house at suppertime, with Alfred Rose at his heels, bursting with the news of Alfred Rose's accomplishment, when he stopped abruptly in the doorway and remembered; *he had almost forgotten his grandmother wasn't there to share the news with anymore.*

Chapter Sixty-Nine *"Boys Bonding"*

Years before, the Snow men had added on to the stable roof a wide, flat awning as a shelter for the horses they kept in the outer pens. Albert had discovered it was a nice place to relax after supper and now Alfred Rose joined him there, to lie on their backs and star-gaze, after the sun had gone down and darkness enveloped Orleans. It was there they talked, for hours sometimes, about life and love and their shared Wampanoag ancestry. It was there a life-long bond was formed, just as if they had known each other all their lives.

From Alfred Rose, Albert learned much more about his grandmother's people, about the unique history of their tribe, about their legends and beliefs. Albert, in turn, educated Alfred Rose in the ways of the white people and introduced him to new foods and customs of the world outside Noepe. They spoke of the re-location and its effects on both of their families. Soon, however, most of their talk was about the war that was coming against the southern states that wanted to secede from the Union over the subject of slavery. It was a hot topic of conversation all over town and now it had taken hold of Albert and Alfred Rose too.

"No man should own another man," Alfred Rose said one night. "Or tell them where they can live or who they can marry."

Albert agreed. "That is what my grandmother used to say," he said. "When she married my grandfather, she had to hide who she really was or be taken away to Mashpee. Luckily, she had light skin and could pass for white."

"I lived in the woods with my father for years," replied Alfred Rose, holding out his arm. "As you can see, we could not hide the color of *our* skin. My parents were both dark like me."

It was true. Albert had never seen anyone as dark as Alfred Rose. It had never occurred to him that a full-blooded Wampanoag could look any different than the half-breeds he had known in Orleans and Mashpee. "*Are you dark all over*?" he blurted out unthinkingly.

Alfred Rose laughed out loud. "Yes, "he said.

"Even your.........?" asked Albert

"Yes," said Alfred Rose. "Even *that.*"

They burst into a fit of laughter and when they had stopped laughing they resumed their conversation.

"Is your father still hiding in the woods?" Albert asked innocently.

"My father's dead," replied Alfred Rose. "And, my mother too. I guess that makes me an orphan. That is why I needed this job."

Albert felt empathy toward his new friend. "My mother died when I was a baby," he said. "I don't even remember her. My grandmother raised me."

"My parents always wanted me to marry a Wampanoag girl," said Alfred Rose. "But, I don't see how that's going to happen now. There are so few of us left."

"There aren't many girls our age in Orleans, *white or Wampanoag*. I think someday I will go west and see what the girls are like out there! Besides, we have a long time to think about marriage!"

"Maybe I will go with you, Albert," replied Alfred Rose. "I have lived near the sea all my life. I could be the first Wampanoag to cross the Great River and live to tell about it!"

Albert got up and climbed down off the roof and Alfred Rose headed for his bed in the loft. "Are you sure you don't want to come sleep at the house?" he asked. "You are more than welcome, you know."

"No, thank you," replied Alfred Rose. "I'm quite comfortable here in the straw."

The following day, and for many days after, their talk turned back to the war, that was now raging in the south.

"All the boys in town are talking about enlisting," Albert said. "Some have already gone. I told Pa, but he said I was too young to join the army."

"You are older than me!" replied Alfred Rose. "We are not babies, Albert. Our people are warriors from the time they can lift a weapon."

"They say they are taking boys as young as sixteen," said Albert. "But, my father would never approve."

"Sometimes we have to disobey our fathers," whispered Alfred Rose, "In order to become *men.*"

It made perfect sense to Albert. They were two perfectly healthy, strong boys who had nothing better to do than care for horses and mules, when they could be off saving the poor blacks in the south from slavery. They began to look for reasons to go to town where they could hang around the local militia office for the latest news. Sometimes, after they had finished their work at the livery, they would practice marching out on the road around the kettle ponds, carrying sticks over their shoulders.

Thomas and Thatcher noticed it too, knowing *the boys were becoming men and that there was very little they could do about it.*

Chapter Seventy *"Runaway Soldiers"*

"Here," whispered Alfred Rose, "Stuff this in your pocket."

"What is it for?" Albert wanted to know.

"It's a tobacco pouch," said Alfred Rose. "*All soldiers chew tobacco.*"

He pinched off a bit of the matted brown contents of the little bag and tied the drawstring back tight. Albert watched curiously as his friend tucked the tobacco into his cheek.

"What does it taste like?" whispered Albert. He took a pinch for himself, and pocketed the pouch.

"Well, not so good, at first," Alfred Rose replied. "You gotta get *used* to it."

His friend was right; the stuff tasted *awful*. Sometimes, becoming a man was distasteful and even *painful*. Albert tried to remember what his grandmother used to say; *that which doesn't kill us makes us stronger.*

And, so the two teenage boys, with their duffle bags slung over their shoulders and their tobacco tucked in their cheeks, ran off down Skaket Road toward the King's Highway in the early morn, even before the old rooster in the backyard had begun to crow. *The country was at war! Every young man in Orleans was enlisting!* They were off to fight against slavery, at the request of President Lincoln, determined to come home victorious. *Nothing, not even the rebel army, was going to deter them!*

"It's best not to say good-bye," Albert had advised. "Or else my pa will make me stay. He'll say I am still too young."

He hated to leave his father and his grandfather, and he knew he would miss Goblin, but the call of duty was loud and strong in his ears and he couldn't ignore it. It had gotten into their blood. While it seemed a little too late to save the Wampanoag, they were out to defend freedom for the oppressed blacks in the south.

"They will be proud of you, once we have won the war against the rebels," Alfred Rose told him. "You'll see."

They had walked all day but still came up a bit short of reaching Barnstable, where they were told they would find the recruiting station. "I need to rest my feet," said Alfred Rose, collapsing to the ground. "I got blisters the size of quarters between my toes and I can't walk another step. Let's sleep here for the night."

Albert had wanted to stop miles before, but he hadn't said a word, thinking *if Alfred Rose could take it, so could he.* He was eager to take off his shoes too and rest his feet in the cool water of the creek that ran past them. "You s'pose they'll give us uniforms?" he asked.

"Of course," said Alfred Rose. "We'll be soldiers, won't we?"

"And, guns too?"

Alfred Rose laughed out loud. "Can't very well kill any rebels without *guns*, now can we?"

And, they went to sleep, under a summer sky, with dreams of glory in their young heads, not knowing exactly what to expect when they reached Barnstable. When they arrived at noon the next day, the recruiters weren't difficult to find, sitting at a long table in a corner of the train depot, with dozens of young men around them. A stout man in a blue uniform looked them over carefully. "You *black*?" he asked Alfred Rose.

"No, Sir!" Alfred Rose replied. "I'm *Wampanoag*, from *Noepe*."

"Well," said the officer. "That's close enough. And, how 'bout you? You ain't Injun, are you?"

Albert wasn't sure quite how to answer the man. *What difference did that make anyhow? They were here to fight the rebels!* "My *grandmother* was part Wampanoag," he started to explain.

"Well, then," the man interrupted. "I'll have to put you with the niggers too, even though you'll stand out like a sore thumb with that white skin of yours." He laughed at the confused look on Albert's face. "Over there."

He pointed to a group of young black boys, sitting outside on the steps of depot, lounging back with their elbows propped against their ragged carpet bags; most of them looked like farm boys straight off the plantation. They approached the group, where the apparent leader of the bunch was silently sizing them up and down. "They puttin' you two with *us*?" he asked. "You *convicts* or somethin'?"

Albert felt the pride rise up in his cheeks. *"No, Sir!"* he said, indignantly. "We aren't *convicts*. We're *Wampanoag*! We're here to fight for you all."

The black boy laughed. He had bad teeth and nappy hair peeking out from under his cap. "Okay by me," he said. "We'll put you two in the *forward division!*"

Albert had no idea what the *forward division* was but he accepted it as a badge of honor.

"Better not put *him* in the front," said another boy, pointing at Albert. "He is so white, them thar rebels will think we're *surrenderin'*!"

All the black boys laughed at that. Albert didn't know what all the fuss was about. *Black. White. Wampanoag. Who cared anyway?* They were all there to fight the rebels.

But, it didn't take long for Albert and Alfred Rose to find out there *was* a difference between being considered "black" and "white", at least as far as the army was concerned. When the white soldiers were issued new blue uniforms and proper footwear, the young recruits in their group were told their uniforms had been *requisitioned.*

"What's *requisitioned* mean?" Albert whispered to Alfred Rose.

"I dunno," Alfred Rose whispered back. "I reckon they ran short and ours are comin' later."

Later, when they lined up again to be assigned their army rifles, their group received shovels instead of weapons. There was grumbling in their midst. "Why ain't we gettin' rifles like them other men?"

"You'll be on *burial* detail for now," an officer told them.

"I didn't enlist to be no *grave-digger*," one black boy said angrily.

The officer chastised him immediately. "You'll get your chance, Son," he said. "For now, just be glad yer *diggin'* the graves and not layin' *in* one!

The march began at dawn, after they spent the night camped out in the train station along with a hundred or so others. Alfred was glad they had brought blankets, for the floor was cold and hard; it had been a restless night, with the snoring and sour odors of a hundred bodies around them. The group of white soldiers marched out first, with their rifles glistening in the morning sun. Albert and Alfred Rose and their group, with their shovels slung over their shoulders, followed behind. They were only told they were on their way to Virginia, to join up with a regiment there they called the *USCT*.

"Do you know what *USCT* stands for?" Albert asked.

"United States Colored Troops," one of the others told them. "You best be ready for the hardest work detail there is. Even *you*, little white nigger!"

Albert looked at the others in the *USCT*; some were even younger than he and Alfred Rose. Most were shoeless, stepping gingerly over the graveled road with the pink soles of their feet already bloodied and blistered from previous journeys afoot. Albert didn't care what names the others called him. He had something they didn't have. *At least, he had shoes on his feet.*

Chapter Seventy-One *"General Ferrero's Men"*

Brigadier General Edward Ferrero was a thirty-three-year-old native of Spain but his ancestry was pure Italian. He had come to America as an infant, where his family settled in New York and they later opened a dance academy for the rich aristocracy who could afford such luxuries. Born into wealth, Ferraro had been interested in military affairs since the days of his youth. He enlisted and soon became a lieutenant colonel in the 11th New York Militia Regiment, where he served for six years.

When Civil War broke out in 1861, the wealthy young colonel decided to raise a regiment at his own expense known as the 51st New York's "Shepard Rifles". For the next three years, he served honorably in places like Roanoke Island, before he was promoted to Brigadier General and transferred to Virginia. It was there that he was given command of the USCT division, the very division Albert Snow and Alfred Rose and the others were marching south to meet. The assignment was a far cry from his previous prestigious missions and Ferrero was not exactly thrilled about it, but he took his orders and headed for Petersburg, nevertheless. Ultimately, *it would not prove to be his shining hour.*

In June of 1864, just before Albert and the others reached Virginia, Grant's army had begun what was to become a nine-month siege of grueling trench warfare, in an attempt to take control of the Confederate capital of Richmond. Focusing in on the town of Petersburg, because it was the main supply center for the capital with access to both railways and navigable rivers, they tried unsuccessfully to breach the line of Confederate earthworks that surrounded the city. When Albert's group arrived it was obvious that they were going to be assigned to digging, although it wouldn't be *graves* at first; they were told they were going to dig trenches around the outskirts of Petersburg. It was going to be back-breaking work, even for those with youth on their side.

They had been assigned to tents that spread out for a mile behind the trench lines, packed in like sardines in a tin, six bodies to a tent. In hopes of escaping the Virginia sun, Albert and the others had escaped to their tents as soon as they were dismissed, rolling up the bottoms of the canvas walls around them to let in some air for they knew the night was going to be unbearably hot. Albert and Alfred Rose had pretty much kept to themselves on the way from Barnstable. Briefly, they had met their new commander, Colonel Ferrero, when they arrived, and then they were immersed into a larger group of older black soldiers.

"My name's Albert Snow," Albert said to the others in his assigned tent, who were arranging their beds for the night and laying claim to the few square inches of space they could call their own. "This is my friend, Alfred Rose. We are from Orleans. Where are you all from?"

They had housed most of the young boys that had just arrived together. Slowly and bashfully, the others introduced themselves as they went around the tent. There was George, a young field worker from Barnstable, Joseph, a smithy apprentice from New York, and William, a cook from Virginia. And, then there was a newcomer named Billy-Ray, who burst into the tent a few minutes after the others. The only one in the group who appeared old enough to shave, he told the others he was a freed-slave who had come all the way from Georgia just to join the *USCT* and it was soon obvious that his second mission was to patronize the others in his tent. "It smells of *boy* in here," he said sarcastically, as soon as he stepped inside. The young man looked around at the wide, innocent eyes staring back at him. "I think I'll take this corner here. It suits me fine."

He was coal-black, with a wide, flat nose that looked like it had been broken more than once and his body was thick and burly like a bear. Not wanting any trouble, Albert and the others gave Billy-Ray a wide berth, moving their belongings quickly out of his way.

"I didn't know I was going to have to *baby-sit* through this war," Billy Ray said, looking directly at Alfred Rose. "Your ma still powder your backside, Boy?"

He laughed and coughed up phlegm at the same time, spitting on the dirt floor of the tent.

"My mother is dead," replied Alfred Rose defiantly, with a scowl across his face. He didn't like this young man, not one bit. "And, seeing as how we all have to *sleep* on this ground you might do your spittin' outside from now on."

"Well, you're a pretty *cocky* little character, aren't you?" asked Billy Ray.

"Nope," replied Alfred Rose, refusing to be intimidated. "I am a soldier, *just like you*."

Billy Ray glanced over at the shovels stacked at one end of the tent. "Looks like you boys are here to *dig*," he said, flippantly stowing his rifle under his bedroll. *"I'm* here to fight with the *real* soldiers."

"I hope we all get the chance to do more than just *dig*," said William, the boy from Virginia. "I thought we'd be a *fightin'* these rebels, not buildin' a moat around them!"

"Well, we have to set up for the battle," said George from Barnstable. "It's all part of General Grant's plan. Besides, *someone's* got to do the diggin'! Might as well be us! We are *used* to hard work in the fields!"

"You know what I mean," William replied. "Don't seem right that as soon as we get *emancipated* they turn us back into slaves as soon as we get here!"

"What do any of you know about *battle plans* anyway?" Billy Ray asked sarcastically. "I expect most you have never been off the farm." Then, his attention turned toward Albert. "And, why are *you* here?" he asked. "You *lost* or somethin'?"

Albert shook his head. "No, I'm not lost," he replied.

"Well, then, don't you think you are in the *wrong* tent? I mean, your skin is a little *pale* for this group, wouldn't you say?"

"I am a *half-breed,*" said Albert. "They put me here because my grandmother was part *Wampanoag.* Not that it should be any concern of *yours.*"

Billy-Ray looked Albert up and down. "Never met me an Injun' a'fore," he said, clearly wanting to have the last word. "You gonna *skin* the rebels after we *shoot* 'em?" He laughed. It was a condescending laugh.

Albert lowered his eyes and took a deep breath. He was not going to let Billy-Ray bully him, even if he *was* older and bigger. "No," he said, calmly. "We don't take scalps anymore." He thought for a moment and glanced over at Alfred Rose. "We might *eat* 'em though, *if they're young and tender enough!*"

The young man's eyes got big and round and he stood there staring, dumbfounded, until he saw Albert break into a grin. "Aw, you're just foolin' with me," said Billy-Ray; the expression in his eyes was still one of suspicion.

"I s'pose it doesn't matter none *what* color our skin is," William chimed in, trying to ease the tension. "We're all gonna bleed *red* before too long anyways."

The conversation ended. Billy-Ray unbuttoned his shirt and laid down in his corner with his head near the few inches of cool air coming in under the canvas wall, while the boys stowed their gear and some left the tent for the chow line.

"C'mon Albert," said Alfred Rose, loud enough for Billy-Ray to hear. "Smells like they're cookin' up *rebels* for dinner and I'm *starving!*"

The only thing worse than a bigot was a bully!

Chapter Seventy-Two *"The Siege of Petersburg"*

The next day they found themselves pulling up their tent stakes and marching once again; all day and into the night, they split up into three separate groups, heading for the James River on the east side of the city. By the time they reached the riverbanks at three in the morning, they were exhausted and ready for sleep. Without enough energy left to pitch their tents, they collapsed onto the grass for a few short hours of slumber before the work began.

Their first mission there was to build a *pontoon bridge* across the river. Albert and Alfred Rose were assigned to the detail moving earth in to shore up the river bank at the base of the bridge, which they did, bucketful by bucketful, lugged in from a nearby field. Then, wagons carrying small canoe-like boats and long rough-hewn planks arrived and the troops began laying the foundation for the bridge. Planks and pontoons began to stretch across the river until, by suppertime on the second day, they reached the banks on the other side. The chow wagons crossed over and they ate their suppers on the opposite banks of the James.

Then came even more marching. When they had reached their final destination, the *real work* started, as they began to carve out what would eventually be thirty miles of battle trenches around Petersburg. For the next several weeks, Albert and the others were awakened every morning at dawn by the shrill call of a bugle, before they lined up at the mess tent for cold oatmeal and black coffee. Each group worked eight hour shifts; the digging never stopped round the clock, while all around them, the sounds of cannon and rifle fire pierced the air.

At night, in their tent, Albert and Alfred Rose found little to talk about, when all they had seen for weeks was the bottom of an endless dirt trench.

"I can't feel my hands anymore," said Alfred Rose, rubbing his calloused and blistered palms together. "And, I've worn holes in my moccasins. When do you think our boots and uniforms will get here?"

Albert was equally as disillusioned. "I'm beginning to think *requisitioned* means *not in this lifetime!*" he said, trying to make light of the situation, for neither boy wanted to give up and admit defeat.

The boy named William reached for his carpet bag and pulled out an old pair of boots.

"My ma made me bring a spare pair," he said. "And, mine seem to be holdin' up ok. Here, Alfred Rose. You can take them."

Alfred Rose took the boots and slid his feet into them. "I thank you kindly, William," he said. "*These will be my lucky boots!*"

The boots were a little large, but with a few pieces of crumpled newspaper stuffed in first they fit quite nicely. The group who shared their tent had all become quite good friends. The one positive development they all could agree on was that they no longer had to tolerate Billy Ray, who had been reassigned to an infantry division. The *downside* was that Albert and the others remained behind to do more *digging.*

Chapter Seventy-Three *"Battle of the Crater"*

The news that was beginning to filter through the ranks and back to the boys of the *USCT* was not *good* news. General Grant's assault on Petersburg was failing. Scrimmage after scrimmage, the Union army was not gaining any ground on the Confederates nor were they getting any closer to capturing the capital of Richmond, and they were losing a lot of men.

It was almost the end of July. With the trench works completed, Albert and his group were again reassigned. Surprisingly enough, the reassignment happened almost simultaneously to the arrival of the requisitioned uniforms and rifles that had been promised them months before. The mood of the boys in the tent that night was almost jubilant; their long hours of slave labor had paid off! Now they would be real soldiers! Now they would be *fighting* instead of just *digging*. As they sat around on their beds, cleaning and polishing their new long rifles and waiting for their orders, there was an infusion of patriotism and honor.

The new plan of attack was a bold one. A lieutenant colonel in one of the infantry divisions, who just so happened to be a mining engineer, had an idea that might once and for all break through the Confederate lines and turn the tide in the Union favor. But, as Albert and Alfred Rose learned much to their dismay, *there would be much more digging involved* before they would be able to use their newly assigned rifles.

The next day they began digging once again; this time it was through the side of the recently excavated trenches, a five-hundred-foot mine shaft below the ground and ending directly under the Confederate defensive line. At the end of the tunnel, it was to spread out in a t-formation, seventy-five feet in both directions, where eight thousand pounds of gunpowder was to be planted. The plan was to explode a gaping hole in the enemy lines and rush the breach, with guns blazing, right through Petersburg and beyond, to the capital. They had to try it; nothing else was working. Grant was frustrated enough to try *anything* to advance his army.

For another long month, Albert and Alfred Rose along with William and George and Joseph and a dozen or so others, dug as if their lives depended upon it, while their new rifles remained in their tent, never-fired, as shiny as the day they were made. Between digging shifts, they were instructed what the plans were when the tunnel was complete. As soon as the explosion happened, they were to grab their rifles and charge through the breach, firing at will. It was incentive enough for them to dig at a furious rate.

Then, the day came when the plan was to come to fruition, when Albert and the other boys of the *USCT* were about to finally show their valor on the battlefield.

But, General Grant had an unexpected visit from another general, George Meade, who had a very different attitude when told of the plan. "Suppose," he told Grant, "Word gets back to the President about this? What will it look like? Ordering the *colored* recruits through *first*? Lincoln will surely chastise us for not sending our more expert marksmen in to clear the way!"

Grant hadn't thought of the political repercussions such a decision could create in Washington. *General Meade had a point.*

"Well," Meade suggested, "Let's make it fair by having the commanders draw lots. That way we are not choosing between the blacks and the whites. It will be strictly by chance!"

Albert's group did not win the first draw; another division under the command of General James Ledlie was chosen to rush through the breach first. Again, they waited until they were under the cover of night. At just before four a.m. the fuses to the explosives were lit in the tunnel. The *USCT* were waiting in reserve, with their rifles loaded and ready. Their adrenaline was pulsing in their veins. As they watched, there was a massive explosion sending earth, men and debris high into the air and creating a huge hole, a hundred and seventy feet long and eighty feet wide, destroying a huge chunk of the Confederate fortifications and killing over three hundred rebel soldiers in the process.

Ledlie's group stood on the edge of the newly formed "crater", waiting for their orders. But General Ledlie could not be found to give the order to his men. When he was finally located, drinking whiskey in the command tent with General Ferrero, the delay had allowed the Confederate troops time to re-group. When the infantry rushed in, it was into a hail of bullets. Seeing the men being slaughtered, the *USCT* were then ordered in to assist.

Albert and Alfred Rose ran in, side by side, through the smoke of a hundred rifles around them. When they reached the place where the Confederate line had once stood, they realized they had a thirty-foot wall of dirt to breach. Looking down on them was a solid line of grey-uniformed soldiers that quickly began firing on them.

"Let's get the hell *outta* here!" William screamed.

They started to retreat, seeing their situation was impossible.

"This way!" Albert yelled through the smoke to Alfred Rose. "Hurry before we are all killed!"

Scrambling over the mounds of upheaved earth and roots and rocks, one by one, the boys of the *USCT* frantically tried to escape what was later called a "turkey shoot" by one of the generals witnessing the carnage. General Grant, himself, called it *the saddest affair I have witnessed in the war.* When the smoke finally cleared, and the few boys left of the *USCT* had collapsed on the ground, finally out of the reach of the rebel rifles, Albert sat up and looked around for his friend, Alfred Rose. But, Alfred Rose was not there.

Albert found William and George and Joseph, who had, like himself, escaped death at the hands of the rebels, all except one. Then, he looked back at the huge crater looming before them in the rising sun. The rifles had silenced as the bodies on both sides were counted. The cold, harsh reality of the daylight reflected on the mangled corpses spread across the mass of dirt and rock. Albert turned to William and said sadly,

"I guess they weren't his lucky boots after all."

PART TWO *"THE IRON HORSE"*

And I looked, and behold a pale horse; and his name that sat on it was Death, and Hades followed with him.
Revelation 6:8 King James Bible.

Chapter Seventy-Four *"The Black Beast"*

Albert stepped onto the station platform on that crisp January morning and tilted his head forward to look down the train tracks. In the distance, he could see a cloud of black smoke against the blue of the not- yet-springtime sky; the train was returning from Provincetown. He knelt down and put his hand on the steel rail at his feet; somewhere he had heard the vibrations of the train approaching could be felt many miles away. He was disappointed that he felt nothing. His eyes watched the smoke cloud, now being carried on the wind toward the west, away from Orleans and everything he had ever known, mostly away from the war that had gone on for another nine months after the death of Alfred Rose. Albert had returned home, sickened and disheartened over the whole affair. No, he had to get away! *The west*, he thought hopefully, *was where he was heading*!

He was early; the train wasn't due in Orleans for another half hour. There was only one other person on the platform that appeared to be waiting for the train, an old man with a cane and a tall felt hat. Pallets of goods were stacked below them, bags of salt, cans of cranberries, open air crates of quahogs, packed in ice, all headed for the mainland, and, Albert Snow, embarking *on the adventure of his life.*

"Where are you headed?" the old man asked.

"Out west," Albert replied. "You?"

The man sat down on a bench and pulled out a whalebone pipe. "I'm going to visit my grandchildren in Boston," he said. "Haven't seen 'em in quite a spell."

"I'm hoping to go into the cattle business," said Albert. "And, maybe settle down in Kansas or Nebraska."

"Cattle business? Is that so?" said the man. "Don't know much about that. Not many cattle herds out here on the cape."

"I hear the herds are *huge* on the plains," said Albert, with anticipation dancing in his eyes. "They say they stretch out for as far as the eye can see!"

"That so?" said the old man. "I reckon that's a hard business."

"I don't know yet," said Albert. "I'll know more when I get there."

By the time the black locomotive finally came into view, a few more passengers had gathered. The arrival of a train in Orleans was not anything unusual; freight trains had been passing through town for years now. But, *this* train was different; this was the first train to bring with it the *first passenger car*. No more hitching rides to Provincetown and back, hiding among the bales and boxes in the open freight cars. No more jumping off as the train slowed down at the Orleans station, to avoid the stationmaster catching him. That was all very exciting in his youth; now he held a bonafide ticket in his pocket. He had given up tempting the railroad authorities to arrest him as a stowaway; now his excitement was *real*. Albert was going to meet his destiny in the west. Exactly *where* he was not sure yet. He had miles of track to cover to think about that.

He thought about Thatcher and Thomas back at home on Skaket Road. Their goodbyes had been simple and brief; the Snow men didn't get *emotional* about such things. They both seemed to understand there wasn't much future in Orleans for a young man any longer. Jobs had become scarce ever since the war, with the free blacks coming north and willing to work for beggars' wages. Albert was good with livestock; in addition to working for his father and grandfather in their livery, he had gained experience working for neighboring farmers, herding their sheep and goats to market, and he could ride a horse better than anyone he knew. Leaving Goblin had been difficult too; they had been together many years. But, his horse was getting on in years and Albert worried that the animal could not make the distance he wanted to go, especially if he signed on with a cattle drive. It would be easier to travel by train and buy another *younger* horse later.

He felt the coins and paper bills he had saved from his mustering-out pay, folded tightly in his pocket, feeling more than a little scared. But, he knew he *had* to get out of Orleans! He just had to make his own way and that meant going west, as far west as west would go!

By the time the Old Colony locomotive finally rumbled into the station, Albert had been joined by a dozen more passengers. He stared at the black iron beast as it pounded the tracks before him, belching out a solid plume of black smoke and blaring out an ear-piercing whistle to announce its arrival. He carried the same carpet bag he had returned with from the war, with an extra set of clothes, his hunting knife and the tobacco pouch Alfred Rose had given him. In his pocket, he had tucked a brochure put out by the railroad, marking the route of the train and the places that sounded interesting to him. Pittsburg, St Louis, Omaha; anywhere there were ranches and livestock, he knew he could find work and survive.

When the train finally rolled to a screeching stop, Albert showed his ticket to the agent and climbed on board. It was the only passenger car in the entire train, nestled between two freight cars. The seats were shiny new and smelled of newly-cured leather, the walls were freshly painted and the aisles were spotless and un-scuffed. The only thing that didn't look spotless were the windows that already had a film of gray soot on them from the coal stacks. He took a seat on the left side of the train, knowing the route they would travel was around Cape Cod Bay on the right. He had *seen* the bay and the ocean all his life. Now, he wanted to see a *different* landscape; he wanted to see wide plains and tall mountains. He leaned in toward the window, watching the porters toting baggage and passengers kissing loved ones goodbye. He thought about poor Alfred Rose, buried back in Virginia. And he realized their conversations had fueled his desire to go west. He looked out over the little town he had grown up in. *Goodbye Orleans!* he thought. *Goodbye Pa and Grampa! Till I see you again!*

A half hour later, the old engine fired up again and its wheels began to turn, ever so slowly, creeping out of the station. Albert watched the familiar places of his youth pass him by, like quickly moving vignettes, disappearing behind them, as the train made its way south to Brewster and Harwich, then west toward Barnstable and Sandwich. By the time they headed north toward Boston, Albert had fallen asleep with his head resting against the window ledge.

He changed trains in the busy Boston station, and Albert was on his way west toward Albany and Buffalo. From there, the brochure said it would be south to Cleveland and then west to Chicago. After that, he hadn't a *clue* which direction he would go.

.

Chapter Seventy-Five *"The Yards"*

The train rumbled into Chicago, after endless miles of bumpy, noisy steel tracks. By then, his pockets were bare and his stomach was equally as empty, having existed on dry biscuits and weak tea for most of his journey. Now, as he picked up his bag and climbed down off the train, he knew he had to find work soon *or starve to death.*

The Chicago train station was much different than the simple whistle stop platform back home in Orleans; it even overshadowed the stations he had come through in Boston and Buffalo. Albert couldn't imagine anything bigger than the high arched ceilings and open steel beams that loomed over his head, at least, until he first stepped out onto the Chicago sidewalk, and found himself staring up at the towering buildings around him. In the shadow of church steeples and clock towers, of huge office and apartment buildings, dotted with hundreds of windows, he entered the street where trolley cars and horse drawn carriages passed before him. *And, so many people*! Albert never would have envisioned such a bustling city; his memory of the quiet streets of Orleans seemed almost *surreal* now.

He walked for a way, around the corner of the train station, where the air was thick with the smell of livestock; the holding pens for the cattle and sheep that had been unloaded from the trains spread out for blocks! Hundreds, perhaps thousands, of bleating, moaning animals were packed together in tiny fenced cubicles and herded down long narrow passageways from the train cars on the tracks. Albert climbed up onto a fence rail to watch the goings on. At his feet, were cattle with long, curved horns, the likes of which he had never seen. Further down, there were pens of huddled, stinking sheep and squealing pigs, being poked and prodded by men on horseback. On one side, were the train tracks and stock-cars; on the other were the meatpacker's buildings. There was no escape for the doomed animals caught in between, *kind of like the men in the battle of the crater*.

Albert jumped down and started down the aisle way, looking for anyone who might be in charge. Most of the men were too busy to notice him but he finally spied a man sitting on a fence post, writing in a notebook. "Are you hiring, sir?" he asked. "I'm looking for work."

The man sized him up and down. "You got any experience, Lad?" he asked, "With *livestock*, I mean."

Albert nodded. "Yes, sir!" he replied. "I herded sheep and goats back home. And, I can ride a horse quite well."

The man seemed uninterested and continued to scribble notes and numbers on his paper.

"I really need a job, Sir," Albert pleaded. "I'm a good worker!"

The man jumped down from the fence. "Ever work in a slaughterhouse before?" he asked.

Albert had to admit he had not, but he had seen slaughter of a different kind in the war and was not afraid of blood. "But, I am a quick learner! Please, Sir, just give me a chance! You won't be sorry!"

The man led Albert into a two-story brick building, where the stench of dead animals in the air was almost overbearing. Albert felt the bile rise up in his throat and he covered his mouth to keep from retching. On one side, there were rows of men with long sledge hammers, standing over a narrow passageway where the cattle were being led in; as the terrified beasts were pushed along below them, the men were knocking them soundly in the heads and sending them crashing to their knees in the muck. At the end of the passageway, more men were lifting the dead bodies up with pulleys and chains, pushing them along toward more men with skinning knives and cleavers, lopping off heads and ripping the hides off. On the other side of the building were rows of skinned carcasses being hosed off by men in bloody, rubber aprons. It was nothing more than a *gauntlet* of death; where animals went in on their feet and came out the other side, hacked pieces of raw meat, ready for packaging. It was a side to the livestock business that Albert could never have imagined.

The man almost forgot that Albert was following along behind him. He turned toward him. "You think you can handle it?" he asked, fully expecting to see the young man bolt and run at his first introduction to the meat packing industry.

Albert swallowed hard. "I am sure I can, Sir," he said weakly. "When would you like me to start?"

"Well, go on the back there," the man said, motioning to a back door. "Tell them you've been hired to work. They'll tell you what to do."

Albert made his way through the clamoring noise, the hideous stench and the screaming of the animals being butchered and, just for a moment, he questioned his reason for being here. He had come an awfully long way, spent every penny he had, to get to this place. What would his father and grandfather have thought, seeing what his eyes were seeing now? Where were the wide, open spaces of the west he had heard so much about, the blue skies and fresh air? Was he doomed to remain here in this crowded city? Was this the exciting life he had dreamed about?

The man outside was no more personable than the first. He was a squat, round man who spoke with a rough Irish brogue. "Come around back to the *pits*," he barked at Albert.

Once again, Albert followed, through a narrow passageway, where men with blood-soaked wheelbarrows were going in and out. And, suddenly, there it was, what the man had called *the pits*. Below him, was a dirt clearing with piles of the remains of animals, bones, hides, hooves and horns, heads with dead black eyes, staring up at him. In the middle of the clearing, the men with the wheelbarrows were dumping more disgusting remains of the slaughtered animals. "Your job is to sort out this stuff," said the man. "Hooves and horns over there," he pointed to one corner. "Hides over *there*. You get the idea?"

Albert rolled up his sleeves. He had to do it if he wanted to eat and have a place to sleep that night. "Might I have a pair of gloves?" he asked the man timidly.

The man laughed, and held up his own bloody hands for Albert to see. "What are you, *some kind of a dandy*?" he asked mockingly. "You want gloves, you gotta buy them yourself!"

Chapter Seventy-Six *"Dandy-Boy"*

Albert struggled through his first day, sorting through the mounds of flesh and bone until his back ached and his hands were caked with dried blood and animal hair. The clothes he wore were soaked and stained and he reeked with the smell of death. When the six o'clock whistle blew from the top of the building, and the other workers were putting away their tools and hanging up their aprons, Albert went to find a faucet to rinse his face and hands. Even after he and Alfred Rose had spent weeks in the trenches outside of Petersburg, he had not felt so filthy.

"You gotta a place to stay, *Dandy-boy*?"

He heard a voice behind him and he turned to see the man who had mocked him before coming towards him. In his hands were a pair of leather gloves. "Here, Lad. I had an old pair I thought you could use," the man said.

Even though the man called him *Dandy-boy*, his voice was not as condescending as before and Albert took the gloves gladly, even if they *were* a little late in coming. "Thank you, Sir," he said. "No, I'm not sure where I will be staying tonight. I have come all the way from Orleans and I am afraid I have spent my last nickel."

"Orleans? Never heard of it," the man said.

"It's on Cape Cod," said Albert. "Massachusetts."

The man reached into his pocket and produced a few pennies. "There's a boarding house down the street," he said. "This should get you a bed and a few meals until payday. You are a long way from home, Dandy-boy. We'll keep you on if you don't mind the work. Some boys run home to their mamas after the first day, puking their guts out."

Albert shook his head. "My mother is *dead*, Sir," he said plainly. "And, I haven't enough money for a train ticket home. Besides, I haven't anything in my stomach to puke."

"Six in the morning till six at night," said the man, "With Sundays off. Be on time and don't be a slacker and you won't starve."

With that, the man turned and disappeared inside the building. Albert pocketed the coins and finished rinsing the filth from his hands and forearms, before he made his way out onto the streets of bustling Chicago.

The boarding house was a pitiful, dilapidated structure, leaning slightly to one side like a crooked top-hat, with peeling paint and weathered wood shingles, wedged so tightly between the houses on either side of it, that there were literally only inches between them. Reaching out of the window of the room he was assigned to by the old lady who owned the place, he could almost touch the house next door. The room was sparse, with only a steel-spring cot topped by a pencil-thin mattress, covered with dingy, gray sheets and a pilled woolen blanket. The dresser was missing its drawer pulls and scratched with initials of all who had slept there before. Seeing how many poor souls had passed through before him only made the place seem more anonymous; he was just one of many faceless tenants, and that was fine with Albert. All he wanted, after a long day of dancing a bloody dance with the corpses of cows, was *sleep* and *a change of clothes.*

"Breakfast is served at five," the woman had told him. "Most of my boarders work in the yards, so I serve meals by their schedule. Is that where you work, Boy?"

"Yes, Ma'am," he had told her politely. "I have to be to work at six."

"Supper is at six-thirty," she said. "And, rent is due again on pay day. *I know when its payday at the yards, Boy, so don't think I won't come collectin'.*" She had pointed up the stairs, toward the landing above, not venturing to make the climb with him. "Number seven is yours."

And, then she had handed him a long brass key and closed her door. Albert was on his own. He climbed the stairs and entered the tiny room, where he stretched out on the hard mattress and closed his eyes, trying to put his empty stomach out of his mind. It could not be quieted, however, and it gurgled and rumbled until he finally drifted off to sleep.

The clamoring of the other boarders loping down the stairs to breakfast startled him awake in the morning and he welcomed the aroma of boiled oatmeal and toasted bread coming up the stairwell. He ate ravenously and so quickly he gave himself the hiccups.

"You started work yesterday?" asked one of the men seated across the table.

"Yes, Sir," said Albert, taking a drink of his coffee to stifle his hiccups.

"Thought I saw you there," said the man. "First week's the toughest. If you can get through *that* you'll be ok. Where you from?"

"Massachusetts," said Albert. *"Cape Cod."*

"Heard that's a place for rich folks," the man said. "What's a rich kid working in the yards of Chicago? You run away from home?"

"All of Cape Cod isn't rich," said Albert. "I come from Orleans. I worked in my father's livery stable."

"Still, it must be a far sight nicer than Chicago," the man said. "You serve in the war, Son?"

"Yes, Sir," replied Albert.

"Bloody war, wasn't it?" the man asked, shaking his head. *"Awful bloody."*

Albert wanted to change the subject; he had seen enough blood on his first day of work to last a lifetime and he had no desire to talk about the war. "I want to work in the cattle business, eventually," he told the man. "You know, where the big cattle ranches are, out west."

"We get loads from just about everywhere," said the man. "Kansas City, Omaha, Fort Worth. You can keep your ears open. But, don't let the boss-man suspect you're looking for another job. There's plenty of men around here willing to step in and take your place."

Albert, being of a quiet sort by nature, had no problem keeping his mouth shut most of the time. Every morning, he pulled on his leather gloves and made his way to the pits, where he spent hours sorting through the endless piles of reeking cow parts. After a while, he grew accustomed to the terrible smell and, after he had earned his first pay and had a few pennies to eat on, even managed to keep his lunch down amidst the stink, sitting with the other workers on the landing high above the bloody gauntlet floor. At night, he would return to the boarding house, eat his supper and fall into bed, exhausted and spent, looking forward only to his next pay day.

Chicago was a young, growing city, although Albert couldn't imagine it getting any bigger, and, he was told, much of its growth could be attributed to the yards. Every day, over two thousand men and women marched in to work along with Albert, where, in an atmosphere of noise and noxious odors, they practiced their art of slaying and flaying cattle and pigs from all over the country. It was a repulsive place, where flies swarmed through the open doors, animals screamed hideously as they were butchered alive and rivers of coagulating blood ran out into the street and down the gutters into the South Fork of the Chicago River. They called it *Bubbly Creek* because of the gases from decomposition that bubbled to the surface of the red water.

Outside, across the train tracks where Albert began to explore on Sundays when he wasn't working, was the only avenue of fresh air to the city, the cool breezes blowing off Lake Michigan. It reminded him of the kettle ponds back home in Orleans, but much bigger. And, when the weather was agreeable, would often sit on the docks there for a while before going back to the boardinghouse, just to clear his head and refresh his mind. The *yards* were not his destiny; he still dreamed of cattle country beyond the city and was determined to get there. He was just waiting for his opportunity.

Chapter Seventy-Seven *"The Late Train"*

Blood and guts. Bones and tendons. Hooves and tails. There was never an end to it. Albert was beginning to smell them in his sleep and hear the screams of the cows as they were butchered and dragged through the gauntlet. Still, his disgusting labors paid for him to eat and sleep in a bed at night. His father and grandfather wouldn't have complained, so he was determined not to either.

The nickname *"Dandy"* had stuck with him at the yards, and, after a while, he didn't let it bother him anymore. Besides, he had been called worse, *half-breed, Injun,* and the worst nickname of all, *white nigger. Why must people have labels anyway?* he wondered, *when they already had perfectly good names given to them by their parents?*

There were others he worked with who had peculiar nicknames as well; there was *Grinder*, who cranked the handle and fed the raw meat through the teeth of the giant processing machine, and *Casey*, who rummaged through the mounds of casings for untorn pieces that were suitable for sausage skins. There was *Jerky Jack*, who collected the meat for the drying room at the Armour plant next door. and *Smokey* who stoked the woodchips over the ever-burning open pit, where the hams were hung to smoke. Without ever a hope of promotion, Albert didn't think about moving up into a less-bloody job; he hoped it was only a matter of time before he would move on and out of smelly Chicago *altogether.*

Albert had made *one* friend, however; ironically it was the same man who had given him his nickname. Angus O'Banion was an Irish immigrant from the old country, having settled in Chicago five years earlier, with his family. He could be a quite likable fellow, once you got to know him, and Albert, who knew no one in Chicago except his fellow boarders with whom he ate his breakfast every morning and his mercenary landlady, was anxious to have a friend. He often thought about the carefree nights, star-gazing on the livery rooftop with his friend, Alfred Rose. It seemed so long ago now. *A lifetime ago.*

They were taking their fifteen-minute break for lunch, sitting on the platform above the gauntlet floor; Angus was munching on a sandwich of soda bread and cold mutton and drinking lukewarm tea from a jar. Albert had tucked some of his breakfast toast into his pocket earlier. Angus offered him a swig of his tea. "You don't eat much, boy," the older man told him. "Havin' a tough time gettin' by are ya?"

Albert shook his head. He didn't want to appear needy. "Oh, I eat all right," he replied, "Back at the boarding house."

"Here, have some of mine," said Angus. "My wife always packs me too much anyway."

They chewed together silently. Albert noticed Angus was missing fingers on his right hand. "What happened to your hand?" he asked.

"Butchering is a dangerous business," said Angus, wiggling the ugly stumps where his fingers had once been in the air. "Be glad you're not on the *cuttin'* floor."

Albert couldn't imagine anything could be worse than his job in the pits. Angus noticed the look his face. "I s'pose workin' the pits isn't that great either, am I right?" he said. "What do you plan to do with yer life? Do you plan to stay in Chicago?"

Albert was wary. He didn't want to lose his job. Remembering what his neighbor at the boarding house had told him, he cautiously phrased his answer. "I don't know, Mr. O'Banion, Sir," he said. "I like it here just fine."

"You can call me Angus, Lad," the Irishman replied. "No need for formality in the yards. We are all just as bloody as the next man. Don't worry. It isn't a sin to *dream* of a better place. You got other interests in your life? Like a sweetheart somewhere?"

"No, Sir," said Albert. "No sweetheart."

"A young man without a sweetheart?" Angus laughed. "Why, that's no good! You need to find yourself a girl. It will make the time in the pits go faster fer sure!"

The boss-man stood up then and stretched his back. "Well, we need to get back to it," he said. "C'mon, Lad. Back to work!"

Albert finished his day in a melancholy mind-set. Angus was right about one thing; he *was* old enough to have a sweetheart and, yet, in all his life the possibility had never even presented itself. It seemed as if all he had done all his life was work at the livery and dig trenches in the war. Sometimes, in his dreams, there would be a young woman. He could conjure up the smell of her sweet talcum and almost taste her lips. But, she never had a face and he could never hear her voice. She was always just beyond his reach, in a sort of misty cloud that eluded him night after night.

You love sick fool, he told himself. *There are more important things to worry about right now!* He had to think about getting further west than Chicago, out where the air wasn't thick with the putrid stench of the yards. Still, he couldn't help but wonder what it would be like, to be coming home to a warm woman rather than a cold, drafty room in a boardinghouse.

When the six o'clock whistle blew, he walked outside, toward the train tracks and the fresh air on the docks for his favorite time of the day, when he could take his leisurely stroll along the lake and forget the horrors of the slaughterhouse. He took a spot on a large, round piling and sat down, watching the sky slowly turn darker, watching the stars pop out one by one above his head. Memories of his grandmother came to him, how she, too, loved sitting under the night sky and sometimes even spoke to the constellations. Love of the stars must have been in his Wampanoag blood. *Was she looking down on him now*, he wondered. *Was she sitting with the old ones and the gods in heaven, watching over him?* He thought of Alfred Rose and the nights they had spent together on the roof of the livery.

Albert sighed deeply. It was time to go home, time to return to his little room at the boarding house and get some sleep before the night was gone and the routine started all over again. He stood up and walked down the dock, with the breezes off the lake at his back. As he approached the train tracks, he heard a whistle blow in the distance and saw the light of an approaching train. He paused at the rails and watched as it came closer and pulled up to the loading platform with several cars full of bleating cattle behind it. It was unusual for the train to be coming in so late, after all the cowhands that unloaded the cattle had left for the day. Albert heard the night watchman yell up at the conductor. "Why are you bringin' them in so late? It's past seven, Man! Everyone's gone home to supper! I've got nobody here to unload em!"

"We had trouble on the line," the conductor yelled back. "Cost us a day and a half gettin' the tracks repaired! It couldn't be helped! We were stuck out in the middle of nowhere! This bunch has been without water for too long. I figured I'd better get them delivered tonight. Would you rather I'd have brought you *dead* cows instead?"

The conductor jumped down from his perch in the locomotive and stood with the watchman trying to figure out what to do. "Who can we get at this hour that can handle a herd?" the watchman mumbled, as he walked right past Albert who was still sitting on the fence. "The boss-man's gonna have my head, if we lose any."

"I can herd them, Sir," Albert said suddenly. "Give me a good horse and I'll bring them down to the pens for you."

The night watchman looked at Albert warily. *"You?"* he said. "You ever herd cattle before, Boy?"

Albert knew he had only herded sheep and goats in Orleans, *but how much different could cattle be?* he thought to himself. *So what if I lie just a little? He and Goblin had done it dozens of times before.* He jumped down off the fence and followed the watchman.

"Well, if you think you know what yer doin'," said the man. "Saddle one of those horses over there and be quick about it! We got to get those cows to water before they start fallin' down dead!"

Albert knew instinctively what to do. He pulled a worn saddle and bridle down from the fence and threw them on the closest horse in the pen. Pulling himself up in the stirrups, he leaned over and opened the gate to the aisle way that led to the train. The watchman opened another gate and yelled to Albert. "When you unload em' bring em' down this way into this empty lot." Another man had appeared from somewhere inside the slaughterhouse. "Sam! Get some more water down here. We have a thirsty herd comin' in."

The gate on the train slid open on its squeaky tracks and Albert watched as the thirsty cows came down the ramp, stumbling and stepping over each other, moaning pitifully. Albert could feel his horse knew exactly what to do; he could feel the tenseness in the animal's withers as they went to work. *It felt like he was riding old Goblin again.* "Heyahhh!" he yelled, slapping his hands on his thighs to urge the cows to move forward. "Heyahhh!"

The horse moved to the right with the slightest touch of the rein to turn the cows to the left. Then, it jumped back, planting its hooves, when Albert wanted the herd to move right. It was a dance he had danced many times. They moved together, Albert and the horse, as one. Not a single cow broke rank and soon the entire herd was unloaded and moved into the holding pen, where they rushed to the troughs and immersed their black noses in the water.

The night watchman came toward Albert as he climbed down out of the saddle and he put out his hand. "I need to shake your hand, Boy," he said. "You saved my life! Where did you learn to handle cattle like that?"

Albert felt a burst of pride in his chest as the man pumped up and down on his arm. "Back in Orleans, Sir," he said, trying to sound humble. "Wasn't anything to it! Cattle, sheep, goats; they're all pretty much the same, if you've got a good horse."

"You work around here, don't you?" asked the man. "I've seen you before."

Albert began to unsaddle the horse. "Yes, Sir," he said. "I've been workin' the pits for a while now."

The man raised his eyebrows. *"The pits?"* he said with surprise. "When you are as good on a horse as *that*? I think you deserve a promotion! I'll be sure the boss-man knows how you handled yourself! And, I thank you kindly!"

Albert was pleased. It was the first *good* thing that had happened since he had arrived in this filthy town. *And, maybe, just maybe, it would be his ticket out.*

Chapter Seventy-Eight *"The Road to Ursa"*

The next day started out just like any other. Albert ate his breakfast and went off to his job in the pits as usual, where, staring up at him, were the same piles of dismembered cow parts he faced every day. By the time the lunch whistle blew, bloodied and stinking, he made his way to the platform above the main floor, where Angus was waiting for him. Albert pulled the dry toast from his pocket and sat down on the platform, swinging his legs over the side.

"I heard you were a *hero* last night," Angus said. "Heard you saved a load of cattle from dyin' of thirst."

Albert laughed. "Oh, it wasn't no big deal," he said. "I just happened to be there and I knew how to ride a horse, that's all."

Angus shook his head. "Heard it was more than that," he replied. "Heard you are pretty darned *good* on a horse! A regular *cowhand*! That's the rumor goin' around this mornin'!"

Albert couldn't help but smile; he *was* proud of the job he had done.

"Thinkin' maybe we should move you out of the pits and put your arse in a saddle."

Albert was happy to hear that. He would surely prefer working on a horse than working in the pits! "Where ever you want to put me, Angus, is fine with me," he said calmly, but on the inside his heart was pounding.

Angus said no more about it and Albert thought the boss-man had forgotten about it altogether. They finished their lunch and went back to work. For the rest of the afternoon, Albert lost himself in his labors, trying not to get his hopes up. *Angus was probably just making conversation*, he told himself, *and probably nothing would ever come of it. So he could ride a horse. So what*? So could a thousand other men in the yards, men with more time on the job than he had. Still his mind wandered a bit; the west was out there, *somewhere*, calling him. *Maybe this wasn't the day. What was it his grandmother used to say? Patience is a virtue?*

By the time the six o'clock whistle blew, Albert had given up any hope that anything more would come of it. He hosed the filth off his arms in the outdoor faucet and stood there, looking out over the miles of cattle pens. Suddenly, someone moved behind him and he turned around to face a stranger standing there. "Is your name *Albert?*" the man asked.

He didn't look like a worker from the yards. He looked like one of the cattle buyers that frequented the livestock pens throughout the day, shopping for good breeding stock. He was dressed in a grey suit with a flashy necktie and his shoes had a spit-shine to them.

"Yes," Albert replied. "*I am Albert Snow.*"

The man looked around and stepped gingerly around the sticky puddles of blood on the cement floor until he found a dry spot near the wall. "I understand you are pretty good on a horse."

Albert's heart lurched. *Maybe this was his day after all!* "Oh, I'm ok, I guess," he said humbly. "Been ridin' since I could walk, almost."

"Yes, so I hear," said the man. "*Frank Purcell's* the name. I'm in the cattle business."

Albert shook the man's hand. "I am happy to meet you, Sir," he said.

"I run cattle down south of here," said Frank. "It was my herd you saved last night. I wanted to thank you for what you did."

So that was it; the man wanted to thank him for getting his dumb cows off the train. Quit wasting my time, thought Albert sourly. *My supper's waitin'.*

The man seemed to be studying Albert, sizing him up and down. "Where are you from, Albert?"

"I'm from Orleans," Albert replied. "*That's on Cape Cod.*"

Now, he's going to ask me what a little rich kid from Cape Cod is doin' in the Chicago yards, thought Albert.

"Well, you're a long way from home," said Frank. "How'd you like to get a little further west?"

Albert blinked. *Was he serious or was he kidding?*

"I've got a job for you, if you're interested," replied Frank. "I'm always looking for good cowhands. My ranch is down around Ursa, near the state line. Do you know where that is?"

"No, Sir," said Albert. "Chicago is as far west as I've been so far."

The man reached into his pocket and produced a crisp twenty-dollar bill. "Here is your train-fare and some food money," Frank said, patting Albert across the shoulders. "Check in with my brother, Larry, as soon as you get down there. You'll have to get off the train at Quincy, and go north to Ursa. You can't miss my ranch. Cows for as far as you can see."

Albert made his way back to the boardinghouse in a stupor. He gathered up his few possessions and had his bag packed at the door. Thinking it wouldn't do to just run out on Angus without even a goodbye, he went to bed, planning to settle up with the landlady first thing in the morning and report to the yards for the last time to tell them he was leaving.

"I can't say as I blame you, Albert," Angus told him the next morning; for the first time he had called Albert by his given name. *No one would ever call him dandy-boy ever again*!

"I know it was partly due to you," said Albert. "Mister Purcell would never have known who I was if you hadn't told him. For that, Angus, I will always be grateful."

Angus slapped Albert across the shoulders, as was his usual way. "Nothin' to it," he said. "I'm gonna miss you, Kid! Stop in and say hello if you ever get back to Chicago!"

And, that was that. Albert boarded the train at half past seven; not since the day he had left Orleans had he felt so elated.

Chapter Seventy-Nine *"The Great River"*

Albert soon got bored looking at his own reflection in the window of the train; there was nothing to see in the darkness outside, so he closed his eyes. Only the periodic announcements from the porter told him where they were, *LaGrange, Naperville, Plano*, names that meant nothing to Albert. He waited and listened for the town of *Quincy* to be announced.

He tried to sleep as the train lumbered along but as soon as he began to drift off, he heard Alfred Rose's voice, muffled and frantic, calling to him in Wampanoag from somewhere in the distance. Albert woke up trembling. *Alfred's not here, you fool*, he said to himself aloud. *He's buried in Petersburg, along with the other soldiers.* Suddenly, he remembered he was not alone and he noticed the startled expressions on the faces of his fellow passengers at his strange utterances. Embarrassed, he turned back toward the window and closed his eyes again. *Poor Alfred Rose*, he thought, for he missed his friend. His death still tormented Albert. *Why had he been lucky enough to have escaped the bullets? Why was Alfred Rose not so lucky?*

It was barely dawn when he finally heard the town of Quincy announced and the train slowly grinded to a halt. When Albert got outside and was finally able to stretch his legs again on the train platform, his eager eyes took in all there was to see. He picked up his bag and ventured out to explore his surroundings and to find a place he could get some breakfast. It was a grand little town, while not so large and bustling as Chicago, but not nearly so filthy either. The main street was only packed clay, but it boasted an impressive row of brick buildings and raised sidewalks just the same. He passed the county courthouse with its green dome and spiraling turrets and checked the time on a huge clock that stood in front of an establishment called the *Cincinnati Store. Seven a.m. on the dot.* He thought about Angus, how he would *already be working at the yards. The yards that were, thankfully, three hundred miles away!*

He entered the store, bustling with train passengers and early-rising farmers, where he purchased two hard boiled eggs from the clerk, stowing them in his pocket, and a cup of coffee. He went back outside, toward a steel truss bridge that was painted the color of pea soup, waiting to take the train over the river. *What was the name Alfred Rose had called it? The great river?* He wandered down to a landing along the shore, where a string of flat, ferry rafts were tied up and available to take people and wagons across. Albert stared at the wide, muddy stretch of water in front of him, not impressed. "Is that the Mississippi?" he asked an old man, who was tending the boats.

"Yes, Sir," said the man. "You want to cross over?"

"What's on the other side?" asked Albert.

"Why, that's the state of *Missouri*, Boy," said the man. "If you want me to take you across, it'll be a nickel, one way."

Albert's mind wandered back, back to something else Alfred Rose had said, how he had wanted to be the first Wampanoag to cross the great river and live to tell about it. Albert smiled and dug in his pocket for *two* nickels. "Take me across and bring me back," he told the old man.

"You just want to go over and come right back?" the man asked.

"Yes," said Albert. "That is exactly what I want to do."

"Well, it's *your* money," the man said, shaking his head. "Watch your step."

Albert boarded the raft and held on to one of the rails that ran down each side, while the old man manned the rudder in the rear and steered the vessel out onto the river. The water swirled around them; the current was swift beneath the creaking timbers as they moved across the water. When they had reached the midpoint, Albert reached in his pocket and pulled out Alfred Rose's tobacco pouch. He looked down at it in his hands. He had never developed a liking for chewing tobacco; that was Alfred Rose's habit. With a smile, he held his hand out over the railing and let the little bag fall into the current where it quickly disappeared beneath the surface. *Now,*

Alfred Rose has crossed the great river, Albert thought; *maybe his spirit will finally rest peacefully.* It was not an attractive river; it was murky and brown and not so *great* in Albert's eyes. But, even his grandmother had called it the *great river; and, beyond it,* she used to say, *was death.* Neither Alfred Rose nor his grandmother had made it this far; *death* had taken them both first. Death was behind them now. *They were just Indian legends,* he thought; he wasn't sure what to believe. And, from what Albert could see*, the great river was just another river.*

He was glad to step onto solid ground again and he thanked the man for taking him on his frivolous voyage. Parting with two nickels was not prudent in his circumstances, but he felt compelled to do it nevertheless. Whether it was out of love for his grandmother or pity for Alfred Rose, he wasn't sure; perhaps it was because there was some Wampanoag blood still running through his veins and he had to prove a point.

The road that led north out of Quincy stretched out across a flat, wide plain with alfalfa fields on both sides and hundreds of haystacks drying in the morning sun. Albert took in a deep breath and closed his eyes for a brief moment. It was the smell his nostrils had been yearning for; the stench of Chicago was only a distasteful memory now. He hastened his steps, eager to get to the Purcell ranch, eager to get in the saddle again.

"How far is Ursa, Sir?" he asked a man passing by him on the sidewalk.

The man turned and pointed north. "About eleven miles, that way," he replied.

"Thank you, kindly," said Albert.

As he walked the length of the main street and glanced down the streets that intersected with it, he got the impression that it was a very *affluent* town. It reminded him of Wellfleet, back home, with its large mansions and well-tended lawns. *Must be a lot of rich folk in Quincy*, he thought to himself, maybe rich cattlemen like Mister Purcell. He was anxious to get a look at the Purcell house in Ursa as he strode happily down the road that took him away from downtown.

The walk took him all day. The actual town of Ursa was hardly a town at all, compared to neighboring Quincy. There was a graveyard, a church and several grain silos on one side of the street; on the other was a small mercantile with some old-timers in overalls sitting on a bench in front. The town had steadily shrunken ever since the railroad had passed it by. "Is it this way to the Purcell ranch?" Albert called to them.

"Yes," one of them yelled back. "Straight ahead."

He saw the cattle first and Mister Purcell had been right; the herds of black and red beasts spread out like a giant shadow across the pastures far beyond what his eyes could see. Then, as he came closer he finally spied the ranch house, sitting back against a hill; three stories tall with open balconies on both the upper floors, it was what Albert envisioned a plantation house would look like in the deep south. Surrounding the house, were miles of white rail fences, and dozens of horses grazing within them, fine-looking, well-muscled cow horses. He looked back at the cattle in the distance that didn't appear to be secured behind any fences at all. Strange, he thought, that the cattle were ranging free. Orleans' farmers had fenced their pastures years before to keep their livestock from wandering off. But, then, he hadn't seen any other ranches on his walk from town. Maybe the Purcell family owned all the land around Ursa and it didn't matter where the cattle wandered.

A man spied Albert making his way up the long drive toward the house. "You there!" the man said. "Can I help you?"

Albert nodded; the man looked familiar, maybe a relative of Mister Purcell. *"Mister Purcell* sent me," he told the man. "He hired me on as a cowhand."
A smile came across the man's face, a *friendly* smile. "Well, welcome to the *Purcell* ranch! C'mon up to the house and we'll talk."

Albert approached the expansive yard that surrounded the big house. The shade of several large oak trees created a canopy over his head.

"I'm *Larry* Purcell," said the man, coming forward. "You must have met my brother, Frank."

"Yes, Sir," replied Albert. "We met at the Chicago yards."

"Then, you must be the young man who saved our cattle," said the man. "For that, you have my gratitude! What's your name, Son?"

"Albert," Albert said. "Albert Snow, Sir."

"Well, I'm pleased to make your acquaintance, *Albert Snow*," said Larry Purcell. "C'mon inside and sit a spell. Did you walk all the way from Quincy? That's quite a hike."

"No, Sir," said Albert. "It wasn't all that far."

"You don't have your own horse?" asked Larry. "Most cowhands have their own horses."

"I had to leave mine behind," explained Albert. "He was getting on in years and I was afraid he wouldn't take the trip too well. I'm from Cape Cod, Orleans, Massachusetts, actually. It was a long way to Chicago. I came out after the war was over."

"Well, no matter," said Larry. "We've got plenty of good horses here on the ranch. We'll let you have your pick."

Albert followed the man up the steps of the big house and through a wide, carved door. The inside was as impressive as the exterior of the house; Albert had never seen such luxury in his lifetime. He was taking it all in, the tapestries on the floors, the chandeliers hanging from the ceilings. Then, *she* walked through an open door and Larry introduced them, while Albert stared, tongue-tied and in awe of the beautiful girl before him.

"This is my sister, *Maggie*," he said. "Maggie, this here is *Albert Snow*, our new cowhand."

Chapter Eighty *"Maggie"*

It wasn't her long blond hair that she kept tied up in a slightly lop-sided ponytail on top of her head. It wasn't her smooth skin, kissed and freckled by the sun. It wasn't even her powder-blue eyes that twinkled like rough-cut diamonds when she spoke. For Albert, that first day, it was the way she was *dressed* that caught him off-guard and impressed him the most. As she strode into the room and they were introduced, she had pulled off one of her leather gloves and extended her bare hand to him. He had never seen a woman in denim pants and pointed boots before; indeed, Albert had never seen a woman in *anything* but a skirt! Her attire was not feminine but there was something very provocative about the way her clothes hugged her body, revealing her womanly curves. "Welcome to the Purcell ranch," she said, her mouth breaking into a warm smile that made Albert feel genuinely welcome. "My brother here says you were quite a hero back in Chicago."

Albert laughed. "Not really," he replied. "I just helped with your father's herd."

Maggie's head tilted slightly and her eyes narrowed. "My *father*?" she asked. "You must mean my big brother, Frank. Our father passed away seven years ago."

"Oh," mumbled Albert. "I just thought, since he was so much older than you...."

Larry explained. "There are seven of us, spread out over twenty years. Ma had babies up until she died having little Horace. And, he's twelve now!"

"I didn't see any new horses in the barn," Maggie said. "Did you bring your own?"

"No," Albert told her. "I had to leave him behind in Orleans. He was getting a bit old for cattle work."

"Sometimes the old ones are the best. You might be surprised how much heart they have," she said. "Too bad about yours. But, we'll find you a good horse, though. Don't you worry."

"I thought maybe you would show Albert around," Larry said. "I've got some business to attend to in town this morning."

"I'd be happy to," she said, flashing that smile again. "C'mon, Albert. We'll start by finding you a new mount!"

They had gone out into the autumn sunshine and Maggie led him to the barn that sat beside the house. As they walked through the open aisle way between the stalls, he watched her closely as she paused at each stall, rubbing the heads of each horse and calling them by name. "We'll be moving all the herds closer to town this week," she said. "We don't like em to be too far away when winter hits."

"How many acres does your father…. I mean, your *brother* own?" Albert asked.

"I'm not sure of the exact acreage," said Maggie. "But, everything from here to Quincy, that's ours, for sure. And, west, to the river."

She paused at a stall door and opened it. "You might like this one," she said. "My father used to ride him; we gentle-broke him as a two-year-old. He's a darned good cattle horse."

Albert followed her into the stall and a horse came through the open door from an outer corral. He was tall and broad-chested, a pale buckskin with dark eyes and a white spot on his dark nose.

"We call him *Spotlight*," said Maggie. "You can see why."

Albert ran his hand down the horse's face and patted his neck.

"He likes you," she said. "He's a good boy. Nothing rattles him, if you know what I mean. We don't raise high-strung horses on the *Purcell*."

"You want to work with me, Boy?" Albert asked the horse.

"You can try him out tomorrow," said Maggie. "You'll be coming along when we move the herds. I think you two will get along just fine."

She showed him, then, where everything was in the barn, where the tack was stored and the tool room.

"Horace does the feeding, so you don't have to worry about that," she told him. "All you have to do is cool him down, hose him off if you need to and brush him dry before you put him away. But, you already know that, I'm sure, having a horse of your own. We take good care of our horses here. Can't work em as hard as we do unless we take good care of them too."

She showed him the big room above the stalls. "These beds will fill up, come roundup time," she said. "But, you can have your pick of them now. We bring on the temporary help in the spring."

Albert immediately found a bed that looked unclaimed situated under a window. "This one will suit me fine," he said.

Chapter Eighty-One *"A New Life"*

They invited him to supper, shared in a plain dining room just off the big kitchen. It didn't look at all like the rest of the grand old house. The floors were bare wood; the long table was unadorned and set with thick porcelain plates. But, then the *Purcells* didn't look like the type of people who would live in the lavish lifestyle that the rest of the house suggested. They were *country* folk, died in the wool, plain and simple. And, as Albert was introduced to the entire family sitting around the table, he liked them all immediately.

Frank, who had not yet returned from Chicago, was the eldest son, followed by a daughter, Pomsilia, who had gone off and married a man from La Grange. Larry was the third child, who ran the ranch in his older brother's absence. Larry was followed by Luther, and then the twins, Aaron and Maggie, and the baby of the family, Horace. At the far end of the table were two hired cowhands, Jed and Joe. Talk commenced as soon as they all had taken their seats about the round up the following day. "I want you two in the flank," said Larry to Jed and Joe. "Albert, you can follow along with them and see how we do things. The object for the next few days will be to bring them down from the high meadows where we can keep an eye out for them when it starts snowing."

"Wolves are already out, scouting," said Luther. "I saw tracks just today. They must be hungry; they're movin' in awful early this year."

Larry nodded and frowned. "Yes, I know. I ran into old man Weatherby in town. He's lost three calves already to the wolves."

"How are you at shootin', Albert?" Luther asked pointedly. "Think you can take down a wolf at a hundred yards?"

"We sometimes had to shoot wolves back in Orleans," replied Albert. "I'm ok, I guess."

"You must've got plenty of shootin' experience in the war," Larry commented. "Did you get to shoot a lot of rebels?"

It was a question Albert hated answering. "I did more *digging* than *shooting*," he said. "Being a soldier isn't all that glamorous, I'm afraid."

"Well, I suppose *someone* has to dig the trenches," said Larry. "Where did you fight?"

"In Virginia, Sir," said Albert politely, wishing someone would change the subject. "Around Petersburg and Richmond, mostly."

"No need to keep calling me *Sir*, Albert. Just *Larry* will do," the boss told him. "Then, you must've got into it late in the fighting, just before Lee surrendered."

"Yes," said Albert. "It was the longest nine months of my life."

"Well, it's all over now," said Luther. "Now, we can all get back to ranchin'."

Maggie was quiet through supper, giving her brothers control of the conversations. She smiled at Albert across the table. Finally, she stood up and said, "I'm going to bed, boys. Five a.m. is going to come early!"

"You are going on the roundup too?" asked Albert; his expression must have shown his surprise.

"Of course," she said. "*All* the Purcells take part in the round-up. Even us *delicate* little girls!"

She was mocking him in a friendly way.

"*Delicate, nothing!*" said Luther. "She can outshoot *and* outride me! Don't let her fool you, Albert!"

"That's not hard to do, Brother," said Maggie. "You are as slow as *molasses in January*."

They all laughed as Maggie left the room. Albert stared after her, with a peculiar admiration. *What a strange girl*, he thought. *Strange and wonderful!*

Five a.m. did come early. Albert was awakened by Jed and Joe as they rolled up their bed rolls and pulled on their boots. As Albert saddled Spotlight, he thought about Goblin back home and he reminded himself that he needed to write his father a letter, now that would be in one place for a while. They headed out together, the entire Purcell family and the hired hands, down the road and across the field, following the long dark shadow that was the herd in the distance. Being in the saddle again felt good to Albert, more comfortable than he had felt in a long time.

They herded cattle until dusk, bringing them down from the high meadows until the Purcell ranch was surrounded with them. Horace had gone ahead and had thrown out piles of hay to entice them away from the green grass and Albert followed Jed and Joe, pulling in the ones who had strayed. It went on for three days, until all of the cows had been accounted for.

A week later, the first snows came, blowing in from across the river. Then, Albert's days consisted of riding guard over the cattle with the others, rescuing some that had fallen into deep snowbanks, pulling sleds piled high with hay over the snow to the hundreds of hungry mouths and breaking ice that had formed on the water troughs. Winter, he soon found out, was the hardest, when the bone-chilling winds whipped through the valley, and Albert's face turned as red as if the summer sun had blistered it. Winters had been cold back in Orleans, but he had never stayed out in it for hours on end or through the night, as he did now when he drew the graveyard shift.

There was a bright spot, however. Coming back to supper in the room off the kitchen where a warm fire crackled in the hearth and the people around the table were as warm as the food that simmered on the stove. And, of course, there was *Maggie*.

Frank had returned from Chicago weeks before with a new bull he had purchased and they had all ridden down to the station in Quincy to unload the beast from the train and get him safely home.

"He's a good-looking animal," Larry told Frank the minute he saw him coming down the ramp.

"Best one in the whole lot," Frank told them. "I think he will sire us some good strong calves."

Albert had never seen an animal so huge and intimidating. His horns were at least four inches around, although they had been filed back on the tips. His chest was enormous, bulging and heaving, as they secured him on both sides with ropes and prepared to lead him down the road toward the Purcell. Surrounded by horses and men on every side, they walked him home through the snow and put him up in the barn.

"He doesn't go out with the herd?" asked Albert.

"We've got another bull we'll have to separate before we introduce him or there'll be blood drawn," said Frank. "I got a good deal on him but I don't want him injured right out of the chute!" He turned to Luther. "Be sure you secure him good. I don't want him bustin' out in the middle of the night."

When Albert finally crawled into his bed, he could still hear the new bull stomping in the stall below and bellowing to the cows across the road. It didn't appear to bother Jed and Joe much; they commenced snoring almost as soon as their heads hit their pillows. But, Albert tossed and turned for a while, unable to sleep. He finally got up and pulled on his clothes to go downstairs. As soon as his feet hit the barn floor, he heard a voice coming from somewhere in one of the stalls, *a familiar feminine voice*. When he strained his ears to listen and followed his ears, he found Maggie, sitting cross-legged just outside the stall door on a bale of straw, singing softly to the new bull. When she saw Albert approaching in the lantern light, she stopped singing. "I'm sorry, Albert," she said. "I didn't mean to wake you. This poor old guy was real restless. He knows there are cows out there somewhere. I was just tryin' to calm him down."

Albert peered over the stall door and the bull was lying there in the straw, sound asleep. "Well, it looks like it worked," said Albert. "He's sleeping like a newborn calf."

She chuckled. "I guess I'll go on up to the house then," she said. "He'll be ok tomorrow, when he gets to meet his new harem. He'll be so tired from now till spring, he'll be *napping* in the afternoon."

Albert laughed. "You're awfully good with animals," he said. "The horses and cows seem to love you. What gave you the idea to sing to him like that?"

"We used to have a family of Indians that lived up along the river," she said. *"Peorias,* I think they were called. Anyway, I went to school with one of the girls. She taught me that the Indians sometimes sing to go to sleep."

Albert was intrigued, remembering the strange customs of the Wampanoag back in Orleans. "I have Indian ancestors myself," he said. "My grandmother was part Wampanoag."

"Wampanoag?" said Maggie. "I don't think I've ever heard of them before."

"Well, my grandmother used to tell me about their customs."

"I thought my friend was *fascinating,"* said Maggie. "She told me lots of stories. What did your grandmother tell you?"

Albert sat down on the barn floor. "Oh, about the *three sisters* and the *sacrifice rock*," he said. "And, of course, the *funeral pyres*. My friend, Alfred Rose, told me they believe that the fires release their spirits and that shooting stars are those spirits riding their chariots through the sky."

"Funeral pyres and sacrifice rocks?" said Maggie. "Wow. Their lives are so much more interesting than ours, don't you think?"

Albert got temporarily lost in his memories. "We had a funeral pyre for my grandmother, just before the war," he said. "I miss her a lot. She was an amazing woman."

"You'll have to tell me about her, sometime when it's not so late. I'm sorry if I kept you up," Maggie said. "Good night, Albert." She picked up the lantern and turned to go.

"If I can't sleep, will you come and sing to me?" Albert asked playfully.

Maggie stopped and turned toward him. In the lantern light, he could see she was smiling. He knew his words had been bold and provocative. He held his breath for her response.

"I might do more than just *sing* to you," she said, laughing flirtatiously.

Then she left, disappearing into the night like water in wet sand, leaving Albert standing in the dark barn with his heart beating wildly and a strong desire to chase after her.

Chapter Eighty-Two *"A Kiss on the Graveyard"*

They had drawn the *graveyard-shift* together. Every night, a team of two rode out to keep watch and to listen for wolves or an occasional bear that might be stalking the herd. On the Purcell, everyone took a turn at even the most monotonous chores; even Frank and Larry did not shrink from the most mundane responsibilities. Winter was winding down but there was still snow on the ground as Albert and Maggie saddled their horses after supper and mounted up for the long night ahead.

They rode up a trail that led to a high ridge, overlooking the valley. Albert had seen something in Maggie's eyes over the supper table that night, something unspoken but profound. It had been a week since their conversation in the barn. At first, Albert thought he had made a terrible mistake, that he had presumed too much and had offended her. But, tonight, her eyes had told him differently. She had taken the lead up the trail; her horse forged ahead, confident and familiar with his surroundings. In the distance, the wolves were already howling. They had to be vigilant tonight and they both had their rifles loaded and stowed beside them.

When they reached the ridge, Maggie got down from her horse and found a familiar rock on which to sit. Albert followed her in the moonlight and sat down only inches away. "The cows are restless tonight," she said. "They know the wolves are near."

"They won't stampede, will they?" Albert was thinking aloud.

"Let's not even *think* about that possibility," replied Maggie. "It's not something you want to see."

"It happens, then?"

"Usually, it takes more than just a few wolves howling in the hills," said Maggie. "I saw lightning strike once and spook the herd. We were chasing cows from here to the river for *days*."

She buttoned the top collar of her jacket and stuffed her hands deep into her pockets. "I'll be glad when spring comes," she said. "I get tired of the cold."

"Have you ever been outside of Ursa?" Albert asked.

"Frank took me to Chicago once," she replied. "I didn't like it much."

"Nor I," said Albert. "It's a dirty, stinking city. So you have never seen the ocean then?"

"I've seen the Mississippi river," she said. "And, Lake Michigan. That's enough water for me."

Albert laughed. "You should see the Atlantic Ocean when the sun comes up and shines across the water."

"Why did you ever leave it if it is such a pretty place?"

Albert wasn't sure he had an answer. "I just had to get away," he said. "From the war, from death, from *childhood*, I guess."

Maggie leaned a little closer in the darkness. "You are not a child anymore," she whispered. "And, are you happy here on the Purcell?"

Of that Albert was sure. "I've never been happier," he said. "But, one day, I might take you to Orleans. Just to see the sunrise."

Maggie laughed. "We have sunrises in Ursa too," she said.

"But, not like back in Orleans," Albert replied. "You'd have to *see* it to understand."

"I can tell you loved it very much," said Maggie.

Albert put his arm around her. He wanted to say *not as much as I love you*. Instead he leaned in close and whispered, "I kinda like it here, too."

He kissed her then, with the moon rising above their heads and the wolves howling in their ears. It was a kiss like none other and he felt it all the way to his toes and fingertips, and, from her response, he could tell she felt it too. Albert had come of age; he had finally met the girl of his dreams. He had so much he wanted to tell her, so much he wanted to learn about her. But, for now, all he wanted to do was kiss her again.

Suddenly, their horses stirred behind them. Maggie pulled away from Albert's embrace just as Larry came riding up out of the darkness. He reined in his horse next to the others.

"Albert, you need to get back down to the ranch," he said. "Frank has another job he wants us to do."

"What's going on?" Maggie asked.

"We've got free-grazers camped out up north," said Larry. "Frank wants to take all the men and run them off."

"Free-grazers?" asked Albert.

"As you know, we don't put up fences on the Purcell," Larry explained. "Sometimes men drive their cattle onto our land and eat up our grass. A few years back, some sheep farmers came across and, before we knew it, had chewed everything down to a nub. There was nothing left for *our* herd." He turned to Maggie. "You think you can handle the graveyard on your own?"

She was almost defiant in her tone. It seemed to be a status symbol for he, *to be as good as her brothers.* "I know how to do my job," she said. "You needn't worry about me. But, why can't *I* go too?"

"It didn't look like you were doing your job a few minutes ago," Larry replied, with a snicker. Albert felt his face get hot with embarrassment. "Besides, there might be trouble. And, *someone* needs to stay behind with the herd. Come on, Albert. Get on your horse. Maybe we can still catch a wink of sleep before we head out at dawn."

There was an awkward silence, as the two men rode down the trail together. *How much had Larry seen?* Albert wondered. *Would her brothers disapprove of his feelings toward Maggie? Could he get fired over it?* "I should probably explain," he began.

"No need," Larry told Albert. "Just remember, Maggie is only seventeen and she has never been away from home."

With that said, he spurred his horse on ahead and the matter was closed.

Chapter Eighty-Three *"The Free-Grazers"*

Before the sun appeared over the hills to the east the next morning, all the men on the Purcell were saddled and ready. With their shotguns at their sides within easy reach, they headed north in the shadowy mist that lingered over the Mississippi. The Purcell cattle were just waking from their damp, grassy beds across the fields and all looked calm. No one knew what they would encounter when they confronted the free-grazers.

They rode all day; it seemed to Albert that the Purcell ranch went on forever, crossing over from Adams County and into Hancock County to the north. Finally, they spotted the free-grazers, camped out in a wide green meadow. It looked to be no more than a half dozen cowhands watching the herd.

"We'll rest our horses down by the river," Frank told them. "We'll go in after dark, after they have bedded down for the night."

"And, what then?" Albert asked.

"We'll disarm them first," said Frank. "Then, we'll force them to move the herd north and off the Purcell."

"Does this happen very often?" asked Albert.

"With a ranch as big as ours," Frank told him, "It's bound to happen from time to time."

"We may have to put up fences one of these days," said Larry with a deep sigh. "Pa would never have approved of it though."

"Well, Pa didn't have to deal with this many cattlemen moving west," Frank replied. "In his day, there was no competition for the grass."

There was a lull in the conversation.

"Larry tells me you are smitten with my little sister," Frank finally said, breaking the silence.

Albert had expected some response but not such a public one, not with all the Purcell brothers and the two hired hands listening to the conversation. "I like her very much, Sir," said Albert.

"There you go again," said Frank, "Calling me *Sir*. Really, Albert, if we are to be all one family you're gonna have to start calling me Frank."

Albert laughed out loud, much to his own surprise. "I thought you all would object," he said. "I didn't know what to expect."

"All of us want her to marry one day and have a family," said Larry. "We had *hoped* it would be with a cattleman like us."

"Yes," Frank agreed. "But, with *one* condition."

"And, that would be?" asked Albert.

"That you treat her good and make her happy," Frank replied.

Having her brothers' approval meant a lot to Albert. *But, what if Maggie didn't want to marry him? Was it possible he had assumed too much?* He hadn't time to think on it; dusk was upon them and they waited on their horses on a rise above the meadow, until it became dark and they could see the campfires. Frank and Larry moved in first, instructing the others to spread out and approach the campsite from the opposite side.

"There's eight of us," said Larry. "If we each take one and disarm him, it should go quickly. Albert, you take the one on the graveyard."

Albert did as he was told. All the men moved forward, down the hill and surrounded the camp. Albert moved close to the herd and spied a man on horseback a few yards away; he reined Spotlight behind some brush and came up behind the man. Suddenly, the man turned and Albert cocked his rifle. "Don't bother trying," he said, when the man reached for his saddle holster. "I've got a scattergun aimed at your back. Just drop your rifle to the ground and there won't be any trouble."

The man, caught unaware, complied and dropped his weapon. "Are you *rustlers*?" the man asked. "You takin' the herd?"

"No," said Albert. "We don't want your herd."

At that moment, Albert heard loud voices from the nearby campsite. "Everyone just stay calm and no one will get hurt," he heard Frank's voice booming in the darkness.

"C'mon" he said to the man. "Get down off your horse and we'll go back to your camp."

When they were all seated around the campfire, and all the guns had been confiscated, Frank gave them instruction. "We're not here to *kill* anybody," he said. "But, we'll shoot if we have to. What I want you to do is get on your horses and turn your herd around. I want you to go north until you are no longer on our land."

"How will we know when we are off your land, Mister?" asked the leader of the group.

"When you get to Carthage," Frank replied. "You can take your cows wherever you want from there. Just know that we might not be so obliging next time."

The men were grumbling, but without their guns, there wasn't much they could do. They quickly saddled their horses and circled the herd. When the cows began to move on, the Purcell men waited until they were a good distance away before they turned around and headed home.

Chapter Eighty-Four *"The Love Nest"*

It seemed like it was meant to be. Maggie and Albert seemed perfect for each other. Both being almost born on horseback and with cattle ranching in their blood, no two people could have been more in tune. They had their wedding in the big house; a minister had come all the way from Quincy to perform the ceremony and they all gathered there in the fancy parlor. But, a romantic honeymoon was out of the question; it was springtime again, time for branding calves and shipping cows off to market. It was time to move the herd back to the new grass that had sprouted up all over the Purcell.

"We have a cabin," Frank told the newlyweds, knowing they would probably not want to stay in Maggie's little room forever. "Up on the high meadow; it was where our parents lived before the big house was built. It's yours if you want it."

Albert was pleased. He felt uncomfortable in the big fancy house. Maggie was excited about it too; she loved her parents' old cabin. "It's beautiful up there," she told Albert. "Wait until you see it. Let's ride out today. I don't think it will take much to get the cabin back into shape."

They rode together up the trail that afternoon as far as the high ridge, where they had shared their first kiss, and veered off the path through a grove of oak trees. There, next to a creek, was the quaint little cabin, built simply from logs and mortar. It only had two windows and a simple little fireplace, but the front porch looked out over the creek that came down from the hills carrying water from the melted snows, in several staggered steps, cascading down in a series of mini-waterfalls.

"We'll have to fix the chinking where it is cracked," said Albert, sizing up the work they would have to do to make the place livable again. "And, shore up that chimney. It's starting to lean."

Inside, they discovered a family of field mice that had taken up residence amongst the cobwebs and several bird families that occupied the nests that dotted the underside of the eaves above the porch. "We'll let the birds stay," said Maggie. "But, the mice will have to go."

Albert realized that it was a far cry from what Maggie had grown accustomed to, living in the big fancy Purcell house all her life. "Are you sure you will be happy here?" he asked. "It's awfully small."

Maggie answered him with a kiss. It was the only answer he needed. And, so began weeks of work on the old cabin, squeezed into the evening hours after their work with the cattle was done. The brothers helped; Frank offered them any of the furniture in the big house that they wanted and Larry helped to build a winter shelter for their horses in the rear. Luther and Aaron brought them a year's supply of firewood, which they stacked all along the outer cabin wall. And, little Horace, not wanting to be the only brother without a wedding gift, brought his sister a picture he had drawn himself to hang on the wall of her new house, a depiction of the sunrise over the hills, with the light shining down on the golden hayfields. "It's a very good picture," Maggie told him. "I know just where I will hang it."

Albert had finally written to his father with the happy news but had, as yet, not received a reply. He was beginning to worry, when, finally, a letter came one morning soon after. It was from his father, Thomas. "My grandfather is dead," Albert told his new bride, after he had read what the letter had to say.

"Was he the grandfather that married your Wampanoag grandmother?" Maggie asked. "What did you say his name was? *Thatcher*?"

"Yes," Albert told her. "We worked together at the livery almost all my life. You would have liked him, I think."

"Perhaps, your father can come for a visit, now that he is all alone."

"It would probably be simpler for me to take you back to Orleans," said Albert. "I am sure my father has never set foot on a train before."

Maggie had just put their supper on the table. It was nigh on to summertime and a refreshing breeze drifted in through the open windows of the cabin. With all the work now complete on their new home, they could finally enjoy their evenings alone, although she enjoyed cooking supper for her brothers when they came to visit.

"Well, I think you should invite him anyway," she said. "It is important to have family."

"*You* are my family, now," said Albert. "I never thought any woman could compare to my grandmother until I met you."

Chapter Eighty-Five *"Cabin Fever"*

In the fall, Maggie gave birth to a daughter they named Emeline and, for the first time in her life, Maggie's days did not revolve around cows and horses. Instead, there was a little girl who immediately ruled the household. Now, when Albert returned home in the evenings, he had *two* women waiting for him. Maggie was always eager to hear the news of the ranch; in many ways it was strange for her to be only *indirectly* involved with the day to day activities. For months, there was a growing concern on the Purcell; they had seen very little rain and the snows were late in coming. The little creek next to the house had slowed to a trickle, so scarce that Albert had to bring buckets of water up the hill so that they would have water to drink and bathe in. But, it was the cows that they worried most about. Without rain, the meadows were turning to dust, forcing the cattle to forage higher and higher in the hills and further and further away from the river.

"We found three more dead today," said Albert at supper. "The poor cows don't know which way to go, up the hill to find grass or down to the river for water. They're doomed either way they go."

Maggie was concerned too. She had seen droughts before, when everything turned brown as the relentless sun scorched the earth. She felt helpless; how could she help when she had a baby to care for? And, she was beginning to grow bored, being isolated from the ranch. When Albert took his turn at graveyard, she thought she would go mad, with no one to talk to and nothing to do.

"I would think the baby would keep you very busy," Albert told her. He had come home from his overnight post, and was looking forward to getting some sleep.

"She sleeps most of the time," Maggie told him. "And, when you come home you just go to bed too!"

"Maggie, I have to sleep *sometime*," Albert said. He didn't understand what she was complaining about. She no longer had to spend her days getting dusty and sweaty working with the cows. She had the sanctity of the trees and the creek; she had little Emmy to keep her company. And, yet, she seemed to grow more restless with every passing day.

Winter crept in silently after a long Indian summer. The sky would occasionally turn a promising shade of gray, but no rain or snow would follow. The clouds would linger for a while, like wanton temptresses, only to move on to the north and east, without leaving a drop of moisture behind. The river had become a shrunken mud pit, thick and undrinkable, and many of the cattle foundered from stomachs full of dirt. The Purcells were worried; if the drought went on much longer, they would be forced to do something drastic.

Albert hurried back to the cabin after every shift, trying to keep Maggie in good cheer, but even he was beginning to get discouraged.

"Why don't you let me take your shift tomorrow?" she asked him one evening. "I'm sure Frank and Larry won't mind. I haven't ridden my horse since before Emmy was born. And, you haven't spent nearly enough time with your daughter."

Albert wasn't sure he liked the idea. "What will I do without you here?" he asked. "I don't know how to change her diapers. And, I can't feed her!"

"You'll do just fine," Maggie said. "Are you saying our daughter is more trouble than a herd of dumb cows?"

In that context, he couldn't very well argue but Albert still wasn't convinced. "Your brothers will laugh at me," he said. "How will it look if *I* stay home to care for the baby and *you* go out to work on the ranch? I will never be able to show my face again!"

Maggie laughed at that. "Is that all you are worried about?" she asked. "My brothers won't laugh at you, I promise. *Please*, Albert. I need to get out or I will go *mad*!"

And, so, the next morning, it was with trepidation that Albert let her go out and saddle her horse, while he held little Emmy in his arms and waved good-bye. The morning air on her face was exhilarating, like the morning dew to the grass. Maggie leaned back in her saddle contentedly, in the seat that molded to her body perfectly. Not in a long time had she felt so happy, not even when little Emmy was born. It was a thought that seeped into her mind whenever she stepped outside, and, although she would never admit it to Albert, she was beginning to think she wasn't cut out to be a *mother*. She was much happier out riding her horse than being cooped up in their little cabin, so isolated from everything and everyone. How could she have been so wrong? She loved Albert; in the beginning their love had been exciting and new. Now, she felt as if her own life was passing her by. She missed her brothers; she missed the horses and the cattle. *Is it possible I don't have any maternal instincts in me?* she wondered, as she reined her horse down the familiar trail. All her life, her brothers had teased her about being a tomboy. Maybe she had soaked up too much of Aaron's testosterone while they shared their mother's womb. *Maybe she was meant to be a boy!*

Her brothers were not as surprised to see her as she thought they would be. "You got poor Albert doing diaper duty?" Larry asked her when she rode up to the barn where they were just saddling their horses for the day.

"Don't you *dare* tease him, Larry Purcell!" she said. "I begged him to let me take his place today."

All the brothers had a good laugh, imagining Albert playing the mother role back at the cabin.

"What's on the board today?" Maggie asked.

"We're movin' the herd farther north where the river is wider and there is a little more clean water," said Larry. "Damned fool cows! We've had to pull a dozen of them out of the mud so far this week!"

Maggie had not yet seen how low the river was, but she could only imagine with the condition of the pastures. She couldn't remember ever seeing it so dry. *Even the lizards were looking for water.* "And, still no rain," she said looking up at the clear sky. "How much longer can this go on?"

Frank mounted his horse and the others followed him. "We will have to make a difficult decision very soon," he said. "We might have to sell the herd to ranchers up in Minnesota where they still have grass. We've got a buyer but we have just been holding onto hope."

"Can you ship them all on the train? Do they have enough cattle cars to accommodate that many?" Maggie wanted to know.

Larry shook his head. "We'll have to drive them up," he told her. "It will be a long haul, but we've got to get them to grass and water if we don't get some rain soon."

It was a sobering thought. *Selling their cattle?* Maggie had never heard her brother sound so serious. *What would happen to the ranch? How would they make a living?* "What will we do without the cattle?" she asked.

"We'll all have to look for work elsewhere," Frank said flatly. "I don't see that we have much choice. The rain seems to be staying up north; there's no telling when we will get it back. If we wait too long, it will be too late."

"You're planning to move the herd in the *dead* of winter?"

"Maggie, there is no *snow* to deal with," said Frank. "This drought spreads clear across Iowa and Missouri too. We have no choice but to go north."

There was not much conversation for the rest of the day; all the brothers were going through the same emotions and Maggie returned home that night with the bad news.

"I knew they were *considering* selling," Albert told her, handing her the baby almost as soon as she came through the door. "Emmy is very happy you are home. I'm afraid her daddy isn't a very good substitute."

"Nonsense," replied Maggie. "She looks fine to me."

She changed out of her dusty clothes and prepared their supper, keeping her true feelings to herself. Her day of freedom had her thinking. She loved Albert; there was no doubt about that, and she wanted to be with him. But, the chains of motherhood, she had decided, were not for her. Maybe, this cattle drive was her way out.

"If Frank decides to move the herd up north and sell them, what will *we* do?" Albert asked.

"Why, we will go with them, of course," said Maggie. "Emmy and I can ride in the chow wagon and I can do the cooking…."

Albert shook his head. "A cattle drive is no place for a woman and baby," he said. "Really, Maggie, you must be more practical!"

"What is the difference between this cabin and a covered wagon?" she said. "Did you plan to leave me all alone for months?"

He hadn't thought of that. "Of course not," he said. "I…. I…don't know *what* I was thinking."

Chapter Eighty-Six *"The Drive"*

The decision was finally made. They were going to sell the herd and move them north to St. Paul. It had to be done. There wasn't enough water and grass left on the Purcell to sustain a thousand head of cattle. The brothers had put it to a vote, to sell out or risk losing the herd to thirst and starvation. Even if they would have purchased hay, with the rest of the Midwest as dry as the ground in Ursa, the price of hay had gone sky-high. What use would it be if they had hay but no water? The groundwater had been depleted and digging new wells was coming up fruitless as well.

The brothers and Albert outfitted the wagon for Maggie and little Emmy, making them a comfortable albeit confined bed amidst the supplies needed for the trip, while Albert slept outside with the men. It was not exactly what Albert had in mind, sleeping apart from his wife the entire journey, but he had no choice in the matter. Everyone was sacrificing *something*; indeed, every member of the Purcell family was losing a great deal. So, they started out on a cold day in late December, with Albert riding up front with Frank to be close to Maggie in the wagon.

They followed the eastern shore of the river or *what was left of it*, which wasn't much. There were only pockets of water, sometimes covered with a hard crust of ice, here and there, where the thirsty cattle would rush in and drain it dry. But most of the riverbed was nothing but a mosaic of dried mud, like an endless cobblestone road, stretching north as far as they could see. The grass was almost non-existent and the dry cornfields, with their withered stalks and stunted ears of dead corn, became the main fodder for the cattle. Day after day, through the mudflats full of dead fish and sandbars with exposed tree roots, they trekked, holding out hope that, around the next bend in the dry riverbed, they would find an oasis of green grass and blue water.

They passed through the little towns of Nauvoo and Moline, then on to La Crosse and Stillwater where other ranchers were experiencing the same plight, no grass and no water. Businesses had closed; farmers had moved north just as they were, chasing nature's illusive blue bounty. When cows died along the way, they quickly butchered them and ate their fill of fresh meat while it lasted, knowing every time it was taking another twenty dollars from their already dwindling profit.

The weather was viciously cold; nights under cloudless skies brought the temperatures so low some of the cows froze to death, with little fat on their bones to keep them warm. Albert and the other men slept around the fire, which they stoked to last throughout the night, while Maggie and little Emmy cuddled under several layers of blankets in the wagon. Even so, the baby caught cold and cried almost continually. It was not a pleasant journey for man *or* beast.

When they finally arrived in St. Paul, Frank and Larry rode into town to locate the man who had promised to buy the herd and he followed them back to inspect the animals he had agreed to purchase."They're nothing but bones!" the man remarked, his warm breath rising white in the cold air. "I'll not pay twenty dollars a head for cattle in this condition!"

Frank was exhausted from the long drive and his patience had worn thin. He knew the man had him at a disadvantage. The market was flooded with cheap cattle for sale; all the cattle from Ursa to St. Paul were starving too and ranchers were willing to sell at any price. "You won't find any cattle in these parts that have any more fat on them than mine," he said.

The man got off his horse and walked amongst the cattle to take a closer look. "Fifteen dollars a head," he said, shaking his head. "I can't pay you any more than that for this pathetic bunch."

Frank and Larry exchanged looks. The younger brothers had already agreed to let the elders of the family make the final decision. It was a decision that practically made itself; the herd would not survive the trip home and there was nothing to go home *to*. They had to settle up with their drovers. They had no choice but to sell. They shook hands and the deal was made.

They rented rooms in a hotel in St. Paul until they all made up their minds where they would go from there.

Albert and Maggie's room looked out across the river to its twin city, Minneapolis, on the other side. Maggie had finally put little Emmy down to sleep. She walked over to the window, where she stood staring at the river below. Albert came up behind her, encircling her waist with his arms and drawing her near to him. "I've missed sleeping with you," he murmured in her ear. "It was a long drive."

Maggie pulled away. *"Don't*, Albert," she said in a tone that surprised him.

"What's wrong?" he asked. "Have I done something to upset you?"

Maggie crossed the room, peering down at Emmy and pulling the blanket up around the little girl's chin. She sighed deeply. "No," she said. "You haven't done anything that *I* haven't done."

"What does *that* mean?" he asked, totally perplexed with his wife's mood.

"Oh, Albert," she said. "What are we going to do now? How will we make a living without the herd?"

Albert was slightly relieved to discover that losing the herd was what was bothering her. He had expected worse; he had thought her melancholy mood was *his* fault somehow. "Frank has paid me fairly," he assured her. "I expect I can find a job quickly with one of the cattle owners up here. I will take care of you and Emmy. You needn't worry about that!"

Maggie's eyes met his. "You will let us go with you, then?"

"Now, Maggie," said Albert, "We've discussed this before. A cattle drive is no place for a woman and a baby. We will find you a nice place to live while I am away. Maybe, I can even find a job on one of the ranches here in St. Paul and not have to leave you at all."

"I don't want to be left behind, Albert," she said. Her words were full of anguish, as if she were about to burst into tears. "Now, that I'm...."

Albert felt like a man in the dark; he had no inkling of what was upsetting her so.

"I'm pregnant again!" she said. "Does that make you happy? *I'm truly doomed!"*

Chapter Eighty-Seven *"The Inside of a Bottle"*

Doomed? Maggie's words stung Albert deeply and he felt tears welling up in his eyes. He couldn't speak; he could hardly *breathe*! *Was this the woman he loved, the woman he thought loved him*? *How could she even think such a thing, let alone say it*? She was acting like a spoiled child! His male ego got the better of him and he grabbed his coat and stormed out of the hotel room, slamming the door behind him.

He was glad he was in a strange town among strangers; this was not something he wanted to discuss with Frank and Larry and the others. It was too personal; it was too painful. He needed to be alone. It didn't take him very long to find sanctuary in a tavern three doors down the street from the hotel and he wandered in, looking for a corner in which he could curl up and nurse his wounded pride.

"Whiskey," he told the barkeep. "*Double.*"

Albert had never tasted anything stronger than beer in his life but this night called for something more potent. *He'd earned the right! By God, he was a husband and a father! He had served his country in the war! He had survived the pits in Chicago! He had the right to get good and drunk if he wanted to!*

The whiskey was bitter on his tongue when he took his first drink and it burned his throat all the way down to his gullet. *Kind of like tasting tobacco for the first time with Alfred Rose.* His tears rose up again at the thought of his friend who now lay in a grave back in Virginia. *In the cold, dark ground,* he thought miserably. *I should've built him a pyre to die on. I shouldn't have let them bury him with the others. Alfred Rose wasn't like the others. He was different. He was a Wampanoag!*

He ordered another drink. *Why were the glasses so damned small?* he wondered. *Why didn't they serve this stuff in a mug that a thirsty man could get his fist around?* He fumbled in his pocket and let several bills fall onto the table. "Keep 'em coming," he told the man.

Above the bar, there was a mirror that reflected the row of bottles in front of it. Tall bottles, short bottles, pudgy, round bottles with bright labels and all sorts of different colored liquors inside them. *Kinda like the men in the USCT,* he thought. *Black, brown, white…. but would they would all bleed red, like William had said? Ha! William had no idea what blood looked like! He had never seen the bloody yards in Chicago! Talk about blood! Bubbly Creek and the gauntlet floor was every bit as bad as the battlefield in Petersburg. No, not quite,* he thought sadly. *Petersburg was where he lost his best friend.* His *only* friend.

A group of men came into the tavern, well-dressed, rich cattlemen, and they pulled up chairs at the table next to him. Laughing and swigging liquor, their voices were muffled and blended in his ears. *What was that they said? A cattle drive?* That was what Albert needed! He needed to do business with these men! He needed another job so that he could take care of his wife and baby! *Making a killing? Who was making a killing?* thought Albert. *Certainly not Larry and Frank Purcell!* The more he listened, the more confused he became; *cattle selling at fifty dollars a head?* That didn't make much sense. *Frank had only gotten fifteen dollars!* He had heard it with his own ears. He had seen Frank sign the papers and shake the man's hand!

He stood up and held on to his chair for balance. The room seemed to be spinning around him. Maybe he would discuss business with these gentlemen at another time. He needed to feel fresh air on his face and he staggered toward the door, where the icy wind blowing in caught him off guard. For a moment, he felt sober, as the bitter night air stung his uncovered cheeks and hands. Then, dizziness set in again and he stumbled down the street in a haze. He put his arms around the street light on the corner, hugging it like he had wanted to hug Maggie, but the iron pole was every bit as cold to his touch as his wife had been. *Still,* he thought with a slight snicker, *street lights didn't talk back!* He couldn't remember his mother ever talking back to his father....no, *wait....* he had never even *known* his mother! She had died just after he was born. He didn't even know what she looked like! He only remembered his grandmother....

now *there* was a wise old woman. *Not a spoiled teenager like the one he married.*

He sank down, sitting on the curb, leaning his back against the pole. The sky was clear, much clearer than his mind at the moment. He found himself watching for shooting stars; for Wampanoag spirits riding their chariots. It all sounded pretty silly to him now, sitting drunk on a street corner. But, there was nothing silly about Alfred Rose. So what, if he believed the only way to heaven was through a fire? Maybe the three sisters and the sacrifice rock *did* exist! Maybe, it was the *white* man's God who was the lie. Who knew? He certainly didn't; who was he to say what was the truth? About all he knew at the moment was that his butt was growing numb on the cold sidewalk, and he was tired and wanted to go to bed.

He pulled himself up and stumbled back in the direction of the hotel. Up the stairs, down the hall, searching for their room number.... *what was their room number again? Number seven? No, that was his room back in Chicago, in the boardinghouse.* Sleep was taking hold of him. He couldn't seem to stay awake any longer. He found the door; at least he *thought* it was the door, and he knocked softly. He didn't want to wake little Emmy. There was no answer; the door did not open. He knocked again. *She wasn't going to let him in. Maggie was being stubborn again.* He leaned his back against the door frame and slid down to the floor, closing his weary eyes.

Things would look better in the morning. They just *had* to!

Chapter Eighty-Eight *"A Hotel on Wheels"*

By morning, the world *didn't* look any better for poor Albert; in fact, it looked and *felt* much worse! Frank had found him in the hall, curled up in a fetal position outside their hotel room door, and he gently woke him. "Albert," he whispered. "C'mon, Man, get up. What are you doing out here in the hallway? Did my sister lock you out?"

Albert rubbed his eyes and then his aching head. "We had a quarrel," he said, sheepishly, not wanting to explain more.

"Well, come join us for breakfast," said Frank. "Are Maggie and the baby up yet?"

"I don't think so," Albert replied. "Let's just let them sleep."

He followed Frank down the stairs to the hotel dining room and they were greeted by Larry and the rest of the crew.

"Looks like old Albert here tied one on last night," said Frank, laughing. "I found him sleeping in the hallway!"

"Just order me a cup of strong coffee," Albert said. "My head feels like it is going to explode."

They all sat down but Albert wanted nothing to eat. "Just coffee," he said.

Frank and Larry had decided to return to the ranch and wait out the drought, but they had made several contacts the night before, hoping to secure jobs for the others. "There is a dairy farmer who is hiring down in Iowa and a cattle drive leaving for the Dakotas next week," Frank told the boys. "We thought the job on the dairy might fit you, Albert. With Maggie and the baby and all, you wouldn't be moving around so much. When things change and we can afford to buy another herd, you will always have a job with us back at the ranch."

Albert thought the dairy job sounded promising. "I'll have to ask Maggie how she feels about it."

At that moment, Maggie entered the dining room, carrying little Emmy on her hip. "Am I invited to breakfast?" she asked curtly. "Or were you boys going to eat everything yourselves?" Albert stood up and pulled another chair up to the table. She sat down and ordered breakfast without looking at Albert. "What's this I hear about another cattle drive?" she asked.

"I'm taking the job on the dairy," said Albert. "Frank and Larry are going back to the ranch."

Maggie was silent as she buttered a piece of toast for the baby to chew on. "How soon do you think you will buy another herd?" she asked Frank.

Frank shook his head. "There's no way of telling," he replied. "Until this damned weather changes, we just have to wait and see."

Albert turned to Maggie; inside he was still licking the wound her words had inflicted on him the night before. "You can go back with your brothers or come with me to Iowa," he told her. "It's up to you." He pushed back his chair and left the dining room.

"What's going on with you two?" asked Frank.

"Oh, we'll be all right," said Maggie. "I'll go talk to him after we finish our breakfast."

After breakfast, Maggie climbed the stairs and found Albert sitting, staring out of the window. She put the baby down and went to him. "I'm sorry about the things I said last night," she said, touching his shoulder. "I didn't mean them, Albert. You know I love you. I think I was just tired from the drive."

Albert nodded. "That's why I decided on the dairy job," he said. "We won't have to be travelling so much." He paused. "You don't have to come with me if you don't want to."

Maggie put her arms around him. *She was so changeable, so unpredictable*, thought Albert. The very trait that had once *endeared* her to him was now driving him mad! "We'll come with you," she said. "We're a *family* now."

They spent the night in each other's arms; it was just as if they had never quarreled at all. The next day her spirits seemed to soar when they boarded the train for Garrison. Maggie had never ridden on a train before! As long as Albert could supply her with new adventures, she seemed content, but still Albert worried about her aversion to having another baby. What did that mean for their marriage, exactly? He wasn't sure. She had him in such a confused state, he had to keep his mind on the job ahead, although the details were still a little vague as to what he would actually be doing. What did it matter? It was a job! After working in the yards, what could be worse?

Albert had purchased three *first class* tickets, *Damn the price*, he thought; he wanted Maggie and the baby to be comfortable. The *Pullman* car, as it was called, had plush velvet seats that folded down into beds with curtains around them for privacy. There were separate washrooms for the men and the ladies, one at each end, and a separate dining car serving meals for seventy-five cents. It was like a fancy hotel on wheels! And, when those great wheels began to turn and the train lurched forward, clanking and bumping together, Maggie was glued to the window, holding little Emmy on her lap, watching the sights as they passed before her. "Look!" she said, pointing out this and that to little Emmy. "Do you see that?" Albert sat down in the seat beside them and he too stared out the window, as the city of St. Paul slowly evaporated behind them. As he looked out through the openings in the steel trusses that were flashing by the train windows, he realized he was once again crossing over the great river. *And, once again, Albert thought of Alfred Rose.*

PART THREE *"THE LAND BEYOND THE GREAT RIVER"*

"The river is everywhere"

Hermann Hesse.

Chapter Eighty-Nine *"The House on Selby Avenue"*

Emmy Snow had inherited the characteristics of her father. Her hair, which she wore long and loose, was as blue-black as shoe polish; her eyes were gray, like storm clouds just before a downpour. She was a smart girl, quick to learn, and she loved to read books, feasting upon any book she could get her hands on. It wasn't surprising that she taught her younger brother, Bert, to read at a very early age. She was sitting on the front porch of the little blue house on Selby Avenue that morning, reading as she always did, and listening for the cable car to come up the hill from downtown St. Paul, the sound that told her brother was home from school. Emmy had taken a job when she finished school but she liked days when she got off early enough to be home when he got there.

Emmy had long since overcome her loneliness with her parents being gone so much of the time, working on cattle ranches down south. Her father, Albert, worked very hard, having spent every nickel he had to buy this little house for them so that his family would always have a place to live. When she and Bert were younger, they sometimes travelled with their parents. In the very beginning, when they were babies, her mother, Maggie, would remain with the children, but she would always grow melancholy and nervous with their father gone. By the time Emmy was mature enough to babysit for little Bert, her mother had started travelling with her father, leaving the children on their own for longer and longer periods of time; once they were teenagers, it seemed she *never* stayed behind. Her parents were like thistles on the wind, never landing too long in any one place. Emmy had grown accustomed to her responsibility and the bond she shared with little Albert was more that of a mother and son than a brother and sister.

She heard the cable car rumbling through the tunnel at the top of the hill and Emmy put her book down. When she got off work early she liked to prepare an afternoon snack for her brother, knowing Bert was always ravenous when he returned from school. He came crashing through the door as usual, dropping his textbooks on the floor, just as she set a tuna sandwich and a glass of milk down on the kitchen table. He draped his jacket over the back of the kitchen chair and sat down to eat. "How was school today?" she asked. "Did you turn in your history assignment?"

Bert nodded between bites of his sandwich. "The teacher only gave me a B."

"*Only a B?*" she asked. "When we spent *hours* on that paper?"

"What can I say, Sis?" asked Bert. "Mister Shepard is a tough teacher. I'm just glad school will be out for the summer soon. I don't intend to *open* another book until September!"

Emmy shook her head. She couldn't understand her brother's aversion to books and reading; she couldn't imagine life without books! She and Bert were different in many ways. She paused and looked at him now, gobbling his sandwich with his face flushed from the sun and his dark hair tousled by the wind that blew off the river. Both of them looked more like their father in their physical appearance, but Bert seemed to have inherited their parents' instinct to roam. Before she could continue their conversation, Bert gulped the last of his milk and dashed out the door. "The guys are getting a ball game going in the park," he hollered. "I'll be home before supper."

"Do you have homework?" Emmy called back into the empty space he left behind. Bert did not answer. He was already halfway down the street, almost knocking the postman down in his eagerness.

"Where *does* he get his energy?" the postman asked, pulling several pieces of mail from his bag and handing them to Emmy who was left standing on the porch. "By this time in the afternoon, after walking up and down these streets all day long, I am *dog-tired*!"

"Yes," agreed Emmy with a smile. "Wouldn't it be nice if we could *harness* all his energy and put it to good use?"

The postman laughed. He tipped his hat and moved on down Selby Avenue and Emmy glanced at the mail in her hands, a bill from the mercantile, the usual weekly postcard from their mother, and another letter postmarked Boston, Massachusetts.

Hope you kids are doing well. We are heading to Charles City tomorrow. Your dad sends kisses. Love, Mom was scribbled on the postcard. Her mother wrote the same words on every card with very little variation, but by the time the card arrived, they would have moved on to another place, another cattle drive, another temporary job on the long list of temporary jobs her father had been through. Nothing ever seemed permanent. But, every month, there would be a check in the mail, enough to pay the bills and buy groceries. She and Bert hadn't been *forgotten*; they were just tucked away, like their old snow boots in the hall closet, waiting for the right time to be brought out. *When would be their right time?* Emmy had wondered most of her life. But, then, they had a roof over their heads and food on the table, so what had she to complain about?

She opened the letter from Boston with more interest than she had in reading her mother's redundant post card. She knew her father had family back east but in the infrequent times they spent together, he rarely spoke of them. This letter was short and to the point. It said simply, *Dear Albert, Your father is dead. I am having him buried in Orleans next to your grandfather. Hope you are doing well. Love, Aunt Susannah*

Emmy showed the letter to Bert when he finally returned home from his ball game in the park. He showed no interest at all. "I guess we had a grandfather and an aunt all this time, living in Massachusetts," she said sadly.

"Who cares?" Bert asked. "What good is *family* when they're never there? *You* are the only family I have ever known, Sis. I can't get all emotional about some old man I never met."

Emmy understood Bert's feelings only too well. Sometimes, it did feel like they were all alone in the world. "I've been thinking about taking on more hours at the millinery," she said. "Now, that you are old enough to take care of yourself."

"Ha!" said Bert. "When have I *not* taken care of myself?"

"Yes," she replied, "I do recall how *adept* you were at changing your own diapers!"

"Aw, Sis!" Bert said, "Cut it out! You know what I mean! But, I think that's a great idea! Make money while you can! It won't be long before our parents are too old to go off running around the country and *you'll* have to stay home and take care of *them*!"

It was a sobering thought. "What about *you*? Aren't you going to stay and help me care for our aging parents when the time comes?"

"Nope," said Bert curtly. "I'm going to hit the road, just like dad, as soon as I am out of school."

Chapter Ninety *"The Prodigal Parents"*

There had been no warning, no mention in the postcards from her mother to let her know that her father had been ill. It was late in the night, half-past midnight and the clock on the wall was slow, when their parents burst through the door of the little house on Selby Avenue. The taxi driver came in, helping them with their bags and quickly bid them goodbye.

"Emmy! Bert! Are you asleep?" Maggie called down the darkened hall.

What else would we be doing at this hour? thought Emmy, as she obligingly rose and wrapped herself in her terry-cloth robe. Bert heard them come in too, but he just rolled toward the wall and went back to sleep.

Emmy could immediately see that her father was not well; he had aged somehow since she had last seen him. She heard him wheezing with every breath.

"The doctor said he has *walking pneumonia*," said Maggie, as Albert made his way to the living room sofa.

"Oh, what do doctors know anyway?" he said. "I just needed a little rest, that's all. And, maybe a glass of something cool. Have you some of that sour lemonade you used to make for us, Emmy?"

Emmy went to the kitchen to fetch her father his lemonade, fighting the feeling of annoyance she felt at the interruption of her sleep. She had to be at work at the millinery at eight a.m. the next morning. How inconsiderate of her parents to just show up in the middle of the night and demand refreshments!

When she returned to the living room, Albert had prostrated himself on the sofa and Maggie had gone down the hall to wake Bert. "Son!" she called. "*Mommie's home!*" Bert could not ignore her once she had planted herself on the edge of his bed. "Wake up, Darling," she cooed. "Mommie and Daddy have come home!"

Bert went through the motions, not knowing himself what he was feeling. There had been a time when he thought his mother was the most beautiful woman in the world, with her long blonde hair and her bright blue eyes. Now, as he sat staring sleepily at her across the room, while she chattered on about their latest adventure, he suddenly felt as if he had *outgrown* her! He was much too old for her nonsense any longer. "Emmy has to be at work in the morning," he told his mother. "She really needs to get her sleep."

"*A job?*" asked Maggie. "You have a *job*, Emmy?"

"Mother, you know that I do," Emmy replied. "I told you about it months ago! Would you mind terribly if we continued this conversation tomorrow, after I have had some sleep?"

Maggie suddenly became the doting mother. "Why, yes, of course, Dear!" she said. "You go on and go back to bed. Your father and I will make ourselves comfortable."

As annoyed as Bert was, there was still a bit of chivalry left in him. "No, Mother," he said. "You and Dad can take my bed. I'll sleep on the sofa."

The next day it became apparent that Albert and Maggie were home for an extended stay. By suppertime, when Emmy returned from her job, Maggie was already busy in the kitchen. "I hope you don't mind, Emmy," she said. "I started supper for your father. The doctor says he needs to keep up his strength."

During their midnight visit, Emmy hadn't had a chance to really *look* at her mother. Now, standing in the kitchen, she noticed that she seemed thinner. Her hair now had streaks of white in between the blond ones. *Her mother was finally showing her age.* "I'm *ever* so sorry we woke you up last night, Emmy," said Maggie, giving her daughter a quick kiss on her cheek. "You can't always predict when the trains will come in. Come, sit and tell me all about your new job and let me do the cooking tonight."

"I only just started working full time," replied Emmy. "Showing ladies' hats and keeping the storeroom tidy. Not all that exciting, I'm afraid."

"Well, you have always loved hats," said Maggie. "Ever since you were little. I remember once when you found one of your father's dirty old hats that he wore on the ranch and you pranced around the house in it. You wanted to wear it to bed as I recall!"

"How long will you and Dad be staying with us this time?" asked Emmy, not at all interested in a trip down memory lane. "Does the doctor think it is wise for him to go back to work? Shouldn't he be in bed, resting? By the way, where *is* he?"

"He went with Bert down to the park," replied Maggie.

"He's not playing ball with the boys, is he? In his condition?" Emmy was surprised but not really shocked. Her father was always testing the limits of human endurance, whether it was breaking a horse or roping a steer or following a herd of cattle across the country. She had never known a tougher, more resilient man.

"You know there is no stopping your father when he decides he wants to *do* something," Maggie said.

"Or *you* either, Mother," said Emmy. "Seems to me you *both* have that trait."

Emmy left the room and returned with the letter from their aunt. "I forgot all about this last night," she said. "Dad will want to know that his father passed away."

Maggie's face turned strangely sad. "I never met the man," she confessed. "I think Albert was much closer to his grandmother growing up. You know his mother died when he was just a baby."

"Yes, I believe he has mentioned that," said Emmy. *And, you just went away*, she thought, wondering if her mother could see the parallel.

"We used to speak of going east," said Maggie. "Your father always wanted me to see the sunrise over the Atlantic." She paused, as if recollecting a poignant memory. "But, somehow, we never made it back there."

"It seems strange sometimes," said Emmy. "To have never known any of our grandparents. Sometimes, I feel like an *orphan*."

Maggie frowned. "That's not a very nice thing to say to your mother," she said. "Haven't we always provided for you and little Bert?"

She didn't want to discuss it. The last thing Emmy wanted to do was quarrel with her mother, who would never understand her feelings. She felt cheated, somehow, of a family. There were many times when she desperately needed her mother, always when her parents were far away and out of touch.

"When you are older, when you are on your own, perhaps you will understand why I went along with your father," she said.

When I am older? thought Emmy. *When I am on my own? Just where do you think I have been all these years? Raising your son while you were out gallivanting around the country! That was when I needed a mother! Not now!* But, she said nothing and went about setting the supper table like nothing was wrong. When Albert and Bert came in, they both collapsed on the sofa. "That was a good game, Son!" said Albert. "You have learned to play well while I've been away."

Emmy came in and showed Albert the letter from Boston. "I forgot to show it to you last night," she said.

Albert, strangely didn't have much of a reaction. He hadn't seen his father in so long, and letters between the two were few and far between. He had never met his aunt. The ones he thought of the most from his past were his grandmother and Alfred Rose.

"It seems that I am the only one of the Snows who made it out of Orleans," he said. "And lived long enough to have crossed the great river!"

He had always spoke of the Mississippi River as if it held some magical qualities and Emmy never understood why. He began to cough from too much excitement and too much ball-playing. Maggie brought him a glass of water from the kitchen. "Here, Albert," she said. "Maybe you should lay down and rest before supper."

"Yes," replied Albert, when his coughing fit had subsided. "Maybe, I will do just that."

When supper was ready, Albert was sleeping soundly. "Let's just eat our supper," Maggie told her children. "I will fix your father something to eat when he wakes up. He needs his rest. This *pneumonia* thing has taken a toll on him."

After she and Emmy had cleared and washed the dishes, Maggie wandered off to bed.

The next thing Emmy and Bert heard was their mother screaming from the bedroom. *"Emmy! Bert*! Someone go for an ambulance! I think your father needs to go to the hospital!"

Chapter Ninety-One *"Bert's Escape"*

Bert had run all the way down Selby Avenue to find the horse-drawn ambulance that would transport his father to the hospital. Maggie rode along with him, leaving Emmy and Bert at home, worried and feeling helpless. They finally went to bed and by morning, Maggie returned on the cable car with the sad news. *Their father was gone.*

Bert had not been thrilled with the news that their parents had come home for good. Now that his father was dead, and Maggie was once again running the house, he was even more eager to finish school and be out on his own. For all intents and purposes, Emmy was the only mother he had ever known. Maggie, (and he had always thought of her as *Maggie*, never *Mother*), was an attractive woman that appeared occasionally with trinkets and gifts from faraway places, someone who hardly knew him at all. Now, it felt like she followed him everywhere, touching his hair and pinching his cheeks and remarking to anyone who would listen, *how grown up her son was.* "You remind me of your father, when he first came to work for us on the ranch," Maggie told him on the day of Albert's funeral. "You and Emmy both have his dark good looks. It must be the Wampanoag blood in you."

The strange thing was that neither Bert nor Emmy knew exactly how to feel. It was hard for them to truly grieve for a father who had been more *out* of their lives than *in* it. They couldn't miss him any more than they had always missed him. They couldn't feel sad over losing someone they felt they never possessed in the first place. "I don't know what I want to do now," he told Emmy that night after their mother had gone to bed. "It was different when it was just you and me."

Emmy had doubts herself. After years of running the house on Selby Avenue, now she was the *second* in command, the *subordinate*. "What will you do?" she asked Bert. "Where will you go? Bert, you can't just go off and leave me alone with her!"

"I've been reading about all the new railroads they are building out west," he told her. "I think I want to hitch a ride out there and look for a job. There is plenty of work. Too bad you are a girl or you could sign up with me!"

Emmy punched her brother playfully. "No, I am quite content working at the millinery. But, what are you going to tell Mother? What if she wants to come with you? You know how she loves a good adventure!"

They laughed together then, but it was a subdued laughter, with a bitter-sweet underpinning; it was more because they knew their days together were numbered than it was over their father's death. Just as Albert's reaction to the news of his own father's death had been tepid, Emmy and Bert could not summon much sorrow for the man they hardly knew.

When school finally let out in June, Bert had received his diploma graciously and endured his mother's tears of joy with only one thought in his head. And, only Emmy knew what that thought was: *Bert was beginning to plan his escape.*

He first took a job at the C.W. Hackett Hardware store in downtown St. Paul, as a delivery boy. It only paid twenty-five cents an hour, not including occasional tips, but it got him out of the house during the day and out from under Maggie's control. After about six months, Mister Hackett promoted him and gave him a job as a shop clerk. Bert had to buy himself a white shirt and a bow tie and he had to polish his shoes every night to pass inspection every morning, but the pay was better.

Every week, Emmy and Bert would sit down at the kitchen table with their paychecks and go through the household bills; now that their father was no longer alive and the monthly checks no longer arrived in the mail, they had to scrimp over the living expenses of a family of three. Maggie never mentioned going to work herself; indeed, the only business she knew was cattle ranching and she was getting a little old for that line of work. But, she did like to *spend*; she ran up bills all over town on just about everything. She was not accustomed to running a house on a tight budget. "Mother," Emmy told her, "We really need to cut back on expenses. Bert and I don't make enough to cover all these bills!"

Maggie had started to cry. "I'm so sorry," she said. "Your father always took care of such things. I fear I have never had a head for numbers!"

At the next moment they had alone together, Emmy and Bert agreed; they had to close all the accounts Maggie had opened all over town and put their mother on a budget.

With every opportunity for a higher salary, Bert would change jobs. By the end of the year, he took a job driving an ice wagon. In the winter, huge blocks of ice were cut from Lake Superior, north of St. Paul, and hauled down by train. In a huge, insulated warehouse, with a vented roof and a drainage floor, the ice could be stored successfully sometimes until late spring. When they received orders for ice, they would saw it off in chunks and load it on the back of the mule driven wagon and Bert would be given a list of deliveries to make.

He endured it for as long as he could. And, then, he made his escape.

Chapter Ninety-Two *"The Impossible Railroad"*

With the few dollars Emmy had given him for his journey, some saved from his pay at the ice house, and a little extra pilfered from the family money jar, Bert purchased a ticket that would take him out of St. Paul, stopping briefly in Chicago and Kansas City before it headed west. He hadn't enough cash in his pocket to ride in a Pullman car, so when darkness fell, he slept in his seat; during the day, he struck up conversations with the porters on every train, to glean whatever they knew about the new railroads that were being planned. The *ATSF*, which was what they called the *Atchison, Topeka and Santa Fe* railroad line, took him as far as El Paso where he transferred to the Southern Pacific train that would take him to Yuma. *Yuma was where they were hiring*, everyone told him, where they were taking on a crew to build the new *San Diego & Arizona Railway*.

The project had earned itself the name of the *impossible railroad* due to the tortuous route it was to follow through undeveloped, hostile territory. Ever since the Mexican War, there had been a loud cry from the people of San Diego for a direct rail line to the east, first out of military necessity and then in the hopes of developing the fledgling Port of San Diego. The earlier train, the Santa Fe, provided only a branch line to Los Angeles, where it then connected with the eastern railroads. But, in San Diego two men, John and Adolph Spreckels, decided it was time they put San Diego on the railroad maps, and they partnered up with Edward Harriman, who controlled the Union Pacific, to do just that.

By the time Bert arrived on the scene, there had already been many disasters for the struggling railroad. First, Harriman had suddenly died in 1909, and his predecessor stopped the flow of money to finance the project, leaving the Spreckels brothers to raise more capital on their own. Slowly, linear foot by linear foot, the rails were laid from San Diego until the first passengers could ride as far as the Tijuana Hot Springs in Lower California and, by the end of the year, they could cross the Tijuana River. But, then, a revolution broke out in Mexico and all the Mexican laborers walked off the job. Bert was hired on as a replacement, not knowing if his status would be permanent when the trouble south of the border was resolved. Luckily for Bert, the work continued and he was able to keep his job. In 1912, the Spreckels brothers were hit with a three-million-dollar lawsuit by the Southern Pacific, to recover the funds the company had advanced under the direction of Harriman, which was not resolved until four years later.

Bert signed on in Yuma, and he, along with other newly-hired men, were shuttled back to the San Diego station. From San Diego, a switch engine transported them to the worksite every other week, returning to San Diego when they needed to load up more supplies. Dozens of flat cars loaded with wooden ties and steel rails and huge bins of iron spikes were sent into the desert. Some of the men were issued shovels to clear debris from their path; others, like Bert, received picks to bust up the rocks for the rail beds. They had reached the valley of *Redondo* in lower California by his first week on the job, a desolate place in the middle of nowhere, where Bert was introduced to rattlesnakes and sagebrush and rocks, *lots of rocks.*

The first night in the desert, sleeping under the stars, was a pleasant one for Bert, however, who was seeing the Mexican wilderness for the first time. Accustomed to the street lights and noisy cable cars of St. Paul, it almost seemed like an oasis to feel the crisp, cool night breezes in the silence of the desert after days of unbearable heat. A band of Mexican women appeared that first night and every night thereafter at dusk on a mule-driven wagon, like camp-followers, with tamales and tequila for a price. Bert and the others would sit around a campfire, commiserating on their aching backs and singing tavern songs, sometimes in Spanish, until, one by one, they would wander off to their bed sacks and sleep. But, the work was hard, *very hard.* Bert's hands became rough and calloused; his chest and arms were soon bronzed from many hours working shirtless in the sun.

The crew's only respite came when they returned to San Diego every other week for supplies, with the men riding in open box cars, Bert would rent a room overnight in a boardinghouse in what locals called the *Horton* district; an eclectic place, where street winos mingled with families listening to concerts in the park and free donuts were handed out by women from the Salvation Army. Bert wrote to Emmy back home every week to tell her of his adventures and rented a box at the local post office so that she could write him back. He found himself looking forward to her letters more and more as time went on and he grew lonelier and lonelier.

The crew celebrated each time they reached a milestone by breaking open a bottle of cheap champagne and partying until they would hit the rails again for the desert. Bert would join the others, catching the trolley from the building yard at the foot of 28th Street, to a tavern in the part of town known as *Stingaree* and, with their wives and sweethearts, and often camp-followers too, they would drink cheap gin and dance to the music of a three-man band there on a saw-dusty, cement floor.

Bert still had no sweetheart and, at times like these, it weighed heavily on his mind. He would watch the couples on the dance floor, clinging to each other stealing kisses in the smoky room, feeling very lonely. By chance, one night, an attractive young woman walked into the tavern. She was blonde haired and blue eyed, tall and slender and very well dressed; she reminded him of his own mother back in St. Paul. At first, he turned away from her *because* of the resemblance. *He wasn't interested in a woman who reminded him of Maggie!*

But, strangely, he couldn't resist glancing back at her and he could see her eyes were fixed on him as well.

"You should stay away from her, my friend," said one of the shop workers who was sitting next to him and noticed Bert staring at her.

"Why do you say that?" Bert asked. "Do you *know* her?"

The man leaned in and whispered, "That's the shop foreman's daughter. She comes down here when she is home from college."

"I've never met a college girl before," Bert told him, intrigued by the very mystery of her.

"You don't understand," replied the man. "She is *forbidden fruit*! Her parents are very religious. *Masonic, Eastern Star* or something like that, I think; they say she was one of those *Job's Daughters* before she went away to college, you know, a *debutante*. Her daddy bought her a new car to go back and forth to school in L.A. Now, when she comes home on break, she always shows up down here and causes a ruckus."

"What kind of ruckus?" asked Bert, watching the tall blonde as she moved through the room as fluidly as a snake through the grass. "She looks harmless to me."

The man laughed at that. "*Harmless*? Ask the *last* guy who tried to get friendly with her! Her old man had him fired the very next day! If her father knew she was down here, he'd be furious! No, you should walk away, man, *if you value your job*."

But it was too late. The girl sat down on a stool next to him. Bert fumbled in his pocket. "Can I buy you a drink?" he asked, politely.

She smiled at him. *Wow, what a smile*! thought Bert. *She's beautiful!* "What's your name?" he asked.

"Jean," she replied. "*Jean Souter*."

"Are you related to *David Souter*, the shop foreman?"

"Yes," she replied demurely as she ordered a gin and tonic from the bartender. "He is my father." She put her index finger to her glossy, red lips in a sign of silence and whispered, "But, don't tell anyone. I'm not supposed to be here."

And, by the end of the evening, the foreman's daughter had stolen Bert's heart. But, alas, there were many miles of train track left to lay in the desert and Bert went back on the rails with the crew the next day, trying unsuccessfully to put Jean Souter out of his mind, while she returned to her classes at the university.

Over the next year, the *impossible railroad* forged ahead in the desert. They built miles of tracks sometimes through bow knots and double horseshoe curves and up steep inclines. In sections, just beneath the sand, they hit solid granite and blasting had to be done, which slowed their progress to a snail's pace. Constructing trestles over deep gorges and boring tunnels through solid rock mountains, they inched their way toward the little border town of Tecate while back in San Diego, the Spreckels brothers were busy buying up all the local railroads, consolidating them into one continuous line from Coronado Island to the Cuyamaca mountains. And, every other week, Bert would look forward to Jean coming home from school in Los Angeles.

Chapter Ninety-Three *"Tombstone Affair"*

In the summer of 1914, a disaster of world-wide proportions hit; *war* had been declared in Europe and wary capitalists were suddenly reluctant to invest in risky ventures such as the San Diego & Arizona Railway. Somehow, the project did not die, even though U.S. relations with the neighbors to the south had become strained and Americans were ordered out of Mexico. Luckily, the Mexican workers had become loyal to the Spreckels brothers and did not abandon them. During this uneasy period, the crew was put to work building the new railway depot, which was later known as the Santa Fe Railway Station on Kettner Blvd in downtown San Diego. They had hoped to reach Yuma before the opening of the Panama-California Exposition in Balboa Park on January first, but, with all the setbacks they had encountered, they still had many miles to go.

And, just when it seemed like it couldn't get much worse, Mother Nature dealt another blow; a devastating flood hit all of southeastern San Diego County. They called it the Hundred Year Flood. The Otay Dam collapsed in January and everything in the valley below it was literally swept away. One train engine was derailed and turned over on its side, sinking into the sand and mud. Temporary tracks had to be installed so that service could continue, which took another month.

During this time, Bert was transferred once again and put to work building replacement tracks in the flooded valley and the calamity actually worked in his favor. He was able to see more of Jean and their love had reached a smoldering pitch. David Souter, who was unaware he was soon to be Bert's father-in-law, was blissfully ignorant to the affair that was going on under his nose. They sought out quieter places than the tavern to spend the few precious hours they had to be alone. It wasn't long before they were talking of running away to the desert together.

Jean had graduated from her classes and had come home to San Diego. Bert was on a brief hiatus while the company was waiting for supplies which were becoming more difficult to obtain since the war was depleting all the steel reserves in the country. "I want to see Tombstone," Jean had told Bert. "Let's go tonight, before they send you away again!"

"Why *Tombstone*?" Bert asked.

"I've always wanted to see the OK Corral," she replied. "And Boot Hill."

"Isn't that a gruesome place for a *honeymoon*?" Bert asked, laughing, knowing he could never deny Jean's demands; *whatever Jean wanted Jean would have!*

So, they stole away in Jean's dark blue Model T Ford, heading out Old Highway 80, west to Tucson and south from there to Tombstone, where they woke a justice of the peace from his sleep and were married. It just so happened that the same night, David Souter, back in San Diego, woke from his sleep with a bad case of indigestion that lasted until dawn.

While the couple was enjoying their brief honeymoon so much they lingered longer than they had planned. Wanting to be free of her parents' control, Jean encouraged Bert to put money down on a little apartment and look for work in Tucson. Unfortunately, jobs in Tucson were as scarce as anywhere. When Jean eventually called her parents to inform them of her marriage, she was already expecting a child. David and Mitzi Souter were not pleased that their oldest daughter had not been properly wed in the church; most of all they were disappointed because they felt that she was throwing away her college degree, marrying a man they had never met and who was now unemployed. "Can't you arrange for him to get his job back with the railroad?" Jean begged her father, but David was of the *old* school; *his daughter had made a rash decision and she had to deal with the consequences on her own.*

"Absolutely not," David told her. "You have both been *irresponsible* and that has cost your husband his job. He can seek employment elsewhere without my assistance."

Their hasty marriage had created a wedge between Jean and her parents that would never be completely bridged ever again. Bert did not rest on his laurels, however. He went out and found odd jobs to keep a roof over their heads. A son was born to them in June and they named him Bert Jr after his father. The U.S. had finally entered into the war and Bert registered for the draft, but the recruiter put his name at the bottom of the roster and told him it was unlikely he would be called upon with his status as a new father.

The couple returned to San Diego, discouraged and broke, where, a year and a half later, another son was born to Jean. They named the second boy Francis, although the nickname *Buster* stayed with him all his life. By November of that year, World War I had ended and all the soldiers were coming home, making employment even harder to find for Bert. Ever searching for work, they moved again, settling in the little town of Fullerton, just south Los Angeles, where he found a job driving a creamery truck.

The Snow family was struggling to survive in the difficult world in which they found themselves.

Chapter Ninety-Four *"A Very Un-Merry Christmas"*

It was the twenty-second of December. The year was 1926. Up and down the main street of Fullerton, the merchants had strung up multi-colored lights on all the storefronts and draped silver tinsel over all the street lights. The Salvation Army bell-ringers were on every corner and every store was playing Christmas carols over the loud speakers. Although there was no snow, for there was never snow in Southern California, it appeared to be a festive scene, a time when all the children were counting the days until Santa Claus and Christmas morning. There was Christmas cheer everywhere it seemed even though the country was in the middle of prohibition and a worsening recession. The war had been over for a while but no one knew that the Great Depression was just around the corner. And, Bert had just been given his pink slip from the creamery company; they had to lay off twenty workers and he had just missed the cut.

For Bert Junior and Buster, it began as a good day, on vacation from school until the New Year. *Beau Geste* starring Ronald Coleman was playing at the Fox Theatre two blocks away and they were standing in line with their quarters clasped tightly in their palms, as the aroma of freshly-popped popcorn drifted through the lobby doors and out into the street. "Do you think Pop will get us those bikes for Christmas?" young Buster asked his big brother. Both boys had their eyes on two shiny new *Mobo* bikes in the Montgomery Ward catalog, even though they knew money was always tight in the Snow household.

"I dunno," the older brother said. "We should probably not get our hopes up. Those bikes are mighty expensive, you know."

Buster pouted a little and sighed. "I wish he could get a good job," he said. "So Mother would quit nagging him so much."

Bert agreed. He was growing tired of the squabbling too. *Christmas was supposed to be a happy time!* But, try as he might, their father couldn't seem to hold onto a job for very long and this year hadn't been any better than years past.

"I think he *tries*," said Bert Junior. "There just aren't many good jobs right now. Maybe, next year will be better."

The line began to move into the theatre and their thoughts moved on from the problems at home to swashbuckling pirates on the big screen and popcorn. *There was always popcorn to make them feel better.*

But, by the time they returned home after the movie had ended, the situation in the little house on East Wilshire Boulevard had gotten worse. Bert had just delivered the bad news of his lay-off to Jean while the boys were away and a loud argument was in progress, which the boys could hear all the way from the front porch.

Bert Junior sat down on the step and Buster took a seat beside him. The boys were very much alike, dark and handsome lads, smart and eager to learn new things, although neither was particularly crazy about school. Neither boy was very vocal about the fighting between their parents; it was like an embarrassing secret they didn't want to discuss. So they sat and listened, silent and sad. *Three days before Christmas!* thought Buster. *We'll probably never get those bikes now!*

"This is the final straw, Bert!" their mother was yelling. "I can't put up with it anymore. It's *Christmas* and we don't even have enough money to buy proper presents for our boys! I have no other choice than to take the boys and go back to live with my parents!"

Young Bert and Buster turned and stared at each other in horror! *Not Grampa Souter's house! Not where they had to go to church twice on Sunday and eat vegetables every night! Things couldn't be that bad!*

"You know I always work when I can, Jean," they heard their father say. "And, I am a *hard* worker. I can't help it if the jobs are only temporary. Maybe, after the first of the year, more jobs will open up. We'll get the boys *something* for Christmas. It might not be those bikes they wanted, but *something*."

Outside both boys sighed deeply. *Another dream shattered.* "Let's go down to the park," said Bert Junior, standing up. "I don't think I want to hear anymore."

When they returned, the house was quiet. As they walked down the hallway toward their bedroom, they passed their parents' room and saw, much to their chagrin, their mother was busy packing suitcases. When she saw them pass, she called out to them. *"Boys, get out your duffle bags and pack some clothes. We are going to Grampa's for a visit."*

Chapter Ninety-Five *"Back to the Desert"*

Bert didn't know which way to go but the only real happiness he had ever known had been in the desert, so he hopped on the first east-bound train, intending to get as far away from California as possible. He had not stayed around long enough to say good-bye to his boys; that was too painful. *I'll write to them*, he told himself, *when I am settled and maybe Jean will let them come visit me.* For now, he just wanted to hide his shame from his sons.

The train passed through Tucson but Bert kept going, watching as the Arizona towns flashed by him outside the windows of the train and then he was in New Mexico, where the train went north from Carlsbad. He hadn't much money but he didn't care. One town was as good as any other. At the next stop, however, Bert looked out and somehow knew he *had* to get off the train.

All his life, Bert had wondered about his name and why his parents had chosen to call him Bertram *Roswell* Snow. To his knowledge, no one in either his mother's or his father's family had been named *Roswell*. Later, when the family became so estranged due to his parents' traveling around the country like gypsies, the subject just never came up. But, Bert had always wondered; maybe it was a place his parents had *visited*. And, there it was! On the signpost outside the train depot: *Roswell, New Mexico! It just had to be his lucky omen!*

He stepped down off the train and laughed out loud in the chilly morning air. This *Roswell* place was even more remote than Tucson or Tombstone; for miles in every direction it was flat without the variation of hills or mountains. The houses in town were built in the *pueblo* style, painted white with red tile roofs, where cactus took the place of trees in the front yards and lots of little raven-haired children played in the sandy dirt. The bed beneath the train tracks was made of the red rock, the same color as the rock that went into the brick tile roofs. It had the look of a poor town, dusty, sleepy, and poor. And, immediately, Bert felt right at home, *as if he belonged there.*

He walked the streets all that day, hoping to see a *Help Wanted* sign, but by the end of the day he had found nothing. Never in his life had Bert felt so all alone and he began to worry about his future. He thought about Jean and how she had cut him to the quick with her harsh words. *Didn't she know he was doing his best? Didn't she understand he would never be able to give her the things her father could?* He thought about Emmy back in St. Paul and wondered momentarily if he should just get back on the train and return to the house on Selby Avenue. At least there he had a home. But, something stopped him. Something drew him to this little town of Roswell.

"Are you lookin' for something?" A man's voice interrupted Bert's thoughts and he realized he had been standing on the same street corner for several minutes. The man was clad in greasy overalls and his hands were black too; he had the look of the men who worked on the train engines back in San Diego.

"No," he replied. "I'm new here. Just getting a good look around."

"You thinkin' of settling in Roswell?" asked the man. *People in small towns were always inquisitive* thought Bert. *He didn't mean any harm. He was just trying to be helpful.*

"Well, I am if I can find a job," said Bert. "You know anyone who is hiring?"

The man looked him up and down. "Well, what can you do? What kind of experience do you have?"

"I worked on the railroad for years," said Bert. "After the war, I drove a truck and did a little bit of everything."

The man seemed to like Bert's looks. "You got a place to stay yet?" he asked.

"No," said Bert. "Not yet."

"How are you with car engines?" asked the man.

Bert had tinkered a bit with Jean's old Model T. He knew enough to get by. "A little," he told the man.

"Well, I might be able to put you up and give you a little work," the man said. "Hinkle's the name. *Horace Hinkle*. I run a little garage over on Virginia Street. There's an attic that I use for storage, but you could stay there and keep an eye on the place at night. You could help me during the day. I think I could keep you busy. Can't pay you much, though, times being what they are."

Bert could not believe his good fortune. He shook the man's hand happily. Maybe Roswell was going to change his streak of bad luck! He followed Horace back to the garage and, together, they rearranged the stuff stored in the attic room. There was a makeshift cot for Bert to sleep on and although it wasn't the Ritz, Bert was satisfied. He had a job and a place to sleep. That was all that mattered for the moment. Getting his family back would have to wait until he could get himself established, at least, to Jean's satisfaction. Horace put him to work that very afternoon, stocking shelves and sweeping floors and fetching tools for him while he worked underneath cars. The day went by quickly and Bert was spent by suppertime.

"There's a little café just down the street," Horace told him. "You're probably gettin' hungry about now."

Bert nodded, but headed up the stairs to his new "room" instead.

"No money, huh?" Horace asked, and dug in his pocket. "Here, you worked hard today. Here is a little advance on your pay."

"Thank you," Bert said sheepishly. He hated being broke and depending on others to feed him. But *it wasn't a handout*, he told himself; *he'd earned that money fair and square*!

"And, you might keep this handy too," said Horace, handing Bert a small revolver. "Just in case anybody tries to break in tonight. We've had a lot of pilfering in town lately. And, bein' so close to the railroad, we get a lot of transients."

Bert nodded but he was laughing on the inside, knowing he was nothing more than a transient himself.

He helped Horace close the garage doors and put the key to the upstairs in his pocket. It was sunset by the time he wandered down the street and found the little café. There was a red reflection in all the windows; red tiles, red sunset, everything had a red hue at that hour. He sat down in a booth and a waitress brought him a menu. He chose the item with the cheapest price; it didn't matter what it was. *Food was food.* The waitress smiled at him, recognizing the look of a man spending his last dime. "Don't worry," she whispered. "You don't have to tip me."

Bert was embarrassed. *Did he look so pathetic that the waitress felt sorry for him?* "Why would you say that?"

he asked her, noticing the plastic tag on her uniform that said her name was Essie. "Of course, I will tip you. What gave you the idea I wouldn't?"

"I didn't mean to offend you, Sir," she said. "I know how things are right now…. for *everybody*…not just *you*."

"No," said Bert. "I know you meant well. It's true I am a little down and out right now. Thank you for understanding."

She smiled. It was a nice smile, warm and friendly. She brought him his dinner of roast chicken and mashed potatoes. "I had the cook give you an extra scoop of potatoes," she whispered. "I told him you were a friend."

"Thank you," Bert said. "That was a nice thing for you to do. I hope I can repay the favor sometime."

He ate his dinner, savoring every mouthful. Somewhere back in the kitchen there was a radio playing *Desert Song. Blue Heaven and you and I and sand……. kissing under a moonlit sky…*it went on, reminding Bert of his honeymoon in Tombstone with Jean. *How would he ever get her back? How could he ever measure up to his father-in-la,; the foreman of the shop at the San Diego Arizona Railway Company? Being a hired laborer was all he had ever done; it was all he knew. Where was the shame in that? Why couldn't Jean see that he was doing the very best he could do?*

The waitress brought him the ticket and he tipped her, even though she told him not to.

"What's your name?" she asked, just as he was putting on his jacket to leave. "I told the cook you were my friend; I should at least know your name!"

"Bert" he replied. "*Bert Snow*. And, I am happy to know you, *Essie*."

Chapter Ninety-Six *"Black Blizzards"*

He had written to Jean to let her know his new address. But, she had not replied in a letter as he had hoped, saying she was sorry and that she was bringing the boys to Roswell. Instead, when he got off work on a Tuesday afternoon and checked his mailbox, he received an official looking divorce document with her signature scribbled hastily at the bottom next to a place for his own. Bert wanted to get good and drunk. He wanted something to take away the pain. But, instead of visiting the tavern on the corner, he went where he knew someone would make him feel good. He found himself sitting in his favorite booth at the café and ordering a big slice of apple pie from Essie. Business was slow. There was no one in the place except Essie and the cook back in the kitchen. She sat down across from him in the booth while he ate his pie. "You ok?" she asked. "You look funny today."

Bert sighed and told her his bad news. "I will probably never see my boys again," he said sadly.

"You shouldn't say that, Bert," she replied. "Don't give up on them yet. Maybe your wife will change her mind."

"You don't know my wife," said Bert. "When she makes up her mind that's all there is to it. She is not understanding like you, Essie."

The truth occurred to him at that moment. *Essie had all the compassion and empathy that his wife lacked*. This little woman who served him his dinner every night brought him much more than food. And, in the weeks and months that followed, he began to see her in an entirely different light. She soon became his reason for living. In May, he proposed and they married in the little Methodist church and moved into a tiny cottage on Sixth Avenue, only two blocks from the train station where Bert had first set foot in Roswell.

Theirs was a different kind of love than he had shared with Jean; while the affair that had begun in Tombstone so many years before had been passionate and consuming, his love with Essie was gentler and more satisfying somehow. She made him feel good about himself again. She gave him hope that things could get better. They talked often of having his boys come for a visit.

But, just when things were looking up for Essie and Bert, however, the country fell into what the news called a *depression*. Bert had no idea what a depression was; nothing seemed any different there in the little town of Roswell, at least, *at first*. People were poor, but they had always been poor. But, gradually things began to change, even in Roswell. Businesses that had been there for years began to close. People born in Roswell moved away to find work elsewhere. Essie lost her job at the café. Bert told her not to worry. He would take care of her.

They couldn't remember exactly *when* the winds began to blow. From over-plowed fields stripped bare year after year, the once rich top soil all across the plains had been slowing turning to dust as fine as talcum powder and soon every town from the Dakotas southward was in its path. It was the first year they actually documented it and gave it a name: *The Dust Bowl*.

It was far worse up north, but the folks of Roswell began to see their share of the dust storms. There was no escaping it. The storms sometimes lasted for hours, sometimes for days. Everything in Horace's garage was covered in dust; it stuck to the crankcase oil and it came through the cracks in the walls, under the doors and around the window frames. Essie would bring Bert his lunch at the garage, wrapped tightly in wax paper to keep the dust out but it was no use; it became a joke between them. "Here comes Essie, bringing me my *sand-wich*," he would say to Horace and they would laugh about it. There was no escaping the dust and sand; it was like living inside an *hourglass*.

Because the cattle were dying from the dust and lack of food, the meat market soon had no meat to sell, not that anyone could afford it anyhow. Essie had to be creative to turn plain beans into something more than a *hobo-meal* every night. They took to wearing long sleeved clothes, even in the hottest summer months, to keep the blowing sand from stinging their skin. In the street, there were more blowing tumbleweeds than cars and the town became overrun with grasshoppers and black-tailed jackrabbits searching for green plants to feed on.

"It's bound to end soon," Essie would tell Bert. "These winds can't blow forever!"

She would take out her four-leaf clover, which she always kept in her pocket, and rub it for good luck. But the winds continued to blow. And, soon, it became obvious, Essie was coming down with what folks called *dust pneumonia.*

"I don't want you to bring me my lunch anymore," Bert told her. "I want you to stay inside out of the dust."

Essie began to stay home but she didn't get any better. In fact, she was getting worse. When Bert heard that they had a special hospital up in Kansas that took care of people suffering from the dust he made plans to take Essie there. It was a charitable hospital, paid for by the government and Bert had to swallow his pride if he wanted to save his wife. "Do you think you can get by without me for a while?" he asked Horace. "I need to get Essie to a doctor who can help her and this hospital seems like the only place I can afford."

Horace shook his head sadly. "I've been meaning to talk to you about that, Bert," he said. "About your job. There's so little business these days, I've been thinkin' I'm gonna have to let you go. I've been holding off because I know your wife has been so sick. I feel just terrible about it."

Bert wasn't surprised. It wasn't Horace's fault. "It's ok, Horace," he told him.

"Maybe things will get better and business will pick up again," said Horace. "Then I would be happy to hire you on again."

They boarded the train the next day for Topeka. Down to their last few dollars, Bert's only thought was to get Essie into the hospital where she would have food to eat and a bed to sleep in. *He would get by.* Essie wouldn't unless she was under a doctor's care.

When they arrived at the hospital, Bert was surprised; it looked more like a giant warehouse than a hospital. It was one enormous room with hundreds of beds and the high ceiling echoed the coughing of all the patients beneath it. It was drafty and even the hospital could not escape the dust; it coated the windowsills and cement floors.

They put Essie in a bed and covered her face with an oxygen mask. She had gotten much worse on their train ride. Bert, feeling helpless, sat by her side, until the nurses would run him away after visiting hours. Then he would wander in the lobby and sleep on any bench he could find so he could be there when she awoke in the morning.

Until the morning they told him Essie was gone and asked him what he wanted to do with her body.

Chapter Ninety-Seven *"The Last Chariot"*

Bert couldn't bear to go home to the empty house on Sixth Avenue. When he stepped down from the train car onto the platform, he could see the car from the funeral home was waiting for them. He watched as they transferred Essie's coffin and drove away. Then, he stood there for a while, not knowing exactly *where* he would go. Twilight was a beautiful hour in the desert, when the setting sun cast its long shadowy fingers across the sandscape, when the cactus flowers were unfurling, unleashing their heavenly scent like a spray of perfume into the air, and the stars were beginning to twinkle and glitter in the endless sky above. Bert was not seeing its beauty, however. Not tonight, *maybe not ever again.*

He thought about Essie, lying there in her hospital bed, so pale and thin. He could hear her raspy breathing in the winds that were still blowing across the dunes. His poor Essie. *How would he ever live without her*? *Why had God taken everything from him that he had held dear in his life? First, Jean, then his boys, now Essie. It didn't seem fair. What did God have against him anyway?* He was not a perfect man, not by a longshot; he had made plenty of mistakes but he had never done anything truly evil. And, yet, here he was, all alone in the world. *Again.*

He started walking north, along the train tracks, wandering, really, for he had no particular destination in mind. The stinging wind bit at his face. Ahead of him were the red cliffs that sunk down to the blue water of Bitter Lake. A flock of mallards flew over his head, going toward the lake, and when he reached the edge of the cliffs he sat down on a waving patch of prairie grass and watched the ducks bobbing up and down on the water below. He could hear the train as the engine fired up again and pulled out of the station, going south to Carlsbad; it was a sound he often heard from their house on Sixth Avenue. But, before, it had been a *comforting* sound. *It was home.* From now on, it would only remind him of the train that had brought Essie's body home.

He laid back on the grass and something hard touched his side; he realized he still had Horace's revolver in his pocket and he pulled it out carefully and placed it beside him on the grass. The stars were beginning to come out above him like tiny points of light across the endless desert sky. *Where was God tonight?* he wondered. He felt something in his other pocket and pulled out the folded tissue that held Essie's four-leaf clover. *Good luck?* *Hardly!* Once he had thought coming to Roswell had been *his* good luck. He remembered an ancient Indian myth his father used to quote about how the earth swallowed the sun in the west every night when Bert knew it would only regurgitate it again the next morning. *Was that all life was? Just a lot of legends and lies?*

Now, here he was, a widower with no job and no hope. He picked up the revolver and put the cold steel barrel against his temple and slowly pulled the trigger.

Four miles away, Horace Hinkle was just closing up the garage for the night. As he stepped out into the street, he happened to glance upward at the sky. At that moment, a shooting star flashed across the heavens.

Chapter Ninety-Eight *"The Letter"*

One week earlier, the postman delivering the mail to the Sixth Avenue neighborhood returned to the post office with a pile of unclaimed mail. He emptied his bag and dropped the stack of unopened letters down on the clerk's desk. "Might as well send these back," he said. "Mail's been piling up. It appears the Snow family don't live at 316 Sixth Avenue anymore."

The woman bundled them up, glancing mindlessly at the pieces of orphaned mail, picking out only those with return addresses written on them. The rest, she immediately pitched into a wire trash basket at her feet. With a red pen, she began to go through the letters, still grainy from the prairie dust, circling the return recipients' names, to put them in the outbox for the next day's pickup. "Electric company's not going to be happy," she said, as she picked through several utility bills marked *Past Due.* "I suppose they must expect it, though, with all the families leavin' town to get outta the dust."

The postman sat down to rest his tired feet and started to empty the grit from his shoes.

"Now, Edgar, don't go dumpin' yer dirt on my floor!" the clerk said, standing up and shooing him away. "Take yer mess outside!"

She went back to sorting the stack of mail. *Just another family long gone*, she thought to herself. *Sad, how many folks just up and moved on.* As she sifted through each envelope, she couldn't help but wonder about the Snow family, what had happened to them, where they had gone. There were several bills from a hospital in Topeka, Kansas and then, at the very bottom of the pile, she sat there staring at an envelope that had come all the way from San Diego, California, addressed to a Mr. Bert Snow from *Buster Snow, at 3994 Florence Street.* She circled the return address. Maybe *that's* where the Snows had gone, *to California.*

She looked around the office. She was not supposed to open the mail; she knew she could get fired for it. But something about the letter in her hands peaked her curiosity; she felt compelled to open it and read it. It wasn't like it was going to ever reach its destination anyway, she rationalized to herself. It was one step away from the *dead* letter office; if it didn't make it this time, there was no resurrectin' the dead! She unfolded the two small sheets of onion-skinned paper tucked inside the envelope and began to read.

Dear Pop,

I don't know if this is still your address. Mother said she didn't know where you had moved to and, even if she did, she probably wouldn't give it to me anyhow. I hope you are doing well. Bert and I are doing ok. He is a senior in high school this year and I am a junior. We have been building a '31 Model A Roadster in Grampa's garage for a while now. Hope to get it running soon.

I don't know if you ever get to California but we would like to see you if you ever come to San Diego.

Your Son,

Buster

How sad, she thought, wondering if the boy would ever find his father again. Slowly, she folded the paper back in half and slipped it into the envelope, licking the flap twice to re-stick it together. Then, she pounded the rubber stamp down on the red ink pad and again across the front of the envelope.

RETURN TO SENDER

Author's Note:

I never met my paternal grandfather, *Bertram Roswell Snow*. He died sixteen years before I was born. My father never even spoke of him that I can recall. It wasn't until many years later that I discovered his tragic story. He is buried now in the desert of New Mexico beside his beloved wife, Essie-Ray, and I hope he has finally found the peace he was seeking.

This will be the final book about the *Snow* family, but definitely not the end of the *family saga*. I hope readers will join me again next year when I will begin to tell the story of the ancestors of *Maggie Purcell Snow*, whom I have traced all the way back to the second century in the land of the midnight sun: *Finland*!

It will be genealogy, history and Norse mythology all colliding in the land of frozen fjords and Viking ships. I look forward to telling the tale of my forefathers as they pillage and plunder through Northern Europe and work their way across the Atlantic. *The Viking series* begins with the book *The Sea Kings*.

See you all again in 2017!

J.A. Snow

Made in the USA
San Bernardino, CA
01 April 2017